OVERWHELMING ACCLAIM FOR
THE SKULL BENEATH THE SKIN

"Levitates right over the boundaries of the genre. . . . Should the elegant ghosts of Jane Austen and Agatha Christie ever collaborate on a detective story, the result might be as good."

—*Cosmopolitan*

"The brooding atmosphere of her island setting, the intriguing nuances and revelations of her highly credible characters, and the beguiling blend of criminal fantasy and social satire all combine to elevate her novel from teasing whodunit to satisfying art."

—*San Francisco Chronicle*

"Marked by powerful and sympathetic characterization . . . an absorbing story, paced and written with fine calculation, a work quite beyond the scope of more than a very few of her contemporaries."

—*New York Times Book Review*

"James's novel has everything you love. . . . All the people who were lamenting the demise of the conventional whodunit can stop their moaning and groaning . . . *The Skull Beneath the Skin* is a fine specimen."

—*Chicago Sun-Times*

"Vastly more than a murder mystery. It is a true novel with a solid plot structure, a richly textured narrative, and solidly drawn characters."

—*John Barkham Reviews*

more . . .

"Mystery writers often deploy stereotypes in similar ways—but not P.D. James. She gives her people fully rounded life, never sacrificing character to plot, and makes deft fun of convention."

—*Newsweek*

"A big, satisfying, and thoroughly traditional whodunit."

—*Philadelphia Inquirer*

"One of the most entertaining and literate mysteries we've read in a long while."

—*Cleveland Plain Dealer*

"James scores with texture: the understated humor, the stately yet unpretentious prose, the psychological insights, the quiet charm—plus, above all, the fundamental warmth and wisdom in every line she writes."

—*Kirkus Reviews*

"A solid mystery . . . deft characterization and wry wit."

—*Booklist*

"Ingenious plotting. . . . With sensitivity and psychological insight, Ms. James reveals the complex relationships and motives of the people involved."

—*Dallas Morning News*

BOOKS BY P. D. JAMES

Original Sin
Cover Her Face
A Mind to Murder
Unnatural Causes
Shroud for a Nightingale
An Unsuitable Job for a Woman
The Black Tower
Death of an Expert Witness
Innocent Blood
The Skull Beneath the Skin
A Taste for Death
Devices and Desires
The Children of Men

NON-FICTION
The Maul and the Pear Tree
(with T. A. Critchley)

Published by
Warner Books

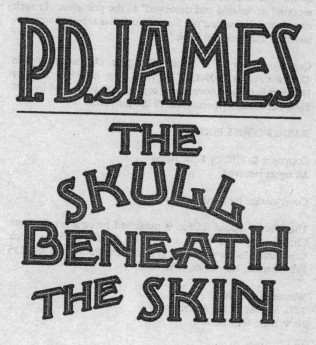

P.D.JAMES

THE SKULL BENEATH THE SKIN

WARNER BOOKS

A Time Warner Company

Quotation from T. S. Eliot's "Whispers of Immortality" in *Collected Poems 1909-1962* by T. S. Eliot; copyright 1936 by Harcourt Brace Jovanovich Inc., copyright © 1963, 1964 by T. S. Eliot. Reprinted by permission of the publisher.

WARNER BOOKS EDITION

Copyright © 1982 by P. D. James
All rights reserved.

Cover design by Daniell Pelavin

This Warner Books Edition is published by arrangement with Charles Scribner's Sons, a division of the Scribner Book Companies, Inc., a subsidiary of Macmillian Publishing Inc., 115 Fifth Avenue, New York, N.Y. 10003

Warner Books, Inc.
1271 Avenue of the Americas
New York, NY 10020

Visit our Web site at
www.warnerbooks.com

W A Time Warner Company

Printed in the United States of America

First Warner Books Printing: October, 1983

Reissued: February, 1996

25 24 23 22

Contents

Contents

Webster was much possessed by death
And saw the skull beneath the skin;
And breastless creatures under ground
Leaned backward with a lipless grin.

Daffodil bulbs instead of balls
Stared from the sockets of the eyes!
He knew that thought clings round dead limbs
Tightening its lusts and luxuries.

From "Whispers of Immortality"
T. S. Eliot

BOOK ONE

CALL
TO AN
OFFSHORE
ISLAND

1

THERE COULD BE NO DOUBT ABOUT IT; the new nameplate was crooked. Cordelia had no need to adopt Bevis's expedient of dodging through the mid-morning traffic which cluttered Kingly Street and squinting at the plaque through a dazzle of grinding delivery vans and taxis to recognize stark mathematical fact: the neat bronze oblong, so carefully designed and so expensive, was half an inch out of true. Lopsided as it was, it looked, she thought, despite the simplicity of its wording, both pretentious and ridiculous, a fitting advertisement of irrational hope and ill-advised enterprise.

PRYDE'S DETECTIVE AGENCY
(Third Floor)
PROP.: CORDELIA GRAY

Had she been superstitious, she might have believed that Bernie's unquiet spirit was protesting against the new plaque with the deletion of his name. And, indeed, it had seemed at the time symbolic, the final obliteration of Bernie at her hands. She had never considered changing the name of the agency; while it remained in being it would always be Pryde's. But it had become increasingly irksome to be asked by her clients, disconcerted as much by her sex as by her youth, "But I thought I would be seeing Mr. Pryde." They might as well know from the start that there was now only one proprietor and she a female.

Bevis rejoined her at the door, his pretty, mobile face a parody of desolation, and said, "I measured it carefully from the ground, honestly, Miss Gray."

"I know. The pavement must be uneven. It's my fault. We should have bought a spirit level."

But she had been trying to limit expenditure from petty cash, ten pounds a week kept in the battered cigarette tin inherited from Bernie with its picture of the battle of Jutland, from which money seemed to drain away by a mysterious process unrelated to actual expenditure. It had been only too easy for her to accept the assurance of Bevis, leaping from his typewriter, that he was handy with a screwdriver, forgetting that, for Bevis, any job was preferable to the one he was actually supposed to be doing.

He said, "If I close my left eye and hold my head like this, it looks all right."

"But we can't rely on a succession of one-eyed, wry-necked clients, Bevis."

Glancing at Bevis's face, which had now fallen into an extreme of despair which would not have been inappropriate to the announcement of an atomic attack, Cordelia felt an obscure desire to comfort him for his own incompetence. One of the disconcerting aspects of being an employer of staff, a role for which she increasingly felt herself almost wholly unsuited, was this oversensitivity to their feelings coupled with a vague sense of guilt. This was the more irrational because, strictly speaking, she didn't directly employ either Bevis or Miss Maudsley. Both were hired from Miss Feeley's employment agency on a weekly basis when the agency's case load warranted it. There was seldom competition for their services; both were invariably and suspiciously available when asked for. Both gave her honesty, conscientious timekeeping, and a fierce loyalty; both would, no doubt, have also given her efficient secretarial service if that had lain in their power. Both added to her anxieties, since she knew that the failure of the agency would be almost as traumatic for them as for her.

Miss Maudsley would suffer the more. She was a gentle, sixty-two-year-old rector's sister, eking out her pension in a bed-sitting-room in South Kensington, whose gentility, age, incompetence, and virginity had made her the butt of the countless typing pools through which she had drifted since her brother's death. Bevis, with his facile, slightly venial charm, was better equipped to survive in the London jungle. He was supposed to be a dancer working as a temporary typist while resting, an inappropriate euphemism when applied to such a restless boy, perpetually fidgeting in his chair or pirouetting on tiptoe, fingers splayed, eyes widened and alarmed, as if poised for flight. He was certificated to type thirty words a minute by an obscure secretarial school long since defunct, but Cordelia reminded herself that even they hadn't guaranteed his proficiency to undertake minor jobs as a handyman.

He and Miss Maudsley were unexpectedly compatible, and a great deal more chat went on in the outer office between the bouts of inexpert typing than Cordelia would have expected from two such discordant personalities, denizens she would have thought of such alien worlds. Bevis poured out his domestic and professional tribulations, liberally laced with inaccurate and occasionally scurrilous theatrical gossip. Miss Maudsley applied to this bewildering world her own mixture of innocence, High Anglican theology, rectory morality, and common sense. Life in the outer office became very cozy at times, but Miss Maudsley had old-fashioned views on the proper distinction to be made between employer and employed and the inner room where Cordelia worked was sacrosanct.

Suddenly Bevis cried out, "Oh, God, it's Tomkins!"

A small black-and-white kitten had appeared at the doorway, shaken one exploratory paw with deceptive insouciance, stretched its tail rigid, then shivered with ecstatic apprehension and darted under a post-office van and out of sight. Bevis, wailing, fled in pursuit. Tomkins was one of the agency's failures, having been repudiated by a spinster of that name who had employed Cordelia to find her missing black kitten with a white eye patch, two white paws, and a striped tail. Tomkins precisely fulfilled the specifications, but his putative mistress had immediately known him for an impostor. Having rescued him from imminent starvation on a building site behind Victoria Station, they could hardly abandon him, and he now lived in the outer office with a dirt tray, a cushioned basket, and access to the roof via a partly opened window for his nightly excursions. He was a drain on resources, not so much because of the rising cost of cat food—although it was a pity that Miss Maudsley had encouraged an addiction to tastes beyond their means by providing the most expensive tin on the market for his first meal and that Tomkins, although in general a stupid cat, could apparently read labels—but because Bevis wasted too much time playing with him, tossing a Ping-Pong ball or drawing a rabbit's foot on string across the office floor with cries of "Oh, look, Miss Gray! Isn't he a clever leaping beastie?"

The clever leaping beastie, having caused chaos among the traffic in Kingly Street, now streaked into the rear entrance of a pharmacy with Bevis in noisy pursuit. Cordelia guessed that neither kitten nor boy was likely to reappear for some time. Bevis picked up new friends as obsessively as others pick up litter, and Tomkins would be a great introducer. Oppressed by the realization that Bevis's morning was now fated to be almost entirely unproductive, Cordelia was aware of a lethargic disinclination to any further effort herself. She stood against the jamb of the doorway, closed her eyes, and lifted her face to the unseasonable warmth of the late-September sun. Distancing herself by an effort of will from the grind and clamor of the street, the pervading smell of petrol, the clatter of passing feet, she played with the temptation, which she knew she would resist, to walk away from it all, leaving the lopsided plaque as a memorial to her efforts to keep faith with the dead Bernie and his impossible dream.

She supposed that she ought to be relieved that the agency was beginning to make a reputation for something, even if it was only for finding lost pets. Undoubtedly there was a need for such a service, and one in which she suspected they had a monopoly; and the clients, tearful, desperate, outraged by what they saw as the callous indifference of the local C.I.D., never haggled at the size of the bill and paid more promptly than Cordelia suspected they might have done for the return of a relative. Even when the agency's efforts had been unsuccessful and Cordelia had to present her account with apologies, the bill was invariably paid without demur. Perhaps the owners were motivated by the natural human need at a time of bereavement to feel that something had been done, however unlikely that something, to achieve success. But frequently there were successes. Miss Maudsley, in particular, had a persistence in door-to-door inquiries, coupled with an almost uncanny empathy with the feline mind, that had restored at least half a dozen cats, damp, half·starved, and feebly mewing, to their ecstatic owners, while occasionally exposing the perfidy of those animals which had been living a double life and had transferred more or less permanently to their second home. She managed to conquer her timidity when in pursuit of cat thieves and on Saturday mornings walked purposefully through the rowdy exuberance and half-submerged terrors of London's street markets as if under divine protection, which no doubt she felt herself to be. But Cordelia wondered from time to time what poor, ambitious, pathetic Bernie would have thought about the debasement of his dream child. Lulled into a trancelike peace by the warmth and the sun, Cordelia recalled with startling clarity that confident, overloud voice: "We've got a gold mine here, partner, if once we get started." She was glad that he couldn't know how small the nuggets and how thin the seam.

A voice, quiet, masculine, and authoritative, broke into her reverie.

"That nameplate's crooked."

"I know."

Cordelia opened her eyes. The voice was deceptive: he was older than she had expected, she guessed a little over sixty. Despite the heat of the day he was wearing a tweed jacket, well tailored but old, with leather patches on the elbows. He wasn't tall, perhaps no more than five feet ten inches, but he stood very upright with an easy, confident stance, almost an elegance, which she sensed concealed an inner wariness as if he were tensed for a word of command. She wondered if he had once been a soldier. His head was held high and fixed, the gray and somewhat sparse hair brushed smoothly back from a high, creased forehead. The face was long and bony, with a dominant nose jutting from cheeks reddened and crossed by broken veins, and a wide, well-shaped mouth. The eyes which scrutinized her, not, she felt, unbenignly, were keen under the bushy eyebrows. The left brow was held higher than the right, and she saw that he had a habit of twitching his brows and working the corners of the wide mouth; it gave his face a restlessness which was singularly at variance with the stillness of his body and which made it slightly embarrassing for her to meet his eyes.

He said, "Better get the job done properly."

She watched without speaking while he put down the briefcase he was carrying, took from a pocket a pen and his wallet, found a card, and wrote on the back of it in an upright, rather schoolboyish hand.

Taking the card, Cordelia noted the single name, Morgan,

and the telephone number, then turned it over. She read: Sir George Ralston, Bt., D.S.O., M.C.

So she was right. He had been a soldier. She asked, "Will he be expensive, this Mr. Morgan?"

"Less expensive than making a nonsense. Tell him I gave you his number. He'll charge what the job's worth, no more."

Cordelia's heart lifted. The lopsided name plaque, gravely surveyed by the critical eye of this unexpected and eccentric knight errant, suddenly seemed to her irresistibly funny, no longer a calamity but a joke. Even Kingly Street was transformed with her mood and became a glittering, sunlit bazaar, pulsating with optimism and life. She almost laughed aloud.

Controlling her trembling mouth, she said gravely, "It's very kind of you. Are you a connoisseur of nameplates or just a public benefactor?"

"Some people think I'm a public menace. Actually, I'm a client; that is, if you're Cordelia Gray. Don't people ever tell you . . ."

Cordelia, unreasonably, was disappointed. Why should she have supposed that he was different from other male clients? She finished the sentence for him: "That it's an unsuitable job for a woman? They do, and it isn't."

He said mildly, "I was going to say, 'Don't they ever tell you that your office is difficult to find?' This street's a mess. Half the buildings aren't properly numbered. Too much change of use, I suppose. But the new plate should help when it's properly fixed. Better get it done. Gives a poor impression."

At that moment Bevis panted up beside them, his curls damp with exertion, the telltale screwdriver protruding from his shirt pocket. Holding the richly purring Tomkins against one flushed cheek, he presented his charming delinquency to the newcomer. He was rewarded by a curt "A botched job, that" and a look which instantly rejected him as officer material. Sir George turned to Cordelia.

"Shall we go up, then?"

Cordelia avoided Bevis's eyes, which she guessed were rolling heavenward, and they climbed the narrow, linoleum-covered stairs in single file, Cordelia leading, past the single lavatory and washroom which served all the tenants in the building (she hoped that Sir George wouldn't need to use it), and into the outer office on the third floor. Miss Maudsley's anxious eyes looked up at them over her typewriter. Bevis deposited Tomkins in his basket (where he at once began washing away the contamination of Kingly Street), gave Miss Maudsley a wide-eyed admonitory look, and mouthed the word *client* at her. Miss Maudsley flushed, half rose from her chair, then subsided and applied herself to painting out an error with a shaking hand. Cordelia led the way into her inner sanctum.

When they were seated, she asked, "Would you like some coffee?"

"Real coffee or ersatz?"

"Well, I suppose you'd call it ersatz. But best-quality ersatz."

"Tea, then, if you have it, preferably Indian. Milk, please. No sugar. No biscuits."

The form of the request was not meant to be offensive. He was used to ascertaining the facts and then asking for what he wanted.

Cordelia put her head outside the door and said, "Tea, please" to Miss Maudsley. The tea, when it arrived, would be served in the delicate Rockingham cups which Miss Maudsley had inherited from her mother and had lent to the agency for the use of special clients only. She had no doubt that Sir George would qualify for the Rockingham.

They faced each other across Bernie's desk. His eyes, gray and keen, inspected her face as if he were an examiner and she a candidate, which in a way she supposed she was. Their sudden, direct, and glittering stare, in contrast to the spasmodically grimacing mouth, was disconcerting.

He said, "Why do you call yourself Pryde's?"

"Because the agency was set up by an ex-Metropolitan policeman, Bernie Pryde. I worked for him for a time as his assistant, and then he made me his partner. When he died he left the agency to me."

"How did he die?"

The question, sharp as an accusation, struck her as odd, but she answered calmly. "He cut his wrists."

She didn't need to close her eyes to see again that remembered scene, garish and sharply outlined as a cinema still. Bernie had lain slumped in the chair in which she now sat, his half-clenched right hand close to the open cutthroat razor, his shrunken left hand, with its scored and gaping wrist, resting palm upwards in the bowl like some exotic sea anemone glimpsed in a rock pool, curling in death its pale and wrinkled tentacles. But no rock pool had ever been so brightly pink. She could smell again the sickly sweet, insistent odor of freshly spilled blood.

"Killed himself, did he?"

His tone lightened. He might have been a golfing partner congratulating Bernie on a well-placed putt, while his quick glance around the office suggested that the action had been in all the circumstances entirely reasonable.

She had no need to see the room through his eyes. What she saw through her own was depressing enough. She and Miss Maudsley had redecorated her office together, painting the walls pale yellow to give an impression of greater light and cleaning the faded carpet with a proprietary liquid; it had dried patchily so that the final impression reminded her of diseased skin. With its newly washed curtains, the room at least looked clean and tidy, too tidy since the absence of clutter suggested no great pressure of work. Every surface was crammed with plants. Miss Maudsley had green fingers, and the cuttings she had taken from her own plants and lovingly tended in a variety of oddly shaped receptacles picked up during her forays into the street markets had flourished despite the poor light. The resulting rampant green-

ery suggested that it had been cunningly deployed to conceal
some sinister defect in the structure or decor. Cordelia still
used Bernie's old oak desk, still imagined that she could trace
the outline of the bowl in which he had bled away his life,
could still identify one particular stain of spilled blood and
water. But then there were so many rings, so many stains.
His hat, with its upturned brim and grubby ribbon, still hung
on the curved wooden coat stand. No jumble sale would take
it, and she found herself unable to throw it away. Twice she
had taken it as far as the dustbin in the backyard but had been
unable to drop it in, finding this final symbolic rejection of
Bernie even more personal and traumatic than the exclusion
of his name from the brass plaque. If the agency did finally
fail—and she tried not to think what the new rent would be
when the present lease came up for renewal in three years'
time—she supposed that she would still leave the hat hanging
there in its pathetic decrepitude for unknown hands to toss
with fastidious distaste into the wastepaper basket.

The tea arrived. Sir George waited until Miss Maudsley
left. Then, measuring milk carefully into his cup, drop by
drop, he said, "The job I'm offering is a mixture of functions. You'd be part bodyguard, part private secretary, part
investigator, and part—well, nursemaid. A bit of everything.
Not everyone's cup of tea. No knowing how it may turn out."

"I'm supposed to be a private investigator."

"No doubt. Shouldn't be too purist in these times. A job's
a job. And you could find yourself involved in detection,
even in violence, although it doesn't seem likely. Unpleasant
but not dangerous. If I thought there was any real risk to my
wife or to you I wouldn't be employing an amateur."

Cordelia said, "Perhaps you could explain what exactly
you want me to do."

He frowned into his tea as if reluctant to begin. But when
he did his account was lucid, concise, and unhesitating.

"My wife is the actress Clarissa Lisle. You may have heard
of her. Most people seem to know of her, although she hasn't

worked much recently. I am her third husband; we married in June 1978. In July 1980 she was employed to play Lady Macbeth at the Duke of Clarence's Theater. On the third night of the advertised six-month run she received what she saw as a death threat. These threats have continued intermittently ever since.''

He began sipping his tea. Cordelia found herself gazing at him with the anxiety of a child hoping that her offering is acceptable. The pause seemed very long. She asked, "You said that she saw the first note as threatening. Are you implying that its meaning was ambiguous? What form exactly do these threats take?"

"Typewritten notes. Variety of machines by the look of it. Each communication surmounted by a small drawing of a coffin or a skull. All are quotations from plays in which my wife has appeared. All the quotations deal with death or dying: the fear of death, the judgment of death, the inevitability of death."

The reiteration of that numinous word was oppressive. But surely it was her imagination that he twisted it on his lips with mordant satisfaction. She said, "But they don't specifically threaten her?"

"She sees this harping on death as threatening. She's sensitive. Actresses have to be, I suppose. They need to be liked. This isn't friendly. I have the notes here, the ones she kept. The first ones were thrown away. You'll need the evidence."

He clicked open the briefcase and took out a stout manila envelope. From it he spilled a heap of small sheets of paper and began spreading them over the desk. She recognized the type of paper at once; it was a popular, medium-quality white writing paper sold over thousands of stationery counters in three sizes with envelopes to match. The sender had been economical and had selected the smallest size. Each sheet bore a typed quotation surmounted by a small drawing about one inch high, of either an up-ended coffin with the initials

R.I.P. on the lid or a skull with crossbones. Neither had
required much skill; they were emblems rather than accurate
representations. On the other hand they were drawn with a
certain sureness of line and decorative sense which suggested
some facility with the pen or, in this case, with a black-tipped
ballpoint. Under Sir George's bony fingers the white slips of
paper with their stark black emblems shifted and rearranged
themselves like the cards for some sinister game, hunt the
quotation, murderer's snap.

Most of the quotations were familiar, words which would
readily come to the mind of anyone reasonably well read in
Shakespeare and the Jacobeans who chose to ponder refer-
ences in English drama to death and the terror of dying. Even
reading them now, truncated and childishly embellished as
they were, Cordelia felt their nostalgic power. The majority
of them were from Shakespeare and the obvious choices were
there. The longest by far—and how could the sender have
resisted it?—was Claudio's anguished cry from *Measure for
Measure*:

Ay, but to die, and go we know not where,
To lie in cold obstruction and to rot,
This sensible warm motion to become
A kneaded clod and the delighted spirit
To bathe in fiery floods, or to reside
In thrilling region of thick-ribbèd ice—
To be imprisoned in the viewless winds,
And blown with restless violence round about
The pendent world

. . . .

The weariest and most loathèd worldly life
That age, ache, penury, and imprisonment
Can lay on nature is a paradise
To what we fear of death.

It was difficult to interpret that familiar passage as a
personal threat, but most of the other quotations could be

seen as more directly intimidating, hinting, she thought, at some retribution for real or imagined wrongs.

He that dies pays all debts.
Oh, thou weed!
Who are so lovely fair and smell'st so sweet
That the sense aches at thee, would thou hadst
  ne'er been born!

Some care had been taken in the choice of illustration. The skull adorned the lines from *Hamlet*—

Now get thee to my lady's chamber, and tell her, let
her paint an inch thick, to this favour she must come

—as it did a passage which Cordelia thought might be from John Webster, although she couldn't identify the play:

Being heretofore drown'd in security,
You know not how to live, nor how to die;
But I have an object that shall startle you,
And make you know whither you are going.

But, even allowing for the sensitivity of an actress, it would take a fairly robust egotism to wrench these familiar words from their contexts and apply them to oneself; that, or a fear of dying so strong as to be morbid. She took a new notebook from her desk drawer and asked, "How do they arrive?"

"Most come by post in the same sort of envelope as the paper and with the address typed. My wife didn't think to keep any of the envelopes. A few were delivered by hand either at the theater or at our London flat. One was pushed under the dressing-room door during the run of *Macbeth*. The first half dozen or so were destroyed—best thing to do with them all in my view. These twenty-three are all we now have. I've numbered them in pencil on the back in the order of receipt as far as my wife can remember and with information about when and how each was delivered."

"Thank you. That should be helpful. Your wife has played a great deal of Shakespeare?"

"She was a member of the Malvern Repertory Company for three years after she left drama school and played a fair amount then. Less in recent years."

"And the first of these—which she threw away—came when she was playing Lady Macbeth. What happened?"

"The first one was upsetting, but she told no one about it. Thought it was an isolated bit of malice. She says she can't remember what it said, only that it had the drawing of a coffin. Then a second came, and a third, and fourth. During the third week of the season my wife kept breaking down and had to be continually prompted. On the Saturday she ran off the stage during the second act and her understudy had to take over. It's all a matter of confidence. If you think you're going to dry up—drying is the theatrical jargon, I believe—then you dry. She was able to return to the part after a week, but it was a struggle to get through the six weeks. After that she was due to appear at Brighton in a revival of one of those thirties murder mysteries, the sort where the ingenue is called Bunty, the hero is Clive, and all the men wear long tennis flannels and keep dashing in and out of french windows. Curious affair. Not exactly her kind of part—she's a classical actress— but there aren't a lot of opportunities for middle-aged women. Too many good actresses chasing too few parts, so they tell me. Same thing happened. The first quotation appeared on the morning the play opened, and they came at regular intervals thereafter. The play came off after four weeks, and my wife's performance may have had something to do with it. She thought so. I'm not so sure. It was a stupid plot; couldn't make sense of it myself. Clarissa didn't act again until she accepted a part in Webster's *The White Devil* at Nottingham, Victoria something or other."

"Vittoria Corombona."

"Was that it? I was in New York for ten days and didn't see it. But the same thing happened. The first note arrived again on the day the play opened. This time my wife went to the police. Not much joy. They took the notes away, thought about them, and brought them back. Sympathetic but not very effective. Made it obvious that they didn't take the death threat seriously. Pointed out that if people are serious about killing, they do it, they don't just threaten. Must say, that was rather my view. They did discover one thing, though. The note which arrived while I was in New York was typed on my old Remington."

Cordelia said, "You still haven't explained how you think I can help."

"Coming to that. This weekend my wife is to play the leading role in an amateur production of *The Duchess of Malfi*. The play is to be given in Victorian dress and will take place on Courcy Island about two miles off the Dorset coast. The owner of the island, Ambrose Gorringe, has restored the small Victorian theater which was first built by his great-grandfather. I understand that the original Gorringe, who rebuilt the ruined medieval castle, used to entertain the Prince of Wales and his mistress, the actress Lillie Langtry, and the guests used to amuse themselves with amateur theatricals. I suppose the present owner is trying to restore past glories. There was an article in one of the Sunday papers about a year ago describing the island, the restoration of the castle, and theater. You may have seen it."

Cordelia couldn't recall it. She said, "And you want me to go to the island and be with Lady Ralston?"

"I hoped to be there myself, but that won't now be possible. I have a meeting in the west country which I can't miss. I propose to motor down to Speymouth with my wife early Friday morning and take leave of her at the launch. But she needs someone with her. This performance is important to her. There's to be a revival of the play at Chichester in the spring, and if she can regain her confidence she might feel that she can do it. But there's more to it than that. She thinks that the threats may come to a head this weekend, that someone will try to kill her on Courcy Island."

"She must have some reason for thinking that."

"Nothing that she can explain. Nothing that would impress the police. Not rational, perhaps. But that's what she feels. She asked me to get you."

And he had come to get her. Did he always procure for his wife whatever she wanted? She asked again, "What precisely am I being employed to do, Sir George?"

"Protect her from nuisance. Take any telephone calls which come for her. Open any letters. Check the set before the performance if you get the chance. Be on call at night; that's when she's most nervous. And bring a fresh mind to the question of the messages. Find out, if you can in just three days, who is responsible."

Before Cordelia could respond to these concise instructions, there came again that disconcerting pierce of gray frown under the discordant brows.

"D'you like birds?"

Cordelia was temporarily nonplussed. She supposed that few people, except those afflicted with a phobia, would admit to not liking birds. They are, after all, one of the most graceful of life's fragile diversions. But she supposed that Sir George was covertly inquiring whether she could recognize a marsh harrier at fifty yards. She said cautiously, "I'm not very good at identifying the less common species."

"Pity. The island's one of the most interesting natural bird sanctuaries in Great Britain, probably the most remarkable of those in private hands, almost as interesting as Brownsea Island in Poole Harbor. Very similar, come to think of it. Courcy has as many rare birds, the blue-eared and Swinhold pheasants as well as Canada geese, black godwits, and oyster catchers. Pity you're not interested. Any questions—about the case, I mean?"

Cordelia said tentatively, "If I'm to spend three days with your wife, ought she not to interview me before any decision is made? It's important that she feel she can trust me. She doesn't know me. We haven't even met.''

"Yes, you have. That's how she knows she can trust you. She was having tea with a Mrs. Fortescue last week when you returned the Fortescue cat—Solomon, I think the brute's called. Apparently you found him within thirty minutes of beginning the search, so your bill was correspondingly small. Mrs. Fortescue is devoted to the animal. You could have charged treble. She wouldn't have queried it. That impressed my wife.''

Cordelia said, "We're rather expensive. We have to be. But we are honest.''

She remembered the drawing room in Eaton Square, a feminine room if femininity implies softness and luxury; a cluttered, cozy repository of silver-framed photographs, an overlavish tea on a low table in front of the Adam fireplace, too many flowers conventionally arranged. Mrs. Fortescue, incoherent with relief and joy, had introduced her guest to Cordelia as a matter of form, but her voice, muffled in Solomon's fur, had been indistinct and Cordelia hadn't caught the name. But the impression had been definite. The visitor had sat very still in her armchair beside the fireplace, one thin leg thrown over the other, heavily ringed hands resting on the arms. Cordelia recalled yellow hair intricately piled and wound above a tall forehead, a small, bee-stung mouth, and immense eyes, deep-set but with heavy, almost swollen lids. She had seemed to impose on the lush conformity of the room a hieratic and angular grace, a distinction which, despite the plainness of the formal suede suit, hinted at some histrionic or eccentric individuality. She had gravely bent her head and watched her friend's effusions with a half-mocking smile. Despite her stillness there had been no impression of peace.

Cordelia said, "I didn't recognize your wife but I remember her very well.''

"And you'll take the job?''

"Yes, I'll take it.''

He said without embarrassment, "Rather different from finding lost cats. Mrs. Fortescue told my wife what you charge per day. This will be higher, I suppose."

Cordelia said, "The daily rate is the same whatever the job. The final bill depends on the time taken, whether I have to use either of my staff, and the level of expenses. These can sometimes be high. But as I'll be a guest on the island, there will be no hotel bills. When do you want me to arrive?"

"The launch from Courcy—it's called *Shearwater*—will be at Speymouth jetty to meet the nine-thirty-two from Waterloo. Your ticket's in this envelope. My wife has telephoned to let Mr. Gorringe know that she's bringing a secretary-companion to help her with various odd jobs during the weekend. You'll be expected."

So Clarissa Lisle had been confident that she would take the job. And why not? She had taken it. And she was apparently equally confident of being able to get her way with Ambrose Gorringe. Her excuse for including a secretary in the party was surely rather thin, and Cordelia wondered how far it had been believed. To arrive for a country-house weekend accompanied by one's private detective was permissible for royalty, but from any less elevated guest showed a lack of confidence in one's host, while to bring one incognito might reasonably be regarded as a breach of etiquette. It wasn't going to be easy to protect Miss Lisle without betraying that she was there under false pretenses, a discovery which would hardly be agreeable for either her host or fellow guests. She said, "I need to know who else will be on the island and anything you can tell me about them."

"There's not much I can tell. There'll be about one hundred people on the island by Saturday afternoon when the cast and invited audience arrive. But the house party is small. My wife, of course, with Tolly—Miss Tolgarth—her dresser. Then my wife's stepson, Simon Lessing, will be there. He's a seventeen-year-old schoolboy, the son of Clarissa's second husband, who drowned in August 1977. He wasn't happy with the relatives who were his guardians, so my wife decided to take him on. I'm not sure why he's invited; music's his interest. Clarissa probably thought it was time he met more people. He's a shy boy. Then there's her cousin, Roma Lisle. Used to be a schoolmistress but now keeps a bookshop somewhere in north London. Unmarried, age about forty-five. I've only met her twice. I think she may be bringing her partner with her, but if so, I can't tell you who he is. And you'll meet the drama critic Ivo Whittingham. He's an old friend of my wife's. He's supposed to be doing a piece about the theater and the performance for one of the color magazines. Ambrose Gorringe will be there, of course. And there are three servants, the butler, Munter, his wife, and Oldfield, who is the boatman and general factotum. I think that's all.''

"Tell me about Mr. Gorringe."

"Gorringe has known my wife since childhood. Both their fathers were in the diplomatic. He inherited the island from his uncle in 1977 when he was spending a year abroad. Something to do with tax avoidance. He came back to the UK in 1978 and has spent the last three years restoring the castle and looking after the island. Middle-aged. Unmarried. Read history at Cambridge, I believe. Authority on the Victorians. I know no harm of him.''

Cordelia said, ''There's one last question I have to ask. Your wife apparently fears for her life, so much so that she is reluctant to be on Courcy Island without protection. Is there any one of that company whom she has reason to fear, reason to suspect?''

She could see at once that the question was unwelcome, perhaps because it forced him to acknowledge what he had implied but never stated, that his wife's fear for her life was hysterical and unreal. She had demanded protection and he was providing it. But he didn't think it was necessary; he believed neither in the danger nor in the means he was employing to reassure her. And now some part of his mind was repelled by the thought that his wife's host and her fellow guests were to be under secret surveillance. He had done what his wife had asked of him, but he didn't like himself any the better for it.

He said curtly, "I think you can put that idea out of your head. My wife has no reason to suspect any of the house party of wishing to harm her, no reason in the world."

2

NOTHING MORE OF IMPORTANCE was said. Sir George looked at his watch and got to his feet. Two minutes later he said a curt good-bye at the street door, neither mentioning nor glancing at the offending nameplate. As she climbed the stairs, Cordelia wondered whether she could have managed the interview better. It was a pity that it had ended so abruptly. There were questions which she wished she had thought to ask, in particular whether any of the people she was to meet on Courcy Island knew of the threatening messages. She would now have to wait until she met Miss Lisle.

As she opened the office door, Miss Maudsley and Bevis looked up over their typewriters with avid eyes. It would have been heartless to deny them a share in the news. They had sensed that Sir George was no ordinary client, and curiosity and excitement had virtually paralyzed them. There had been a suspicious absence of clacking typewriters from the outer office during his visit. Now Cordelia told them as little as was compatible with telling them anything worth hearing, emphasizing that Miss Lisle was looking for a companion-secretary who would protect her from an irritating but unimportant poison-pen nuisance. She said nothing about the nature of the threatening messages or of the actress's conviction that her life was seriously threatened. She warned them that this assignment, like all other jobs, even the most trivial, was to be treated as confidential.

Miss Maudsley said, "Of course, Miss Gray. Bevis understands that perfectly well."

Bevis was passionate in his assurances. "I'm more reliable than I look. I won't utter, honestly. I never do, not about the agency. But I'll be no good if anyone tortures me for information. I can't stand pain."

Cordelia said, "No one's going to torture you, Bevis."

By general consent they took an early lunch hour. Bevis fetched sandwiches from the Carnaby Street delicatessen and Miss Maudsley made coffee. Sitting cozily in the outer office, they gave themselves over to happy speculation about where this interesting new assignment might lead. And the hour wasn't wasted. Unexpectedly, both Miss Maudsley and Bevis had helpful information to give about Courcy Island and its owner, pouring out a spate of antiphonal chat. It wasn't the first time this had happened. Their more orthodox skills might be suspect, but they not infrequently provided a bonus in the way of useful gossip.

"You'll enjoy the castle, Miss Gray, if you're interested in Victorian architecture. My brother took the Mothers' Union to the island for their summer outing the month before he died. Of course, I'm not a full member; I couldn't be. But I usually went on the outing, and this one was so interesting. I particularly enjoyed the pictures and the porcelain. And there's one delightful bedroom which is almost a museum to the Victorian Arts and Crafts Movement: De Morgan tiles, Ruskin drawings, Mackmurdo furniture. It was quite an expensive outing, I remember. Mr. Gorringe—he's the owner—

allows parties only once a week during the season, and he restricts the numbers to twelve at a time, so I suppose he has to charge rather a lot to make it worthwhile. But no one grumbled, not even Mrs. Baggot, who was always, I'm afraid, rather inclined to complain at the end of the day. And the island itself—so beautiful and varied, and such peace. Low cliffs, woods, fields, and marshes. It's like England in miniature."

"Darlings, I was actually in the theater when she dried, Clarissa Lisle, I mean. It was ghastly. It wasn't just that she forgot the lines, though I don't see how anyone can forget Lady Macbeth; the part practically speaks itself. She dried completely. We could hear the prompter positively shrieking at her from where Peter—he was my friend—and I were sitting. And then she gave a kind of gasp and ran offstage."

Bevis's outraged voice recalled Miss Maudsley from her happy recollection of Orpen portraits and William Morris tapestries.

"Poor woman! How terrible for her, Bevis."

"Terrible for the rest of the cast. For us, too. Altogether shamemaking. After all, she is a professional actress with something of a reputation. You don't expect her to behave like a hysterical schoolgirl who's lost her nerve at her first amateur performance. I was amazed when Metzler offered her Vittoria after that *Macbeth*. She started all right and the notices weren't that bad, but they say that things got pretty dodgy before it folded."

Bevis spoke as one who had been privy to all the negotiations. Cordelia had often wondered at the assurance which he assumed whenever they spoke of the theater, that exotic world of fantasy and desire, his promised land, his native air. He said, "I'd love to see the Victorian theater on Courcy Island. It's very small—only a hundred seats—but they say it's perfect. The original owner built it for Lillie Langtry when she was mistress to the Prince of Wales. He used to visit the island and the house party would amuse themselves with amateur theatricals."

"How do you get to know these things, Bevis?"

"There was an article about the castle in one of the Sundays soon after Mr. Gorringe completed the restoration. My friend showed it to me. He knows I'm interested. The auditorium looked charming. It even has a royal box decorated with the Prince of Wales feathers. I wish I could see it. I'm madly envious."

Cordelia said, "Sir George told me about the theater. The present owner must be rich. It can't have been cheap, restoring the theater and the castle and collecting the Victoriana."

Surprisingly, it was Miss Maudsley who replied. "Oh, but he is! He made a fortune out of that best-seller he wrote. *Autopsy*. He's A. K. Ambrose. Didn't you know?"

Cordelia hadn't known. She had bought the paperback, as had thousands of others, because she had got tired of seeing its dramatic cover confronting her in every bookshop and supermarket and had felt curious to know what it was about, a first novel that could earn a reputed half a million before publication. It was fashionably long and equally fashionably violent, and she remembered that she had indeed, as the blurb promised, found it difficult to put down, without now being able to remember clearly either the plot or the characters. The idea had been neat enough. The novel dealt with an autopsy on a murder victim and had told at length the stories of all the people involved: forensic pathologist, police officer, mortuary attendant, family of the victim, victim, and finally, the murderer. You could, she supposed, call it a crime novel with a difference, the difference being that there had been more sex, normal and abnormal, than detection and that the book had attempted with some success to combine the popular family saga with mystery. The writing style had been nicely judged for the mass market, neither good enough to jeopardize popular appeal nor bad enough to make people ashamed of being seen reading it in public. At the end she had been left dissatisfied, but whether that was because she had felt manipulated or because of a conviction that the pseudonymous A. K. Ambrose could have written a better book had he chosen, it was hard to say. But the sexual interludes, cunningly spaced, all written with undertones of irony and self-disgust, and the detailed description of the dissection of a female body certainly had a salacious power. Here at least the writer had been himself.

Miss Maudsley was anxious to disclaim any implied criticism in her question. "It's not surprising that you didn't know. I wouldn't have known myself, only one of the members on the summer outing had a husband who keeps a bookshop and she told us. Mr. Ambrose doesn't really like it to be known. It's the only book he's written, I believe."

Cordelia began to feel a lively curiosity to see the egregiously talented Ambrose Gorringe and his offshore island. She sat musing on the oddities of this new assignment while Bevis collected the coffee cups, it being his turn to wash up.

Miss Maudsley had fallen into a pensive silence, hands folded in her lap. Suddenly she looked up and said, "I do hope you won't be in any danger, Miss Gray. There's something wicked, one might say evil, about poison-pen letters. We had a spate of them once in the parish and it ended very tragically. They're so frighteningly malevolent."

Cordelia said, "Malevolent, but not dangerous. I'm more likely to be bored by the case than frightened. And I can't imagine anything very terrible happening on Courcy Island."

Bevis, precariously balancing the three mugs, turned around at the door. "But terrible things have happened there! I don't know what exactly. The article I read didn't say. But the present castle is built on the site of an old medieval castle which used to guard that part of the Channel, so it's probably inherited a ghost or two. And the writer did mention the island's violent and bloodstained history."

Cordelia said, "That's just a journalistic platitude. All the past is bloodstained. That doesn't mean that its ghosts still walk.''

She spoke entirely without premonition, glad of the chance of a real job at last, happy at the thought of getting out of London while the warm autumnal weather still lasted, seeing already in her mind the soaring turrets, the gull-loud marshes, the gentle uplands and woods of that miniature England, so mysterious and beautiful, lying waiting for her in the sun.

3

AMBROSE GORRINGE now visited London so rarely that he was beginning to wonder whether the subscription to his town club was really justified. There were parts of the capital in which he still felt at home, but too many others in which he had previously walked with pleasure now seemed to him grubby, despoiled, and alien. When business with his stockbroker, agent, or publisher made a visit desirable, he would plan a program of what he described to himself as treats, an adult reenactment of school holidays, leaving no portion of a day so unprovided for that he had time to ponder on his stupidity in being where he was. A visit to Saul Gaskin's small antique shop near Notting Hill Gate was invariably in his program. He bought most of his Victorian pictures and furniture at the London auction houses, but Gaskin knew and partially shared his passion for Victoriana and he could be confident that there would be, awaiting his inspection, a small collection of the trivia which were often so much more redolent of the spirit of the age than his more important acquisitions.

In the unseasonable September heat, the cluttered and ill-ventilated office at the back of the shop smelled like a lair in which Gaskin, with his white, pinched face, precise little hands, and grubby moleskin waistcoat, scurried around like a tenacious rodent. Now he unlocked his desk drawer and reverently laid before this favored customer the scavengings of the last four months. The Bristol blue decanter engraved with a design of grapes and vine leaves was attractive, but there were only five glasses and Gorringe liked his sets complete; and one of a pair of Wedgwood vases designed by Walter Crane was slightly chipped. He was surprised that Gaskin, knowing that he demanded perfection, had bothered to keep them for him. But the ornately trimmed menu for the banquet given by the Queen at Windsor Castle on October 10, 1844, to celebrate the appointment of King Louis Philippe of France as a Knight of the Garter was a happy find. He played with the idea that it would be amusing to serve the same meal at Courcy Castle on the anniversary, but reminded himself that there were limits both to Mrs. Munter's culinary skills and to the capacity of his guests.

Gaskin had saved the best until last. He now brought out, with his customary grave air of serving at some secular mass, two heavy mourning brooches, beautifully wrought in black enamel and gold, each with a lock of hair intricately twisted into whorls and petals; a widow's black peaked bonnet, still in the hatbox in which it was delivered; and a marble carving of a baby's plump truncated arm reposing on a purple velvet cushion. Gorringe took the cap in his hands and stroked the coffered satin, the streamers of ostentatious woe. He wondered what had happened to its owner. Had she followed her husband to an untimely grave, desolated by grief? Or had the bonnet, an expensive contraption, merely failed to please? Both it and the brooches would be an addition to the bedroom in Courcy Castle which he called Memento Mori and where he kept his collection of Victorian necrophilia: the death masks of Carlyle, Ruskin, and Matthew Arnold; the black-edged memorial cards with their weeping angels and sentimental verses; the commemorative cups, medals, and mugs; the wardrobe of heavy mourning garments, black, gray, and mauve. It was a room Clarissa had entered with a shudder, only once, and now pretended didn't exist. But he had noted with pleasure that those of his guests who were lovers, acknowledged or furtive, liked occasionally to sleep there, rather, he thought, as eighteenth-century whores had copulated with their clients on the flat tops of tombs in London's East End graveyards. He watched with a sardonic and slightly contemptuous eye this symbiosis of eroticism and morbidity, as he did all those human foibles which he happened not to share.

He said, "I'll take these. And probably the marble too. Where did you find it?"

"A private sale. I don't think it's a memorial piece. The owner claimed that it was a duplicate of one of the marble limbs of the royal children at Osborne, carved for Queen Victoria. This one is probably the arm of the infant Princess Royal."

"Poor Vicky! What with her formidable mother, her son, and Bismarck, not the happiest of princesses. It's almost irresistible, but not at that price."

"The cushion is the original. And if it is the arm of the princess, it's probably unique. There's no record as far as I know of any duplicates of the Osborne pieces."

They entered into their usual amicable pattern of bargaining, but Gorringe sensed that Gaskin's heart wasn't in it. He was a superstitious man, and it was apparent to Gorringe that the marble, which he seemed unable to bring himself to touch, both fascinated and repelled him. He wanted it out of his shop.

Hardly had the business concluded when there was a ring on the locked street door. As Gaskin left to answer it,

Gorringe asked if he might use the telephone. It had occurred to him that with some slight hurry he could catch an earlier train. As usual, it was Munter who answered the ring.

"Courcy Castle."

"Gorringe, Munter. I'm ringing from London. I find that I shall, after all, be able to catch the two-thirty train. I should be at the quay by four-forty."

"Very good, sir. I will instruct Oldfield."

"Is all well, Munter?"

"Quite well, sir. Tuesday's dress rehearsal was hardly a success, but I understand that this is considered propitious for the actual performance."

"The lighting rehearsal was satisfactory?"

"Yes, sir. If I may say so, the company is more fortunate in the talent of its amateur electricians than in its actors."

"And Mrs. Munter? Have you been able to get all the help she needs for Saturday?"

"Not quite all. Two of the girls from the town have defaulted, but Mrs. Chambers is bringing her granddaughter. I have interviewed the girl and she seems well intentioned if untrained. If the Courcy play is to be an annual event, we may have to reconsider our staffing needs, at least for this one week of the year."

Gorringe said calmly, "I don't think that either you or Mrs. Munter need assume that the play will be an annual event. If you feel the need to plan for twelve months ahead, it would be safer to assume that this is the last performance which Lady Ralston will give on Courcy."

"Thank you, sir. I should tell you that Lady Ralston telephoned. Sir George has an unexpected meeting to attend and is unlikely to arrive before Saturday afternoon and, possibly, not until after the performance. Lady Ralston proposes to solace marital deprivation by inviting a secretary-companion, a Miss Cordelia Gray. She will arrive with the rest of the party on Friday morning. Lady Ralston appeared to think that she need not speak to you personally about this arrangement."

Munter's disapproval came over the line as clearly as his carefully controlled irony. He was adept at judging just how far he could safely go, and since his veiled insolence was never directed against his employer, Gorringe was indulgent. A man, particularly a servant, was entitled to his small recalcitrant bolsterings of self-respect. Gorringe had noted early in their relationship how Munter's persona, modeled as it was on Jeeves and his near namesake Bunter, became markedly closer to parody when any of his carefully contrived domestic arrangements was upset. During Clarissa's visits to the castle he became almost intolerably Bunterish. Relishing his manservant's eccentricities, the contrast between his bizarre appearance and his manner, and totally uncurious about his past, Gorringe now hardly bothered to wonder whether a real Munter existed and, if so, what manner of man he might be.

He heard him say, "I thought that Miss Gray could be companionable in the De Morgan room, subject to your agreement."

"That would seem suitable. And if Sir George does arrive for Saturday night he can have Memento Mori. A soldier should be inured to death. Do we know anything about Miss Gray?"

"A young lady, I understand. I take it that she will eat in the dining room."

"Of course."

Whatever Clarissa thought she was up to, it would at least even the numbers at his dinner table. But the thought of Clarissa with a secretary-companion, and a woman at that, was intriguing. He hoped that her addition to the party wouldn't make the weekend more complicated than it already promised to be.

"Good-bye, Munter."

"Good-bye, sir."

When Gaskin returned to the office, he found his customer sitting contemplatively holding the marble arm. He gave an involuntary shiver. Gorringe replaced the marble on its cushion and watched while Gaskin busied himself finding a small cardboard box and lining it with tissue paper.

He said, "You don't like it?"

Gaskin could afford to be frank. The limb was sold, and Mr. Gorringe had never yet rejected a piece once the price was agreed. He lowered the arm into its box, taking care to touch only the cushion.

"I can't say I'm sorry to see it go. I usually do very well with those porcelain models of the human hand which the Victorians were so fond of, ring stands and so on. I had a nice one in last week but the wrist frill was chipped. It wouldn't have interested you. But a child's arm! And cut off like that! I call it brutal, almost morbid. It's just a feel I have about the piece. You know how I am. It reminds me of death."

Gorringe took a final look at the brooches before they were wrapped and boxed.

"Less rationally, surely, than should the jewelry and the widow's cap. I agree with you; I doubt whether this is a memorial marble."

Gaskin said firmly, "They're different. They don't worry me; memorials never have. But this is different. To tell you the truth, I took against it as soon as it came into the shop. Whenever I look at it, I keep imagining that it's oozing blood."

Gorringe smiled. "I must try it on my houseguests and watch their reactions. The Courcy play this weekend is *The Duchess of Malfi*. If this were a full-size male hand we could use it for one of the props. But even the duchess in her extremity could hardly mistake this for the dead hand of Antonio."

The allusion was lost on Gaskin, who had never read

Webster. He murmured, "No indeed, sir," and smiled his sly, sycophantic smile.

Five minutes later, he saw his customer and his parcels formally off the premises, congratulating himself with premature satisfaction—for despite his carefully nurtured sensitivity he had never claimed to be a clairvoyant—that he had seen and heard the last of the arm of the dead princess.

4

LESS THAN TWO MILES AWAY in a Harley Street consulting
room, Ivo Whittingham slipped his legs over the edge of the
examination couch and watched Dr. Crantley-Mathers shuffle
back to his desk. The doctor, as always, was wearing his old
but well-tailored pinstripe suit. Nothing so clinical as a white
coat ever intruded into his consulting room, and the room
itself, with its patterned Axminster carpet, its Edwardian
carved desk holding the silver-framed photographs of Sir
James's grandchildren and distinguished patients, its sporting
prints, and the portrait of some solidly prosperous ancestor
holding pride of place above the carved marble mantel shelf,
looked more like a private study than a consulting room. No
apparent effort was made to keep infection at bay; but, then,
thought Whittingham, germs would know better than to lurk
in the well-upholstered armchair in which Sir James's patients
awaited his advice. Even the examination couch looked
unclinical, being covered with brown leather and mounted by

way of elegant eighteenth-century library steps. The assumption was that, although a number of Sir James's guests might wish for some private whim to take off their clothes, that eccentricity could have nothing to do with the state of their health.

Now he looked up from his prescription pad and asked, "That spleen troubling you?"

"As it must weigh twenty pounds and I look and feel like a lopsided pregnant woman, yes, you could say that it's troubling me."

"The time may come when it's better out. No hurry, though. We'll have another think in a month's time."

Whittingham went behind the painted oriental screen where his clothes were folded over a chair and began to dress, drawing his trousers up over the heavy belly. It was, he thought, like carrying one's own death, feeling it drag at the muscles, a fetus-like incubus which never stirred, reminding him with its dead weight, by the deformity which he saw in his mirror every time he bathed, what it was he bore within him. Looking over the screen, he said, his voice muffled by his shirt, "I thought you explained that the spleen is enlarged because it's taken over the manufacture of the red blood corpuscles, which my blood's no longer producing."

Sir James didn't look up. He said with careful unconcern, "That's more or less what's happening, yes. When one organ ceases to function, another tends to take over."

"So would it be tactless to inquire which organ will obligingly take over the job when you've whipped out the spleen?"

Sir James guffawed at this witticism. "Let's cross that bridge when we come to it, shall we?"

He had never, thought Whittingham, been a man for originality of speech.

For the first time since his illness had begun, Whittingham would have liked to ask his doctor directly how much time remained for him. It wasn't that there were affairs that he needed to put in order. He was divorced from his wife, alienated from his children, and living now alone; his affairs, like his obsessively tidy flat, had been depressingly in order for the last five years. The need to know was now little more than a mild curiosity. He would be glad to learn that he was to be spared another Christmas, his most disliked time of the year. But he realized that the question would be in the worst of taste. The room itself had been designed to make it unsayable; Sir James was adept at training his patients not to ask questions which they knew it would distress him to have to answer. His philosophy—and Whittingham wasn't altogether in disagreement with it—was that patients would realize in their own good time that they were dying and that, by then, physical weakness would ensure that the realization would be less painful than a sentence of death pronounced when the blood still ran strong. He had never believed that the loss of hope did anyone any good; and besides, doctors could be wrong. This last assertion was a conventional gesture to modesty. Sir James did not privately believe that he personally could be wrong, and indeed he was a superb diagnostician. It was hardly his fault, thought Whittingham, that the ability of the medical profession to diagnose is so far in advance of its ability to cure. Slipping his arms through his jacket sleeves, he spoke aloud Brachiano's words from *The White Devil:* " 'On pain of death, let no man name death to me: / It is a word infinitely terrible.' "

It was a view Sir James obviously shared. It was surprising, supposing he knew the words, that he hadn't carved them over his door lintel.

"I'm sorry, Mr. Whittingham. I didn't quite catch what you said."

"Nothing, Sir James. I was merely quoting Webster."

Escorting his patient to the consulting-room door at which an exceedingly pretty nurse was waiting to see him finally on his way, the doctor asked, "Are you going out of London this weekend? It's a pity to waste this weather."

"To Dorset, actually. To Courcy Island, off Speymouth. An amateur company with some professional support is putting on *The Duchess of Malfi*, and I'm doing a piece for one of the color supplements." He added, "It's chiefly about the restoration of the Victorian theater on the island and its history."

Immediately he despised himself for the explanation. What was it but a way of saying that dying he might be, but he wasn't yet reduced to reviewing amateurs.

"Good. Good." Sir James boomed out a note of approval which might have sounded excessive even for God on the seventh day.

When the imposing front door had closed behind him, Whittingham was tempted to hire the taxi which had just drawn up, presumably to deposit another patient. But he decided he might manage a mile of the walk to his Russell Square flat. And there was a new coffeehouse in Marylebone High Street where the young couple who owned it ground the beans freshly and made their own cakes, and where a few chairs under umbrellas gave the locals the illusion that the English summer was suitable for eating outdoors. He might rest there for ten minutes. It was extraordinary how important these trivial self-indulgences had become. As he resigned himself to the accidiae of mortal illness, he was beginning to acquire some of the foibles of old age: a liking for small treats, a fussiness about routine, a reluctance to bother with even his oldest acquaintances, an indolence which made even dressing and bathing a burden, a preoccupation with his bodily functions. He despised the half-man he had become, but even this self-disgust had some of the querulous resentment of senility. Sir James was right. It was difficult to feel regret about losing a life so diminished; by the time this sickness had finished with him, death would be no more than the final disintegration of a body from which the spirit had already seeped away, worn out by pain, by weariness, and by a malaise which went deeper than physical weakness, some

brittle-armed traitor of the heart which had never mustered
the will to fight.

As he made his way down Wimpole Street through the
mellow autumn sunlight he thought of the great performances
he had seen and reviewed and mentally spoke the names like
a roll call: Olivier's Richard the Third, Wolfit playing Malvolio,
Gielgud's Hamlet, Richardson's Falstaff, Peggy Ashcroft's
Portia. He could recall them, could remember the theaters,
the directors, even some of the most quoted extracts from his
reviews. It was interesting that after thirty years of playgoing,
it was the classics which had lasted longest for him. But he
knew that even if he were this night to take his accustomed
seat in the third row of the stalls, formally dressed as he
always was for a first night, listening to that anticipatory hum
which is unlike any other sound in the world, nothing that
happened when the curtain rose would move or excite him
beyond a mild, detached interest. The glory and the wonder
had departed. Never again would he feel that tingle between
the shoulder blades, that almost physical surge of the blood
which, for all his youth, had been his response to great
acting. It was ironic that now, all passion spent, he was about
to review his last play, and that an amateur production. But
somehow he would find the energy for what he had to do on
Courcy Island.

The island was reputed to be beautiful and the castle an
interesting example of high Victorian panache. Seeing them
would probably be worth the effort of the journey, which was
as close as he could now get to enthusiasm. But he was less
sure about the company. Clarissa had mentioned that her
cousin Roma Lisle was to be there with a friend. He hadn't
met Roma, but had had to listen to Clarissa's caustic dispar-
agement of her for too many years to relish being under the
same roof as them both, and the careful omission of the
friend's name hadn't been reassuring. And the boy was to be
with them, apparently. Clarissa's decision to take on the son
of her drowned husband, Martin Lessing, had been one of her

more spectacular impulses; he wondered who was regretting it more, benefactress or victim. On the three occasions on which he had met Simon Lessing, two at the theater and one at a party at Clarissa's Bayswater flat, he had been struck by the boy's gaucherie and by a sense of deep personal wretchedness which he thought had less to do with adolescence than with Clarissa. There had been something doglike in his servility, a desperate need to win her approval without the least idea what it was she wanted of him. Whittingham had seen that same look in his father's eyes; the prick of memory hadn't been comfortable. Simon was supposed to be a talented pianist. Probably Clarissa had seen herself splendidly cantilevered in one of the front boxes at the Royal Festival Hall while her prodigy, adoring eyes glancing upwards, took his triumphant bow. It must be disconcerting for her to be faced instead with the moodiness and the physical gracelessness of adolescence. He found himself possessed of a slight interest in seeing how the two of them were doing. And there would be other minor satisfactions; not the least would be watching how Clarissa Lisle was coping with her own neurosis. If this were to be his last performance, there was some satisfaction in knowing that it might well be hers. She would know that he was dying. She had the use of her eyes. But he wouldn't grudge her any pleasure she could get from observing the process of his physical disintegration. There were subtler pleasures than that; watching mental disintegration might, he suspected, be among them. He was discovering that even hatred died a little at the end. But it still lasted longer than desire, longer even than love. Walking slowly in the sunshine and thinking of the weekend ahead, he smiled at the realization that what was most alive in him now was the capacity for mischief.

5

IN THE BASEMENT of a small shop in a passageway of the north end of Tottenham Court Road, Roma Lisle was on her knees unpacking and sorting a box of secondhand books. The room, which had originally been a kitchen and which still contained an old porcelain sink, a row of wall-mounted cupboards, and a disconnected gas stove so heavy that the combined efforts of Colin and herself had been unable to shift it, was oppressively hot despite the tiled floor. Outside, the accumulated heat of the dying summer seemed to have concentrated in the area beneath the iron railings, pressing against the one small window like a sweaty, fume-soaked blanket, cutting off air as well as light. Above her the single pendant light threw shadows rather than illumination; it was ridiculous to have to be using expensive electricity on such a day. She must have been mad ever to have thought that this hole could be transformed into an intimate, invitingly cozy secondhand books department, a browser's delight.

42

The books, she now saw, were a poor lot. She had bid for them and bought them cheaply at a country-house sale. Now the first real inspection revealed that it hadn't been cheap enough. The best had been on the top. The rest were a motley collection of Victorian sermons, reminiscences of retired generals, biographies of minor politicians as undistinguished in death as they had been in life, novels which provoked no interest except a wonder that anyone should have chosen to publish them.

Her knees were numb against the tiles, her nostrils choked with the smell of dust, of moldering cardboard and rotting paper. In her imagination it was to have been so different: Colin kneeling beside her, the happy rummaging, the exclamations of pleasure as each treasure came to light, the laughter, the planning, the fun. She remembered their last day at Pottergate Comprehensive: the farewell party with its cheap sherry and inevitable crisps and cheese savories; the barely concealed envy of their colleagues that she and Colin were getting out, setting up business together, saying good-bye to timetables, mark sheets, examinations, the daily dispiriting struggle to impose order on a class of forty in an inner-city comprehensive where teaching had always to be subordinated to the struggle to maintain some semblance of discipline.

And that was only nine months ago! Nine months in which everything they had bought, everything they needed, had become more expensive, in which the shop had been as dead as if boarded up and bankrupt. Nine months of overwork and dwindling returns, of fading hope and half-acknowledged panic. Nine months—could it be?—of the slow death of desire. She almost cried out in protest, shoving her strong hands against the box as if the thought and its pain could be physically pushed from her mind. And then she heard his step on the stairs. She turned her face to his, making herself smile. He had hardly spoken over luncheon. But that was three hours ago. Sometimes his moods didn't last. His first words destroyed hope.

"My God, this place stinks."

"It won't, once we get it cleaned up."

"And how long will that take? It needs an army of cleaners and decorators. And even then it'll still look what it is, a basement slum."

He slumped down on an unopened box of books and began turning over the pile she had unpacked, letting them drop with careful disdain in an untidy heap. In the dim light his handsome, petulant face looked lined with weariness. Why? she wondered. It was she who had been doing the work. She held out her hand, and after a moment he took it in a limp grasp.

She thought, Oh, God, I love you! We love each other. Don't take that away from me.

He slid his hand from hers almost furtively and began to pretend an interest in one of the books. As he opened it, a small sheet of thick and faded paper fluttered out.

She said, "What's that?"

"Some kind of old woodcut by the look of it. I shouldn't think it has any value."

"We could ask Ambrose Gorringe when we get to Courcy Island. He knows about these things even if they aren't his period."

They peered at it together. It was certainly old, early seventeenth century she guessed from the antiquated spelling, and it was in remarkably good condition. The paper was headed with a crude woodcut of a skeleton holding in its right hand an arrow and in its left an hourglass. Beneath was the title, "The Gt Meffenger of Mortality," followed by the verse. She read the first four lines aloud.

Fair lady lay your costly robe afide,
No longer may you glory in your pride,
Take leave of all yr carnal vain delight,
I'm come to fummon you away tonight.

The undated subscription gave the printer's name as John Evans of Long Lane, London.

Roma said, "It reminds me of Clarissa."

"Of Clarissa? Why?"

"I don't know. I don't know why."

He pressed her, sounding irritably insistent, as if it mattered, as if she had intended something.

"It's just something I said, something that came into my mind. It didn't mean anything. Put the paper by the sink, on the draining board. We'll show it to Ambrose Gorringe." He did so and returned moodily to his box. He said, "It was a mistake, buying this junk. We should have stuck to the new stock. London seems to have a surfeit of bookshops. And God knows why I let you talk me into buying all that left-wing stuff upstairs. No one wants it. The left wing already have enough cozy haunts in this neighborhood and it only repels the other buyers. Those pamphlets are just gathering dust. I must have been mad."

She knew that he wasn't referring only to the left-wing literature. The injustice stung her into anger. She knew even as she spoke that it was folly. He needed to be cajoled, humored, comforted. The quarrels which he seemed increasingly to provoke only left him sulky and resentful and herself exhausted. But she had had enough.

"Look, you didn't take on this place to oblige me. You were just as keen to get out of Pottergate. You loathed teaching. Remember? I was fed up with it, I admit, but I wouldn't have resigned if you hadn't made the first move."

"You mean it's all my fault."

"All! What all? It isn't anyone's fault. We both did what we wanted."

"Then what are you complaining about?"

"It's just that I'm tired of being made to feel as if I'm some kind of encumbrance, worse than a wife, as if you're keeping on the shop only because of me."

"I'm keeping it—we're keeping it on—because there's no

alternative. Pottergate wouldn't take us back even if we apply."

And where else could they apply? He didn't need her to tell him about the unemployment in the teaching profession, the expenditure cuts, the desperate search for jobs even by the best qualified.

She said, knowing even as she spoke that argument was folly, that it would only fuel his irritation, "If you do chuck it, it'll please Stella. I suppose that's what she's been waiting for. She can say, 'I told you so' and hand you over, neatly trussed, a sacrificial victim to dear Daddy and the family business. My God, she must be praying for our bankruptcy! It's a wonder she doesn't lurk outside counting the customers."

His protest was sulky rather than vehement. It was, after all, an argument they had had before.

"She knows I'm worried, obviously. She's worried herself. She has a right to be. Half the money I put in here was hers."

As if that needed saying. As if Roma didn't know exactly how much cash from Daddy's generous allowance Stella had graciously handed over. And that it was generous of her, generous or stupid or cunning. Or all three. Because she must have known that Colin was going into partnership with his mistress; she wasn't that blind. Oh, she'd known all right! Stella couldn't understand what he saw in Roma—she wasn't unique in that—but she'd known the score. And had this been her revenge, the money to set up a partnership which was bound to fail, given their inexperience, their small capital, their self-delusions, a failure that would draw him back, suitably chastened, to the place where he belonged—the place, come to think of it, that he'd never really left? And then what would there be for him but Daddy's business, the store in Kilburn which sold cheap plywood furniture on the installment plan to customers too ignorant to know when they were being cheated or too proud in their poverty to rummage around the street markets and buy good solid oak, second-hand? The stuff he dazzled them with—cocktail cabinets, room dividers, ornate suites—would fall or be kicked to pieces long before they'd finished paying for it. Was that what Colin wanted to do with his life? Had he left teaching for that? And had Stella thought all this out for herself, or had Daddy had a hand in it? The money she had lent them, hadn't it been carefully calculated, enough to make the enterprise possible but not enough to enable them to succeed? She was sharp enough. She had a shrewd little mind to go with those sharp painted nails, those white childlike teeth. And she had other weapons, Justin and Joanna. Possessiveness and acquisitiveness had been sanctified by maternity. She had the twins. And, by God, she knew how to use them! With every childhood infection, every school speech day, every dental appointment, every family holiday, every Christmas demanding his presence at home, it was as if she were saying, "He may sleep with you, play at keeping shop with you, imagine that he's in love with you, confide in you. But he'll never give you children. And he'll never divorce me to marry you."

Appalled at her thoughts, at what was happening to them, she cried, "Look, darling, don't let's quarrel. We're tired, we're hot, and it's a bloody day. On Friday we shut the door on the whole scene and take off for Courcy Island. Three days of peace, sunshine, good wines, first-class food, and the sea. The island's only three miles by two and a half, so Clarissa says, but there are marvelous walks. We can get away from the rest of the party. Clarissa will be busy with the play. I don't suppose Ambrose Gorringe will care a damn what we do. No creditors, no people, just peace. And, my God, don't I need it."

She was going to add, "And I need you, my darling. More and more. Always." But then she looked up and saw his face.

It wasn't an unfamiliar look, that mixture of shame, irritation, embarrassment. She had seen it before. This, after all, had been the pattern of their lives, the plans so confidently, so

happily, made, the last-minute cancellations. But never before
had it mattered so desperately. Tears scalded her eyes. She
told herself that she had to stay calm, that she mustn't break
down; but when she could speak, the note of angry recrimina-
tion was unmistakable even to her own ears and she saw the
look of shame harden into defiance.

"You can't do this to me! You can't! You promised! And
I've told Clarissa I'm bringing my partner. It's all arranged."

"I know and I'm sorry. But Stella's father telephoned at
breakfast to say that he's coming for the weekend. I've got to
be there. I've told you what he's like. He was pretty fed up
about my leaving teaching. We've never got on. He thinks I
don't appreciate her enough; you know how it is with an only
child. He's not going to be pleased if he finds I'm away for a
long weekend, leaving her to cope with the kids. And he
won't believe the story about attending a book sale. I don't
think even Stella does."

So that was it. Daddy was arriving. Daddy, who paid the
twins' school fees, provided the car, the annual holiday, the
luxuries which had become necessities. Daddy, who had his
own ideas about his son-in-law's future.

She said in a voice that was almost a wail, "What is
Clarissa going to think?"

"Well, isn't it rather what she'd think if I did come? She
knows I'm married. I mean, you must have let that drop.
Wouldn't it look rather odd, the two of us arriving together?
And it's not as if we could have shared a room or anything
like that."

"By 'anything like that' I suppose you mean that we couldn't
have slept together. Why not? Clarissa isn't exactly a model
of purity, and I don't suppose Ambrose Gorringe creeps down
his corridors at night checking that his guests are in their
own rooms."

He muttered, "It's not that. I explained. It's Stella's
father."

"But this weekend might have freed you from him and her.

I thought we could have spoken to Clarissa, told her about the shop, asked if she couldn't help. That's why I wangled the invitation. After all, a third of her money comes to me if she dies without a child. It's all in Uncle's will. It wouldn't harm her to part with some when it's most needed. We'd only be asking for a loan.''

She tried not to see the hope brightening in his face. Then it faded. He said sulkily, ''I couldn't ask a woman for money.''

''You wouldn't have to. I'd do the asking. What I thought was that she'd meet you, like you. She'd be seeing you under the best possible conditions. Then I could speak to her when the time seemed right. It's worth a try, darling. Even twenty thousand would mean all the difference.''

''What would you get if she died?''

''I'm not sure. About eighty thousand, I think. It could be more.''

He turned away. ''And that's about what we'd need if I were to leave Stella, get a divorce. But Clarissa isn't going to die just to convenience us. Twenty thousand might just save the shop. But that's about all it would do. And why should she part with it? Anyone with an ounce of financial sense would see that it would be throwing good money after bad. It's no use. I can't come this weekend.''

Above them the floor creaked. Someone had come into the shop. He said quickly, gratefully, ''Sounds like a customer. Look, I'll close promptly at five if there's nothing doing and give you a hand down here. We'll get this room together somehow.''

When he had gone, she went over and stared out the window, standing rigidly, grasping the edges of the sink so tightly that her knuckles were white. Her eyes were unfocused, staring beyond the railings, the crumbling stucco on the basement wall, to where the brightly patterned reds, greens, and yellows of the fruit stall on the opposite pavement fused and shivered. From time to time feet passed, voices called, the narrow street broke momentarily into life. And still that silent figure at the window stood unmoving. Then she gave a little sigh. The taut shoulders relaxed, the fingers loosened their grip. She took up the woodcut from the draining board and studied it as if she hadn't seen it before. Then she opened her shoulder bag and folded it carefully away.

6

SIMON LESSING stood at the open window of his study at Melhurst and gazed out over the wide lawns to where the river cut its slow stream between the horse chestnuts and the limes. In his hand he held Clarissa's still-unopened letter. It had arrived by the morning post, but there had been an excuse for not opening it then. He had had an early practice period. And that had been followed by the sixth-form seminar. He had told himself that he would wait until break. But the morning had passed and now it was the lunch hour. In less than five minutes the bell would sound. He couldn't delay indefinitely. It was ridiculous and humiliating to be so afraid, to stand like a first-former holding a dreaded school report, knowing that however long and cunningly deferred, the moment of truth must come at last.

He would wait until the bell actually sounded, and then he would read it, quickly, uncaring, and with his mind on luncheon. And at least he could do so in peace. From the

51

middle school upwards, every boy at Melhurst had his own study. The importance of a daily period of silence and privacy was one of the more enlightened precepts of the school's pious seventeenth-century founder, and, largely because it had been incorporated into the almost monastic architecture, it had endured through three hundred years of changing educational fashion. It was one of the things about Melhurst which Simon most valued, one of the privileges which Clarissa's patronage, Clarissa's money, had procured for him. Neither she nor Sir George had ever considered another choice of school, and Melhurst had made no difficulty about finding a place for the stepson of one of its more distinguished alumni. Its motto, in Greek rather than in the more usual Latin, extolled the virtues of moderation, and for three hundred years, in obedience to Theognis's dictum, the school had been moderately famous, moderately expensive, and moderately successful.

No other school could have suited Simon better. He recognized that its traditions and occasionally bizarre rituals, which he quickly learned and sedulously observed, were designed as much to discourage too personal a commitment as to promote a corporate identity. He was tolerated but left alone, and he asked nothing more. Even his talents were acceptable to the ethos of the school, which, perhaps because of a strong personal antipathy between a nineteenth-century headmaster and Dr. Arnold of Rugby, by tradition eschewed muscular Christianity and almost all manifestations of the team spirit and espoused High Anglicanism and the cult of the eccentric. But music was well taught; the school's two orchestras had a national reputation. And swimming, the only physical skill at which he excelled, was one of the more acceptable sports. Compared with the Norman Pagworth Comprehensive, Melhurst seemed to him a haven of civilized order. At Pagworth he had felt like an alien set down without a phrase book in a lawless, ill-governed, and alien country whose language and customs, crudely harsh as the playground in which they were born, were terrifyingly incomprehensible. The prospect of having to leave Melhurst and return to his old school had been one of his worst terrors since he began to sense that things were going wrong between himself and Clarissa.

It was strange that fear and gratitude should be so mixed. The gratitude was genuine enough. He only wished that he could experience it as it surely ought to be experienced, as a graciousness, a reciprocal benison, free of this dragging load of obligation and guilt. The guilt was the worse to bear. When its weight became almost too much for him, he tried to exorcise it by rational thought. It was ridiculous to feel guilty, ridiculous and unnecessary even to feel too oppressive an obligation. Clarissa owed him something after all. It was she who had destroyed his parents' marriage, enticed away his father, helped kill his mother through grief, left him an orphan to endure the discomforts, the vulgarities, the suffocating boredom of his uncle's house. It was Clarissa, not he, who should feel guilt.

But even to let this thought creep traitorously into his mind only increased his burden of obligation. He owed her so much. The trouble was that everyone knew just how much. Sir George was seldom there, but when he was, he presented himself to Simon as a silent, accusing personification of all those masculine qualities which he knew were alien to his own personality. He sometimes sensed in Clarissa's husband an inarticulate goodwill which he would have liked to put to the test if only he could summon the courage. But most of the time he imagined that Sir George had never really approved of Clarissa's taking him on and that their secret marital conversations were punctuated with the phrases "I told you so. I warned you." Miss Tolgarth knew; Tolly, whose eyes he dared not meet for fear of encountering one of those judgmental gazes in which he thought he detected dislike, resentment, and contempt. Clarissa knew it, probably to the last penny. Increasingly he had come to feel that Clarissa repented of a generosity which at first had held all the charm of novelty, the magnificent gesture, superbly theatrical at the time in all its eccentricity, but which she now saw had lumbered her with a spotty, inarticulate adolescent, ill at ease with her friends; with school bills, holiday arrangements, dental appointments; with all the minor irritations of motherhood and none of its essential compensations. He sensed that there was something she required of him which he could neither identify nor give, some return, unspecified but substantial, which would one day be demanded of him with all the brutal insistence of a tax collector.

She seldom wrote to him now, and when he did see in his cubbyhole that tall, curved hand—she disapproved of personal letters being typed—he had to steel himself to open the envelope. But the apprehension had never before been as bad as this. The letter seemed to have stuck to his hand, to have grown heavy with menace. And then the one o'clock bell clanged out. With sudden vehemence he tore at the corner of the envelope. The pale blue linen-based paper which she always used was tough. He wrenched in his thumb and tore a jagged slit through envelope and letter, as roughly as a lover who cannot wait to know his fate. He saw that the letter was short, and his immediate reaction was a moan of relief. If she was throwing him out, if there was to be no last term at Melhurst, no chance of a place at the Royal College of Music, no more allowance, surely the excuse, the justification, would require more than half a page. The first sentence did away with his worst fears.

This is to let you know the arrangements for next weekend. George will drive Tolly and me down to Speymouth before breakfast on Friday but it will be best if you arrive with the rest of the house party in time for lunch. The launch will meet the nine-thirty-two from Waterloo. Be at the harbor at Speymouth by eleven-forty. Ivo Whittingham and my cousin Roma will be on the train and you'll also meet a girl, Cordelia Gray. I shall need some extra help during the weekend and she is a kind of temporary secretary, so there will be someone young on the island for you to practice talking to. You should also be able to get some swimming so you won't need to be bored. Bring your dinner jacket. Mr. Gorringe likes to dress in the evenings. And he knows something about music so you may as well select some of your best pieces, the ones you know, nothing too heavy. I've written to your housemaster about the extra days' leave. Did Matron give you that acne lotion I sent last month? I hope you've been using it.

Love,
Clarissa

It was odd how soon relief could change to a new and different anxiety, even to resentment. Reading the letter for the second time, he wondered why he should have been invited to the island. It was Clarissa's doing, of course. Ambrose Gorringe didn't know him and would hardly be likely to include him among his guests if he did. He remembered vaguely having heard about the island, the restored Victorian theater, the plans to stage the Webster tragedy, and he sensed that the performance was important to Clarissa, amateur production though it was. But why should he be there? He was expected to keep out of her way, not to make a nuisance of himself; that much was evident. He could disport himself in the sea or the pool. He supposed that there would be a pool and pictured Clarissa, pale and golden, stretched out in the sun, and beside her this new girl, this Cordelia Gray, with whom he was supposed to practice making conversation. And what else did Clarissa want him to practice? Making himself agreeable? Paying compliments? Knowing what jokes women like and when to make them? Flirting? Showing himself to be a susceptible heterosexual male? The prospect made his mouth dry with terror.

It wasn't that he disliked the idea of a girl. He had already created in his mind the girl he would like to be with on Courcy Island, on any island: sensitive, beautiful, intelligent, kind, and yet wanting him, wanting him to do to her those terrifyingly exciting and shameful things which would no longer be shameful because they loved each other, acts which would reconcile for him in sweet responsive flesh, finally and forever, that dichotomy between romanticism and desire which so occupied his daydreaming hours. He didn't expect to meet this girl, on Courcy or anywhere else. The only girl with whom he had so far had anything to do had been his cousin Susie. He hated Susie, hated her bold, contemptuous eyes, her perpetually chewing mouth, her voice which alternately whined and yelled, her dyed hair, her grubby beringed fingers.

But even if this girl were different, even if he liked her, how could he get to know her when Clarissa would be watching them, marking him for articulacy, attraction, wit, checking up on his social performance, as she and this Ambrose Gorringe would be checking up on his musicianship? The reference to his music made his cheeks burn. He was insecure enough about his talent without having it diminished by this coy reference to his pieces as if he were a child showing off to the neighbors at a suburban tea party. But the instruction was clear enough. He was to bring with him something showy or popular or both, something he could play with practiced bravado so that she wouldn't be disgraced by any nervous misfingerings, and she and Ambrose Gorringe would together decide whether he had enough talent to justify a final year at school, a chance to try for a place at the Royal College or the Academy.

And suppose the verdict went against him? He couldn't return to Mornington Avenue, to his aunt and uncle. Clarissa couldn't do that to him. After all, it was she who had brought the order of release. She had arrived unannounced on a warm afternoon during the summer holidays, when he had been in the house alone as usual, reading at the sitting-room table. He couldn't remember how she had announced herself, whether he had been told that the silent, upright man with her was her new husband. But he remembered how she had looked, golden and effulgent, a cool, sweet-smelling, miraculous vision who had immediately taken hold of his heart and his life as a rescuer might pluck a drowning child from the water and set him firmly on a sunlit rock. It had been too good to last, of course. But how marvelous in memory shone that long-dead summer afternoon.

"Are you happy here?"

"No."

"I don't see how you could be, actually. This room's pretty gruesome. I've read somewhere that a million copies of that print have been sold, but I didn't realize people actually hung it on their walls. Your father told me that you're musical. Do you still play?"

"I can't. There isn't a piano here. And they only teach percussion at school. They have a West Indian steel band. They're only interested in music where everyone can join in."

"Things which everyone can join in usually aren't worth doing. They shouldn't have put two different papers on the walls. Three or four might have been bizarre enough to be fun. Two are just vulgar. How old are you? Fourteen, isn't it? How would you like to come and live with us?"

"For always?"

"Nothing is for always. But perhaps. Until you grow up, anyway."

Without waiting for his reply, without even looking into his face to watch his initial response, she turned to the silent man at her side. "I think we can do better than this for Martin's boy."

"If you are sure, my dear. Not a thing to decide quickly. Shouldn't make an impulse buy of a child."

"Darling, where would you be if I hadn't made an impulse buy? And he's the only son I'm ever likely to give you."

Simon's eyes were turning from one face to the other.
He remembered how Sir George had looked, the features
stiffening as if the muscles were bracing themselves against
pain, against vulgarity. But Simon had seen the hurt,
visible, unmistakable, before Sir George had turned silently
away.

She had turned to him. "Will your aunt and uncle
mind?"

The misery, the grievances, had spilled out. He had had to
prevent himself from clutching at her dress.

"They won't care! They'll be glad! I take up the spare
room and I haven't any money. They're always telling me
how much it costs to feed me. And they don't like me. They
won't mind, honestly."

And then, on impulse, he had done the right thing. It was
the only time he had done exactly the right thing where
Clarissa was concerned. There had been a pink geranium in a
pot on the window ledge; his uncle was a keen gardener and
grew cuttings in the lean-to greenhouse at the side of the
kitchen. One of the flower heads was small and as delicate as
a rose. He had broken it off and handed it to her, looking up
into her face. She had laughed aloud and taken it from him
and slipped it into the belt of her dress. Then she had looked
at her husband and had laughed again, a peal of happy
triumph.

"Well, that seems to have decided itself. We'd better stay
until they come home. I can't wait to see the owners of this
wallpaper. And then we'll take you to buy some clothes."

And so, with such promise, in such an exhilaration of
surprised joy, it had all begun. He tried now to recall when
the dream had faded, when things had first started to go
wrong. But, apart from that first meeting, had they ever
really gone right? He sensed that he was worse than a failure,
that he was the last of a series of failures, that earlier
disappointments had reinforced her present discontent. He
was beginning to dread the holidays, although he saw little

either of Clarissa or of Sir George. Their official life together, such as it was, was lived in the London flat overlooking Hyde Park. But they were seldom there together. Clarissa had a flat in Regency Square in Brighton, her husband a remote flint cottage on the marshes of the east coast. It was there that their real lives were lived, she in the company of her theatrical friends, he in bird-watching and, if rumor were correct, in right-wing conspiracy. Simon had never been invited to either place, although he often pictured them in those other secret worlds: Clarissa in a whirl of gaiety, Sir George conferring with his mysterious, hard-faced, and nameless confederates. For some unexplainable reason, these imaginings, which occupied a disproportionate part of his holiday hours, were in the guise of old films. Clarissa and her friends, dressed in the waistless shifts of the twenties, hair shingled, and flourishing long cigarette holders, flung out their legs in a hectic Charleston, while Sir George's friends arrived at their rendezvous in veteran cars, trench-coated, their wide-brimmed trilbys pulled down over secretive eyes. Excluded from both these worlds, Simon spent the holidays in the Bayswater flat, looked after occasionally by an almost silent Tolly or coping on his own, eating his dinner each night, by arrangement, in a local restaurant. Recently the meals had become poorer; dishes he chose were no longer available although they were served to others; he was shown to the worst table and kept waiting. Some of the waiters were almost openly offensive. He knew that Clarissa was no longer getting value for money, but he dared not complain. Who was he, so expensively bought and maintained, to talk about value for money?

It was time to go if he wanted any luncheon. He crumpled the letter in his hand and stuffed it into his pocket. Shutting his eyes against the brightness of grass and trees and shimmering water, he found himself praying, petitioning the God in whom he no longer believed, with all the desperate urgency, all the artless importunity, of a child.

"Please let the weekend be a success. Don't let me make a fool of myself. Please don't let the girl despise me. Please let Clarissa be in a good mood. Please don't let Clarissa throw me out. Oh, God, please don't let anything terrible happen on Courcy Island."

7

It was TEN O'CLOCK on Thursday night, and in her top-floor flat off Thames Street in the City, Cordelia was completing her preparations for the weekend ahead. The long, uncurtained windows were fitted with wooden slatted blinds, but these were still up and as she moved from the single large sitting room to her bedroom she could see spread below her the glittering streets, the dark alleyways, the towers and steeples of the city, could glimpse beyond them the necklace of light slung along the Embankment and the smooth, light-dazzled curve of the river. The view, in daylight or after dark, was a continual marvel to her, the flat itself a source of astonished delight.

It had only been after Bernie's death and at the end of her own first traumatic case that she had learned that her father's small estate had at last been wound up. She had expected nothing but debts, and it had been a surprise to discover that he had owned a small house in Paris. It had, she imagined, been purchased years before when he had been comparatively well off to provide a safe house and occasional refuge for the comrades and himself; such a dedicated revolutionary would surely otherwise have despised the acquisition of even so dilapidated and insalubrious a piece of real estate. But the area had been zoned for development and it had sold surprisingly well. There had been enough money, when the debts were paid, for her to finance the agency for another six months and to begin her search for a London flat cheap enough to buy. No building society had been interested in a sixth-floor apartment at the top of a Victorian warehouse with no lift and the barest amenities, or in an applicant with an income as uncertain as it was erratic. But her bank manager, apparently to his surprise as much as hers, had been sympathetic and had authorized a five-year loan.

She had paid for the installation of a shower and for the fitting out of the small kitchen, narrow as a galley. She had done the rest of the work herself and had furnished the flat from junk shops and suburban auctions. The immense sitting room was in white with one wall covered by a bookcase made from painted planks resting on columns of bricks. The dining and working table was scrubbed oak, and the heating was provided by an ornate wrought-iron stove. Only the bedroom was luxurious, an intriguing contrast to the spartan bareness of the sitting room. As it was only eight feet by five, Cordelia had felt justified in extravagance and had chosen an expensive and exotic hand-printed paper with which she had covered the ceiling and cupboard door as well as the walls. At night, with the window which occupied almost all of one wall wide open to the sky, she would lie, warmly cocooned in eccentric luxury, feeling that she was drawn up in her bright capsule to float under the stars.

She guarded her privacy. None of her friends and no one from the agency had ever been in the flat. Adventures occurred elsewhere. She knew that if any man shared that narrow bed, for her it would mean commitment. There was only one man she ever pictured there, and he was a commander of New Scotland Yard. She knew that he, too, lived in the City; they shared the same river. But she told herself that the brief madness was over, that at a time of stress and frightening insecurity she had only been seeking her lost father. There was this to be said for a smattering of amateur psychology: it enabled one to exorcise memories which might otherwise be embarrassing.

A narrow ledge with a parapet ran outside all the windows, wide enough for rows of potted herbs and geraniums and for a single deck chair in summer. Underneath were warehouses and offices, mysterious businesses symbolized rather than identified by a double row of ancient nameplates. By day the building had a secretive, many-tongued, and sometimes raucous life. But by five o'clock this began to seep away, and at night it held a vast, almost unbroken silence. One of the tenant firms imported spices. To Cordelia, climbing up to her flat at the end of the day, that pungent, alien smell permeating the stairs represented security, comfort, her first real home.

The most onerous part of the preparation for this new case was deciding which clothes to pack. In her more puritanical moments Cordelia despised women who spent an inordinate amount of time and money on their appearance. Such a total preoccupation with externals must, she felt, argue a need to compensate for some deficiency at the heart of personality. But she was quick to recognize that her own interest in clothes and makeup, although spasmodic, was intense while it lasted and that she had never known the state of not caring how she looked. In this, as in all other matters, she preferred to travel light, and the whole of her wardrobe could be comfortably accommodated within one cupboard and three drawers which were fitted along a wall of her bedroom.

She opened them now and considered what would be necessary for a weekend which, apart from detection, might offer anything from sailing and rock climbing to amateur theatricals. The creamy fawn pleated skirt in fine wool and the matching cashmere two-piece, both bought at Harrod's in the July sale, should, she felt, take care of most occasions; the cashmere's understated extravagance might, with luck, inspire confidence in the agency's prosperity. If the warm weather held, her brown corduroy knickerbockers might be warm for sleuthing or walking, but they were tough and she liked the jerkin and jacket, either of which looked good with them. Jeans and a couple of cotton tops were an obvious choice, as was her guernsey. The evenings were more difficult. Few people now dressed for dinner; but this was a castle, Ambrose Gorringe might well be an eccentric, and anything was possible. She would need something cool and reasonably formal. In the end she packed her only long dress, in Indian cotton in subtle shades of pink, red, and brown, and a pleated cotton skirt with matching top.

She turned with relief to the more straightforward business of checking her scene-of-crime kit. It was Bernie who had first devised it, basing it, she knew, on the kit issued to the Murder Squad of New Scotland Yard. His had been less comprehensive, but all the essentials had been there: envelopes and tweezers for the collection of specimens, dusting powder to detect fingerprints, a Polaroid camera, a pocket torch, fine rubber gloves, a magnifying glass, scissors and a sturdy penknife, a tin of Plasticine for taking impressions of keys, test tubes with stoppers for the collection of blood samples. Bernie had pointed out that, ideally, these should hold a preservative and an anticlotting agent. Neither had ever been necessary, then or now. Rescuing lost cats, shadowing errant husbands, tracing runaway teenagers, had required persistence, good feet, comfortable footwear, and infinite tact rather than the esoteric lore which Bernie had so enjoyed teaching her, compensating in those long summer sessions in Epping Forest of stalking, tracking, physical combat, and even gun lore for his own professional failure, trying to re-create through Pryde's Agency the lost hierarchical and fascinating world of the Metropolitan C.I.D.

She had made only a few alterations to the kit since Bernie's death, dispensing with the original case and using instead a canvas shoulder bag fitted with inner pockets which she had bought in a store which sold ex-army equipment. And since her first case she had included an additional item, a long leather belt with a buckle, the belt with which that first victim had been hanged. She had no wish to dwell on the case which had promised so much and had ended so tragically, one which had left her with its own legacy of guilt. But the belt had once saved her life, and she recognized an almost superstitious attachment to it, justifying its inclusion with the thought that a length of strong leather always came in useful.

Last she took a manila envelope file and wrote the name CLARISSA LISLE in capitals on the cover, taking care to make the letters neat and even. She had often thought that this was the most satisfying part of a new investigation, a moment of hope spiced with anticipatory excitement, the pristine folder and crisp lettering themselves symbolic of a fresh beginning. She glanced through her notebook before adding it to the folder. Except for Sir George and his briefly seen wife, her companions on the island were still only names, a roll call of putative suspects—Simon Lessing, Roma Lisle, Rose Tolgarth, Ambrose Gorringe, Ivo Whittingham—sounds written on paper but holding the promise of discovery, of challenge, of the fascinating variety of human personality. Like planets they circled the golden figure of Clarissa Lisle: her stepson, her cousin, her dresser, her host, her friend.

She spread out the twenty-three quotations on the table to study them before filing them in the case folder in the order of their receipt by Miss Lisle. Then she took from her shelf her two volumes of quotations, the paperback *Penguin Dictionary of Quotations* and the second edition of the *Oxford Dictionary*. As she had expected, all the passages appeared in one or the other, all but three in the paperback. Almost certainly that had been the dictionary used; it could be bought in almost any bookshop and its size would make it easy to conceal and light to carry about. To select the quotations would take no great trouble or time, merely a look at the index under *death* or *dying* or a quick read through the forty-five pages devoted to the plays of Shakespeare, the two which covered Marlowe and Webster. And it would not be too difficult to discover which plays Clarissa Lisle had appeared in. She had been a member of the Malvern Repertory Company for three years, and Shakespeare and the Jacobean dramatists were their forte. Any program note covering her career, then or later, would list her main appearances. But it was a safe bet that, given the exigencies of a Shakespearean production with the resources of a medium-sized repertory company, she would have had at least a walk-on part in all the plays.

Only two of the quotations which she had tentatively identified as Webster were not in the Penguin dictionary. But these could be found by studying the texts. All the quotations were familiar; she herself had had no difficulty in recognizing most of them even if she wasn't always sure of the play. But typing them accurately from memory was another matter. In each passage the lines were set out correctly and the punctuation was faultless, another reason for concluding that the typist had worked with the Penguin dictionary at his or her elbow.

Next she studied them under her magnifying glass, wondering as she did so how much attention the Metropolitan police had thought it worthwhile to give them. As far as she could judge, only three were typed on the same machine. The quality as well as the size of the letters varied; some were uneven, others faint or partly broken. The typing wasn't particularly expert, the work of someone who was used to a machine perhaps for his own correspondence but didn't type professionally. She thought that none had been typed on an electric typewriter. And who would have access to twenty-one different machines? Obviously someone who dealt in second-hand typewriters or someone who owned or worked in a secretarial school. It was unlikely to be a secretarial agency; the quality of the machines wasn't good enough. And it needn't necessarily be a secretarial school. Probably most modern comprehensives taught shorthand and typing; what was to prevent any member of the staff, whatever his or her subject, from staying after school hours and making private use of the machines?

And there was another way in which the messages could have been produced and one which she thought the most likely. She had bought cheap secondhand machines for her own agency, visiting the shops and showrooms where they were chained on display and trying them out, moving unhindered and unregarded from machine to machine. Anyone armed with a pad of paper and the dictionary of quotations could have provided himself—or herself—with a sufficient supply to keep the menace going, making a series of short visits to a variety of shops in districts where he was unlikely to be recognized. A reference to the yellow pages of the telephone directory would show him where to find them.

Before filing the messages in the folder she looked closely at the one which Sir George had told her had been typed on his machine. Was it her imagination that the skull and crossbones had been drawn by a different, a more careful, less assured, hand? Certainly the heads of the two crossing bones were differently shaped and slightly larger than in the other examples, the skull broader. The differences were small but, she thought, significant. The drawings of the other skulls and the coffin were practically identical. And the quotation itself, typed with erratic spacing of the letters, had no venom in its admonition:

On pain of death let no man name death to me:
It is a word infinitely terrible.

It wasn't a quotation known to her, and she couldn't find it in the Penguin dictionary. Webster, she thought, rather than Shakespeare; perhaps *The White Devil* or *The Devil's Law*

Case. The punctuation looked accurate enough, although she would have expected a comma after the first word *death*. Perhaps this quotation had been remembered, not looked up; certainly it had been typed by a different and less expert hand. And she thought she knew whose.

The remaining quotations varied in the degree of their menace. Christopher Marlowe's bleak despair—

Hell hath no limits, nor is circumscribed
In one self place; for where we are is hell,
And where hell is, must we ever be

—could only doubtfully be described as a death threat, although its stark contemporary nihilism might well be unwelcome to a nervous recipient. The only other Marlowe quotation, received six weeks earlier—

Now hast thou but one bare hour to live,
And then thou must be damned perpetually!

—was direct enough, but the threat had proved baseless; Clarissa had lived out more than her hour. But it seemed to Cordelia that since these earlier messages, the quotations had increased in menace, had been selected to build up to some kind of climax, from the sinister threat typed underneath a coffin—

I wish you joy o' the worm

—to the brutally explicit lines from *Henry VI*:

Down, down to hell; and say I sent thee thither.

Seen together the sonorous reiteration of death and hatred was oppressive, the silly childish drawings limned with menace. She began to understand what this carefully organized program of intimidation might do to a sensitive and vulnerable woman, to any woman come to that, darkening the mornings, making terrible such ordinary events as the arrival of the post, a letter on the hall salver, a note pushed under the door. It was easy to advise the victim of a poison pen to flush the messages down the lavatory like the rubbish they were. But in all societies there was an atavistic fear of the malevolent power of a secret adversary, working for evil, willing one to failure, perhaps to death. There was a horrible and rather frightening intelligence at work here, and it wasn't pleasant to think that the person responsible might be one of that small group who would be with her on Courcy Island, that the eyes which would meet hers over the dining table could be hiding such malignancy. For the first time she wondered whether Clarissa Lisle could be right, whether there really was a threat to her life. Then she put the thought aside, telling herself that the messages were beginning to exercise their malevolence even on her. A murderer did not advertise his intention over a period of months. But was that necessarily true? To a mind consumed with hatred, might not the act of killing be too swift, too momentary in its satisfaction? Could Clarissa Lisle have an enemy so bitter that he needed to watch her suffer, to destroy her slowly with terror and failure before he moved in for the kill?

She shivered. The warmth of the day was already dissipating; the night air drifting through the open window, even in this city aerie, held the taste and tang of autumn. She put away the last message and closed the folder. Her own instructions had been clear: to safeguard Clarissa Lisle from any worry or distress before Saturday's performance of *The Duchess of Malfi* and, if possible, to discover who was sending her the messages. And that, to the best of her ability, she would do.

BOOK TWO

DRESS
REHEARSAL

1

VICTORIAN SPEYMOUTH, which to the surprise of its citizens had converted its street lamps to gas without explosion or other disaster, had seen no reason to reject the new railway or, while accepting its inevitability, to banish it as had Cambridge to an inconvenient distance from the town. The charming little station was only a quarter of a mile from the statue of Queen Victoria which marks the center of the promenade, and when Cordelia stepped out into the sunlight, bag in one hand and portable typewriter in the other, she found herself gazing down over a jumble of brightly painted houses to a stone-enclosed harbor, tiny as a pool, and beyond it to the stunted pier and the shimmering sea. She was almost sorry to leave the station. With its gleaming white paint and its curved roof of wrought iron, delicate as lace, it reminded her of the summer issues of her weekly childhood comic where the sea had been always blue, the sand a bright yellow, the sun a golden ball, and the railway a highly colored

73

toy-town welcome to these imagined joys. Mrs. Wilkins, the poorest of all her foster mothers, had been the only one to buy her a comic, the only one whom Cordelia remembered with affection. Perhaps it was a happy augury that she should think of her now.

There was already a small queue waiting for the taxis, but she saw no reason to join it. The road was downhill and the quay clearly in sight. She stepped out, almost oblivious of the weight of her luggage in the pleasure of the day. The little town was bathed in sunshine, and the rows of Georgian terraced houses, simple, unpretentious, and dignified with elegant façades and wrought-iron balconies, looked as charmingly artificial and as brightly lit as a stage set. In the bay the gray shape of a small warship rested stiffly immobile as a child's cutout toy. She could almost imagine putting out her hand and plucking it from the water. As she made her way down a steep cobbled street, terraces of fawn, pink, and blue houses curved upwards toward a glimpse of distant hills, while below the brightly painted statue of Queen Victoria, majestically robed, pointed her scepter imperiously toward the public lavatories.

And everywhere there were people, jostling on the pavements, spilling from the esplanade onto the beach, laid in sunburned rows on the gritty sand, lumped in sagging deck chairs, queuing at the ice-cream kiosk, peering from the windows of cars in search of a parking place. She wondered where they had all come from on this mid-September weekday when the holiday season was surely over, the children back at school. Were they all truants from work or schoolroom, drawn out from autumn's hibernation by this resurgence of summer, with their mottled red faces above white necks, their glistening chests and arms, recently covered against September's chills, revealing again the unlovely evidence of harsher suns? The day itself smelled of high summer, of seaweed, hot bodies, and blistering paint.

The busy little harbor was a confusion of rocking dinghies

and furled sails, but the launch with *Shearwater* painted on its
bow was soon identified. It was about thirty feet long with a
central low-roofed cabin and a slatted seat in the stern. One
wizened seaman seemed to be in charge. He was squatting on
a bollard, his thin legs clamped, wearing sea boots and a blue
jumper with *Courcy Island* emblazoned across the chest. He
looked so like Popeye that Cordelia suspected that the pipe,
which he slowly took from his apparently toothless gums on
seeing her approach, was sucked for effect rather than solace.
He touched his hat and grinned when she gave her name but
he didn't speak. He took the typewriter and her bag and
stowed them in the cabin, then turned to offer her his hand.
But Cordelia had already jumped on board and had seated
herself in the rear. He resumed his seat on the bollard and
together they waited.

Three minutes later a taxi drew up at the mouth of the
quay, and a boy and a woman got out. The woman paid the
fare—not, it seemed, without some argument—while the boy
stood uneasily to one side, then loitered to the edge of the
quay to stare down at the water. She joined him and they
moved together to the launch, he a little behind her like a
reluctant child. This, thought Cordelia, must be Roma Lisle
with Simon Lessing in tow, neither apparently pleased with
the chance that had forced them into sharing a taxi.

Cordelia observed her as she allowed herself to be handed
aboard. Superficially, she had nothing in common with her
cousin except the shape of the lower lip. She was too fair, but
it was an ordinary Anglo-Saxon blondness in which the
strong sun already revealed a glint of gray. Her hair was short
and expensively shaped to her head. She was taller than her
cousin and moved with a certain assurance. But her face with
its lines scored across the forehead and from nose to mouth
had a look of brooding discontent, and there was no peace in
the eyes. She was dressed in an extremely well-tailored fawn
trouser suit with blue braid facing the collar and a high-
necked sweater striped in fawn and pale blue, an outfit which

seemed to Cordelia to combine superficial suitability for a holiday weekend with an inappropriate smartness, perhaps because she was wearing it with high-heeled shoes which made the descent into the launch less than graceful. The color, too, was unflattering to her skin. It was impossible not to recognize that here was a woman who cared about clothes without having any clear idea what suited either her or the occasion. About the young man there was less chance to make a judgment, sartorial or otherwise. He glimpsed Cordelia in the stern, blushed, and scuttled into the cabin with an alacrity which suggested that he was unlikely to add to the gaiety of the weekend. Miss Lisle seated herself in the bow while the boatman again took his seat on the bollard. They waited in silence while the launch gently rocked against the fender of old tires slung against the stones of the quay and small boats gently edged past them on the way to the open sea.

After a few minutes Miss Lisle called out, "Oughtn't we to be moving off? We're expected for lunch."

"One more a-comin'. Mr. Whittingham."

"Well, he couldn't have been on the nine-thirty-two. He'd have been here by now. And I didn't recognize him at the station. Perhaps he's driving down and has been delayed."

"Mr. Ambrose said he'd be a-comin' by train. Said to wait for him."

Miss Lisle frowned and gazed fixedly out to sea. Two more minutes passed.

Then the boatman called out, "Here he be. He's a-comin' now. That'll be Mr. Whittingham." The triple assurance given, he rose and began making ready to move off. Cordelia looked up and saw through a distorting dazzle of sun what seemed at first like a death's head on stilts jerking across the quay toward her, its skeleton fingers grasping a canvas holdall. She blinked and the picture composed itself, moved into focus, became human. The skull clothed itself in flesh, stretched and gray over the fineness of the bones, but still human flesh. The sockets moistened into eyes, keen and a little amused. The figure was still the thinnest and most desperately sick man she had ever seen moving on his own feet, but the voice was firm, and the words were easy and comfortable.

"Sorry to hold you up. I'm Ivo Whittingham. The quay looked deceptively close. And having started walking, I couldn't, of course, find a taxi."

He brushed aside Oldfield's proffered arm but without impatience and lowered himself into a seat in the bow, wedging his bag between his legs. No one spoke. The final end of rope spilled free from the bollard and was wound aboard. The engine shuddered into life. Almost imperceptibly the launch crept away from the quay and made for the harbor mouth.

Ten minutes later they seemed no closer to the island toward which, crabwise, they were edging, although the shore was visibly receding. The fishermen on the end of the pier shrank into matchstick men with fairy wands; the bustle of the town was swallowed up in the noise of the engine and finally shaken off; the royal statue became a colored blur. The horizon was a pale purple curdling into low clouds from which there separated great islands of creamy whiteness which rose to float almost motionless against a clear azure blue. The small waves seemed to be leaping with light, absorbing it from the bright air and reflecting it back to the paler blue of the sky. Cordelia thought that the sea and the distant shore were like a Monet painting, bright color laid in streaks against bright color, light itself made visible. She leaned over the edge of the boat and plunged her hand into the leaping wake. The cold made her gasp, but she held her arm under the water, spreading her fingers so that three small wakes spouted into the sunlight, watching the hairs on her forearm catch and hold the shining drops.

Suddenly her mood was broken by a woman's voice. Roma Lisle had made her way around the cabin and come up beside her. She said, "It's typical of Ambrose Gorringe just to send Oldfield and leave his guests to introduce themselves. I'm Roma Lisle, Clarissa's cousin."

They shook hands. Her fingers were firm and pleasantly cool.

Cordelia gave her name. She said, "But I'm not a guest. I'm going to the island to work."

Miss Lisle's glance went to the typewriter. She said, "Good Lord, Ambrose isn't writing another blockbuster, is he?"

"Not as far as I know. I'm employed by Lady Ralston." It might, thought Cordelia, have been more accurate to say that she was employed by Sir George, but she sensed that this might only lead to complications. But sooner or later some explanation of her presence would have to be given. It might as well be now. She prepared for the inevitable questions.

"By Clarissa! Doing what, for God's sake?"

"Dealing with her correspondence. Making telephone calls. Generally easing things along while she concentrates on the play."

"She's got Tolly to ease things along. What does she think of this—Tolly, I mean?"

"I haven't the least idea. I haven't met her yet."

"I can't see her liking it." She gave Cordelia a look in which suspicion mingled with puzzlement.

"I've read of those stagestruck oddballs, without talent themselves, who try to buy themselves into the club by attaching themselves to one of their idols, cooking, shopping, running errands, acting as a kind of poodle. They either die of overwork or end up with nervous breakdowns. You're not one of that pathetic breed, are you? No, I can see that you aren't. But don't you find your job, well . . . odd?"

"What do you do? And is your job any less odd?"

"I'm sorry. I was being offensive. Put it down to the fact that I'm a failed schoolteacher. At present I work in a bookshop. It may sound pretty orthodox, but I assure you it has its moments. You'd better meet Clarissa's stepson, Simon Lessing. He's probably nearer your age than anyone else on this benighted weekend.''

Hearing his name, the boy came out of the cabin and blinked in the sun. Perhaps, thought Cordelia, he preferred a voluntary appearance to being dragged out by Miss Lisle. He held out his hand and she shook it, surprised that his clasp should be so firm. They murmured a conventional greeting. He was better-looking than a first glimpse had suggested, with a long, sensitive face and widely spaced gray eyes. But his skin was pitted with the scars of old acne, with a fresh outcrop along the forehead, and his mouth was weak. Cordelia knew that with her wide brow, high cheekbones, and catlike face she looked younger than her age, but she couldn't imagine any time when she wouldn't have felt older than this shy boy.

And then there was a fresh voice. The last passenger was making his way astern to join them. He said, ''When the Prince of Wales came to Courcy Island in the eighteen-nineties, puffing across the bay in a steam launch, old Gorringe used to have his private band waiting on the quay to play him ashore. They were dressed, for some reason not recorded, in Tyrolean costume. Do you suppose that Ambrose's love affair with the past extends to laying on a similar welcome for us?''

But before anyone had a chance to respond, the launch had turned, and the eastern edge of the island and the castle itself came suddenly into sight.

2

ALTHOUGH CORDELIA WASN'T AWARE that she had consciously thought about the architecture of Courcy Castle, it had, nevertheless, formed itself in her mind as a gray-stoned, massive, crenellated sham, overornate in its Victorian solidity, an unsatisfactory compromise between domesticity and grandeur. The reality, suddenly presented to her in the clarity of the morning sunlight, made her catch her breath with wonder. It stood on the edge of the sea, almost as if it had risen from the waves, a castle of rose-red brick, its only stonework the pale flush lines and the tall curved windows which now coruscated in the sun. To the west soared a slender round tower topped with a cupola, solid yet ethereal. Every detail of the mat-surfaced walls, the patterned buttresses, and the battlements was distinct, unfussy, confident. The whole was compact, even massive, yet the high, sloping roofs and the slender tower gave an impression of lightness and repose which she hadn't associated with High Victorian architecture. The southern façade overlooked a wide terrace—surely wave-swept in winter—from which two flights of steps led down to a narrow beach of sand and shingle. The proportions of the castle seemed to her exactly right for its site. Larger and it could have looked pretentious; smaller and there would have been a suggestion of facile charm. But this building, compromise though it might be between castle and family house, seemed to her brilliantly successful. She almost laughed aloud at the pleasure of it.

She was unaware that Ivo Whittingham had come up beside her until he spoke. "This is your first visit, isn't it? What do you think of it?"

"It's remarkable. And unexpected."

"You're interested in Victorian architecture."

"Interested, but not at all knowledgeable."

"I shouldn't tell Ambrose that. He'll devote the whole weekend to educating you in his passions and prejudices. I've done my homework, so I'll forestall him by telling you now that the architect was E. W. Godwin, who worked for Whistler and Oscar Wilde and was associated with the aesthetes. What he aimed for—so he tells us—was the careful adjustment of solids and voids. Well, he's achieved that here. He did some perfectly awful town halls, including one at Northampton—not that Ambrose would admit to its awfulness—but I think that he and I will agree about this achievement. Are you taking part in the play?"

"No, I'm here to work. I'm Miss Lisle's secretary, her temporary secretary."

His quick glance was surprised. Then his lips curved in a smile. "So I should imagine. Clarissa's relationships tend to be temporary."

Cordelia said quickly, "Do you know anything about the play? I mean, which company is acting in it?"

"Didn't Clarissa explain? They're the Cottringham Players, said to be the oldest amateur company in England. They were started in 1834 by the then Sir Charles Cottringham, and the

family have more or less kept them going ever since. The
Cottringhams have been mad about acting for over three
generations, their enthusiasm invariably in inverse proportion
to their talent. The present Charles Cottringham is playing
Antonio. His great-grandfather used to take part in the revels
here until he was imprudent enough to cast a lascivious eye
on Lillie Langtry. The Prince of Wales made his displeasure
known, and no Cottringham has spent the night under the
castle roof since. It's a convenient tradition for Ambrose. He
need only entertain the leading lady and a few private guests.
Judith Cottringham has a house party for the producer and the
rest of the cast. They'll all come over tomorrow by launch.''

"Where did they act before Mr. Gorringe offered the
castle?''

"It was offered, I imagine, by Clarissa rather than Gorringe.
They gave an annual performance in the old assembly rooms
at Speymouth, an occasion more social than cultural. But
tomorrow shouldn't be too discouraging. A Speymouth butcher,
appropriately enough, is playing Bosola, and he's reputed to
be good. Ferdinand is taken by Cottringham's agent. Hardly
Gielgud, but Clarissa tells me that he knows how to speak
verse.''

The sound of the engine died to a gentle shudder and the
launch slowly edged toward the jetty. The stone quay curved
from the terrace in two arms to form a miniature harbor. At
intervals, steep steps festooned with seaweed led down to the
water. At the end of the eastern and longer arm was a
charming folly, a circular bandstand of delicate wrought iron,
painted white and pale blue with slender pillars supporting a
curved canopy. Beneath this stood the welcoming party, a
group of two men and two women, as immobile and carefully
positioned as a tableau. Clarissa Lisle was a little to the front,
her host attendant at her left shoulder. Behind them, waiting
with the impassive, careful noninvolvement of servants, stood
a dark-clad man and woman, the man outtopping the group in
height.

But the dominant figure was Clarissa. The immediate impression, whether by chance or by design, was of a goddess of classical mythology with her attendants. As the launch drew alongside the quay, Cordelia saw that she was wearing what looked like shorts and a sleeveless top in closely pleated cream muslin with over it a loose-fitting, almost transparent shift of the same material, wide-sleeved and corded at the waist. Beside this deceptively simple, cool, flowing elegance Roma Lisle in her trouser suit seemed to exude a sweaty and eye-dazzling discomfort. The waiting group, as if under instruction, held their pose until the launch gently bumped the landing steps. Then Clarissa fluted a small cry of welcome, spread bat wings of fluttering cotton, and ran forward. The pattern was broken.

During the chatter which followed the formal introductions and while Ambrose Gorringe was supervising the unloading of luggage and the humping ashore of boxes of supplies from a locker in the stern, Cordelia studied her host. Ambrose Gorringe was of middle height with smooth black hair and delicate hands and feet. He gave an impression of spry plumpness, not because he carried excess fat but because of the feminine softness and roundness of his arms and face. His skin gleamed pink and white; the circular flush on each cheekbone looked almost artificial. His eyes were his most striking feature. They were large and sparkling, bright as black sea-washed pebbles, the surrounding whites clear and translucent. Above them the brows curved in a strong arch as tidily as if they had been plucked. The ends of the mouth curved upwards in a fixed smile so that the whole face held the shining, humorous animation of a man enjoying a perpetual internal joke. He was wearing brown cotton trousers and a black short-sleeved singlet. Both were highly suitable for the weather and the occasion, yet to Cordelia they seemed incongruous. Something more formal was needed to define and control the latent strength of what she guessed was a complex and, perhaps, a formidable personality.

In his way the manservant, now supervising the loading of
the luggage and crates of supplies onto a small motorized
truck, was equally remarkable. He must, thought Cordelia, be
well over six feet in height, and with his dark suit and heavy
white lugubrious face he had the spurious gloom of a Victorian
undertaker's mute. His long, rather pointed head sloped to a
high and shiny forehead topped with a wig of coarse black
hair, which made absolutely no pretensions to realism. It was
parted in the middle and had been inexpertly hacked rather
than trimmed. Cordelia thought that such a bizarre appearance could hardly be inadvertent, and she wondered what
perversity or secret compulsion had led him to contrive and
present to his world a persona so uncompromisingly eccentric. Could it be revulsion against the tedium, the conformity,
or the deference demanded of his job? It seemed unlikely.
Servants who found their duties frustrating or uncongenial
nowadays had a simple remedy. They could leave.

Intrigued by the man's appearance, she scarcely noticed his
wife: a short, round-faced woman who stood always at her
husband's side and didn't speak during the whole course of
the disembarkation.

Clarissa Lisle had taken absolutely no notice of Cordelia
since their arrival, but Ambrose Gorringe came forward,
smiled, and said, "You must be Miss Gray. Welcome to
Courcy Island. Mrs. Munter will look after you. We've put
you next to Miss Lisle."

Cordelia waited until the Munters had finished unloading
the launch. As the three of them walked together behind the
main party, Munter handed his wife a small canvas bag with
the words "Not much post this morning. The parcel from the
London Library hasn't come. That means Mr. Gorringe probably won't get his books until Monday."

The woman spoke for the first time. "He'll have plenty to
do this weekend without new library books."

At that moment Ambrose Gorringe turned and called to
Munter. The man moved forward, changing his quick steps to

a stately, unhurried walk which was probably part of his act. As soon as he was out of earshot Cordelia said, "If there's any post for Miss Lisle, it comes first to me. I'm her new secretary. And I'll take any telephone calls for her. Perhaps I'd better take a look at the post. We're expecting a letter."

Rather to her surprise, Mrs. Munter handed over the bag without demur. There were only eight letters in all, held together in a rubber band. Two were for Clarissa Lisle. One, in a stout envelope, was obviously an invitation to a dress show. The name, but not the address, of the prestigious designer was engraved on the flap. The second, an ordinary white envelope, was addressed in typing to:

> The Duchess of Malfi
> c/o Miss Clarissa Lisle
> Courcy Island
> Speymouth
> Dorset

She walked a few steps ahead. She knew that it would be wise to wait until she reached the privacy of her room, but restraint was impossible. Controlling her excitement and curiosity, she slipped her finger under the flap. It was loosely gummed and came apart easily. She guessed the communication would be short and it was. Inside, on a small sheet of the same paper was a neatly drawn skull and crossbones, and typed underneath just two lines which she instinctively knew rather than recognized were from the play:

Call upon our dame aloud,
And bid her quickly don her shroud!

She put the message back into the envelope and slipped it quickly into her jacket pocket, then lingered until Mrs. Munter had caught her up.

Cordelia saw that the main rooms opened onto the terrace with a wide view of the Channel, but that the entrance to the castle was on the sheltered eastern side away from the sea.

They passed through a stone archway which led to a formal walled garden, then turned down a wide path between lawns and finally through a high arched porch and into the great hall. Pausing at the doorway, Cordelia could picture those first nineteenth-century guests, the crinolined ladies with their furled parasols, followed by their maids, the leather round-topped trunks, the hatboxes and gun cases, the distant beat of the welcoming band as that heavy Germanic prince carried his imposing paunch before him under Mr. Gorringe's privileged portals. But then the great hall would have been ostentatiously overfurnished, a lush repository of sofas, chairs, and occasional tables, rich carpets, and huge pots of palms. Here the house party would congregate at the end of the day before slowly processing in strict hierarchical order through the double doors to the dining room. But now the hall was furnished only with a long refectory table and two chairs, one on each side of the stone fireplace. On the opposite wall was a six-foot tapestry which she thought was almost certainly by William Morris: Flora, rose-crowned, with her maidens, her feet shining among the lilies and the hollyhocks. A wide staircase, branching to left and right, led to a gallery which ran around three sides of the hall. The eastern wall was almost entirely taken up by a stained-glass window showing the travels of Ulysses. Motes of colored light danced in the air, giving the great hall something of the quiet solemnity of a church. She followed Mrs. Munter up the staircase.

The main bedrooms opened out of the gallery. The room into which Cordelia was shown was charming with a lightness and delicacy which she hadn't expected. The two windows, high and curved, had curtains of a lily-patterned chintz which was used also for the bed cover and the fitted cushion of the mahogany cane-backed bedside chair. The simple stone fireplace had a paneled frieze of six-inch tiles, their patterns of flowers and foliage echoed in the larger tiles which surrounded the grate. Above the bed was a row of delicate watercolors, iris, wild strawberry, tulip, and lily. This, she thought, must be the De Morgan room of which Miss Maudsley had spoken. She glanced around with pleasure and Mrs. Munter, noting her interest, assumed the role of guide. But she recited the information without enthusiasm as if she had learned the facts by rote.

"The furniture here is not as old as the castle, miss. The bed and chair were designed by A. H. Mackmurdo in 1883. The tiles here and in the bathroom are by William De Morgan. Most of the tiles in the castle are by him. The original Mr. Herbert Gorringe, who rebuilt the castle in the eighteen-sixties, saw a house that he'd done in Kensington and had all the original tiles here ripped out and replaced by De Morgan. That mahogany and pine cabinet was painted by William Morris and the paintings are by John Ruskin. What time would you like your early tea, miss?"

"At half past seven, please."

After she left, Cordelia went through to the bathroom. Both rooms faced west, and any broad view of the island was blocked by the tower which rose immediately to her right, a phallic symbol in patterned brick, soaring to pierce the blue of the sky. Gazing up at its smooth roundness, she felt her head swim and the tower itself reeled dizzily in the sun. To her left she could just glimpse the end of the southern terrace and, beyond it, a wide sweep of sea. Beneath the bathroom window a wrought-iron fire escape led down to the rocks, from which, presumably, it was possible to reach the terrace. Even so, the escape route seemed to her precarious. In a high storm one would surely feel trapped between fire and sea.

Cordelia had started to unpack when the communicating door between her room and the adjoining one opened and Clarissa Lisle appeared.

"Oh, here you are. Come next door, will you? Tolly will see to your unpacking for you."

"Thank you, but I'd rather do my own."

Apart from the fact that the few clothes she had brought could be hung up in minutes and she preferred to do these

things for herself, Cordelia had no intention of letting other
eyes see the scene-of-crime kit. She had already noticed with
relief that the bottom drawer of the cabinet had a key.

She followed Clarissa into her bedroom. It was twice as
large as her own and very different in style; here opulence and
extravagance replaced lightness and simplicity. The room was
dominated by the bed, a mahogany half-tester with canopy,
cover, and side curtains of crimson damask. The head and
footboard were elaborately carved with cherubs and swags of
flowers, the whole surmounted by a countess's coronet. Cordelia
wondered whether the original owner, thrusting his way
upwards through the Victorian social hierarchy, had commissioned it to honor a particularly important guest. On either
side of the bed was a small bow-fronted chest and, across its
foot, a carved and buttoned chaise longue. The dressing table
was set between the two tall windows from which, between
the looped curtains, Cordelia saw only an expanse of blue
untroubled sea. Two ponderous wardrobes covered the opposite wall. There were low chairs and a screen of Berlin
woolwork before the marble fireplace in which a small pile of
sticks had already been laid. Ambrose Gorringe's chief guest
was to have the luxury of a real fire. She wondered whether
some housemaid would creep in during the early hours to
light it, as had her Victorian counterpart when the long-dead
countess stirred in her magnificent bed.

The room was very untidy. Clothes, wraps, tissue paper,
and plastic bags were flung across the chaise longue and the
bed, and the top of the dressing table was a jumble of bottles
and jars. A woman was walking about, calmly and un-
censoriously gathering up the clothes over her arm.

Clarissa Lisle said, "This is my dresser, Miss Tolgarth.
Tolly, meet Miss Cordelia Gray. She's come to help with my
correspondence. Just an experiment. She won't be in anyone's way. If she wants anything done, look after her, will
you?"

It wasn't, thought Cordelia, an auspicious introduction.

The woman neither smiled nor spoke, but Cordelia didn't feel that the steady gaze which met her own held any resentment. It didn't even hold curiosity. She was a heavily busted, rather sturdy woman with a face that looked older than her body and with remarkably elegant legs. Their shape was enhanced by very fine stockings and high-heeled court shoes, an incongruous touch of vanity which emphasized the plainness of the high-necked black dress, its only ornament a gold cross on a chain. Her dark hair, parted in the middle and drawn back into a bun at the nape of the neck, was already streaked with gray, and there were lines as deep as clefts across the forehead and at the ends of the wide mouth. It was a strong, secretive face, not, Cordelia thought, the face of a woman willingly subservient.

When she had disappeared into the bathroom, Clarissa said, "I suppose we'll have to talk, but it can't be now. Munter has set lunch in the dining room. It's ridiculous on a day like this. We ought to be in the sun. I've told him that we shall eat on the terrace, but that means he'll see that we don't get it until one-thirty, so we may as well make a quick tour of the castle. Is your room comfortable?"

"Very, thank you."

"I suppose I'd better give you some letters to type just to allay suspicion. There are one or two that need answering. You may as well do some work while you're here. You can type, I suppose."

"Yes, I can type. But that's not why I'm here."

"I know why you're here. I was the one who wanted you. And I still want you. But we'll talk about that tonight. There won't be a chance until then. Charles Cottringham and the other principals are coming across after lunch for a run-through of one or two scenes, and they won't be gone until after tea. You've met my stepson, haven't you, Simon Lessing?"

"Yes, we were introduced on the boat."

"Find him, will you, and tell him there's time for him to have a swim before lunch. There's no point in his trailing

round the castle with us. You'll probably ind him hiding in
his room. It's two down from your own."

Cordelia thought that the message could more suitably have
come from Clarissa. But she reminded herself that she was
supposed to be a secretary-companion, whatever that meant,
and that the job probably included running errands. She
knocked on Simon's door. He didn't call out, but after what
seemed an inordinate delay, the door slowly opened and his
apprehensive face appeared. He blushed when he saw who it
was. She gave him Clarissa's message, suitably edited, and
he managed a smile and a whispered "Thank you" before
quickly reclosing the door. Cordelia felt rather sorry for him.
It couldn't be altogether easy, having Clarissa as a stepmother. She wasn't sure that it would be any easier having her as a
client. For the first time she felt some of her euphoria drain
away. The castle and the island were even lovelier than she
had pictured. The weather was glorious and no change
threatened in this balmy resurgence of summer. It promised to
be a weekend of comfort, even of luxury. And, above all, the
envelope in her pocket confirmed that the job was real, that
she would pit her brain and her wits against a human
adversary at last. Why, then, should she have to struggle
against a sudden and overwhelming conviction that her task
was doomed to disaster?

3

"AND NOW," announced Clarissa, leading the way down the staircase and across the great hall, "we'll end with a visit to Ambrose's private chamber of horrors."

The tour of the castle had been hurried and incomplete. Cordelia sensed that the sun-warmed terrace beckoned and that the thoughts of the party were less on Ambrose's treasures than on their pre-luncheon sherry. But there were treasures, and she promised herself that if she had the chance, she would enjoy later and at leisure what was a small but comprehensive museum of the artistic achievements and spirit of Victoria's long reign. The tour had been too rushed. Her mind was a confusion of form and color; porcelain, pictures, glass, and silver jostled for place: pottery exhibited at the Great Exhibition of 1851, jasper, Grecian ware terra-cotta, majolica; cabinets of painted Wedgwood dishes and delicate pâte-sur-pâte made by M. L. Solon for Minton; part of a Coalport dinner service presented by Queen Victoria to the

Emperor of Russia and decorated with English and Russian
Orders surrounding the Russian royal crown and eagles.

Clarissa had floated on ahead, waving her arms and produc
ing a stream of doubtfully accurate information. Ivo had
lingered when he was allowed to and had said little. Roma
stumped behind them with an expression of careful uninterest
and from time to time made an acid comment about the
misery and exploitation of the poor represented by these
glittering monuments to wealth and privilege. Cordelia felt
some sympathy with her. Sister Magdalen, who had taught
nineteenth-century history at the convent, hadn't shared the
view of some of the sisters that since the pleasures of the
world were to be rejected, so might some of its vicarious
sorrows, and had attempted to instill a social sense into her
privileged pupils. Cordelia couldn't see a picture of that
pudding-faced queen with her plain, discontented-looking
children around her without seeing also the wan, aching-eyed
seamstresses working their eighteen-hour day, the factory
children half asleep at their looms, the bobbin-lace makers
bent double over their cushions, and the steaming tenements
of the East End.

Cordelia had found more to interest her than to admire in
Ambrose's collection of pictures. Everything that she most
disliked in High Victorian art was here: the strained eroticism, the careful naturalism which had nothing to do with
nature, the vapid anecdotal pictures, and the debased religios
ity. But he did have a Sickert and a Whistler.

As they passed along the gallery, Roma said to her,
"There's a William Dyce in my room called *The Shell
Gatherers*. Not badly painted; rather good, in fact. A crinolined
group of ladies examining their finds on a Kentish beach. But
what's the reality? A group of overfed, overclad, bored, and
sexually frustrated upperclass females with nothing to do with
their time but collect shells to make their useless shell boxes,
paint insipid watercolors, entertain the gentlemen after dinner

at the pianoforte, and wait for a man to give status and purpose to their lives.''

It was while Cordelia and Roma were standing in front of a Holman Hunt, neither of them finding anything to say, that Ambrose had come up to them.

''Not, perhaps, one of his best. The Victorians may have got their money from the dark satanic mills, but they had a passionate craving for beauty. It was their tragedy that, unlike us, they understood only too well how far they fell short of achieving it.''

The tour was now almost at an end. Clarissa led them down a tiled passageway to Ambrose's business room. Here, apparently, was the promised Chamber of Horrors.

It was a smaller room than most in the castle and looked out over the lawn which faced the eastern entrance. One wall was hung with a framed collection of Victorian popular gallows literature, the crudely printed and illustrated broadsheets which were sold to the mob after a notable trial or execution. Roma seemed particularly interested in them. Murderers, looking remarkably slim and elegant in their breeches, sat penning their last confessions under the high barred window of the condemned cell, listened in the chapel at Newgate to their last sermon with their coffins placed at hand, or drooped from the rope end as the robed chaplain stood, his book in hand. Cordelia disliked the pictures of hanging and moved to join Ambrose and Ivo, who were examining a wall shelf of Staffordshire figures. Ambrose identified his favorites.

''Meet my Victorian murderers and murderesses. That pair are the notorious Maria and Frederick Manning, hanged in November 1847 in front of Horsemongers Lane Gaol before a riotous crowd of fifty thousand. Charles Dickens saw the execution, and he wrote afterward that the behavior of the crowd was so indescribable that he thought he was living in a city of devils. Maria wore black satin for her part in the entertainment, a choice which did absolutely nothing for its subsequent fashionable appeal. The gentleman appropriately clad in a shooting jacket is William Corder, aiming his pistol at poor Maria Marten. Notice the red barn in the background. He might have got away with it if her mother hadn't repeatedly dreamed that her daughter's body was buried there. He was hanged at Bury St. Edmunds in 1828, also in front of a large and appreciative audience. The lady next to him in the bonnet and carrying a black bag is Kate Webster. The bag contains the head of her mistress, whom she beat to death, cut into pieces, and boiled in the kitchen boiler. She is said to have gone round the local shops offering cheap dripping for sale. She was turned off, as they used to say, in July 1879.''

Leaving the business room, they paused at two elegant rosewood display cases which stood on each side of the door. The left-hand one contained a clutter of small objects which were all neatly labeled: a doll and a solitaire set with small colored marbles, both of which had belonged to the Queen as a child; a fan; early Christmas cards; scent bottles of crystal, silver gilt, and enamel; and a collection of small silver objects, waist hook, chatelaine, prayer book, and posy holder. But it was the righthand case which drew their eyes. Here were less agreeable mementos, an extension of Ambrose's museum of crime.

He explained: "That tag end of rope is part of the executioner's rope which hanged Dr. Thomas Neill Cream, the Lambeth poisoner, in November 1892. The stained linen nightdress with the *broderie anglaise* frills was worn by Constance Kent. It's not the nightdress she had on when she slit the throat of her small stepbrother, but it has a certain interest all the same. That pair of handcuffs with the key were used on young Courvoisier who murdered his master, Lord William Russell, in 1840. The spectacles are a pair which belonged to Dr. Crippen. As he was hanged in November 1910 he's really nine years out of my period, but I couldn't resist them.''

Ivo asked, "And the marble of a baby's arm?''

"That hasn't any criminal interest as far as I know. It

should be in Memento Mori or in the other cabinet, but I hadn't time to rearrange the exhibits. But it doesn't look out of place among the props of murder. The man who sold it to me would approve. He told me that he kept imagining that the limb was oozing blood."

Clarissa hadn't spoken, and glancing at her, Cordelia saw that her eyes were fixed on the marble with a mixture of fear and repulsion which none of the other exhibits had evoked. The arm, a chubby replica in white marble, lay on a purple cushion bound with cord. Cordelia herself thought it an unpleasant object, sentimental and morbid, useless and undecorative, and to that extent not untypical of the minor art of its age.

Clarissa said, "But it's perfectly hateful! It's disgusting! Where on earth did you pick it up, Ambrose?"

"In London. A man I know. It may be the only extant copy of one of the limbs of the royal children made for Queen Victoria at Osborne House, said to be by Mary Thornycroft. This one could be poor Vicky, the Princess Royal. It's either that or a memorial piece. And if you dislike it, Clarissa, you should see the Osborne collection. They look like the remnants of a holocaust, as if the Prince Consort had descended on the royal nursery with a machete, as he may well have been tempted to do, poor man."

Clarissa said, "It's repulsive! What on earth possessed you, Ambrose? Get rid of it."

"Certainly not. It may be unique. I regard it as an interesting addition to my minor Victoriana."

Roma said, "I've seen the Osborne pieces. I find them repulsive too. But they throw an interesting light on the Victorian mind, the Queen's in particular."

"Well, this throws an interesting light on Ambrose's mind," Ivo said quietly. "As a piece of marble, it's rather well done. It's the association you find unpleasant, perhaps. The death or mutilation of a child is always distressing, don't you think, Clarissa?"

But Clarissa appeared not to have heard. She turned away and said, "For God's sake, don't start arguing about it. Just get rid of it, Ambrose. And now I need a drink and my lunch."

4

HALF A MILE from the shore, Simon Lessing stopped his slow and regular crawl stroke, turned on his back, and let his eyes rest on the horizon. The sea was empty. Faced with that shuddering waste of water, he found it possible to imagine that there was emptiness also behind him, that the island and its castle had gently subsided under the waves, silently and without turbulence, and that he floated alone in a blue infinity of sea. This self-induced sense of isolation excited but didn't frighten him. Nothing about the sea ever did. Here was the element in which he felt most at peace; guilt, anxiety, failure, washed away in a gentle and perpetual baptism of redemption.

He was glad that Clarissa hadn't wanted him tagging along behind her on the tour of the castle. There were rooms he would be interested to see, but there would be time enough to explore on his own. And it would give him another excuse to keep out of her way. He couldn't swim more than twice a day at most without its seeming odd and deliberately unsociable, but it would seem perfectly natural to ask if he might wander off to explore the castle. Perhaps the weekend might not be so terrifying after all.

He had only to thrust himself upright to feel the bite of the cold undercurrent. But now he floated, spread-eagled under the sun, feeling the sea creep over his chest and arms as softly warm as a bath. From time to time he let his face submerge, opening his eyes on the thin film of green, letting it wash lightly over his eyeballs. And deep down there was the knowledge, unfrightening and almost comforting, that he only had to let himself go, to give himself up to the power and gentleness of the sea, and there need never again be guilt or anxiety or failure. He knew that he wouldn't do it; the thought was a small self-indulgence which, like a drug, could be safely experimented with as long as the doses were small and one stayed in control. And he was in control. In a few minutes it would be time to turn and strike for the shore, to think about luncheon and Clarissa and getting through the next two days without embarrassment or disaster. But now there was this peace, this emptiness, this wholeness.

It was only at moments like this that he could think without pain of his father. This was how he must have died, swimming alone in the Aegean on that summer morning, finding the tide too strong for him, letting himself go at last without a struggle, without fear, giving himself up to the sea he loved, embracing its majesty and its peace. He had imagined that death so often on his solitary swims that the old nightmares were almost exorcised. He no longer awoke in the darkness of the early hours as he had in those first months after he had learned of his father's death, sweating with terror, desperately tearing at the blankets as they dragged him down, living every second of those last dreadful minutes, the stinging eyes, the agony as he glimpsed through the waves the lost, receding, unattainable shore. But it hadn't been like that. It couldn't have been like that. His father had died secure in his great love, unresisting and at peace.

It was time to turn back. He twisted under the water and began again his steady, powerful crawl. Now his feet found the shingle and he pulled himself ashore, colder and more tired than he had expected. Looking up, he saw with surprise that there was someone waiting for him, a dark-clad still figure standing like a guardian beside his pile of clothes. He shook the water from his eyes and saw it was Tolly.

He came up to her. At first she didn't speak but bent and picked up his towel and handed it to him. Panting and shivering, he began patting dry his arms and neck, embarrassed by her steady gaze, wondering why she was there.

Then she said, "Why don't you leave?"

She must have seen his incomprehension. She said again, "Why don't you leave, leave this place, leave her?" Her voice, as always, was low but harsh, almost expressionless. He stared at her, wildeyed under the dripping hair.

"Leave Clarissa! Why should I? What do you mean?"

"She doesn't want you. Haven't you noticed that? You aren't happy. Why go on pretending?"

He cried out in protest. "But I am happy! And where can I go? My aunt wouldn't want me back. I haven't any money."

She said, "There's a spare room in my flat. You could have that for a start. It isn't much, a child's room. But you could stay there until you found something better."

A child's room. He remembered hearing that she had once had a child, a girl who had died. No one ever spoke about her now. He didn't want to think about her. He had thought enough about dying and death. He said, "But how could I find somewhere? What would I live on?"

"You're seventeen, aren't you? You're not a child. You've got five 'O' levels. You could find something to do. I was working at fifteen. Most children in the world start younger."

"But doing what? I'm going to be a pianist. I need Clarissa's money."

"Ah, yes," she said, "you need Clarissa's money."

And so, he thought, do you. That's what this is all about.

He felt a surge of confidence, of adult cunning. He wasn't a child to be so easily fooled. Hadn't he always sensed her dislike of him, caught that contemptuous glance as she set down his breakfast on those days when she and he were alone in the flat, watched the silent resentment with which she gathered up his laundry, cleaned his room? If he weren't there, she wouldn't need to come in except twice a week to check that all was well. Of course she wanted him out of the way. Probably she expected to be left something in Clarissa's will; she must be ten years younger even if she didn't look it. And she was only a servant after all. What right had she to upset him, to criticize Clarissa, to patronize him, offering her sordid little room as if it were a favor? It would be as bad as Mornington Avenue; worse. The small seductive devil at the back of his mind whispered its enticement. However difficult things might be at times, he would be crazy to give up the patronage of Clarissa, who was rich, to put himself at the mercy of Tolly, who was poor.

Perhaps something of this reached her. She said, almost humbly but with no trace of solicitation, "You'd be under no obligation. It's just a room."

He wished she would go. Yet he couldn't walk away, couldn't start dressing while that dark, oppressive figure stood there, seeming to block the whole beach. He drew himself up and said as stiffly as his shivering body would permit, "Thank you, but I'm perfectly happy as I am."

"Suppose she gets tired of you like she did your father."

He gaped at her, clutching his towel. Above them a gull shrieked, shrill as a tormented child. He whispered, "What do you mean? She loved my father! They loved each other! He explained to me before he left us, mother and me. It was the most marvelous thing that had ever happened to him. He had no choice."

"There's always a choice."

"But they adored each other! He was so happy."

"Then why did he drown himself?"

He cried, "It isn't true! I don't believe you!"

"You don't have to if you don't want to. Just remember it when your turn comes."

"But why should he do it? Why?"

"To make her feel sorry, I suppose. Isn't that usually why people kill themselves? But he should have known. Clarissa doesn't understand about guilt."

"But they told me that there was an inquest. They found that it was accidental death. And he didn't leave a note."

"If he did they didn't see it. It was Clarissa who found his clothes on the beach."

Her eyes fell to where his own trousers and jacket were jumbled under a stone. A picture came unbidden into his mind, so clear that it might have been memory. The gritty sand, hot as cinders, an alien sea layered in purple and blue to the horizon, Clarissa standing with the wind billowing her sleeves, the note in her hand. And then the tattered scraps of white, fluttering down like petals, briefly littering the sea before floating and dissolving in the surf. It had been three weeks before his father's body, what was left of it, was washed up. But bones and flesh, even when the fish have finished with it, last longer than a scrap of paper. It wasn't true. None of it was true. As she had told him, there is always a choice. He would choose not to believe.

He looked down so that he need not meet her eyes, that compelling stare which was much more convincing than any words she could speak. There was a swath of seaweed wound around his calf, brown as a gash on which the blood has dried. He bent and plucked at it. It tightened, a slimy ligature. He knew that she was watching him.

Then she said, "Suppose she died. What would you to then?"

"Why should she die? She isn't sick, is she? She never said anything to me about being sick. What's wrong with her?"

"Nothing. Nothing's wrong with her."

"Then why are you talking about dying?"

"She thinks she's going to die. Sometimes when people think that strongly enough they do die."

His heart surged with relief. But that was ridiculous! She was trying to frighten him. Everything was plain to him now. She had always been jealous of him, just as she had been jealous of his father. He picked up his jacket and tried to sound dignified through the chattering of his teeth.

"If she does die I'm sure you'll be remembered. I shouldn't worry if I were you. And now perhaps you'll let me get dressed. I'm cold and it's time for luncheon."

As soon as the words were out he felt ashamed. She turned away without another word. And then she looked back and their eyes met for the last time. He knew what she must see in his: the shame, the fear. He was prepared to encounter anger and resentment. But what he hadn't expected to see was pity.

5

A LONG ARCADE, brick-built but with columns and arches of patterned stonework, led from the west side of the castle, past a rose garden and formal pool to the theater. Making his solitary way, rather late, to watch part of the final run-through, Ivo could picture the slow after-dinner procession of Victorian guests passing under the arches, pale arms and necks above the richness of satin and velvet, jewels sparkling on bosoms and in the intricately piled hair, the white shirt fronts of the men gleaming in the moonlight.

The theater itself surprised him, less by the perfection of its proportions, which he had expected, than by its contrast to the rest of the castle. He wondered whether it was the work of a different architect; he would have to ask Ambrose. But if Godwin had been responsible, it was apparent that his client's insistence on opulence and ostentation had prevailed over any inclination he himself might have had for lightness or restraint. Even now, with only half the house lights lit, the

theater glowed with richness. The deep red velvet of the
curtains and seats had faded but was still remarkably well
preserved. The candle lighting had been replaced by
electricity—the conversion must have given Ambrose a pang—
but the delicate convolvulus light shades were still in use and
the original crystal chandelier still glittered from the domed
ceiling. Everywhere there was ornament, sumptuous, florid,
occasionally charming, but always splendid in its craftsmanship.
Across the front of the boxes gilded plump-buttocked cherubs
held swags of flowers or lifted trumpets to pouting mouths,
and the richly carved royal box with its Prince of Wales
feathers and twin seats, regal as thrones, must have satisfied
even the most ardent monarchist's view of what was owing to
the heir apparent.

Ivo had settled himself at the end of the fourth row of the
stalls with no intention of staying for more than an hour. He
was eager to disabuse the cast of any idea they might have
that he was on the island primarily to review their performance, and this casual appearance to watch the final rehearsal
would remind them that he was less interested in what they
managed to make of Webster's tragedy than in the glories,
scandals, and legends of the theater itself. He was glad that
the seats, designed for broad Victorian rumps, were so
luxuriously comfortable. The afternoon was always the worst
time for him when his luncheon, however frugal, lay heavily
on his distorted stomach and the monstrous spleen seemed to
grow and harden under his supporting hands. He twisted
himself more comfortably into the velvet plush, aware of
Cordelia sitting silent and upright farther along the row, and
tired to fix his attention on the stage.

The cast had obviously decided, or been instructed by
DeVille, to concentrate on the sense and let the verse look
after itself, a ploy which would have been disastrous with
Shakespeare but which succeeded well enough with Webster's rougher meter. And at least it made for pace. Ivo had
always believed that there was only one way to direct Web-

ster: as a highly stylized drama of manners, the characters more ritual personifications of lust, decadence, and sexual rapacity, moving in a pavane toward the inevitable orgiastic triumph of madness and death. But DeVille, half sunk in lugubrious disgust at finding himself actually directing amateurs, was obviously aiming at some semblance of realism. It would be interesting to see how he dealt with the more gratuitous horrors. He would be lucky to get away with the proffered severed hand and the gaggle of madmen without a suppressed giggle or two. Revenge tragedy was hardly a genre for the inexperienced; but, then, what classic was? Certainly this charnelhouse poet, heaping horror on horror until the appetite sickened and then suddenly piercing the heart with lines of redeeming beauty, demanded more than the present enthusiastic bunch of playactors. Still, DeVille had to get only one performance out of them. It wasn't what you could raise yourself to on one night, but what you could continue to do, night after night and two matinees a week, for three months or more, that distinguished the professional from the amateur. He had known that the play was to be done in Victorian costume. The idea had seemed to him an eccentric, slightly ludicrous conceit. But he could see that it had its uses. The stage and the small auditorium fused into one claustrophobic cockpit of evil; the high-necked dresses and the bustles hinted at a sexuality which was the more lascivious because covert, overlaid with Victorian respectability. And there was some wit in the decision to dress Bosola as a kilted Highlander, although it was hard to imagine Victoria's good old Brown in this complex creature of nihilism and thwarted nobility.

The four principals had been rehearsing now for nearly fifty-five minutes. DeVille had been leaving them pretty much to themselves, his heavy froglike face expressing nothing but a settled gloom. Probably he had resented being dragged away from his postprandial nap and subjected to yet another sea trip merely to indulge Clarissa's wish for a final run-through in costume of her more important scenes. Ivo glanced at his watch. Boredom was taking hold of him as he had known it would, but the effort of moving seemed too great. He glanced along the row and watched Cordelia's face, upturned to the stage, the firm yet delicate chin, the sweet curve of the throat. He thought, Two years ago I should have been mildly agonizing over her, scheming how I might get into her bed before the weekend was out, fretting at the possibility of failure. He recalled his past exploits, less with disgust than with a detached wonder that so much time and thought and energy should have been expended on such petty expedients against boredom. The trouble had been so disproportionate to the satisfaction, the desire less urgent than the need to prove himself still desirable. What, after all, would getting into bed with her have meant but a small fillip to the ego, ranking only a little higher than the quality of the food and wine and the wit of the after-dinner conversation as an index of the success of the weekend? Always he had aimed to conduct his affairs on the level of a civilized, uncommitted exchange of pleasure. And always they had ended in rows, recriminations, in messiness and disgust. It had been no different with Clarissa except the rows had been more bitter, the disgust more lasting. But, then, with Clarissa he had made the mistake of letting himself become involved. With Clarissa, at least for those first six months when he had been cuckolding Simon's father, he had known again the agonies, the ecstasies, the uncertainties of love.

He made himself look again at the stage. They were playing the second scene of act three. Clarissa, dressed in a voluminous lace-trimmed dressing gown, was seated at her looking glass with Cariola in attendance, hairbrush in hand. The dressing table, like all the other props, was authentic, borrowed, he supposed, from the castle. There was more than one advantage in staging the play in the 1890s. The scene was being played to the accompaniment of a music box which had been placed on the dressing table and which tinkled out a medley of Scottish airs. That too was probably another of Ambrose's pieces of Victoriana, but he suspected that the idea was Clarissa's.

The scene began well enough. He had forgotten how Clarissa could take on an almost luminous beauty, the power of that high, slightly cracked voice, the grace with which she used her arms and body. She wasn't a Suzman or a Mirren, but she did manage to convey something of the high erotic excitement, the vulnerability, and the rashness of a woman deeply in love. That wasn't surprising; it was a part she had played often enough in real life. But to produce such conviction with a leading man who obviously saw Antonio as an English country gentleman sinning above his station was something of an achievement. But Cariola was a disaster, nervous and skittish, tripping across the stage in her goffered cap like a soubrette in a French farce. When she had stumbled for the third time over her lines, DeVille called out impatiently, "You've only to remember three lines, God help you. And cut out the coyness. You're not playing *No, No, Nanette*. All right. Take it from the beginning of the scene."

Clarissa protested, "But it needs pace, lightness. I lose the impetus if I have to keep going back."

He reiterated, "Take it from the beginning."

She hesitated, shrugged, then sat silent. The cast glanced at each other furtively, shuffled, waited. Ivo's interest suddenly rekindled. He thought, She's losing her temper. With her, that's halfway to losing her nerve.

Suddenly she took the music box and slammed down the lid. The crack was as sharp as a gunshot. The tinkling little tune stopped. It was followed by absolute silence as the cast seemed to hold their breath. Then Clarissa came forward to the footlights.

"That bloody box is getting on my nerves. If we have to have background music in this scene, surely Ambrose can find something more suitable than those damn Scottish tunes.

They're driving me mad, so God knows what they'll do to the audience.''

Ambrose called quietly from the back of the auditorium. Ivo was surprised to hear him and wondered how long he had been silently sitting there.

"It was your idea, as I remember."

"I wanted a music box but not a bloody Scottish medley. And do we have to have an audience? Cordelia, can't you find something useful to do? God knows, we're paying you enough. Tolly could do with some help ironing costumes, unless you propose to sit on your ass all afternoon."

The girl got to her feet Even in the half-light, Ivo could detect the flush rising on her throat, could see her mouth half open in protest, then close resolutely. Despite those candid, almost judgmental eyes, the disconcerting honesty, the impression of controlled competence, she was at heart a sensitive child. Anger rose in him, satisfyingly strong and uncomplicated. He rejoiced that he could feel it. With difficulty he pulled himself erect. He was aware that all eyes had turned toward him. He said calmly, "Miss Gray and I will take a walk. The performance hasn't been exactly riveting so far and the air outside will be fresher."

When they were outside, their going silently watched by the cast, she said, "Thank you, Mr. Knightley."

He smiled. Suddenly he felt well, extraordinarily well, his whole body mysteriously lighter. "I'm afraid I'd make a poor dancer in my present state, and if I had to cast you as any character in *Emma* it certainly wouldn't be poor Harriet. You must excuse Clarissa. When she's nervous, she's apt to become rude."

"That may be her misfortune, but I don't find it particularly excusable."

He added, "And public rudeness provokes in me the kind of childish retort which is only satisfying for the second after it's spoken. She'll apologize very prettily when she next sees you alone."

"I'm sure she will." Suddenly she turned to him and smiled. "Actually, I should like a walk if you won't find it too exhausting."

She was, he thought, the only person on the island who could say that to him without making him feel either irritated or embarrassed. He said, "What about the beach?"

"I'd like that."

"It'll be slow going, I'm afraid."

"That doesn't matter."

How very sweet she was, with that gentle, self-contained dignity. He smiled and held out his hand to her. " 'Upon such sacrifices, my Cordelia, / The Gods themselves throw incense ' Well, shall we go?"

6

THEY TRUDGED SLOWLY side by side along the very edge of the tide where the firmer sand made the going easiest. The beach was narrow, cut by rotting breakwaters and bounded by a low stone wall beyond which rose the tree-covered, friable cliffs. Much of the bank must once have been planted. Between the beeches and the oaks were clumps of laurel, old rosebushes twined among the thicker foliage of rhododendrons, woody geraniums distorted by the wind, hydrangeas in their autumn shades of bronze, lime yellow, and purple, so much more subtle and interesting, thought Cordelia, than the gaudy heads of high summer. She felt at peace with her companion and wished, for a moment, that she could confide in him, that her job needn't impose such a weight of deception.

For ten minutes they walked in undemanding silence. Then he said, "This may be a stupid question. Gray isn't an uncommon name. But you're not by any chance related to Redvers Gray?"

"He was my father."

"There's something about the eyes. I only met him once, but his was a face one didn't forget. He had a great influence on my generation at Cambridge. He had the gift of making rhetoric sound sincere. Now that the rhetoric and the dream are not only discredited, which is discouraging, but unfashionable, which is fatal, I suppose he is almost forgotten. But I should like to have known him."

Cordelia said, "So should I."

He glanced down at her. "It was like that, was it? The revolutionary idealist dedicated to mankind in the abstract but not much good at caring for his own child. Not that I can criticize. I haven't done too well with mine. Children need you to talk to them, play with them, give time to them when they're young. If you can't be bothered, it isn't surprising if, when they're adolescents, you find that you don't much like each other. But, then, by the time mine were adolescents I didn't much like their mother either."

Cordelia said, "I think I could have liked him if we'd had time. I did spend six months with him and the comrades in Germany and Italy. But then he died."

"You make death sound like a betrayal. And so, of course, it is."

Cordelia thought of those six months. Half a year of cooking for the comrades, shopping for the comrades, carrying messages, sometimes not without danger, finding rooms, propitiating landladies and shopkeepers, sewing for the comrades. They and her father believed implicitly in equality for women without troubling to acquire the basic domestic skills which would have made that equality possible. And it was for that precarious nomadic existence that he had taken her from the convent, made it impossible for her to take up her place at Cambridge. She no longer felt any particular resentment. That period of her life was passed, finished. And she hoped that they had given something to each other, if only trust. She had early dropped Redvers from her name, telling herself that it was an unnecessary piece of cabin luggage. She had been reading Browning at the time. Now she wondered if it had been a more significant rejection, even a small revenge. The thought was unwelcome and she thrust it away.

She heard Ivo say, "And what about your education? One was always seeing pictures of him being dragged off by the police. That's all very admirable in youth, no doubt. In middle age it begins to look embarrassing and ridiculous. I don't remember hearing about a daughter, or a wife for that matter."

"My mother died when I was born."

"And who looked after you?"

"I was placed with foster parents for most of the time. Then, when I was eleven, I won a scholarship to the Convent of the Holy Child. That was a mistake, not the scholarship but the choice of school. They muddled my name with another C. Gray, who was a Roman Catholic. I don't think Father much liked it, but by the time he bothered to reply to the education officer's letter I was settled and they didn't like to move me. And I wanted to stay."

He laughed. "Redvers Gray with a convent-educated daughter! And they didn't succeed in converting you? That would have taught Papa, dedicated atheist, to answer his letters more promptly."

"No, they didn't convert me. But, then, they didn't try. I didn't believe, but I was happy in my invincible ignorance. It's rather an enviable state. And I liked the convent. I suppose it was the first time I felt secure. Life wasn't messy anymore."

She had never before spoken so freely of her time at the convent, she who was so slow to confide. She wondered whether this unusual frankness was possible only because she knew he must be dying. The thought seemed to her ignoble and she tried to put it from her.

He said, "You agree with Yeats. 'How but in custom and in ceremony are innocence and beauty born?' I can see that it must have been reassuring, even having one's sins neatly categorized into venal and mortal. Mortal sin. I like the expression even if I reject the dogma. It has a note of splendid finality. It dignifies wrongdoing, almost gives it form and substance. One can imagine oneself saying, 'What have I done with my mortal sin? I must have put it down somewhere.' One could carry it around, neatly packaged.''

Suddenly he stumbled. Cordelia put out her hand to steady him. His palm in hers was cold, the dry skin sliding over the bones. She saw that he looked very tired. The walk over the shingle had not, after all, been easy.

She said, "Let's sit for a while."

There was a kind of grotto above them, cut out of the cliff, with a mosaic terrace, now fractured and almost overgrown, and a curved marble seat. She helped pull him up the slope, watching as his feet found convenient clumps of grass and half-hidden stone steps. The back of the seat, warmed by the sun, still struck a little chill through her thin shirt. They sat side by side, untouching, and lifted their faces to the sun. Above them hung a beech tree. Its trunk and boughs had the tender luminosity of a girl's arm, its leaves, just beginning to burn with their autumn gold, were veined marvels of reflected light. The air was very still and quiet, the silence pierced only by the occasional cry of a gull, while below them the sea hissed and withdrew in its everlasting restlessness.

After a few minutes, his eyes still closed, he said, "I suppose a mortal sin has to be something special, something more original and momentous than the expedients, the meannesses, the small delinquencies which make up everyday living for most of us."

Cordelia said, "It's a grievous offense against the law of God, which puts the soul at risk of eternal damnation. There has to be full knowledge and consent. It's all laid down. Any R.C. will explain it to you."

He said, "Something evil, if the word means anything to you, if you believe in the existence of evil."

Cordelia thought of the convent chapel, altar candles flickering fitfully, her own bowed lace-covered head among the ranks of muttering conformists. "And deliver us from evil." For six years she had repeated those words at least twice a day long before she had ever asked herself what it was from which she craved deliverance. It had taken her first case, after Bernie's death, to teach her that. She could still recall, in sleeping and waking dreams, the horror which she had not in fact actually seen: a white, elongated neck, a boy's disfigured face drooping from the noose, the twisting feet pointing to the floor. It was when she had finally stared into the face of his murderer that she had known about evil.

She said, "Yes, I believe in the existence of evil."

"Then Clarissa once did something which you might dignify as evil. I don't know whether the good sisters would designate it as mortal sin. But there was knowledge and consent. And I've a feeling that, for Clarissa, it could prove mortal."

She didn't speak. She wouldn't make it easy for him. But there was no self-control in her silence. She knew he would go on.

"It happened during the run of *Macbeth* in July 1980 Tolly—Miss Tolgarth—had had an illegitimate daughter four years earlier. There was no particular secret about it; most of us in Clarissa's set knew about Viccy. She was a sweet child Gravefaced, rather silent, intelligent I think, as far as one can judge at that age. Sometimes, but only rarely, Tolly would bring her to the theater, but most of the time she kept her private and her working life separate. She paid a child-minder to look after Viccy while she was working, and it must have been convenient having mainly an evening job. She wouldn't take any money from the father. I think she was too posses sive about Viccy to want to share even the cost of her food Then two days before Clarissa opened in *Macbeth* it happened. Clarissa was at the theater—there was a final rehearsal—and the minder was in charge of Viccy. The child had slipped out into the street and was playing with something in the gutter behind a parked lorry. It was the usual tragedy. The driver didn't see her and reversed. She was horribly injured. They rushed her to hospital and operated, and she stood that very well. We thought that she'd make it. But on the first night of *Macbeth* the hospital telephoned at nine-forty-five to say that there had been a relapse and to ask Tolly to go at once. Clarissa took the call. She had just come offstage for her costume change before the third act. She was appalled at the thought of losing her dresser at that moment. She took the message and put down the receiver. Then she told Tolly that the hospital wanted her to visit but that there was no hurry, after the performance would be all right. When Tolly wanted to ring back she wouldn't let her. And shortly after the performance ended, the hospital rang again to say that the child was dead."

"How do you know this?"

"Because I took the trouble to get in touch with the hospital and ask about that first message. And because I was there in Clarissa's dressing room when it came. You could say I was in something of a privileged position at the time. I wasn't with them when Clarissa finally told Tolly that she couldn't leave. I'd have stopped that; at least I hope I would. But I was there when the call came through. Then I went back to my seat. When the play ended and I went backstage to take Clarissa out to supper, Tolly was still there. And fifteen minutes later the hospital telephoned to say the child was dead."

"And when you learned what had happened, was that when you stopped being a privileged person?"

"I should like to be able to tell you that it was. The truth is less flattering. She became my mistress for two reasons: first because I'd gained some reputation and Clarissa has always found power an aphrodisiac, and second because she imagined that a lay a week would ensure her good notices. When she discovered her mistake—like most other men I'm capable of betrayal but not of that particular betrayal—the privileges ceased. There are some favors it is unwise to pay for in advance."

"Why are you telling me this?"

"Because I like you. Because I don't want to have this weekend spoiled by watching yet another person I respect being seduced by her charm. She has charm even if she hasn't bothered yet to exercise it on you. I don't want to see you behaving like all the others. I suspect that you may be possessed of that divine common sense which is impervious to the blandishments of egotism, whether sexual or other, but who can be sure? So I am committing one more small act of betrayal to strengthen you against temptation."

"Who was the child's father?"

"No one knows, except presumably Tolly, and she isn't saying. The question is who did Clarissa think he was."

Cordelia glanced at him. "Not her husband?"

"Poor besotted Lessing? Possible, I suppose, but hardly probable. He and Clarissa had been married only a year. Admittedly, she was already giving him hell, but I can't see him choosing that way of revenge. My guess is that it was DeVille. His only requirements are that the woman be comely and willing and not an actress. He's reputed to be impotent with anyone who holds an equity card, but that may be only his device for keeping his professional and private lives separate."

"The man who is directing the Webster? The one who's here now? Do you think that Clarissa was in love with him?"

"I don't know what Clarissa means by that word. She may have wanted him if only to prove that she could get him. One thing's certain: if he wouldn't play, she wouldn't easily forget an affair with her own dresser."

"Why do you think he's here? He's famous; he doesn't have to bother with an amateur production, particularly out of London."

"Why are any of us here? He may see the island as a future dramatic Glyndebourne, a world-famous center for experimental drama. This may just be a way of getting his foot in the door. After all, he's not exactly sought after now. His tricks were much admired in their day, but there are some clever young dogs coming along now. And Ambrose, if he's prepared to spend money, could make something of his Courcy Festival. Not commercially, of course; a theater which seats only a hundred comfortably can hardly be that, particularly when it could always be cut off by a storm on the first night. But he could have some fun with it once he's got rid of Clarissa.''

"And does he want to get rid of Clarissa?"

"Oh, yes," said Ivo easily. "Hadn't you noticed that? She's trying to take him over, him and his theater and his island. He likes his private kingdom. Clarissa is a particularly persistent invader.''

Cordelia thought of the child, lying alone on her high aseptic hospital bed behind the drawn curtains. Had she been conscious? Had she known that she was dying? Had she perhaps cried out for her mother? Had she gone frightened and alone into that last good night? She said, "I don't see how Clarissa can live with that memory.''

"I'm not sure that she can. When people are terrified of dying, it could be because with one part of their minds they feel that they deserve it.''

"How do you know she's terrified?"

"Because there are some emotions which even an actress as experienced as Clarissa can't altogether hide.''

He turned to her, saw the expression on her face, upturned to the glitter of shuddering green and gold, and said quietly, "There are, perhaps, excuses one should make for her. And if not excuses, explanations. She was about to make an important costume change. She couldn't have managed it herself, and there wasn't another dresser available.''

"Did she even try to find one?"

"I don't suppose so. You see, from her point of view, she wasn't in the world of hospitals and sick children. She was

Lady Macbeth. She was at Dunsinane Castle. I doubt whether she would have left the theater to go to her own dying child, not at that moment. It didn't occur to her that someone else might want to."

Cordelia cried, "But you can't excuse it! You can't explain it. You don't really believe that a play, any play, any performance, is more important than a dying child."

"I don't suppose for one moment that she really believed the child to be dying, assuming that she gave the matter thought."

"But is that what you believe? That a performance, any performance, could be more important?"

He smiled. "Now we're edging toward that old philosophical mine field. If the building's on fire and you can rescue only a syphilitic old tramp or a Velázquez, which, or who, gets incinerated?"

"No, we aren't. We're talking about a dying child wanting her mother, balancing that need against a performance of *Macbeth*. And I get tired of that old burning-building analogy. I should throw the Velázquez out the window and start lugging the tramp to safety. The real moral choice is when you find that he's too heavy. Do you escape alone or keep trying and risk getting incinerated with him?"

"Oh, that's easy. Obviously you escape alone and without leaving the decision too conscientiously to the last possible moment. About the child: no, I don't believe that any performance could be more important, certainly none that Clarissa is capable of giving. Does that satisfy you?"

"I don't understand how Miss Tolgarth can go on working for her. I couldn't."

"But you will. I confess I'm intrigued about your precise function here. But presumably you won't throw in your hand."

"But that's different; at least I shall persuade myself that it is. I'm just a temporary employee. But Tolly believed Clarissa when she was told that there was no immediate danger; she trusted her. How can she stay with her now?''

"They've been together almost all their lives. Tolly's mother was Clarissa's nurse. The family with a small *f* served the Family with a large *F* for three generations. They're born to be served; she was born to serve them. Perhaps, given the habit of subservience, a dead child here or there doesn't make any difference.''

"But that's horrible! It's ridiculous and degrading. It's Victorian!''

"Don't you believe it! The instinct for worship is remarkably persistent. What else is religious belief? Tolly's lucky to have her god walking the earth with shoes that need cleaning, clothes that need folding, hair that needs brushing.''

"But she can't want to go on serving. She can't like Clarissa.''

"What has liking to do with it? 'Though she slay me yet shall I trust her.' It's a perfectly common phenomenon. But I admit I do sometimes wonder what would happen if she faced the truth about her own feelings. If any of us did, come to that. It's getting colder, isn't it? Don't you feel it? Perhaps it's time we were getting back.''

7

THEY HARDLY SPOKE on the way back to the castle. For Cordelia, the sunlight had drained out of the day. The beauty of sea and shore passed unregarded by her desolated heart. Ivo was obviously very tired by the time they reached the terrace and said that he would rest in his room; he wouldn't bother with tea. Cordelia told herself that it was her job to stay close to Clarissa, however unwelcome that might be to both of them. But it took an effort of will before she could make her way back to the theater, and it was a relief to find that the rehearsal still wasn't over. She stood for a minute at the back of the auditorium, then made her way to her own room. The communicating door was open and she could see Tolly moving from bathroom to bedroom. But the thought of having to speak to her was intolerable and Cordelia made her escape.

Almost on impulse she opened the door next to her own, which gave access to the tower. A circular staircase of elaborately decorated wrought iron curved upwards into semi-darkness lit only by occasional slit windows less than a brick in width. She could see there was a light switch, but preferred to climb steadily upwards in the gloom in what seemed an endless spiral. But at last she reached the top and found herself in a small, light-filled, circular room with six tall windows. The room was unfurnished except for one cane armchair with a curved back and was obviously used to store acquisitions for which Ambrose hadn't yet found a place or which he had inherited from the previous owner, chiefly a collection of Victorian toys. There was a wooden horse on wheels, a Noah's ark with carved animals, three china dolls with bland faces and stuffed limbs, a table of mechanical toys including an organ grinder with his monkey, a set of cat musicians on a revolving platform, gaudily dressed in satin, each with an instrument, a toy grenadier soldier with a drum, a wooden music box.

The view was spectacular. The whole island, seen as if from an aircraft, was a neatly patterned colored map precisely placed in a crinkled sea. To the east was a smudge which must be the Isle of Wight. To the north the Dorset coast looked surprisingly close; she could almost make out the stunted pier and the colored terraces. She gazed down over the island, at the northern marshes fringed with white gulls, the central uplands, the fields, small patches of green amid the many-hued curdle of autumnal trees, the brown cliffs sliding down to the shore, the spire of the church rising amid the beeches, the roof of the arcade leading to a toy theater. From his cottage in the stable block the fore-shortened figure of Oldfield crept, a bucket in either hand, and as she watched, Roma emerged from the copse of beech trees which lined the lawn and made her way, hands hunched in her pockets, toward the castle. Across the grass a peacock stalked, dragging its tattered tail.

Here, slung between earth and sky in a brick-enclosed aerie, the sound of the sea was a low moan almost indistinguishable from the sighing of the wind. Suddenly Cordelia felt immensely lonely. The job which had promised so much seemed now a humiliating waste of time and effort. She no longer cared who was sending the messages or why. She felt that she hardly cared whether Clarissa lived or died. She wondered what was happening at Kingly Street, how Miss Maudsley was coping, whether Mr. Morgan had come to see to the nameplate. And thinking of him reminded her of Sir George. He had paid her to do a job. She was here to protect Clarissa, not to judge her. And there were only two more days to be got through. By Sunday it would all be over and she would be free to get back to London, need never hear Clarissa's name again. She recalled Bernie's words when he had once rebuked her for being overfastidious: "You can't make moral judgments about your clients in this job, mate. Start that and you may as well shut up shop."

She turned from the window and, on impulse, opened the music box. The cylinder slowly revolved and the delicate metal filaments plucked out the tune "Greensleeves." Then one by one she set the other mechanical toys in motion. The grenadier thumped his drum; the cats revolved, mouths grinning, jerking their satined arms; cymbals clashed; the plaintive "Greensleeves" was lost in the discordant din. And thus, in a gentle cacophony of childish sounds, which couldn't entirely shut out from her mind the image of a dying child but which helped to release some tension in her, Cordelia stared down over Ambrose's colored kingdom.

8

IVO HAD BEEN WRONG. Clarissa didn't apologize for her behavior at the rehearsal, but she did exert herself to be particularly charming to Cordelia over tea. It was a boisterous and protracted feast of sandwiches and overrich cake, and it was after six before the launch bearing DeVille and the other principals back to Speymouth finally drew away from the quay. Clarissa spent the hour before it was time to dress for dinner playing Scrabble in the library with Ambrose. She played noisily and badly, constantly calling out to Cordelia to look up challenged words in the dictionary or to support her against Ambrose's allegations that she was cheating. Cordelia, happily engrossed in old copies of *The Illustrated London News* and *The Strand* magazine, in which she could read the Sherlock Holmes stories as they had originally appeared, wished that she could have been left in peace. Simon was apparently to entertain them with music after dinner, and the distant sound of Chopin from the drawing room where he was practicing was pleasantly restful and evocative of her school days. Ivo was still in his room, and Roma sat in silence with the weekly journals and *Private Eye*.

The library, with its barrel roof and carved brass-fronted bookcases set between the four tall windows, was one of the most beautifully proportioned in the castle. The whole of the southern wall was taken up with one immense window decorated with round panes of colored glass. In the daytime the window framed nothing but a view of sea and sky. But now the library was in darkness except for the three pools of light from the desk lamps, and the great window rose like a sheet of rain-washed marble, blue-black and smudged with a few high stars. It was a pity, thought Cordelia, that, even here, Clarissa was incapable of occupying herself in peaceable silence.

When it was time to dress they went up together, and Cordelia unlocked both rooms and made a check on Clarissa's bedroom before she went in. All was well. She dressed quickly, put out the light, and then sat quietly at her window, looking out at the distant clumps of trees, black against the night sky, and the faint shimmer of the sea. Suddenly a light flashed from the south. She watched. In three seconds it flashed again and then for a third and last time. She thought that it must be some kind of signal, perhaps in answer to one from the island. But why and from whom? But then she told herself that the thought was childish and melodramatic. It was probably some solitary sailor on his way back to Speymouth harbor casually flashing a light over the quay. But there remained something discomforting and almost sinister about that threefold flash, as if someone were signaling that the cast was assembled, the leading lady ensconced in splendor under the castle roof, that the drawbridge could be drawn up and the play begin. But this was a castle without a drawbridge, its moat the sea. For the first time since her arrival, Cordelia was touched by a sense of claustrophobic unease. Here their only lifelines were the telephone and the launch, both easily put out of commission. She had been drawn to the mystery and loneliness of the island; now she missed the solid reassurance of the mainland, of towns and fields and hills ranged at her back. It was then that she heard Clarissa's door close and Tolly's departing footsteps. Clarissa must be ready. Cordelia went through the communicating door and they made their way together to the hall.

The dinner was excellent, artichokes followed by poussins and spinach au gratin. The south-facing room still held the warmth of the day, and the wood fire had been lit more for its sweet-smelling and comforting glow than because it was needed. The three tall candlesticks threw a steady light on the epergne of colored glass and Parian, the rich gold, green, and rose of the Davenport dinner service, and the engraved table glasses. Above the fireplace was an oil painting of the two daughters of Herbert Gorringe. Their poses were awkward, almost angular, and the faces with their bright exophthalmic eyes under the strong Gorringe brows and the moist half-open mouths looked flushed and feverish, while the reds and deep blues of the evening dresses shone as brightly as if the paint had recently dried. Cordelia found it difficult to keep her eyes from the picture, which so far from being tranquil or domestic seemed to her charged with a hectic sexual energy. Watching her gaze, Ambrose said, "It's by Millais, one of the comparatively few social portraits which he did. The dinner service we're using was a wedding gift to the elder daughter from the Prince and Princess of Wales. Clarissa insisted that I bring it out for tonight."

It seemed to Cordelia that there was a great deal which Clarissa insisted on at Courcy Castle. She wondered if she also proposed to supervise the washing up.

It should have been a festive meal, but the pleasure didn't match the food or the excellence of the wines. Beneath the glittering surface and the easy social chat flowed a current of unease, which from time to time spurted into antagonism. No one but Simon and herself with their youthful appetites did

justice to the food, and he shoved it in furtively, watching
Clarissa from the corners of his eye like a child allowed up
for his first diningroom meal and expecting any minute to be
banished to the nursery. Clarissa, elegant in her high-necked
dress of blue-green chiffon, began by teasing her cousin about
the absence of her partner, who had apparently been expected
for the weekend, a topic which she seemed reluctant to let go.

"But it's so odd of him, darling. Surely we didn't frighten
him away? Who are you ashamed of, us or him?"

Roma's face was an unbecoming pink above the harsh blue
of her taffeta dress.

"We're expecting an American customer to drop into the
shop this Saturday. And Colin has got behind with the
accounts. He's hoping to get them finished before Monday."

"On a weekend? How conscientious of him. But I'm
relieved to hear that you have some accounts worth doing.
Congratulations."

Cordelia, finding that she could make little headway with
Simon, who seemed afraid to speak, withdrew her interest
from her fellow guests and concentrated on her meal. When
she next took notice it was to hear Roma's belligerent voice.
She was addressing Ambrose across the table, clutching her
fork as if it were a weapon.

"But you can't opt out of all responsibility for what's
happening in your own country! You can't just say that you're
not concerned, not even interested!"

"But I can. I didn't collude in the depreciation of its
currency, the spoliation of its countryside, the desecration of
its towns, the destruction of its grammar schools, or even the
mutilation of the liturgy of its church. For what am I personally expected to feel a responsibility?"

"I was thinking of aspects which some of us see as more
important. The growth of fascism, the fact that our society is
more violent, less compassionate, and more unequal than it
has been since the nineteenth century. And then there's the
National Front. You can't ignore the Front!"

"Indeed I can, together with Militant Tendency, the Trots, and the rest of the rabble. You'd be surprised at my capacity for ignoring the ignorable."

"But you can't just decide to live in another age!"

"But I can. I can live in any century I wish. I don't have to choose the dark ages, old or new."

Ivo said quietly, "I'm grateful that you don't reject modern amenities or modern technology. If I should enter into the final process of dying during the next few days and need a little medical help to ease the way, I take it you won't object to using the telephone."

Ambrose smiled around at them and raised his glass. "If any of you decides to die in the next few days, all necessary measures will be taken to ease you on your way."

There was a short, slightly embarrassed silence. Cordelia looked across at Clarissa, but the actress's eyes were on her plate. For a second, the long fingers trembled and were still.

Roma said, "And what happens to Eden when Adam, solaced with no Eve, finally returns to dust?"

"It would be pleasant to have a son to follow one here, I admit, almost worth marrying and breeding for. But sons, even supposing they came to order and if the process of getting them, deceptively simple physiologically, weren't so fraught with practical and emotional complications, are notoriously unreliable. Ivo, you're the only one here with experience of children."

Ivo said, "It's unwise, certainly, to look to them for vicarious immortality."

"Or anything else, wouldn't you say? A son might easily convert the castle into a casino, lay down a nine-hole golf course, make the air hideous with speedboats and waterskiing, and hold pretentious Saturday hops for the locals, eight-fifty a head, three-course dinner included, evening dress obligatory, no extras guaranteed."

Clarissa looked across at Ivo. "Talking of children, what's

the news of your two, Ivo? Is Matthew still living in that Kensington squat?''

Cordelia saw that Ivo's chicken had been pushed almost untouched to the side of his plate and that although he was forking his spinach into shreds, little of it was reaching his mouth. But he had been drinking steadily. The claret decanter was on his right hand and he reached for it again, adding to a glass which he seemed not to realize was already three-quarters full. He looked across at Clarissa's eyes, bright in the candlelight.

"Matthew? I suppose he's still with the Children of the Sun or whatever they call themselves. As we don't communicate, I'm not in a position to say. Angela, on the other hand, writes a filial letter at boring length every month. I have two granddaughters now, she informs me. Since Angela and her husband refuse to visit a country where they might find themselves sharing a dining table with a black and I have a distaste for sharing a table with my son-in-law, I am unlikely to make their acquaintance. My ex-wife, in case you meant to inquire, is with them in Johannesburg, which she calls Jo'burg, and is said to be enchanted with the country, the climate, the company, and the kidney-shaped swimming pool.''

Clarissa laughed, a small bell note of triumph. "Darling, I wasn't asking for a family history.''

"Weren't you?" he said easily. "Oh, I rather thought you were.''

The table fell into a silence which, to Cordelia's relief, lasted with few interruptions until the meal was at last over and Munter opened the door for the women to follow Clarissa into the drawing room.

IVO WANTED NEITHER COFFEE nor liqueur, but he carried the decanter of claret and his glass with him into the drawing room and settled himself in an armchair between the fire and the open french windows. He felt no particular social responsibility for the rest of the evening. The dinner had been sufficiently grim, and he had every intention of getting quietly but thoroughly drunk. He had listened too much to his doctors. Throw physic to the dogs; he'd have none of it. Obviously, what he needed was to drink more, not less; and if it could be wine of this quality and at Ambrose's expense, so much the better. Already his self-disgust at allowing Clarissa to provoke him into that spurt of angry revelation was fading under the influence of the wine. What was taking its place was a gentle euphoria in which his mind became supernaturally clear, while the faces and words of his companions moved into a different dimension, so that he watched their antics with bright sardonic eyes as he might actors on a stage.

Simon was preparing to play for them, arranging his music on the stand with uncertain hands. Ivo thought, Oh, God, not Chopin followed by Rachmaninoff. And why, he wondered, was Clarissa draping herself over the boy, ready to turn the pages? It wasn't as if she could read music. If this was to be the start of her usual system of alternate kindness and brutality, she would end by driving the boy out of his wits as she had his father. Roma, in the taffeta dress which would have looked too young on an ingenue of eighteen, was sitting rigidly on the edge of her chair like a parent at a school concert. Why should she care how the boy performed? Why should any of them care? Already his nervousness was communicating itself to his audience. But he played better than Ivo expected, only occasionally attempting to disguise the misfingerings by too fast a tempo and the overuse of the loud pedal. Even so, it was too like a public performance to be enjoyable, the pieces chosen to show off his technique, the occasion made more important than anyone wanted. And it went on too long.

At the end Ambrose said, "Thank you, Simon. What are a few wrong notes among friends? And now, where are the songs of yesteryear?"

The decanter was now less than a quarter full. Ivo stretched himself more deeply in the chair and let the voices come to him from an immense distance. They were all around the piano now, roaring out sentimental Victorian drawing-room ballads. He could hear Roma's contralto, invariably late and slightly off-key, and Cordelia's clear soprano, a convent-trained voice, a little unsure but clear and sweet. He watched Simon's flushed face as he bent over the keys, the look of intense, exultant concentration. He was playing with more assurance and sensitivity now than he had alone. For once, the boy was enjoying himself.

After about half an hour Roma drifted away from the piano and walked over to look at two oils by Frith, crowded anecdotal canvases showing rail travelers going to the Derby by first class and third class. Roma walked from one to the other, studying them intently as if to check that no detail of social or sartorial contrast had been neglected by the artist. Then Clarissa suddenly dropped her hand from Simon's shoulder, swept past Ivo, her chiffon floating against his knee, and went out onto the terrace alone. Cordelia and Ambrose were left singing together. The three of them at the piano were linked by their enjoyment, seemingly unaware of their audience, transposing and consulting, choosing and comparing and collapsing into laughter when a piece proved beyond their range or competence. Ivo recognized only a few of the songs: Peter Warlock's Elizabethan pastiches, Vaughan Williams's "Bright Is the Ring of Words." He was listening now with the nearest he had come to happiness since his illness had been diagnosed. Nietzsche was wrong; it wasn't action but pleasure which bound one to existence. And he had become afraid of pleasure; to admit even the possibility of joy to his shriveled senses was to open the mind to anguish and regret. But now, listening to that sweet voice blending with Ambrose's baritone and floating past him out and over the sea, he lay back, weightless, in a dreamy contentment which was without bitterness and without pain. And gradually his senses began to tingle into life. He was aware of the cool stream of air from the window on his face, nothing as inconvenient as a draft, but a barely perceptible sensation like a stroking finger; of the sharp red of the wine glowing in the decanter and its softness against his tongue; of the smell of the wood fire, evocative of lost boyhood autumns.

And then his mood was broken. Clarissa stormed into the room from the terrace. Simon heard her and stopped playing in midbar. The two voices sang on for a few notes, then broke off.

Clarissa said, "I'll have enough of amateurs before the weekend's finished without you three adding to the boredom. I'm going to bed. Simon, it's time you called it a day. We'll go together; I want to see you to your room. Cordelia, ring for

Tolly, will you, and tell her I'm ready for her, then come up in fifteen minutes; I want to discuss arrangements for tomorrow. Ivo, you're drunk."

She waited with a shiver of impatience until Ambrose had opened the door for her, then swept out, merely pausing briefly to offer him her cheek to kiss. He bent forward but was too late, and his pursed lips pecked ludicrously at the air. Simon bundled up his music with shaking hands, looked around as if for help, and ran after her. Cordelia went across to where the embroidered rope hung by the side of the fireplace.

Roma said, "Black marks all round. We should have realized that we're here to applaud Clarissa's talent, not to demonstrate our own. If you plan to make a career as secretary-companion, Cordelia, you'll have to learn more tact."

Ivo was aware of Ambrose bending over him, of his flushed face and the black eyes bright and malicious under the strong half circles.

"Are you drunk, Ivo? You're remarkably quiet."

"I thought I was, but I seem not to be. Sobriety has overtaken me. But if you would open another bottle I could begin the agreeable process again. Good wine is a good familiar creature, if it be well used."

"But shouldn't you keep your mind clear for the task of tomorrow?"

Ivo held out the empty decanter. He was surprised to see that his hand was perfectly steady. He said, "Don't worry. I shall be sober enough for what I have to do tomorrow."

10

CORDELIA WAITED exactly fifteen minutes, refused Ambrose's offer of a nightcap, then made her way upstairs. The communicating door between her room and Clarissa's was ajar, and she went through without knocking. Clarissa, in her cream satin dressing gown, was sitting at the dressing table. Her hair was tugged back from her face and tied with a ribbon at the nape of the neck; her hairline was bound with a crepe band. She was scrutinizing her face in the glass and didn't look around.

The room was lit by only one bright light on the dressing table and the softer glow of the bedside lamp. A thin wood fire crackled in the grate and threw leaping shadows over the richness of damask and mahogany. The air smelled of wood smoke and perfume, and the room, dim and mysterious, struck Cordelia as smaller and more luxurious than it had been in its daytime brightness. But the bed was more than ever dominant, glowing under its scarlet canopy, sinister and

portentous as a catafalque. Cordelia saw that Tolly must have
been there before her. The sheets were turned back and
Clarissa's nightdress had been laid out, its waist pinched. It
looked like a shroud. In the shadowed half-light it was easy to
imagine that she stood in the doorway of a bedroom in Amalfi
with Webster's doomed duchess bright-haired at her toilet
while horror and corruption stalked in the shadows and,
beyond the half-open window, a tideless Mediterranean lay
open to the moon.

Clarissa's voice broke into her mood. "Oh, here you are.
I've sent Tolly away so that we can talk. Don't just stand
there. Find yourself a chair."

On each side of the fireplace was a low spoon-backed chair
with carved arms and feet. Cordelia slid one forward on its
casters and seated herself to the left of the dressing table.
Clarissa peered at herself in the glass, then unscrewed a jar of
cleansing pads and began wiping off her eye shadow and
mascara. Thin, black-stained scraps of tissue crept over the
polished mahogany. The left eye, wiped clean of makeup,
looked diminished, almost lifeless, giving her suddenly the
mask of a lopsided clown. She peered at the denuded lid,
frowned, then said, "You seem to have enjoyed yourself this
evening. Perhaps I should remind you that you were hired as
a detective, not an after-dinner entertainer."

It had been a long day and Cordelia couldn't summon the
energy for anger. "Perhaps if you were honest with them and
told them why I'm here they'd be less likely to treat me as a
fellow guest. Private detectives aren't expected to sing, at
least I wouldn't think so. They probably wouldn't even want
to eat with me. A private eye is hardly a comfortable dining
companion."

"What good would that do? If you don't mix with them,
how can you watch them? Besides, the men like you. I've
seen Ivo and Simon looking at you. Don't pretend that you
don't know it. I hate that kind of sexual coyness."

"I wasn't going to pretend anything."

Clarissa was busy now with an immense jar of cleansing cream, smearing dollops of the cream over face and neck and wiping them off with strong upward sweeps of cotton wool. The discarded greasy balls were added to the mess on the dressing table. Cordelia found herself studying Clarissa's face with as much intensity as did its owner. The eyes were a little too far apart; the skin was thick, unluminous, but almost without lines; the cheeks were flat and wide; the mouth with its pouting lower lip too small for beauty. But it was a face that could take on loveliness at Clarissa's will, and even now, bandaged, unenhanced, and sunk in repose, it held the assurance of its latent, eccentric beauty.

Suddenly, she asked, "What do you think of Simon's playing?"

"I'm not really qualified to judge. Obviously, he has talent." She was about to add that he might make a more successful accompanist than solo performer, then thought better of it. It was perfectly true: she wasn't competent to judge. And she had the feeling that ignorant though she was, some kind of decision might depend on her answer.

"Oh, talent! That's common enough. One doesn't invest six thousand pounds or so in mere talent. The thing is, has he the guts to succeed? George thinks not, but he may as well be given his chance."

"Sir George knows him better than I do."

Clarissa said sharply, "But it isn't George's money, is it? I'll consult Ambrose, but not until after the play. I can't worry about anything until then. He'll probably damn the poor boy. Ambrose is such a perfectionist. But he does know something about music. He'd be a better judge than poor George. If only Simon had taken up a stringed instrument, he might eventually try for a place in an orchestra. But the piano! Still, I suppose he could always work as an accompanist."

Cordelia wondered whether she should point out that the job of a professional accompanist, so far from being an easy option, required a formidable combination of technical ability and musicality, but she reminded herself that she hadn't been employed to advise on Simon's career. And this talk of Simon was wasting time. She said, "I think we should discuss the messages and our plans for the weekend, especially tomorrow. We ought to have spoken earlier."

"I know, but there hasn't really been time what with the rehearsal and Ambrose showing off his castle. Anyway, you know what you're here for. If there are any more messages, I don't want to receive them. I don't want to be shown them. I don't want to be told about them. It's vital that I get through tomorrow. If I can only get back my confidence as an actress, I can face almost anything."

"Even the knowledge of who is doing this to you?"

"Even that."

Cordelia asked, "How many of the people here know about the messages?"

Clarissa had finished cleaning her face and now began removing the varnish from her nails. The smell of acetone overlaid the smell of scent and makeup.

"Tolly knows. I haven't any secrets from Tolly. Anyway, she was with me in my dressing room when some of them were brought in by the doorman, the ones sent by post to the theater. I expect Ivo knows; there's nothing happens in the West End that he doesn't get to hear about. And Ambrose. He was with me in my dressing room at the Duke of Clarence when one was pushed under the door. By the time he'd picked it up for me and I'd opened it, whoever it was had gone. The corridor was empty. But anyone could have got in. Backstage at the Clarence is like a warren, and Albert Betts used to drink and wasn't always on the door when he should have been. They've sacked him now, but he was still working there when the note was delivered. And my husband knows, of course. Simon doesn't, unless Tolly has told him. I can't think why she should."

"And your cousin?"

"Roma doesn't know, and if she did, she wouldn't care."

"Tell me about Miss Lisle."

"There's not much to tell and what there is, is boring. We're first cousins, but George has told you that. It's quite a common story. My father made a sensible marriage and his younger brother ran off with a barmaid, left the army, drank, and made a general mess of his life, then expected Daddy to help out. And he did, at least as far as Roma was concerned. She was always staying with us when I was a child, particularly after Uncle died. Poor Little Orphan Annie. Glum, badly dressed, and perpetually miserable. Even Daddy couldn't stand her for long. He was the most marvelous person; I adored him. But she was such a bore, and so plain, worse than she is now. Daddy was one of those people who really couldn't bear ugliness, particularly in women. He loved gaiety, wit, beauty. He just couldn't make himself look at a plain face."

Cordelia thought that Daddy, who sounded like a self-satisfied humbug, must have spent most of his life with his eyes shut, depending, of course, on his standard of ugliness.

Clarissa added, "And she wasn't a bit grateful."

"Should she have been?"

Clarissa seemed to feel that the question deserved serious thought, or as much as she could spare from the business of filing her nails. "Oh, I think so. He didn't have to take her in. And she could hardly expect him to treat her the same as me, his own child."

"He could have tried."

"But that's not reasonable, and you know it. You wouldn't behave like that, so why expect him to? You really must guard against becoming just a bit of a prig. Men don't like it."

Cordelia said, "I don't much like it myself. Someone once told me that it's the result of having an atheist father, a convent education, and a nonconformist conscience."

There was silence between them, not uncompanionable. Then Cordelia said on impulse, "These notes—could Miss Tolgarth have anything to do with them?"

"Tolly! Of course not. Whatever put that idea into your head? She's devoted to me. You mustn't be put off by her manner. She's always been like that. But we've been together since I was a child. Tolly adores me. If you can't see that, you're not much of a detective. Besides, she can't type. The messages are typed, in case you hadn't noticed."

Cordelia said gravely, "You should have told me about her child. If I'm to help I need to know anything that might be relevant." She waited, apprehensive, for Clarissa's response. But the hands, busy with their self-ministrations, didn't falter.

"But that isn't relevant. It was all a mistake. Tolly knows that. Everyone knows it. I suppose Ivo told you. That's typical of his malice and disloyalty. Can't you see that he's sick? He's dying? And he's eaten up with jealousy. He always has been. Jealousy and malice."

Cordelia wondered whether she could have asked the question more tactfully, whether it had been wise to ask it at all. Ivo hadn't asked her not to betray their conversation, but presumably he had hoped for discretion. And the weekend promised to be difficult enough without setting two of the guests at each other's throats. Direct lying had never been easy for her. She said cautiously, "No one has been disloyal. Obviously I did some tactful research before I arrived here. These things do get talked about. I have a friend in the theater." Well, that was true enough anyway, even if poor Bevis was more often out than in. But Clarissa was uninterested in putative theatrical friends.

"I'd like to know what right Ivo has to criticize me. Do you realize how many careers he's ruined by his cruelty? Yes, cruelty! I've seen actors—actors, mind you—in tears after one of his reviews. If he could have resisted the impulse to be clever, he might have been one of the great British critics. He could have been a second Agate or a Tynan. And what is he now? Dying on his feet. He's no right to come here looking as he does. It's like having a death's head at table. It's indecent."

It was interesting, thought Cordelia, the way in which death had replaced sex as the great unmentionable, to be denied in prospect, endured in decent privacy, preferably behind the drawn curtains of a hospital bed, and followed by discreet, embarrassed, uncomforted mourning. There was this to be said about the Convent of the Holy Child: the views of the sisters on death had been explicit, firmly held, and not altogether reassuring; but at least they hadn't regarded it as in poor taste.

She said, "Those first messages, the ones that came when you were playing Lady Macbeth, the ones you threw away. Were they the same as the later ones, typed and on white paper?"

"Yes, I suppose so. It was a long time ago."

"But you can't have forgotten!"

"They must have been the same, mustn't they? What does it matter? I don't want to talk about it now."

"It's the only chance we may get. I haven't been able to see you alone today, and tomorrow isn't going to be any easier."

Clarissa was on her feet now, pacing between the dressing table and the bed. "It wasn't my fault. I didn't kill her. She wasn't properly cared for. If she had been she wouldn't have had the accident. What's the point of having a child—a bastard, too—if you don't look after it?"

"But wasn't Tolly at work, looking after you?"

"The hospital had no right to phone like that, upsetting people. They must have known that it was a theater that they were calling, that West End curtains rise at eight, that we'd be in the middle of a performance. She couldn't have done anything if I had let her go. The child was unconscious; she wouldn't have known her. It's sentimental and morbid, this sitting by the bedside waiting for people to die. What good does it do? And I had three changes in the third act. Kalenski designed the banquet costume himself: barbaric jewelry, a crown set with great dollops of red stones like blood, a skirt so stiff I could hardly move. He meant me to be weighed down, to walk stiffly like an overencumbered child. 'Think of yourself as a seventeenth-century princess,' he said, 'wonderingly loaded with inappropriate majesty.' Those were his words, and he made me keep moving my hands down the side of the skirt as if I couldn't believe that I was actually wearing so much richness. And of course it made a marvelous contrast with the plain cream shift in the sleepwalking scene. It wasn't a nightgown; they used to sleep naked apparently. I used it to wipe my hands. Kalenski said, 'Hands, darling, hands, hands; that's what this part is all about.' It was a new interpretation, of course. I wasn't the usual kind of Lady Macbeth, tall, domineering, ruthless. I played her like a sex kitten but a kitten with hidden claws.''

It was, thought Cordelia, a novel interpretation of the part, surely not altogether consonant with the text. But perhaps Kalenski, like other Shakespearean directors whose names came to mind, didn't let that bother him. She said, ''But was it true to the text?''

''Oh, my dear, who cares about the text? I don't mean that exactly, but Shakespeare's like the Bible: you can make it mean anything. That's why directors love him.''

''Tell me about the child.''

''Macduff's son? Desmond Willoughby played him, an intolerable child. A vulgar Cockney accent. You can't find a child actor now who knows how to speak English. Too old for the part too. Thank God I never had to appear with him.''

One biblical text came into Cordelia's mind, brutally explicit in its meaning, but she didn't speak it aloud:

''Whoso shall offend one of these little ones which believe in me, it were better that a millstone were hanged about his neck, and that he were drowned in the depth of the sea.''

Clarissa turned and looked at her. Something in Cordelia's face must have pierced even her egotism. She cried, ''I'm not paying you to judge me! What are you looking like that for?''

"I'm not judging you. I want to help. But you have to be honest with me."

"I am being honest, as honest as I know how. When I first saw you, that day at Nettie Fortescue's, I knew I could trust you, that you were someone I could talk to. It's degrading to be so afraid. George doesn't understand; how could he? He's never been afraid of anything in his life. He thinks I'm neurotic to care. He went to see you only because I made him."

"Why didn't you come yourself?"

"I thought you might be more likely to accept the job if he asked you. And I don't enjoy asking people for favors. Besides, I had a fitting for one of my costumes."

"There wasn't any question of a favor. I needed the job. I probably would have taken almost anything if it wasn't illegal and didn't disgust me."

"Yes, George said that your office was pretty squalid. Well, pathetic rather than squalid. But you aren't. There's nothing squalid or pathetic about you. I couldn't have put up with the usual kind of female private eye."

Cordelia said gently, "What is it that you're really afraid of?"

Clarissa turned on Cordelia, her softly gleaming, cleansed, uncolored face looking for the first time, in its nakedness, vulnerable to age and grief, and gave a sad, rather rueful smile. Then she lifted her hands in an eloquent gesture of despair.

"Oh, don't you know? I thought George had told you. Death. That's what I'm afraid of. Just death. Stupid, isn't it? I always have been, even when I was a child. I don't remember when it began, but I knew the facts of death before I knew the facts of life. There never was a time when I didn't see the skull beneath the skin. Nothing traumatic happened to start it off. They didn't force me to look at my nanny, dead in her coffin; nothing like that. And I was at school when Mummy died and it didn't mean anything. It isn't the death of other people. It isn't the fact of death. It's my death I'm afraid of. Not all the time. Not every moment. Sometimes I can go for weeks without thinking about it. And then it comes, usually at night, the dread and the horror and the knowledge that the fear is real. I mean, no one can say, 'Don't worry, it may never happen.' They can't say, 'It's all your imagination, darling, it doesn't really exist.' I can't really describe the fear, what it's like, how terrible it is. It comes in a rhythm, wave after wave of panic sweeping over me, a kind of pain. It must be like giving birth, except that I'm not delivering life; it's death I have between my thighs. Sometimes I hold up my hand, like this, and look at it and think, Here it is, part of me. I can feel it with my other hand, and move it and warm it and smell it and paint its nails. And one day it will hang white and cold and unfeeling and useless, and so shall I be all those things. And then it will rot. And I shall rot. I can't even drink to forget. Other people do. It's how they get through their lives. But drink makes me ill. It isn't fair that I should have this terror and not be able to drink! Now I've told you, and you can explain that I'm stupid and morbid and a coward. You can despise me.''

Cordelia said, ''I don't despise you.''

''And it's no good saying that I ought to believe in God. I can't. And even if I could, it wouldn't help. Tolly got converted after Viccy died, so I suppose she believes. But if someone told Tolly that she was going to die tomorrow, she'd be just as unwilling to go. I've noticed that about the God people. They're just as frightened as the rest of us. They cling on just as long. They're supposed to have a heaven waiting but they're in no hurry to get there. Perhaps it's worse for them: judgment and hell and damnation. At least I'm only afraid of death. Isn't everyone? Aren't you?''

Was she? Cordelia wondered. Sometimes, perhaps. But the fear of dying was less obtrusive than more mundane worries: what would happen when the Kingly Street lease ran out, whether the Mini would pass inspection, how she would face

Miss Maudsley if the agency no longer had a job for her. Perhaps only the rich and successful could indulge the morbid fear of dying. Most of the world needed its energies to cope with living.

She said cautiously, knowing that she had no comfort to offer, "It doesn't seem reasonable to be afraid of something which is inevitable and universal and which I shan't be able to experience, anyway."

"Oh, those are just words! All they mean is that you're young and healthy and don't have to think about dying. 'To lie in cold obstruction and to rot.' That was in one of the messages."

"I know."

"And there's another for you to add to the collection. I've been keeping it for you. It came by post to the London flat yesterday morning. You'll find it at the bottom of my jewel case. It's on the bedside table, the left-hand side."

The instruction as to the side was unnecessary; even in the subdued light and amid the clutter of Clarissa's bedside table, the softly gleaming casket was an object that caught the eye. Cordelia took it in her hands. It was about eight inches by five, with delicately wrought clawed feet, the lid and sides embossed with a representation of the judgment of Paris. She turned the key and saw that the inside was lined with cream quilted silk.

Clarissa called, "Ambrose gave it to me when I arrived this morning, a good-luck present for the performance tomorrow. I took a fancy to it when I saw it six months ago but it took a time before he got the message. He has so many Victorian baubles that one less can't make any difference. The casket we're using in act three is his; well, most of the props are. But this is prettier. More valuable too. But not as valuable as the thing I'm keeping in it. You'll find the letter in the secret drawer. Not so very secret, actually. You just press the center of one of the leaves. You can see the line if you look carefully. Better bring it here. I'll show you."

The box was surprisingly heavy. Clarissa pulled out a
tangle of necklaces and bracelets as if they were cheap
costume jewelry. Cordelia thought that some of the pieces
probably were, bright beads of colored stone and glass
intertwined with the sparkle of real diamonds, the glow of
sapphires, the softness of milk-white pearls. Clarissa pressed
the center of one of the leaves which decorated the side of the
box and a drawer in the base slid slowly open. Inside
Cordelia saw first a folded cutting of newsprint. Clarissa took
it out.

"I played Hester in a revival of Rattingan's *The Deep Blue
Sea*, at the Speymouth Playhouse. That was in 1977, Jubilee
Year, when Ambrose was abroad on his year's tax exile. The
theater's closed now, alas. But they seemed to like me.
Actually, that's probably the most important notice I ever
had."

She unfolded it. Cordelia glimpsed the headline. "Clarissa
Lisle Triumphs in Rattigan Revival." Her mind busied itself
for only a second on the oddity of Clarissa's attaching so
much importance to the review of a revival in a small
provincial town, and she noticed, almost subconsciously, that
the cutting was oddly shaped and larger than the space taken
by the notice. But her interest fastened on the letter. The
envelope matched the one handed to her by Mrs. Munter
from the morning post bag, but the address had been typed on
a different and obviously older machine. The postmark was
London, the date two days earlier, and like the other it was
addressed to the Duchess of Malfi but at Clarissa's Bayswater
flat. Inside was the usual sheet of white paper, the neat black
drawing of a coffin, the letters *R.I.P.* Underneath was typed a
quotation from the play:

Who must despatch me?
I account this world a tedious theatre
For I must play a part in 't 'gainst my will.

Cordelia said, "Not very appropriate. He must be getting to the end of suitable quotations."

Clarissa tugged off her hair band. In the glass her reflection gazed back at them both, a ghost face, hung about with pale, disheveled hair, the huge eyes troubled under their heavy lids.

"Perhaps he knows that he won't need many more. There's only tomorrow. Perhaps he knows—who better?—that tomorrow will be the end."

BOOK THREE

BLOOD
FLIES
UPWARDS

1

CORDELIA SLEPT MORE DEEPLY and for longer than she had
expected. She was awakened by a quiet knock at the door.
Instantly she was fully conscious and throwing her dressing
gown around her shoulders as she went to open it. It was
Mrs. Munter with early-morning tea. Cordelia had meant to
be up well before she arrived. It was embarrassing to be
discovered sleeping behind a locked door as if she were
confusing Courcy Castle with a hotel. If Mrs. Munter was
surprised at this eccentricity she gave no sign, but placed the
tray on the bedside table with a quiet "Good morning, miss,"
and left as unobtrusively as she had arrived.

It was half past seven. The room was filled with the
smudged half-light of dawn. Going to the window, Cordelia
saw that the eastern sky was just beginning to streak into
brightness and that a low mist hung over the lawn and curled
like smoke between the treetops. It was going to be another
lovely day. There was no sign of any bonfire, yet the air held

149

the smoky wood-fire smell of autumn, and the great mass of the sea heaved, gray and silver, as if it exuded its own mysterious light.

She crept to the communicating door and opened it very gently. It was heavy, but it swung open without a creak. The curtains were drawn across the windows, but there was enough light from her own room to show her Clarissa, still sleeping, one white arm curved around her pillow. Cordelia tiptoed up to the bed and stood very still, listening to the quiet breathing. She felt a sense of relief without knowing exactly why. She had never believed that there was a real threat to Clarissa's life. And their precautions against mischief had been thorough. Both the doors to the corridor had been locked and the keys left in the locks. Even if someone had a duplicate there was no way in which he could have got in. But it was only after this reassurance that she felt free to drink her tea in comfort.

And then she saw the paper, a pale oblong gleaming against the carpet. Another message had been delivered, pushed under the door. So whoever was responsible was here, on the island. She felt her heart jolt. Then she took hold of herself, angry that she hadn't thought of the possibility of a missive under the door, resenting her own fear. She crept across to pick up the paper and took it into her own room, shutting the door behind her.

It was another passage from *The Duchess of Malfi*, eleven short words surmounted by a skull:

Thus it lightens into action,
I am come to kill thee.

The form was the same, but the paper was different. This message was typed on the back of an old woodcut headed "The Gt Meffenger of Mortality." Beneath the title was the crude figure of death bearing an hourglass and an arrow, followed by four stanzas of verse.

She gulped down her tea, pulled on her trousers and shirt,

and went in search of Ambrose. She had hardly hoped to find him so early, but he was already in the breakfast room, coffee cup in hand, gazing out over the lawn. It was one of the rooms which she had seen on Friday's quick tour of the castle, the furniture and fittings all designed by Godwin. There was a simple refectory table with a set of fretwork-backed chairs, and one long wall was entirely covered by a set of cupboards and open shelves, charmingly carved in light wood and surmounted by a tiled frieze in which orange trees in bright blue pots alternated with highly romanticized scenes from the legend of King Arthur and the Round Table. At the time Cordelia had thought it an interesting example of the architect's move toward the simplicities of the Aesthetic Movement, but now its self-conscious charm was lost on her.

Ambrose turned at her entrance and smiled. "Good morning. It looks as if we're going to be lucky in the weather. The guests should arrive in sunshine and get back without risk of parting with their supper. The crossing can be treacherous in bad weather. Is our leading lady awake?"

"Not yet."

Cordelia made a sudden resolution. It could do no harm to tell him. The woodcut almost certainly came from his house. Clarissa had told her that he already knew about the poison-pen messages. And Clarissa was his guest. Above all, she wanted to see his reaction to the paper. She held it out and said, "I found this pushed under Clarissa's door this morning. Does it belong to you? If so, someone has mutilated it for you. Look on the back."

He studied it briefly, then turned it over. For a moment he was silent. Then he said, "So the messages are still coming. I did wonder. Has she seen this?"

There was no need to ask whom he meant. "No. And she won't."

"Very wise of you. I take it that weeding out this kind of nuisance is one of your duties as secretary-companion?"

"One of them. But does it belong to you?"

"No. It's interesting, but not my period."

"But this is your house. And Miss Lisle is your guest."

He smiled and wandered over to the sideboard. "Will you have coffee?"

She watched while he went over to the hot plate, poured her cup, and refilled his own. Then he said, "I accept the implied criticism. One's guests certainly have the right not to be harassed or menaced while under one's roof. But what do you suggest I can do? I'm not a policeman. I can hardly interrogate my other houseguests. That, apart from its certain lack of success, would only result in six aggrieved persons instead of one. I doubt whether Clarissa would thank me. And, forgive me, aren't you taking this a little too seriously? I admit that it's a practical joke in poor taste. But is it any more than a joke? And surely the best response to this kind of nonsense is a dignified silence, even a certain amused contempt. Clarissa is an actress. She should be able to simulate one response or the other. If there is someone on the island who is trying to spoil her performance, he—or more likely she—will soon give up if Clarissa demonstrates total unconcern."

"That's what she will do, at least until after the play. She won't see this. I can trust you not to tell her?"

"Of course. I have a strong interest in Clarissa's success, remember. You didn't put the thing there yourself by any chance."

"No."

"I thought not. Forgive my asking, but you see my difficulty. If it wasn't you, it was presumably her husband—except that he isn't here at the moment—her stepson, her cousin, her faithful dresser, or one of her oldest friends. Who am I to start probing these family and long-standing relationships? Incidentally, that woodcut belongs to Roma."

"To Roma! How do you know?"

"You do sound fierce, quite like a schoolmistress. Roma used to teach, you know. Geography and games, Clarissa tells me. A strange combination. I can't quite picture Roma, whistle at the lip, panting down the hockey field exhorting the girls to greater efforts, or plunging into the deep end of the swimming pool. Well, perhaps I can believe that. She has aggressively muscular shoulders.''

Cordelia said, ''But the woodcut?''

''She told me that she found it in a secondhand book and thought I might be interested in seeing it. She showed it to me yesterday, just before the rehearsal, and I left it on the blotter on my desk in the business room.''

''Where anyone could have seen and taken it?''

''You sound like a detective. As you say, where anyone could have seen and taken it. It looks, incidentally, as if the message was typed on my machine. That, too, is kept in the business room.''

The typing, at least, would be easy enough to check. She might as well do it now. But before she could make the suggestion Ambrose said, ''And there's another thing. Forgive me if I find it rather more annoying than Clarissa's poison pen. Someone has broken the lock of the display cabinet outside the business room and taken the marble arm. If during your duties as secretary-companion you should happen to learn who it is, I'd be grateful if you would suggest that he or she put it back. I admit that the marble's not to everyone's taste, but I have a fondness for it.''

Cordelia said, ''The arm of the Princess Royal? When did you notice that it had gone?''

''Munter tells me that it was in the display case when he locked up last night. That was at ten minutes past midnight. He unlocked this morning shortly after six but didn't look at the display case, although he thinks that he might have noticed if the arm had gone. But he can't be sure. I myself saw that it was missing and that the lock had been forced when I went to the kitchen to make tea just before seven.''

Cordelia said, ''It couldn't have been Clarissa. She was asleep when I got up this morning. And I doubt whether she'd have the strength to break a lock.''

"Not much strength was required. A strong paper knife would have done the trick. And, conveniently enough, there was a strong paper knife on the desk in the business room."

Cordelia asked, "What are you going to do?"

"Nothing, at least until after the play. I can't see how it affects Clarissa. It's my loss, not hers. But I take it you would prefer her not to know?"

"I think it's vital that she doesn't find out. The least thing could upset her. We'll just have to hope no one else notices that the arm has gone."

He said, "If they do, I suppose I can say that I've removed it since Clarissa found it so displeasing. It's humiliating to have to lie when there's no need, but if you think it important that Clarissa isn't told . . ."

"I do. Very important. I'd be grateful if you'd say and do nothing until after the play."

It was then that they heard the footsteps, firm, quick, clanging on the tiled floor. Both turned simultaneously and gazed at the door. Sir George Ralston appeared, tweed-coated and holding a grip. He said, "I got through the meeting late yesterday. Drove most of the night and slept in a turnoff. Thought Clarissa would like me to put in an appearance if I could make it."

Ambrose said, "But how did you get to the island? I didn't hear a launch."

"Found a couple of early fishermen. They put me ashore in the small bay. Got my feet wet but nothing worse. I've been on the island a couple of hours. Didn't like to disturb you. Is that coffee?"

A jumble of thoughts ran through Cordelia's mind. Was she still wanted? She could hardly ask Sir George directly with Ambrose present. She was supposed to be on the island as Clarissa's secretary, a job that was unlikely to be affected by his sudden appearance. And what about her room? Presumably he would wish to move next door to his wife. She was uncomfortably aware that she must look less than pleased to see him and that Ambrose was glancing at her with a sardonic, wryly amused look which recognized her discomfiture. Murmuring an excuse, she slipped away.

Clarissa was stirring, although Tolly hadn't yet brought in the early tray. Cordelia drew back the curtains and unlocked the door. She stood by the bed until Clarissa opened her eyes, then said, "Your husband has just arrived. Apparently the meeting ended sooner than he expected."

Clarissa heaved herself up from her pillows. "George? But that's ridiculous! He isn't expected until late tonight at the earliest."

"Well, he's here."

Cordelia thought that it was as well that she had warned Clarissa. Sir George could hardly have been gratified at her reception of the news. She sat up and stared straight ahead, her face expressionless. Then she said, "Tug on that bell rope, will you? The one by the fireplace. It's time Tolly brought in my tea."

Cordelia said, "I wondered whether you'll still want me."

Clarissa's voice was sharp, almost frightened. "Of course I still want you! What possible difference does this make? You know what you're here to do. If someone's out to get me, he isn't going to stop because George has arrived."

"I could move out of the next-door room if you like."

Clarissa swung her legs out of bed and made for the bathroom. "Oh, don't be so bloody naive, Cordelia! Stay where you are. And tell George I'm awake if he wants to see me."

She disappeared. Cordelia decided to wait in the bedroom until Tolly arrived with the tea. If she could help it, there would be no time between now and the rise of the curtain when Clarissa would be left unguarded.

Clarissa returned from the bathroom and climbed back into bed.

Cordelia said, "Before Miss Tolgarth arrives, could you tell me what the program is today?"

"Oh, don't you know? I thought I'd explained it all. The curtain is due to rise at three-thirty. Ambrose is arranging an early lunch, about midday, and I shall rest up here alone from one until two-forty-five. I don't want to spend too long in my dressing room before a performance. You can call me at two-forty-five and we'll decide what, if anything, I want you to do during the play. The launch will fetch the Cottringham party from Speymouth. They should arrive at two-thirty or shortly afterward. There is a larger hired launch for the guests and that is due at three. We have tea in the interval at four-thirty, set out under the arcade if it's warm enough, and supper at seven-thirty in the great hall. The launches are ordered for nine."

Cordelia said, "And this morning? What is planned for the three hours between breakfast and luncheon? I think we should try to stay together."

"We shall all stay together. Ambrose has suggested that we might like a trip round the island in *Shearwater*, but I've told him that we're not a party of his five-pounds-a-day summer trippers. I've thought of a better plan. There are sights on Courcy that he hasn't shown us yet. I don't think you need worry about being bored. We'll start with a visit to the skulls of Courcy."

Cordelia said, "The skulls of Courcy? Do you mean real skulls, here in the castle?"

Clarissa laughed. "Oh, they're real enough. In the crypt of the church. Ambrose will recite the famous legend. They should put us all nicely in the mood for the horrors of Amalfi."

Tolly with the tea tray and Sir George arrived simultaneously. He was received very prettily. Clarissa held out a languid arm. He raised her hand to his lips, then bent with a stiff, graceless movement and briefly laid his face against hers.

She cried, her voice high and brittle, "Darling, how lovely! And how clever of you to find someone to bring you across."

He didn't look at Cordelia. He said gruffly, "You're all right?"

"Darling, of course. Did you think I wasn't? How touching! But, as you see, here I am, Duchess of Malfi still."

Cordelia left them. She wondered whether Sir George would find an opportunity of speaking to her privately and, if so, whether she should tell him about the woodcut pushed under the door. It was, after all, he who had employed her. But it was Clarissa who had sent for her, Clarissa who was her client, Clarissa she was paid to protect. Some instinct urged her to keep her counsel, at least until after the play. And then she remembered the missing marble. In the surprise of Sir George's arrival it had slipped from the front of her mind. But now its pale image gleamed in her imagination with all the sinister force of an omen. Ought she at least to warn Sir George that it was missing? But warn him against what? It was only the carved replica of a baby's limb, the limb of a long-dead princess. How could it harm anyone? Why should it hold in its chubby fingers such a weight of portentous power? She couldn't even explain to herself why she thought it so important that Clarissa not be told about the loss, except that the marble had repelled her and that any mention of it would be upsetting. Surely she had been right in asking Ambrose to say nothing, at least until after the play. So why tell Sir George? He hadn't even seen the limb. It would be time enough for them all to be told when Ambrose started inquiring and looked for it after the play. And that would be this evening. There was only today to be got through.

She was aware that she wasn't thinking very clearly. And one thought in particular surprised and fretted her. Surely the presence of Clarissa's husband on Courcy Island ought to make her job easier. She should be feeling relieved at a sharing of responsibility. Why, then, should she see this unexpected arrival as a new and unwelcome complication? Why should she feel for the first time she was caught in a charade in which she stumbled blindfold, while unseen hands spun her around, pushed and pulled at her, in which an unknown intelligence watched, waited, and directed the play?

2

BREAKFAST WAS A long-drawn-out meal to which the members of the house party came singly, ate at leisure, and seemed reluctant to finish. The dishes would have done justice to Herbert Gorringe's Victorian notions of a proper start to the day. As the lids of the silver dishes were raised, the discordant smells of eggs and bacon, sausages, kidneys, and haddock filled the breakfast room, stifling appetite. Despite the early promise of another warm day, Cordelia sensed that the party was ill at ease and that she wasn't the only one present who was mentally counting the hours to nightfall. There seemed to be an unspoken conspiracy not to upset Clarissa, and when she announced her plan to visit the church and the crypt the murmur of agreement was suspiciously unanimous. If anyone would have preferred a trip around the island or a solitary walk, no one admitted it. Probably they were well aware how precarious was her control before a performance, and no one wanted to risk being held responsible if that control broke. As they walked in a group along the arcade, past the theater and under the shadow of the trees which led to the church, it seemed to Cordelia that Clarissa was surrounded by the solicitous care afforded to an invalid or—and the thought was disagreeable—to a predestined victim.

Sir George was the one most at ease. When they entered the church and the rest of the party gazed around with the air of people resolved to find something positive to say, his reaction was immediate and uncompromising. He obviously found its nineteenth-century fusion of religious enthusiasm with medieval romanticism unsympathetic and viewed the richly decorated apse with its mosaic of Christ in glory, the colored tiles, and the polychromatic arches with a prejudiced eye.

"It looks more like a Victorian London club—or a Turkish bath come to that—than a church. I'm sorry, Gorringe, but I can't admire it. Who'd you say the architect was?"

"George Frederick Bodley. My great-grandfather had quarreled with Godwin by the time he came to rebuild the church. His relationships with his architects were always stormy. I'm sorry you don't like it. The paintings on the reredos are by Lord Leighton, by the way, and the glass is by William Morris's firm, which specialized in these lighter hues. Bodley was one of the first architects to use the firm. The east window is considered rather fine."

"I don't see how anyone could actually pray in the place. Is that the war memorial?"

"Yes. Put up by my uncle from whom I inherited. It's the only architectural addition he ever made to the island."

The memorial was a plain stone slab set in the wall to the south of the altar which read:

In memory of the men of Courcy Island
who fell on the battlefields of two world wars
and whose bones lie in foreign soil.
1914–1918
1939–1945

This at least met with Sir George's approval.

"I like that. Plain and dignified. Wonder who put the wreath there. Been there some time by the look of it."

Ambrose had come up behind them. He said, "There'll be a fresh one on the eleventh of November. Munter makes them from our own laurels and hangs one up each year. His father was killed in the war, in the navy I think. Anyway, he was drowned. He told me that much."

Roma asked, "And do you assist at this charade?"

"No, he hasn't asked me. It's a purely private ceremony. I'm not sure that I'm even supposed to know that it happens."

Roma turned away and said, "It throws a new light on Munter though. Who would suspect him of that streak of romanticism? But I wouldn't have thought that the memorial was particularly appropriate. His father didn't live or work on the island, did he?"

"Not to my knowledge."

"And if he drowned, his bones won't be buried in any soil, foreign or otherwise. It all seems rather pointless. But, then, Remembrance Day is pointless. No one seems to know any longer what it's supposed to be for."

Sir George said, "It's for remembering the good chaps who've gone. Once a year. For two minutes. You wouldn't think that was too much to ask. And why degrade it into a sentimental mass love-in? At our last Parade the padre preached a sermon about the Third World and the World Council of Churches. I could see that some of the older chaps in the Legion were getting restless."

Roma said, "I suppose he thought his sermon had something to do with world peace."

"Armistice Day isn't to do with peace. It's to do with war and remembering one's dead. A nation that can't remember its dead will soon cease to be worth dying for. And what's so peaceful about the Third World?"

He turned quickly away, and for a moment Cordelia thought that his eyes were moist. But then she saw that it was just a

trick of the light and was embarrassed at her naiveté. He
might be remembering his own good chaps and the lost,
forgotten, and discredited causes for which they had died.
But he was remembering without tears. He had seen so many
bodies, so many deaths. Could any death now, she wondered,
be more to him than a single statistic?

A door in the vestry led down to the crypt. To make their
way down narrow stone steps lit by Ambrose's pocket torch
was to descend into a different world, a different time. Here
alone was there any trace of the original Norman building.
The roof was so low that Ivo, the tallest of them, could hardly
stand upright, and the heavy, squat pillars strained as if
bearing on their capitals the weight of nine centuries. Ambrose
put out his hand to a wall switch and the claustrophobic
chamber sprang into harsh, unflattering light. They saw the
skulls at once. One whole wall was patterned with them, a
grinning parade of death. They had been ranged on rough oak
shelves and were so tightly wedged that Cordelia judged that
it would be impossible to separate them except by hacking
them apart. Little care had been taken in the arrangement. In
some places cement had been poured over them, fixing mouth
to mouth in the parody of a kiss. In others, the grit of the
years had seeped between them, binding them into cohesion,
blocking the nasal cavities, collecting in the eye sockets, and
laying over the smooth domes a patina of dust like a shroud.

Ambrose said, "There's a legend about them, of course;
there always is. In the seventeenth century the island was held
by the de Courcy family; they had, in fact, been here since
the fourteen-hundreds. The de Courcy at that time was a
particularly unpleasant representative of his breed. Someone
must have told him about Tiberius's little doings on Capri—I
don't suppose he could himself read—and he started to
emulate them here. You can imagine the kind of thing: local
maidens from the mainland abducted, *droit du seigneur* exer-
cised on a scale which even the most compliant tenants found
unreasonable, mutilated bodies brought in on the tide to the

general disapproval of the locals. Speymouth was a small fishing village then. The town only reached any size or importance in the Regency—a sort of West Country Brighton. But the word got around. No one did anything, of course. The story is that the father of one of the abducted girls, whose tortured body floated ashore three weeks later, laid information against him with the local magistrate. De Courcy was subsequently tried at the assizes but acquitted. One supposes it was managed in the usual way: a venal judge, perjured witnesses, bribed jurymen, a mixture of subservience and fear. And, of course, there was no direct evidence. At the end of the trial the father—he was an immensely powerful man according to the legend—rose up in court and cursed de Courcy and all his clan in the customary dramatic terms of dead firstborn, revolting diseases, the castle falling into ruins, the line extinct. Everyone must have enjoyed that part immensely. And then in 1665 came the plague.''

Cordelia thought that Ambrose's pause, if intended for dramatic effect, was unnecessary. The little group ranged around him were gazing at him with the rapt attention of foreign tourists whose guide, for once, is giving value for money. Ambrose went on.

''The plague raged particularly fiercely on this coast. It was said to have been brought here by a family from Cheapside who had relations in the village and fled here for safety. One by one the local families fell victim. The parson and his family died early, and there was no one to say the rites over the dead. Soon there was only one old man willing to bury them. Anarchy reigned. The island felt itself to be safe and de Courcy threatened death to anyone who landed. The story is that a boatload of women and children with one adult male to manage the boat did try. But if they were hoping to arouse de Courcy's compassion they were disappointed. He was behaving perfectly reasonably in this instance, of course. The only way to escape the pestilence was quarantine. It wasn't quite as reasonable to drive holes in the planks in the bottom of the boat before forcing it out to sea so that the human cargo drowned before they could reach shore, but that may be only a gloss on the story. About those seventeenth-century boat people, I think we ought to give him the benefit of the doubt. And now for the climax."

Ivo murmured, "This story has everything but costumes by Motley and background music by Menotti." But Cordelia saw that he was as interested as any of them.

"I don't know whether you know about the bubonic plague, the symptoms, I mean. The victims would first have the sensation that they could smell rotting apples. After that came the dreaded pink rash on the forehead. The day came when the father of the murdered girl smelled the smell, saw in his glass the mark of death. It was a summer night but unruly, the sea turbulent. He knew that he hadn't long to live; the plague killed swiftly. He launched his boat and set sail for the island.

"De Courcy and his private court were at dinner when the door of the great hall opened and he appeared, this great shambling sea-drenched figure, stumbling toward his enemy, eyes blazing. There was a moment when they were all too astounded for action. And in that moment he reached de Courcy, flung his great arms around him, and kissed him full on the mouth."

No one spoke. Cordelia wondered whether they would break into polite applause. The story had been well told and it had, in its simplicity, its terror, its almost symbolic confrontation of innocence with evil, a remarkable power.

Ivo said, "That story would make an opera. You've got the libretto. All you need is a Verdi or a second Benjamin Britten."

Roma Lisle, gazing at the skulls in fascinated distaste, asked, "And did the curse come true?"

"Oh, yes. De Courcy and all his people here caught the plague and were wiped out. The line is now extinct. It was four years before anyone came here to bury them. By then a kind of superstitious awe surrounded the island. The landsfolk averted their eyes from it. Fishermen, remembering the old religion, crossed themselves when they sailed in its shadow. The castle crumbled. It remained a ruin until my great-grandfather bought the place in 1864, built himself a castle in the modern style, reclaimed the land, cleared the undergrowth. Only the ruins of the old church remained standing. De Courcy and his islanders hadn't been buried in the churchyard. The locals hadn't thought that they merited Christian burial. As a result Herbert Gorringe kept turning up the skeletons when planting his pleasure garden. His men collected the skulls and arranged them here, a nice compromise between Christian disposal and tossing them on the bonfire.''

Roma said, ''There's something carved about the top shelf, words and numbers. The carving's a bit crude. It could be a biblical reference.''

''Ah, that's a personal comment by one of the Victorian workmen who thought that the setting up of this row of Yoricks might be an opportunity to point a moral and adorn a tale. No, I shan't identify it for you. Look it up for yourselves.''

Cordelia didn't need to look it up. A convent-born knowledge of the Old Testament and a lucky guess led her unerringly to the text. ''Judgement is mine saith the Lord. I will repay.'' It was, she thought, an inappropriate comment on a vengeance which, if Ambrose's story was true, had been so singularly, so satisfyingly, human.

It was very cold in the crypt. Conversation had died. They stood in a ring looking at the row of skulls as if those smooth domes of bone, the ragged nasal orifices, the gaping sockets, could be made to yield the secret of their deaths. How unfrightening they were, thought Cordelia, those age-long symbols of mortality, set up like a row of grinning devils to frighten children at a fairground and, in their denuded anonymity, stripping human pretensions to the risible evidence that what lasted longest in man were his teeth.

From time to time during Ambrose's story she had glanced

at Clarissa, wondering what effect this recital of horrors might have on her. It seemed to her strange that the crudely drawn caricature of a skull could produce such fear while the reality provoked no more than an exaggerated frisson of distaste. But Clarissa's refined sensibilities were apparently capable of sustaining any amount of assault, provided the horrors were anesthetized by time and there were no threats to herself. Even in the harsh, draining glare of the crypt her face looked flushed and the immense eyes shone more brightly. Cordelia doubted whether she would be happy to visit the crypt alone, but now, feeling herself the center of the company, she was enjoying a thrill of vicarious dread like a child at a horror movie who knows that none of the terror is real, that outside is the familiar street, the ordinary faces, the comfortable world of home. Whatever Clarissa feared, and Cordelia couldn't believe that the fear was faked, she had no sympathy with these long-dead tormented souls, no dread of a supernatural visitation in the small hours. She was expecting that, when her fate came and in whatever guise, it would still wear a human face.

But now excitement had made her euphoric. She said to Ambrose, "Darling, your island's a repository of horrors, charming on the surface and seething underneath. But isn't there something closer in time, a murder which really did happen? Tell us about the Devil's Kettle."

Ambrose avoided looking at her. One of the skulls was unaligned with its fellows. He took the white ball between his hands and tried to grind it back into place. But it couldn't be shifted and, suddenly, the jawbone came apart into his hands. He shoved it back, wiped his hands on his handkerchief, and said, "There's nothing to see. And the story is rather beastly. Only interesting really to those who relish in imagination the contemplation of another's pain."

But the warning and the implied criticism were wasted on her. She cried, "Darling, don't be so stuffy! The story's forty years old at least and I know about it anyway. George told

me. But I want to see where it happened. And I've got a
personal interest. George was here on the island at the time.
Did you know that George was here?''

Ambrose said shortly, ''Yes, I know.''

Roma said, ''Whatever it is, you may as well show us.
Clarissa won't give you any peace until you do, and the rest
of us are entitled to have our curiosity satisfied. It can hardly
be worse than this place.''

No one else spoke. Cordelia thought that Clarissa and her
cousin were unlikely allies even in persuasion and wondered
whether Roma was genuinely interested or merely hoped to
get the story over with so that she could get out of the crypt.

Clarissa's voice assumed the wheedling note of an impor-
tunate child. ''Please, Ambrose. You promised that you
would some time or other. Why not now? After all, we're
here.''

Ambrose looked at George Ralston. The look seemed to
invite consent, or at least comment. But if he was hoping for
support in resisting Clarissa, he was disappointed. Sir George's
face was impassive, its restlessness for once stilled.

Ambrose said, ''All right, if you insist.''

He led them to a low door at the west end of the crypt. It
was made of oak, almost black with age and with strong
bands of iron and a double bolt. Beside it on a nail hung a
key. Ambrose shot back the bolts, then inserted the key in the
lock. It turned easily enough, but he needed all his strength to
pull open the door. Inside he reached up and switched on a
light. They saw before them a narrow vaulted passage only
wide enough for two to walk abreast. Ambrose led the way
with Clarissa at his shoulder. Roma walked alone, followed
by Cordelia and Simon with Sir George and Ivo at the rear.

After less than twenty feet, the passage gave way to a flight
of steep stone steps which curved to the left. At the bottom it
widened, but the roof was still so low that Ivo had to stoop.
The passage was lit by unshaded but protected light bulbs
hung from a cable, and the air, although fusty, was fresh

enough to breathe without discomfort. It was very quiet and their footsteps echoed on the stone floor. Cordelia estimated that they must have covered about two hundred yards when they came to a turn in the passage and then a second flight of steps, steeper than the first and rougher as if hewn out of the rock. And it was then that the light failed.

The shock of instantaneous and total blackness after the artificial brightness of the tunnel made them gasp, and one of the women—Cordelia thought that it was Clarissa—gave a cry. She fought against a moment of panic, calming by an act of will her suddenly pounding heart. Instinctively she stretched out her hand into the darkness and encountered a firm warm arm under thin cotton, Simon's arm. She let go but almost immediately felt her hand grasped by his. Then she heard Ambrose's voice.

"Sorry, everyone. I'd forgotten that the lights are on a time switch. I'll find the button in a second."

But Cordelia judged that it must have been fifteen seconds before the light came on. They blinked at each other in the sudden glare, smiling a little sheepishly. Simon's hand was immediately withdrawn as if scalded, and he turned his face from her.

Clarissa said crossly, "I wish you'd warn us before playing silly tricks."

Ambrose looked amused. "No trick, I assure you. And it won't happen again. The chamber above the Devil's Kettle has an ordinary light system. Only another forty yards to go. And you did insist on this excursion, remember."

They went down the steps with the aid of a looped rope which had been threaded through rings bolted into the rock. After another thirty yards the passage widened to form a low roofed cave.

Ivo said, his voice sounding unnaturally loud, "We must be forty feet below ground. How is it ventilated?"

"By shafts. One of them comes up into the concrete bunker built in the war to guard the southern approach to the island. And there are a number of others. The first of them is believed to have been installed by de Courcy. The Devil's Kettle must have had its uses for him.''

In the middle of the floor was an oak trapdoor furnished with two strong bolts. Ambrose drew them back and pulled open the flap. They crowded around and six heads bent to peer down. They saw an iron ladder leading down to a cave. Below them heaved seawater. It was difficult to tell which way the tide was running, but they could see the light streaming in from an aperture shaped like a half-moon, and they heard for the first time the faint susurration of the sea and smelled the familiar salty seaweed tang. With each wave the water gushed almost silently into the cave and swirled around the rungs of the ladder. Cordelia shivered. There was something remorseless, almost uncanny, about that quiet, regular spouting.

Clarissa said, "Now tell!"

Ambrose was silent for a minute. Then he said, "It happened in 1940. The island and the castle were taken over by the government and used as a reception and interrogation center for foreign nationals of the Axis powers trapped in the United Kingdom by the war, and others, including a number of British citizens who were suspected, at worst, of being enemy agents or at best of being Nazi sympathizers. My uncle was living in the castle with only his one manservant, and they were moved out to the cottage in the stable block now occupied by Oldfield. What went on in the castle was, of course, top secret. The internees were kept here for only a relatively short time, and I've no reason to suppose that their stay was particularly uncomfortable. A number were released after interrogation and clearance; some went on to internment on the Isle of Man; some, I suppose, eventually came to less agreeable ends. But George knows more about the place than I do. As Clarissa says, he was stationed here as a young officer for a few months in 1940.''

He paused, but again there was no response. He had

spoken as if Sir George were no longer with them. Cordelia saw Roma glance at Ralston, surprised, a little wary. She half opened her mouth, then thought better of it. But she kept her gaze on him with a stubborn intensity, rather as if she were seeing him for the first time.

Ambrose went on, "I don't know any of the details. Someone does, I suppose, or as much of the truth as came out. There must be an official record of the incident somewhere, although it was never published. All I know is what my uncle told me on one of my rare visits, and that was mostly rumor."

Clarissa permitted herself a display of nicely judged impatience. It was, thought Cordelia, as artificial as the simulated moue of distaste with which she had first regarded the shelf of skulls. Clarissa had no need of impatience; Clarissa knew exactly what was coming.

Ambrose spread plump hands and shrugged, as if resigned to a recital he would have preferred to avoid. But he could have avoided it, thought Cordelia, if he had really tried. And for the first time she wondered whether the conversation, even the visit to the crypt, had been the result of collusion.

He said, "In March 1940 there were about fifty internees on Courcy and, among them, a hard core of dedicated Nazis, most of whom were Germans trapped in Britain at the outbreak of war. They suspected one of their number, a boy of twenty-two, of having betrayed their secrets to the British authorities during interrogation. Perhaps he did. On the other hand, he may have been a British undercover agent who had infiltrated their group. All I know are rumors, and second-hand rumors at that. What does seem beyond dispute is that the group of Nazis convened a secret court in the crypt of the church, convicted their comrade of treason, and condemned him to death. Then they gagged him, bound his arms, and brought him down the passageway to this cave. It's called the Devil's Kettle. As you can see, it has a narrow opening which leads to the east cove, but the cave is always flooded at high tide. They bound their victim to that iron ladder and left him to drown. He was a very tall young man. He died slowly in the darkness, and he died hard. Later one of them crept back to untie him and let the body float out to sea. When it was washed up only two days later, the wrists were cut through almost to the bone. One of his fellow internees told a story of the young man's mounting depression, and it was suggested that he had bound his wrists to prevent himself from swimming and had leaped into the sea. None of his judges or executioners ever spoke."

Roma asked, "Then how was the story ever known?"

"Someone talked eventually, I suppose, but not until after the war. Oldfield was living in Speymouth at the time and was employed here by the army. He may have heard rumors. He doesn't admit it now, but someone on the island must have suspected. Someone may even have condoned what happened, or at least closed his eyes. After all, the army were in charge here. Yet the gang got their hands on the keys to the crypt and the secret passage and managed to return them undetected. That suggests, well, let's say a certain degree of official carelessness on someone's part."

Clarissa turned to her husband. "What was he called, darling, the boy who died?"

"His name was Carl Blythe."

Clarissa turned to the company. Her voice was as out of key as a hysteric's: "And the most extraordinary thing is that he was English—well, his father was anyway; his mother was German—and George was at school with him, weren't you, darling? They were both at Melhurst. He was three years older and rather a horrid boy, cruel really, one of those bullies who make other boys' lives a torment to them, so he and George weren't exactly friends. In fact George hated him. And then to find him here and at his mercy. Wasn't it odd?"

Ivo said easily, "Not particularly. The British public schools produced their share of Nazi sympathizers, and this is where you'd expect to find them in 1940."

Cordelia stared down at the iron ladder. The light in the passage, fierce and garish, did nothing to mitigate the horror; rather it intensified it. In the old days the cruelty of man to man was decently shrouded in darkness; the mind dwelt on airless, unlit dungeons, on light filtering through the slits of narrow windows. But the modern interrogation rooms and torture chambers were ablaze with light. The technocrats of pain needed to see what they were at. Suddenly the place become intolerable to her. The chill of the passageway intensified. She had to tauten her arms and clench her fists to prevent herself visibly shaking. In her imagination the tunnel behind them stretched to infinity and they were doomed to rush down its contracting brightness like terrified rats. She felt a bead of sweat roll down her forehead and sting her eyes and knew that it had nothing to do with the cold. She made herself speak, hoping that her voice didn't betray her.

"Can't we get out of here? I feel like a voyeuse."

Ivo said, "And I feel cold."

Taking her cue promptly, Clarissa shivered. Then Sir George spoke for the first time. Cordelia wondered whether it was her confused senses or the echo from the low roof which made his voice sound so different.

"If my wife has satisfied her curiosity, perhaps we might go." Then he made a sudden jerk forward. Before they could guess what was coming, he put his foot behind the open trapdoor and pushed. It crashed down. The walls seemed to crack and the passage shook under their feet. They must all have cried out, their voices thin screams in the echoing, reverberating roar. When it had faded no one spoke. Sir George had already turned on his heel and was making his way toward the entrance.

Cordelia found herself a little ahead of the others. Fear, and a deadening sense of misery which was stronger than fear and which added to her claustrophobia, urged her forward. Even the crypt with its neatly disposed ossuary was preferable to this horrible place. She stooped to pick up the neatly folded oblong of paper almost instinctively and without curiosity, without even turning it over to see if it was addressed. In the harsh light of the single bulb the neatly drawn skull and the typed quotation were starkly clear, and she realized that she had known from the first what it must be.

Thy death is plotted; here's the consequence of murder,
We value not desert nor Christian breath
When we know black deeds must be cured with death.

It was not, she thought, completely accurate. Surely the first word should be *My*, not *Thy*. But the message was plain enough. She slipped it into her trouser pocket and turned to wait for the rest of the party. She tried to recall where they had all been standing when the lights went out. Surely it had been at about this spot where the tunnel curved. It would have taken only a few seconds for one of them to dart back under cover of the darkness, someone who had the message ready, someone who didn't care, might even have been pleased, that Clarissa would know that her enemy was one of this small party. And if anyone other than she had seen it first, or if the group had been together, it would have been placed in Clarissa's hands. It was addressed to her in the same typed letters. Ambrose was perhaps the most likely culprit. That light had failed very conveniently. But any of the others could have done it, any except Simon. She had felt his hand firmly in hers.

And then they came into view. She stood under the light and scanned their faces. But none betrayed anxiety, none showed any surprise, no eyes dropped to the ground. Joining them, she felt that she fully understood for the first time why it was that Clarissa was so afraid. Until now the messages had seemed little more than a childish persecution which no intelligent woman would think worth more than a moment's real anxiety. But they were a manifestation of hatred, and hatred, whatever else it was, could never be petty. They were childish, but there was an adult and sophisticated malice behind the childishness, and the danger they threatened might, after all, be real and imminent. She wondered whether she was right in keeping this message and the earlier ones from Clarissa, whether it might not be safer to put her on increased guard. But her instructions had been clear: to save Clarissa from any anxiety or annoyance before the performance. There would be time enough after the play to decide what else should be done. And there were less than four hours now before the curtain rose.

While they were passing the row of skulls, this time without a glance, Cordelia found herself walking with Ivo. His speed, whether by necessity or by design, was slower than that of the others and she kept pace with him. He said, "That was an instructive episode, don't you think? Poor Ralston! I take it that the whole episode and his subsequent moral scruples were an offering of conjugal unreserve. What did you think of it all, O wise Cordelia?"

"I thought that it was horrible." And both of them knew that she wasn't thinking only of that poor renegade's last agony, his lonely and terrible death.

Roma came alongside them. Cordelia saw that, for once, she looked animated, her eyes brightly malicious. She said, "Well, that was an unedifying performance. For those of us fortunate enough to be unmarried it makes holy matrimony seem a pretty unholy estate. Almost terrifying."

Ivo said, "Marriage is terrifying. At least I've found it so."

Roma was unwilling to let the matter rest. "Does she always need to psych herself up with an exhibition of cruelty before a performance?"

"She's nervous certainly. It takes people different ways."

"But this is only an amateur performance, for God's sake! The theater can't hold more than eighty or so. And she's supposed to be a professional. What do you think George Ralston was feeling back there?"

The note of satisfaction was unmistakable. Cordelia wanted

to say that one had only to have looked at his face to see what Sir George was thinking. But she didn't speak.

Ivo said, "Like most professional soldiers, Ralston is a sentimentalist. He takes the great absolutes, honor, justice, loyalty, and binds them to his heart with hoops of steel. I find it rather appealing. But it does make for a certain . . . rigidity."

Roma shrugged. "If you mean that he's abnormally controlled, I agree. It will be interesting to see what happens if ever the control snaps."

Clarissa turned and called to them, her voice happily imperious, "Come on, you three. Ambrose wants to lock the crypt. And I want lunch."

3

THE CONTRAST between the sun-warmed terrace, where, once
again, luncheon was set out on a linen-covered trestle table,
and the dark, rank-smelling pit of the Devil's Kettle was so
great that Cordelia felt disoriented. That brief descent into the
hell of the past could have happened in a different place and
time. Looking out across the light-flecked sea to where the
canvases of the Saturday sailors curved to catch the breeze,
she found it possible to imagine that it hadn't happened at all,
that de Courcy's plague-ridden court, Carl Blythe's agony as
he struggled against the horror of his long dying, were the
remnants of a nightmare which had no more reality than the
crude caricatures of a horror comic.

It was a light meal, a watercress-and-avocado salad followed
by salmon soufflé, chosen, perhaps, to soothe a nervous
digestion. But, even so, no one ate with appetite or evident
enjoyment. Cordelia took one glass of the cool Riesling and
forced down the salmon, knowing, rather than tasting, that it

176

was delicious. Clarissa's brittle euphoria had given way to a silent preoccupation which no one liked to disturb. Roma crouched on the step at the end of the terrace, her unregarded plate in her lap, and gazed moodily out to sea. Sir George and Ivo stood together but neither spoke. But all of them, except Clarissa and herself, drank steadily. Ambrose said little but moved among them, refilling the glasses, his bright eyes amused and indulgent as if they were children behaving predictably under stress.

Unexpectedly, Simon was the liveliest of the party. He was drinking heavily, apparently unnoticed by Clarissa, swilling the wine down as if it were beer, his hand a little unsteady, his eyes bright. At about ten to one, he suddenly announced loudly that he would go for a swim, looking around at them rather as if he expected them to take an interest in this news. No one did, but Clarissa said, "Not so soon after a meal, darling. Take a walk first."

The endearment was so unexpected that they all looked up. The boy blushed, gave them a stiff little bow, and disappeared. Shortly afterward, Clarissa put down her plate, looked at her watch, and said, "Time to rest. No coffee, thank you, Ambrose. I never take it before a performance. I thought you knew that. Will you ask Tolly to bring up the tea tray at once? China tea. She knows the kind I have. George, would you come up in five minutes? I'll see you later, Cordelia. Better make it ten past one."

She made her slow way across the terrace with the graceful deliberation of a stage exit. For the first time, she seemed to Cordelia to be vulnerable, almost pathetic, in her lonely, self-absorbed fear. She felt an impulse to follow, but knew that it would only arouse Clarissa's fury. And she had no fear of Clarissa's finding another message thrust under her door. Cordelia had checked the room immediately before coming down to lunch. She knew now that the person responsible had been one of the small party who had visited the Devil's Kettle, and all of them had been under her eye throughout the meal. Only Simon had left early. And she did not believe for one moment that the culprit was Simon.

Suddenly Roma struggled to her feet and hurried out after her cousin, almost running from the terrace. The eyes of Ambrose and Ivo met but neither spoke, inhibited, perhaps, by the presence of Sir George. He walked to the end of the terrace, his back to them, coffee cup in hand. He seemed to be counting the minutes. Then he glanced at his watch, replaced his cup on the table, and made for the french windows. Looking around, foot on the step, he asked, "What time does the curtain rise, Gorringe?"

"At three-thirty."

"And we change before then?"

"That's what Clarissa expects. There won't be time afterward, anyway. Supper is at seven-thirty."

Sir George nodded and was gone.

Ivo said, "Clarissa organizes her helots with the brutal precision of a military commander. Ten minutes before you need report for duty, Cordelia. Time surely for a second cup of coffee."

When Cordelia unlocked her bedroom and went through the communicating door, Sir George was with his wife, standing by the window looking out over the sea. The round silver tea tray with its single cup and saucer, its elegant matching pot, was on the bedside chest, as yet untouched. Clarissa, still in her Bermuda shorts and shirt, was pacing up and down, her color high.

"She asked me for twenty-five thousand, came out with it, red-faced, as if she were a child asking for an increase in pocket money. And now of all times! She couldn't even wait until after the performance. Talk about crass stupidity! Is she deliberately trying to upset me or something?"

Sir George spoke without turning. "Important to her, I expect. Couldn't bear the suspense of waiting. Had to know. It's not easy to get you alone."

"She never had any sense of timing, even as a child. If

there was a wrong moment for anything, trust Roma to pick it. Part of her general insensitivity. By God, she's chosen the wrong moment now!''

The voice from the window said quietly, "Would there have been a right one?''

Clarissa seemed not to have heard. "I told her that I wasn't prepared to hand over capital to support a lover who hadn't even the guts or decency to come and ask for it himself. I gave her some advice. If you have to buy yourself a man, he's not worth having. And if you can't get sex without buying it, buy cheaper. She's madly in love with him, of course. That's what this shop of theirs is all about, a ploy to get him away from his wife. Roma in love! I could almost feel sorry for him if he wasn't such a fool. When a plain virgin of forty-five falls in love for the first time and gets her first taste of sex, God help the man.''

"My dear, is that our concern?''

She said sharply, "The money's my concern. Apart from anything else, they haven't a chance of making a go of it. No capital, no experience, no sense. Why should I throw good money after bad?'' She turned to Cordelia. "You'd better go and get yourself dressed. Then lock your room and come out this way. I don't want you fussing about next door while I'm resting. I suppose you'll be wearing that Indian thing again. It shouldn't take long to get into that.''

Cordelia said, "None of my clothes take long to get into.''

"Nor to get out of, no doubt.''

Sir George swung around, his voice low. "Clarissa!''

She smiled, gratified, went up to him, and gently tapped his cheek. "Dear George. Always so gallant.'' She might have been patting a dog.

Cordelia said, "I wondered whether you'd like me to stay next door while you rest. The communicating door could be open or locked as you like. I wouldn't make any noise.''

"I've told you! I don't want you next door, or anywhere near me for that matter. I might want to speak some of the

verse and I can't do that when I know someone's listening.
With the three doors locked and no telephone in the room I
suppose I can hope to be left in peace." Suddenly she called
out, "Tolly."

Tolly came out of the bathroom, dark-clad, expressionless
as ever. Cordelia wondered how much, if anything, she had
heard. Without being asked, she went to the wardrobe and
brought out Clarissa's satin robe and folded it over her arm.
Then she went and waited silently beside her mistress. Clarissa
unbuttoned her shirt and let it fall. Tolly made no move to
pick it up but unhooked the back of Clarissa's brassiere. That
too fell away and was plucked off by Clarissa, held out, and
let drop. Last Clarissa unbuttoned the front of her shorts and
eased them off, together with her pants, letting them fall
together over her knees to the floor. She stood there for a
moment immobile, her pale body dappled in the sunlight, the
full, almost heavy breasts, the narrow waist, the jutting
angular hips, and the smudge of corn-gold hair. Without haste
Tolly unfolded the dressing gown and held it out for Clarissa's
arms. Then she knelt, collected the bundle of discarded
clothes, and returned to the bathroom. Cordelia thought that it
had been a ritualistic display of almost innocent sensuality,
less vulgar than she would have expected, narcissistic rather
than provocative. A conviction came to her, as certain as it
was irrational, that this was the image of Clarissa that she
would remember all her life. And, whatever its motive,
Clarissa's moment of frank exultation in her beauty seemed to
have calmed her. She said, "Don't take any notice of me,
darlings. You know what it is before a performance." She
turned to Cordelia. "Just get anything you want from your
room and let me have both the keys. I'll set the alarm for
two-forty-five, so come up about then and I'll let you know if
there's anything I want you to do during the performance.
And don't rely on being able to watch up front. I may want
you backstage."

Cordelia left them still together and went into her room by

the communicating door. As she substituted her long cotton dress for shirt and jeans, she thought about Roma's extraordinary request. Why hadn't she done the obvious thing and waited until after the performance when she might have hoped to catch her cousin in the euphoria of success? But perhaps she had seen this as the most propitious, perhaps the only possible, time. If the performance were a fiasco, Clarissa would be unapproachable; it was possible that she might even leave the island without waiting for a celebratory party. But surely Roma must have known her cousin well enough to see that whatever moment she chose, hers was a hopeless cause. What was she hoping for; that Clarissa would once again indulge in the grand generous gesture as she obviously had with Simon Lessing, that she wouldn't be able to resist the insidiously gratifying role of patron and deliverer? Cordelia thought that two things were certain: Roma must be in desperate need of the money; and Roma, for one, wasn't betting on Clarissa's success.

She brushed her hair vigorously, gave a final look at herself in the glass without enthusiasm, and locked her bedroom door, leaving the key in the lock. Then she knocked at the communicating door and went through. The key to that door was in the lock on Clarissa's side. Sir George and Tolly had left, and Clarissa was seated at the dressing table, brushing her hair with long, firm strokes. Without looking around she said, "What have you done with your key?"

"Turned it and left it in the lock. Shall I lock the communicating door now?"

"No. I'll see to it. I want to check that you've locked your outside door."

Cordelia said, "I'll stay within call. If you want me I'll be at the end of the corridor. I can perfectly well get a chair from my room and sit there with a book."

Clarissa's anger flared. "Can't you understand English? What are you trying to do, spy on me? I've told you! I don't want you next door and I don't want you pussyfooting up and down the corridor. I don't want you, or anyone, near me. What I want now is to be left in peace!''

The note of hysteria was new and unmistakable. Cordelia said, "Then will you roll up one of your towels tightly and wedge it against the door? I don't want any notes delivered to you by hand."

Clarissa's voice was sharp. "What do you mean? Nothing has happened since I arrived, nothing!"

Cordelia said soothingly, "I just want to ensure that it stays that way. If whoever is responsible should land on Courcy Island, he might make one last attempt to get a message to you. I don't in the least think that it will happen. I'm sure it won't. The notes have probably stopped for good. But I don't want to take any risks."

Clarissa said ungraciously, "All right. It's not a bad idea. I'll block the bottom of the door."

There seemed nothing else to say. As Cordelia went out, Clarissa followed her, firmly closed the door on her, and turned the key. The scrape of metal, the small click, were faint, but Cordelia's keen ears heard them distinctly. Clarissa was locked in. There was nothing more that she could do until two-forty-five. She looked at her watch. It was just one-twenty.

4

THERE WAS ONLY an hour and a half to be got through, but Cordelia found herself possessed of an irritable restlessness which made the slow minutes stretch interminably. It was a nuisance that her room was barred to her and that before locking it she had forgotten to pick up her book. She went to the library, hoping to pass an hour with old bound copies of *The Strand* magazine. But Roma was there, not reading but sitting upright, close to the telephone, and the look she gave Cordelia was so unwelcoming that it was obvious that she was expecting or hoping for a call and wanted to take it in private. Closing the door, Cordelia thought with envy of Simon, probably even now enjoying his solitary swim, and of Sir George, striding out with his binoculars at the ready. She wished that she could be with him, but her long skirt was unsuitable for walking, and in any case she felt that she shouldn't leave the castle.

She made her way to the theater. The house lights were

already on and the crimson-and-gold auditorium with its rows
of empty seats seemed to be waiting in a hushed, portentous,
nostalgic calm. Backstage, Tolly was checking the main
women's dressing room, setting out boxes of tissues and a
supply of hand towels. Cordelia asked if she needed any help
and received a polite but definite refusal. Then she remembered
that there was something she could do. Sir George, when he
was at Kingly Street, had mentioned checking the set. She
wasn't sure what he had had in mind. Even if the poison pen
managed to secrete a missive on the set or among the props,
Clarissa would hardly open and read it in the middle of a
performance. But Sir George had been right. It was a sensible
precaution to check the set and the props and she was glad to
have something definite to do.

All was well. The set for the first scene, a Victorian garden
outside the palace, was simple: a blue back cloth, bay trees
and geraniums in stone urns, a highly sentimental statue of a
woman with a lute, and two ornate cane armchairs with
cushions and footrests. At the side of the stage stood the
props table. She checked over the assortment of Ambrose's
Victoriana assembled for the indoor scenes: vases, pictures,
fans, glasses, even a child's rocking horse. A suede glove
stuffed with cotton wool was placed ready for the prison
scene and did, indeed, look unpleasantly like a severed hand.
The music box was there, as was the silver-bound jewel chest
for the second act. Cordelia opened it, but no missive lurked
in its rosewood depths.

There was nothing else she could usefully do. There was
still an hour before she was due to wake Clarissa. She walked
for a time in the rose garden, but the sun was less warm here
on the westerly side of the castle, and in the end she returned
to the terrace and sat in the corner of the bottom step leading
to the beach. It was a small sun trap; even the stones struck
warm to her thighs. She closed her eyes and lifted her face to
the sun, relishing the soft air on her eyelids, the smell of

pines and seaweed, and soothed by the gentle hiss of the waves on the shingle.

She must have dozed briefly, but was roused by the arrival of the launch. Ambrose and both the Munters were there to receive the cast, Ambrose already changed and wearing a voluminous silk cloak over his dinner jacket, which gave him the appearance of a Victorian music-hall conjurer. There was a great deal of excited chatter as the cast, some of the men already in Victorian costume, jumped ashore and disappeared through the archway which led to the eastern lawn and the main entrance to the castle. Cordelia looked at her watch. It was two-twenty; the launch was early. She settled down again but didn't dare risk closing her eyes. And twenty minutes later, she set off through the french windows to call Clarissa.

She paused outside the bedroom door and glanced at her watch. It was two-forty-two. Clarissa had asked to be called at two-forty-five but a few minutes could hardly matter. She knocked, quietly at first, and then more loudly. There was no reply. Perhaps Clarissa was already up and in the bathroom. She tried the door; to her surprise it opened, and looking down, she saw that the key was in the lock. The door opened easily with no obstructing wedge of towel. So Clarissa must have finished her rest.

For some reason which she was never able afterward to understand, she felt no premonition, no unease. She moved into the dimness of the room calling gently, "Miss Lisle, Miss Lisle. It's nearly two-forty-five."

The lined and heavy brocade curtains were drawn across the windows, but brightness pierced the paper-thin slit between them, and even their heavy folds couldn't entirely exclude the afternoon sun which seeped through as a gentle diffusion of pinkish light. Clarissa lay, ghostlike, on her crimson bed, both arms gently curved at her sides, the palms upwards, her hair a bright stream over the pillow. The bedclothes had been folded down, and she was lying on her back, uncovered, the pale satin dressing gown drawn up almost to her knees. Lifting her arms to draw back the curtains, Cordelia thought that the subdued light in the room played odd tricks; Clarissa's shadowed face looked almost as dark as the canopy of the bed, as if her skin had absorbed the rich crimson.

As the folds of the second curtain swung back and the room sprang into light, she turned and saw clearly for the first time what it was on the bed. For a second of incredulous time her imagination whirled crazily out of control, spinning its fantastic images: Clarissa had applied a face mask, a darkening, sticky mess which had even seeped into the two eye pads; the canopy was disintegrating, dripping its crimson fibers, obliterating her face with its richness. And then the ridiculous fancies faded and her mind accepted the stark reality of what her eyes had seen. Clarissa no longer had a face. This was no beauty mask. This pulp was Clarissa's flesh, Clarissa's blood, darkening and clotting and oozing serum, spiked with the brittle fragments of smashed bones.

She stood at the side of the bed, shaking. The room was full of noise, a regular drumming which filled her ears and pounded against her ribs. She thought, I must get someone; I must get help. But there was no help. Clarissa was dead. And she found that her limbs were rooted; only her eyes could move. But they saw things clearly, too clearly. Slowly she turned them from the horror on the bed and fixed them on the bedside chest. Something was missing, the silver jewel casket. But the small round tray of tea was still there. She saw the shallow cup, delicately painted with roses, the pale dregs of tea with two floating leaves, the smear of lipstick on the rim. And beside the tray there was something new: the marble limb, thick with blood had seeped over the paper, almost obliterating the familiar skull and crossbones, but the typed message had escaped that insidious stream and she could read it clearly:

Other sins only speak; murder shrieks out:
The element of water moistens the earth,
But blood flies upwards and bedews the heavens.

And then it happened. The alarm clock on the other bedside cabinet rang, making her leap with terror. Her limbs were galvanized into life. She dashed around the bed and tried to silence it, grabbing it with hands so shaking that the clock clattered on the polished wood. Oh, God! Oh, God! Would nothing stop it? Then her fingers found the button. The room was silent again, and in the echo of that dreadful ringing she could hear once again the thudding of her heart. She found herself looking at the thing on the bed as if terrified that the din had waked it, that Clarissa would suddenly jerk up stiff as a marionette and confront her with that faceless horror.

She was calmer now. There were things she must do. She must tell Ambrose. Ambrose would have to ring the police. And nothing must be touched until the police arrived. She found herself looking around the room, noticing all the details with great intensity: the balls of cotton wool smeared with makeup on the dressing table, the bottle of eye lotion still unstoppered, Clarissa's embroidered slippers neatly placed on the hearth rug, her makeup box open on a fireside chair, her copy of the script fallen by the bed.

As she turned to the door it opened, and she saw Ambrose with Sir George behind him, his binoculars still around his neck. They stared at each other. No one spoke. Then Sir George pushed past Ambrose and moved up to the bed. Still without a word he stood gazing down at his wife, his back rigid. Then he turned. His face was taut, all its restlessness stilled, the skin almost green. Then he swallowed and put his hand to his throat as if he were about to retch. Cordelia made an instinctive movement toward him and cried, "I'm sorry. I'm so very sorry!"

The words in all their futile banality appalled her as soon as she had uttered them. And then she saw his face, a mask of astonished horror. She thought, Oh, God, he thinks I'm confessing! He thinks I killed her.

She cried, "You employed me to look after her. I was here to keep her safe. I should never have left her."

She watched the horror drain from his face. He said calmly, almost crisply, "You couldn't have known. I didn't believe she was in any danger; no one did. And she wouldn't have let you stay with her, you or anyone. Don't blame yourself."

"But I knew that the marble had been taken! I should have warned her."

"Against what? You couldn't have expected this." He said again, sharply as if he were giving a command, "Don't blame yourself, Cordelia."

It was the first time he had used her Christian name.

Ambrose was still at the door. He said, "Is she dead?"

"See for yourself."

He moved up to the bed and looked down at the body. His face flushed a deep red. Watching him, Cordelia thought that he looked more embarrassed than shocked. Then he turned away. He said, "But this is incredible!" Then he whispered, "Horrible! Horrible!"

Suddenly he darted to the communicating door and turned the knob. It was unlocked. They followed him into Cordelia's room and through into the bathroom. The window to the fire escape was open as she had left it.

Sir George said, "He could have got out this way and down the fire escape. We'd better organize a search of the island. The castle too, of course. How many men can we muster, including those in the play?"

Ambrose made a rapid calculation. "About twenty-five of the players and six of us, including Oldfield. I don't know whether Whittingham will be much use."

"That's enough for four search parties, one for the castle, three to cover the island. It needs to be systematic. You'd better ring the police at once. I'll get the men organized."

Cordelia could imagine the disruption that thirty or more people tramping over the house and island would cause. She said, "We mustn't touch anything. Both these rooms must be locked. It's a pity that you handled the doorknob. And we'd better prevent the audience from landing. About the search; mightn't it be better to wait for the police?''

Ambrose looked uncertain. Sir George said, "I'm not prepared to wait. That's not possible. It's not possible, Gorringe!" His voice was fierce. His eyes looked almost wild.

Ambrose said soothingly, "No, of course not.''

Sir George asked, "Where's Oldfield?''

"In his cottage, I imagine. The stable block."

"I'll get him to take out the launch and patrol the channel between here and Speymouth. That'll block any escape by sea. And then I'll join you in the theater. Better warn the men that I'll be wanting them.''

He was gone.

Ambrose said, "It's best that he should have something to keep him busy. And I don't suppose they'll do any harm.''

Cordelia wondered what Oldfield was supposed to do if he did intercept a boat leaving the island. Board it and tackle a murderer single-handed? And did either Ambrose or Sir George seriously expect to find an intruder on Courcy? Surely the significance of that bloody arm couldn't have escaped them.

Together they checked the door in Cordelia's room leading to the corridor. It was locked from the inside with the key still in place. So the murderer couldn't have left by that route. Next they closed and locked the communicating door. Finally they locked Clarissa's room behind them and Ambrose pocketed the key.

Cordelia said, "Are there any duplicate keys?''

"No, none. The spare bedroom keys were missing when I inherited and I've never bothered to have others made. It wouldn't have been easy, anyway. The locks are complicated; these are the original keys.''

As they turned from the door they heard footsteps, and Tolly appeared around the corner of the gallery. Acknowledging them with only a nod, she went up to Clarissa's door and knocked. Cordelia's heart thumped. She looked at Ambrose, but he seemed bereft of speech. Tolly knocked again, this time more loudly. Then she turned to Cordelia.

"I thought you were supposed to call her at two-forty-five. She should have left it to me."

Cordelia said, through lips which were so dry and swollen that she thought they would crack, "You can't go in. She's dead. Murdered."

Tolly turned and knocked again.

"She's going to be late. I have to go to her. She always needs me before a performance."

Ambrose took a step forward. For a moment Cordelia thought that he was going to lay a hand on Tolly's shoulder. Then his arm dropped. He said in a voice which seemed unnaturally harsh, "There isn't going to be a performance. Miss Lisle is dead. She's been murdered. I'm just about to ring the police. Until they arrive no one can go into that room."

This time she understood. She turned and faced him, her face expressionless but so white that Cordelia, thinking she would faint, put out a hand and grasped her arm. She felt Tolly shudder, a small spasm of rejection, almost of revulsion, which was unmistakable, as shocking as a blow in the face. Quickly she withdrew her hand.

Tolly said, "The boy. Does the boy know?"

"Simon? Not yet. No one knows except Sir George. We've only just discovered the body."

His voice held a trace of aggrieved impatience, like that of an overworked servant. Cordelia almost expected him to protest that he couldn't see to everything at once.

Tolly still fixed her eyes on him. She said, "You'll break it gently, sir. It will be a shock to him."

Ambrose said curtly, "It's a shock for us all."

"Not for one of us, sir."

She turned and left them without another word.

Ambrose said, "Extraordinary woman! I've never understood her. I doubt whether Clarissa did. And why this sudden concern for Simon? She's never shown any particular interest in the boy. Oh, well, we'd better get on with telephoning the police."

They made their way down the stairs and through the great hall. There preparations for the buffet supper was already under way. The long refectory table was covered with a cloth and rows of wineglasses were ranked at one end. The door to the dining room was open, and Cordelia could see Munter pulling the chairs from the table and putting them in line, presumably before carrying them into the hall.

Ambrose said, "Wait here a moment, will you?"

A minute later he was back. He said, "I've told Munter. He'll get down to the quay and prevent the launches from tying up."

They went together into the business room. Ambrose said, "If Cottringham were here, he'd probably insist on speaking to the chief constable personally. But I suppose the Speymouth police are the ones to ring. Ought I to ask for the C.I.D.?"

"I should just ring the Speymouth station and leave it to them. They'll know the procedure."

She looked up the number for him and waited while he got through. He gave the facts succinctly and without emotion, mentioning that Lady Ralston's jewel box was missing. Cordelia was interested that he had noticed its absence; nothing had been said about it while they were in the bedroom. There was a certain amount of delay from the other end of the line and then the crackle of a voice. She heard Ambrose say, "Yes, we've already done that," and, later, "That is what I propose doing as soon as I get off the line." Shortly afterward he put down the receiver and said, "Much as you expected. Lock the rooms. Don't touch anything. Keep people together. Don't let anyone land. They're sending a Chief Inspector Grogan."

In the theater the house lights were already on. A door to

the left of the proscenium led backstage. From the open doors of the two main dressing rooms came laughter and a confusion of voices. Most of the cast had already changed and were now making up with a great deal of giggling advice from their friends. The atmosphere was reminiscent of an end-of-term frolic. Ambrose knocked on the closed doors of the two rooms reserved for the principals, then called out loudly, "Will you all come on stage please, immediately."

They tumbled out in an unruly bunch, some clutching their clothes around them. But one glance at his face silenced them, and they trooped onto the stage, subdued and expectant. Partly costumed and half made up as they were, their faces white except for the garish patches of rouge, they looked, thought Cordelia, like the clients and inmates of some Victorian bawdy house pulled out by the police for interrogation.

Ambrose said, "I'm afraid I have some very shocking news for you. Miss Lisle is dead. It looks very much like murder. I've telephoned the police and they'll be here shortly. In the meantime, they've asked that you all stay together here in the theater. Munter and his wife will bring you all some tea and coffee and anything else you need. Perhaps, Cottringham, you'd take charge here. There are still people I have to tell."

One of the women, a blonde, pert-faced girl dressed as a parlor maid in a frilled apron and goffered cap with long streamers, said, "But what about the play?"

It was a question born of shock which Cordelia thought she would probably remember with shame all her life. Someone gasped, and she blushed scarlet.

Ambrose said curtly, "The performance is canceled."

Then he turned on his heel and left.

Cordelia followed. She said, "What about the search parties?"

"I'll leave that to Ralston and Cottringham to sort out. I've told the cast to stay together. I can't cope with trying to enforce police instructions against the determination of the bereaved husband to demonstrate his competence. Where do you suppose are the rest of the party?" He sounded almost peevish.

Cordelia said, "I suppose Simon is swimming. Roma was in the library, but she's probably dressing by now. I imagine that Ivo is in his room, resting."

"See them, will you, and break the news. I'll go and find Simon. Then we'd better stay together until the police arrive. I suppose it would be courteous if I kept company with my guests in the theater, but I'm not in the mood to cope with a gaggle of agitated women all hurling questions at me."

Cordelia said, "The less they're told until the police arrive, the better."

He glanced at her with his sharp bright eyes. "I see. You mean we should keep quiet about the actual cause of death?"

"We don't know the actual cause of death. But, yes, I think we should say as little as possible to anyone."

"But surely the cause of death was obvious. Her face had been battered in."

"That may have been done after death. There was less blood than one would expect."

"There was more than enough blood for me. You're remarkably knowledgeable for a secretary-companion."

"I'm not a secretary-companion. I'm a private detective. There's no point in carrying on the charade any longer. Anyway, I know that you'd already guessed. And if you're going to say that I've been useless, I know that too."

"My dear Cordelia, what more could you have done? No one could have expected murder. Stop blaming yourself. We're going to be stuck here together at least until the inquest, and it will be boring enough being grilled by the police without having you sunk in lugubrious self-reproach. It doesn't suit you."

They had reached the door which led from the arcade into the castle. Glancing around, they saw Simon in the distance, towel slung around his shoulders, making his way down the

long grass slope which led upwards from the rose garden
between the avenue of beeches to the crown of the island.
Without speaking, Ambrose went to meet him. Cordelia stood
in the shadow of the doorway and watched. Ambrose didn't
hurry; his walk was little more than a leisurely stroll. The two
figures came together and stood in the sun, their heads bent,
their shadows staining the bright grass. They didn't touch.
After a moment, still distanced, they began walking slowly
toward the castle. Cordelia passed into the great hall. Coming
down the staircase was Ivo with Roma at his side. He was in
his dinner jacket; Roma was still wearing her trouser suit.

She called down to Cordelia, "Where is everyone? The
place is dead as a morgue. I've just been telling Ivo I've no
intention of changing and I'm not coming to the play. You
two can do what you like, but I'm damned if I'll climb into
an evening dress in the middle of a warm afternoon just to
watch a bunch of amateurs make fools of themselves and
pander to Clarissa's megalomania. You all indulge her nonsense as if you're terrified of her. Someone should put a stop
to Clarissa."

Cordelia said, "Someone has."

They froze on the stairway, gazing down at her.

She said, "Clarissa's dead. Murdered."

And then her control broke. She gave a gasp and felt the
hot tears coursing down her face. Ivo ran down to her and she
felt his arms, thin and strong as steel rods, pulling her toward
him. It was the first human contact, the first sympathetic
gesture, which anyone had made since the shock of finding
Clarissa's body, and the temptation to give way and cry like a
child against his shoulder was almost irresistible. But she
gulped back her tears, fighting for control, while he held her
gently without speaking. Looking up over his shoulder, she
saw, through her tears, Roma's face hanging above her, a
streaked amorphous pattern of white and pink. Then she
blinked and the features came into focus: the mouth, so like
Clarissa's, hanging loose; the eyes staring wide; the whole

face blazing with an emotion which could have been terror or triumph.

She wasn't sure how long they stayed there, she locked in Ivo's arms, Roma staring down at them. Then she heard footsteps behind her. She broke free, murmuring over and over again, "I'm sorry. I'm sorry. I'm sorry."

Ambrose spoke: "Simon's gone to his room. He's very shocked and he wants to be alone. He'll be down as soon as he feels ready."

Ivo asked, "What happened? How did she die?"

Ambrose hesitated and Roma cried out, "You've got to tell us! I insist that you tell us!"

Ambrose looked at Cordelia. He gave a shrug of resigned apology. "Sorry, but I'm not prepared to do the work of the police. They have a right to know." He looked up at Roma. "She was battered to death. Her face has been smashed to pulp. It looks as if the weapon used was the limb of the dead princess. I haven't told Simon how she was killed and I think it better that he shouldn't know."

Roma sank down on the stairs and grasped the banister. She said, "Your marble? The killer took your marble? But why? How did he know it was there?"

Ambrose said, "He, or she, took it from the display cabinet some time before seven o'clock this morning. And I'm afraid that the police are only too likely to take the view that he knew it was there, because, yesterday before luncheon, I myself showed it to him."

5

TEN MINUTES LATER Roma, Ivo, and Cordelia stood at the drawing-room window and looked down over the terrace to the landing stage. All three of them were now outwardly calm. The first shock had been replaced by a restlessness, almost an unhealthy prurient excitement, which they recognized in themselves and each other and which was as shaming as it was unexpected. They had all resisted the temptation to take alcohol, perhaps feeling that it would be unwise to face the police with its smell on their breath. But Munter had served strong coffee in the drawing room and it had been almost as effective.

Now they watched as the two heavily loaded launches rocked dangerously at the quayside, the passengers in their evening clothes crowding to one side like a gaudily clad cargo of aristocratic refugees fleeing from some republican holocaust. Ambrose was talking to them, with Munter standing at his shoulder like a second line of defense. There was a great deal of gesticulating. Even at this distance, Ambrose's pose, the slightly bent head, the spread hands, conveyed regret, distress, and some embarrassment. But he was standing firm. The sound of chattering came to them, faint but high like the squeaking of distant starlings. Cordelia said to Ivo, "They look restless. I expect they want to stretch their legs."

"Want to pee I expect, poor dears."

"There's someone standing up on the gunwale taking photographs. If he's not careful, he'll go overboard."

"That's Marcus Fleming. He's supposed to be taking the pictures to illustrate my article. Oh, well, he'll be able to phone a scoop of sorts to London if they don't capsize with excitement before they reach shore."

"The fat lady seems very determined, the one in mauve."

"That's Lady Cottringham, the formidable dowager. Ambrose had better watch her. If she gets one foot on the quay there'll be no holding her. She'll dash in to give poor Clarissa the once-over, subject us all to third degree, and solve the crime before the police get here. Ah, victory for Ambrose! The launches are pulling away."

Roma said quietly, "And here come the police."

Around the corner of the island came four bright wings of spray. Two sleek dark blue launches were approaching, their long wakes feathering the paler blue of the sea.

Roma said, "Odd that one feels so apprehensive. Stupid, too. It's like being a schoolgirl again. One always felt and looked most guilty when one was totally innocent."

Ivo said, "Totally? That's an enviable state. I've never managed to achieve it. But I shouldn't worry. The police have a formula for these occasions. The suspects are ranked in strict order of priority: first the husband, then the heirs, then the family, then close friends and acquaintances."

Roma said dryly, "As I'm both an heir and a relation, I can hardly find that reassuring."

They watched in silence as the two brightly laden launches drew clumsily away and those sleek blue hulls came rapidly closer.

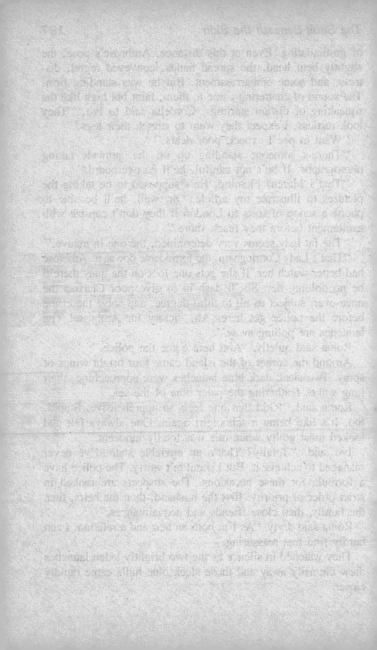

BOOK FOUR

THE
PROFESSIONALS

1

SERGEANT ROBERT BUCKLEY was young, good-looking, and intelligent and well aware of these advantages. He was also, less commonly, aware of their limitations. He had gained three A-level subjects with respectable grades at the end of his two years in the sixth, an achievement which would have justified going on to university in company with friends similarly qualified. But it wouldn't have been the university of his choice. He suspected that his intelligence, although keen, was superficial, that he couldn't compete with real scholars, and he had no intention of joining the overeducated unemployed at the end of another three years of mildly boring academic grind. He judged that success would come quickest in a job for which he was over- rather than under-qualified and where he would be competing with men who were less rather than better educated than himself. He recognized in himself a streak of sadism which found a certain mild

satisfaction in the pain of others without necessarily needing
actively to inflict it.

Buckley was an only child of elderly parents who had
begun by doting on him, moved on to admiring him, and had
ended by being a little afraid of him. That too he found
agreeable. His choice of career had been natural and easy, the
final decision made while he was loping with long, easy
strides over the Purbeck hills, watching the earth move in
streaks of fawn and green. There had been only two possibilities, the army or the police, and he had quickly rejected the
first. He was aware of some social insecurity; there were
traditions, mores, a public-school ethos, about the army for
which he felt a wary distrust. This was an alien world which
might expose him, even reject him, before he had had a
chance to master it. The police, on the other hand, given
what he had to offer, ought to be pleased to have him. And to
do them justice, they had been pleased.

Sitting now in the bow of the launch, he felt particularly
pleased with the world and with himself. He made a practice
of concealing his enthusiasm as he did his imagination. Both
were like fascinating but wayward friends, to be enjoyed
rarely and with caution since they had about them the taint of
treachery. But as he watched Courcy Island steadily taking
form and color across a dazzle of sea, he was aware of a
heady mixture of exultation and fear. He exulted at the
promise that here, at last, was the murder case of which he
had dreamed since he had gained his sergeant's stripes. He
feared that it might yet collapse, that they would be met at the
jetty with those depressingly familiar words: "He's waiting
for you upstairs. We've got someone watching him. He's in a
terrible state. He says he doesn't know what came over him."

They never did know what came over them, those self-
confessed murderers, as pathetic in defeat as they were
incompetent in their killing. Murder, the unique and ultimate
crime, was seldom the most interesting forensically or the
most difficult to solve. But when you did get a good one there

was no excitement like it: the heady combination of a manhunt with a puzzle; the smell of fear in the air, strong as the metallic smell of blood; the sense of randy well-being; the fascinating way in which confidence, personality, morale, subtly changed and deteriorated under its contaminating impact. A good murder was what police work was about. And this promised to be a good one.

He glanced across to where his chief sat, his red hair glinting in the sun. Grogan looked as he always did before a case, silent and withdrawn, the eyes hooded but wary, the muscles tensed under the well-cut tweed, the whole of that powerful body gathering its energies for action like the predator he was. When Buckley had been introduced to him three years earlier, he had been at once reminded of pictures in his boyhood comics of an Indian brave and had mentally crowned that carved and ruddy head with ceremonial feathers. But the comparison had in some subtle way been inaccurate. Grogan was too large a man, too English, and too complicated for so uncompromisingly simple an image. Buckley had only once been invited briefly into the stone cottage outside Speymouth where, separated from his wife, Grogan lived alone. It was rumored that he had a son and that there was some trouble with the boy; what exactly no one seemed to know. The cottage had revealed nothing. There were no pictures, no mementos of old cases, no photographs of family or colleagues, few books apart from what looked like a complete set of the Famous Trials series, little but bare stone walls and a bank of expensive stereo equipment. Grogan could have packed his bags and been out of it in half an hour, leaving nothing of himself behind. Buckley still didn't understand him, although after two years of working under him he knew what to expect: the alternate taciturnity and volubility during which he would use his sergeant as a sounding board, the occasional sarcasm, the ruthlessness, and the impatience. He only partly resented being used as a combination of clerk, shorthand writer, pupil, and audience. Grogan did too much of the work himself. But you could learn from him, he got results, he wasn't tainted with failure, and he was fair. And he was nearing retirement; only two years to go. Buckley took what he wanted from him and bided his time.

There were three figures waiting for them on the jetty, motionless as statues. Buckley guessed who two of them must be before the launches had chugged to a stop: Sir George Ralston, standing almost at attention in his old-fashioned shooting jacket; Ambrose Gorringe, more relaxed but incongruously formal in his dinner jacket. Both of them watched the arrivals disembark with wary formality like the commanders of a besieged castle awaiting the armistice negotiators and watching with undeluded eyes for the first hint of treachery. The third man, dark-clad and taller than the other two, was obviously some kind of servant. He stood a little behind them and gazed stolidly past them out to sea. His stance conveyed that certain guests were welcome on Courcy but that the police were not among them.

Grogan and Gorringe made the introductions. Buckley noticed that his chief expressed no sympathy, spoke no words of formal regret to the widower. But, then, he never did. He had once explained why: "It's offensively insincere, and they know it. There's enough duplicity in police work without adding to it. Some lies are insulting." And if Ralston or Gorringe noticed the omission, neither made a sign.

Ambrose Gorringe did all the talking. As they moved between wide lawns toward the castle entrance, he said, "Sir George has organized a search of the castle and the island. The castle has been searched but the three groups covering the island aren't back yet."

"My men will take that over now, sir."

"So I supposed. The rest of the cast are in the theater. Sir Charles Cottringham would be glad of a word with you."

"Did he say what about?"

"No. Merely a matter, I imagine, of letting you know that he's here."

"I know that already. I'll see the body now, and then I'd be grateful for the use of a small and quiet room for the rest of the day and, possibly, until Monday."

"I thought that my business room would be the most suitable. If you will ring from Miss Lisle's room when you're ready, I'll show you where it is. And Munter will get you anything you need. My guests and I will be in the library when you want us."

They moved through a large hall and up the staircase. Buckley noticed nothing of his surroundings. He walked with Sir George immediately behind Grogan and Ambrose Gorringe and listened while Gorringe gave his chief a succinct but remarkably comprehensive account of the events leading up to Miss Lisle's death: how she came to be on the island; brief particulars of the rest of the house party; the threatening letters; the fact that she had thought it necessary to bring her own private detective with her, a Miss Cordelia Gray; the loss of the marble limb; the discovery of the body. It was an impressive performance, as carefully impersonal and factual as if it had been rehearsed. But, then, thought Buckley it probably had.

Outside the door the party paused. Gorringe handed over three keys. He said, "I locked all three doors after the discovery of the body. These are the only keys. I take it you don't want us to come in."

Sir George spoke for the first time: "When you need me, Chief Inspector, I'll be with my wife's stepson in his room. Boy's upset. Natural in the circumstances. Munter knows where to find me." He turned abruptly and left them.

Grogan answered Gorringe's question. "You've been very helpful, sir. But I think we can manage here on our own."

She was an actress even in death. The scene in the bedroom was extraordinarily dramatic. Even the set had been cleverly designed for melodrama in the grand manner, the props glittering and ostentatious, the dominant color red. And there she lay, sprawled under the crimson canopy, one white leg carefully raised to show an expanse of thigh, her face plastered with artificial blood, while director and cameraman stepped around her, contemplating the best angles, careful not to touch or disturb that artfully provocative pose. Grogan stood at the right of the bed and looked down at her, frowning as if wondering whether the casting director had been right in choosing her for the role. Then he leaned down and sniffed at the skin of her arm. The moment was bizarre. Buckley thought: Is thy servant a dog that he should do this thing? Almost he expected her to shudder with outrage, sit up and stretch out groping hands, demand a towel to wipe the mess from her face.

The room was overcrowded but the experts in death— investigating officers, fingerprint officers, photographer, and scene-of-crime searchers—were adept at keeping out of each other's way. Grogan, as Buckley knew, had never reconciled himself to the use of civilian scene-of-crime officers, which was odd when you considered that he had come from the Met where the employment and training of civilians had gone about as far as it could go. But these two knew what they were about. They moved as delicately and confidently as a couple of cats prowling their familiar habitat. He had worked with both of them before, but he doubted whether he would recognize them in the street or the pub. He stood back out of the way and watched the senior of them. It was always their hands that he watched, hands sheathed in gloves so fine that they looked like a second glistening skin. Now those hands poured the remnants of the tea into a collecting flask; stoppered, sealed, and labeled it; gently eased the cup and saucer into a plastic bag; scraped a sample of blood from the marble limb and placed it in a specially prepared tube; took up the limb itself, touching it only with the tips of the fingers, and lowered it into a sterile box; delicately picked up a note with tweezers and insinuated that gently into its transparent enve- lope. At the bed his colleague was busy with magnifying glass and tweezers, collecting hairs from the pillow, seemingly oblivious of that shattered face. When the Home Office pathologist had completed his examination, the bedclothes would be bundled into a plastic bag, sealed, and added to the other exhibits.

Grogan said, "Doc Ellis-Jones is visiting his mother-in-law at Wareham, conveniently for us. They've sent an escort. He should be here within the next half hour. Not that there's much he can tell us that we can't see for ourselves. And the time of death is fixed within pretty tight limits anyway. If you reckon the loss of body heat on this kind of day at about one and a half degrees an hour for the first six hours, he's unlikely to be able to put it any closer than we already know, sometime between twenty past one when the girl left her alive, so Ambrose Gorringe tells us, and two-forty-three when the same girl found her dead. To be the last one to see the victim and the one to find the body suggests that Miss Cordelia Gray is either careless or unfortunate. We may be able to judge which when we see her."

Buckley said, "From the appearance of the blood, sir, I'd say that she died sooner rather than later."

"Yes. My guess would be within about thirty minutes of being left. That quotation under the marble limb. You recognized it, Sergeant?"

"No, sir."

"I'm relieved to hear it. From *The Duchess of Malfi*, so Ambrose Gorringe informs us, the play in which Miss Lisle was cast in the title role. 'Blood flies upwards and bedews the heavens.' I applaud the sentiment even if I couldn't identify the source. But it isn't particularly apposite. The blood didn't fly upwards, or not to any great extent. This systematic destruction of the face was done after death. And we know the possible reasons for that."

It was rather like a viva-voce examination, thought Buckley. But this question was an easy one.

"To conceal identity. To obscure the real cause of death.

To make absolutely sure. An explosion of anger, hatred, or fear."

"And then, after that brainstorm of violence, our literary-minded murderer calmly replaces the eye pads. He has a sense of humor, Sergeant."

They moved together into the bathroom. Here was a compromise between period opulence and modern functional-ism. The great bath was marble and encased in a mahogany surround. The seat of the lavatory was mahogany, too, with a high flush. The walls were tiled, each tile painted in blue with a different posy of wild flowers, and there was a cheval glass, its frame decorated with cherubs. But the towel rail was heated, there was a bidet, a shower had been installed above the bath, and a shelf over the handbasin held a formidable assortment of bath essences, powder, and expensive wrapped soaps.

Four white towels were untidily hung over the rail. Grogan sniffed each of them and rumpled them in his huge hands. He said, "It's a pity about that heated rail. They're completely dry. And so are the bath and handbasin. There's no way of telling whether she had time to bath before she was killed, not unless Doc Ellis-Jones can isolate traces of powder or bath essence from her skin, and even that wouldn't be conclusive. But the towels look as if they've been recently used and they're slightly scented. So is the body, and it's the same smell. My guess is that she did have time. She drank her tea, took off her makeup, and bathed. If Miss Gray left her at twenty past one, that would bring us to about twenty minutes to two."

The senior scene-of-crime officer was waiting at the door. Grogan stood aside for him, then went back into the bedroom and stood at the window, looking out to where a hairline of purple separated the darkening sea from the sky. He said, "Have you heard of the Birdhurst Rise Poisonings?"

"In Croydon, wasn't it, sir? Arsenic."

"Three members of the same middle-class family murdered

with arsenic between April 1928 and March 1929, Edmund Duff, a retired colonial civil servant, his sister-in-law, and her widowed mother. In each case the poison must have been administered in food or medicine. It could only have been a member of the family or the household, but the police never made an arrest. It's a fallacy to suppose that a small circle of suspects, all known to each other, makes a case easier to solve. It doesn't; it only makes failure indefensible.''

Failure wasn't a word which Buckley could remember having heard before on Grogan's lips. His euphoria gave way to a small weight of anxiety. He thought of Sir Charles Cottringham, even now cooling his heels in the theater, of the chief constable, of Monday's publicity. ''Baronet's Wife Battered to Death in Island Castle.'' ''Well-known Actress Slain.'' This wasn't a case which any officer ambitious for his future could afford to lose. He wondered what it had been about this room, this victim, this weapon, perhaps the air of Courcy Island itself, which had evoked that depressing note of caution.

For a moment neither of them spoke. Then there was sudden roar and a speedboat rounded the eastern tip of th. island and swept a wide, curving wake toward the quay.

Grogan said, ''Doc Ellis-Jones is making his usual dramatic appearance. Once he's told us what we already know, that she's a female and she's dead, and has explained what we can work out for ourselves, that it wasn't accident or suicide and it happened between one-twenty and two-forty-three, we can get down to the business of finding out what our suspects have to say for themselves, beginning with the baronet.''

2

IT WAS NEARLY half past four, and Ambrose, Ivo, Roma, and
Cordelia were standing together on the jetty looking out to
sea as *Shearwater*, taking the cast back to Speymouth, moved
beyond the eastern tip of the island and out of sight.

Ambrose said, "Well, they may have been done out of
their moment in the spotlight, but they can't complain that the
day has been dull. Clarissa's murder will be all over the
county by dinner time. That means we can expect a press
invasion by dawn."

Ivo said, "What will you do?"

"Prevent anyone from landing, although not with the
brutal effectiveness of de Courcy at the time of the plague.
But the island is private property. And I'll instruct Munter to
refer all telephone inquiries to the police at Speymouth.
They've presumably got a public-relations department. Let
them cope."

Cordelia, still in her cotton dress, shivered. The bright day was beginning to fade. Soon would come that transitory and lovely moment when the setting sun shines with its last and brightest rays, intensifying the color of grass and trees so that the air itself it stained with greenness. Now the shadows lay long and heavy over the terrace. The Saturday sailors had turned for home and the sea stretched in an empty calm. Only the two police launches rocked gently against the quay, and the smooth bricks of the castle walls and turrets, which for a moment had glowed with a richer red, darkened and reared above them, ponderous and forbidding.

As they passed through the great hall, the castle received them in an unnatural silence. Somewhere upstairs the police were busy with their secret expertise of death. Sir George was either being questioned or was with Simon in his room. No one seemed to know and no one liked to ask. The four of them, still awaiting their formal questioning, turned by common consent into the library. It might be less comfortable than the drawing room, but at least it offered plenty of material for those who chose to pretend that they wanted to read. Ivo took the only easy chair and lay back with his eyes turned to the ceiling, his long legs stretched. Cordelia sat at the chart table and slowly turned the pages of an 1876 bound copy of *The Illustrated London News*. Ambrose stood with his back to them, looking out over the lawn. Roma was the most restless, regularly pacing between the bookshelves like a prisoner under compulsory exercise. It was a relief when Munter and his wife brought in the tea, the heavy silver teapot, the brass kettle with the wick burning under it, the Minton tea service. Munter drew the curtains across the tall windows and put a match to the fire. It crackled into life. Paradoxically, the library became at once cozier but more oppressive, enclosed in its shadowed hermetic calm. They were all thirsty. No one had much appetite, but ever since the finding of the body they had craved the comfort and stimulus of strong tea or coffee, and busying themselves with cups and saucers at least gave them something to do.

Ambrose settled himself beside Cordelia. Stirring his tea, he said, "Ivo, you have all the London gossip. Tell us about this man Grogan. I confess that, on first acquaintance, I don't take to him."

"No one has all the London gossip. London, as you very well know, is a collection of villages, socially, occupationally, as well as geographically. But theatrical gossip and police gossip do occasionally overlap. There's an affinity between detectives and actors as there is between surgeons and actors."

"Spare us the dissertation. What do you know about him? You've spoken to someone, I suppose?"

"I admit I did telephone a contact; from this room actually, while you were busy receiving Grogan and his minions. The story is that he resigned from the Met because he was disgusted with the corruption in the C.I.D. That, of course, was before the latest purge. He is, apparently, a proper William Morris man: 'No more now my knight, or God's knight any longer, you/Being than they so much more white, so much more pure and good and true.' That should reassure you, Roma."

"Nothing about the police reassures me."

Ambrose said, "I suppose I'd better be careful about offering him a drink. It could be construed as an attempt to bribe or corrupt. I wonder if the chief constable, or whoever it is who decides these things, sent him here to fail."

Roma said sharply, "Why should anyone do that?"

"Better the incomer than one of your own men. And he could very easily fail. This is a storybook killing: a close circle of suspects, isolated scene of crime conveniently cut off from the mainland, known *terminus a quo* and *terminus ad quem*. It should be perfectly possible to tie it up—that's the jargon, isn't it?—within a week. Everyone will expect it to be solved quickly. But if the killer keeps his head clear and his mouth shut, I very much doubt whether he or she is in real danger. All he needs to do—let's be chivalrous and assume it's a man—is to stick to his story; never excuse, never embellish, never explain. It isn't what the police know or suspect; it's what they can prove."

Roma said, "You sound as though you don't want it solved."

"Without having strong feelings on the matter, I should prefer to have it solved. It would be tedious to spend the rest of one's life as a suspected murderer."

"It'll bring in the summer tourists, though, won't it? People love blood and horror. You'll be able to show the scene of the crime—for an extra twenty pence, of course."

Ambrose said easily, "I don't pander to sensationalism. That's why summer visitors don't get shown the crypt. And this is a murder in poor taste."

"But aren't all murders in poor taste?"

"Not necessarily. It would make a good parlor game, classifying the classical murder cases according to their degree of tastelessness. But this one strikes me as particularly bizarre, extravagant, theatrical."

Roma had drained her first cup of tea and was pouring a second. "Well, that's appropriate enough." She added, "It's odd that we've been left here alone, isn't it? I thought that there'd be a plainclothes underling sitting in and taking a note of all our indiscretions."

"The police know the limit of their territory and of their powers. I've given them the use of the business room and, naturally, they've locked the two guest rooms. But this is still my house and my library and they come in here by invitation. Until they decide to charge someone, we're all entitled to be treated as innocent. Even Ralston, presumably, although as husband he has to be elevated to chief suspect. Poor George! If he really loved her, this must be hell for him."

Roma said, "He stopped loving her six months after the wedding. He must have known by then that she wasn't capable of fidelity."

Ambrose asked, "He never showed the least sign, did he?"

"Not to me, but then I hardly ever saw them. And what could he do, faced with that particular insubordination? You can hardly deal with an unfaithful wife as if she were a recalcitrant subaltern. I don't suppose he liked it. But if he didn't kill her, and I don't for one moment believe that he did, he's probably not entirely ungrateful to whoever did. The money will come in useful to subsidize that fascist organization he runs. The Union of British Patriots, U.B.P. Wouldn't you know from the name that it's a fascist front?"

Ambrose smiled. "Well, I wouldn't expect it to be full of Trots and international socialists certainly. It's harmless enough. A *Boys' Own Paper* mentality and a geriatric army."

Roma slammed down her cup and began again her restless pacing.

"My God, you're good at deceiving yourselves, aren't you? It's nasty, it's embarrassing, and most unforgivable of all, the people concerned actually take themselves seriously. They really believe in their dangerous nonsense. So let's all laugh at it, and perhaps it will go away. When the chips are down, who do you think this geriatric army are going to be defending? The poor bloody proles? Not likely!"

"I rather hope they'll be defending me."

"Oh, they will, Ambrose, they will! You and the multinational corporations, the establishment, the press barons. Clarissa's money will do its bit toward keeping the rich man in his castle, the poor man at his gate."

Ambrose said mischievously, "But don't you get some of the money? And won't it come in useful to you?"

"Of course; money always does. But it isn't important. I'll be glad enough of it, I suppose, when it actually comes, but I don't need it. It certainly isn't important enough to kill for. Come to that, I don't know what is."

"Oh, come on, Roma, don't be naive! A cursory read of the daily papers will tell you what people find important enough to kill for. Dangerous and destructive emotions, to begin with. Love, for example."

Munter was at the door. He coughed, rather, thought Cordelia, like a stock butler in a play, and said, "The Home Office pathologist, Dr. Ellis-Jones, has arrived, sir."

Ambrose looked for a moment distracted as if wondering whether he was expected to greet the newcomer formally. He said, "I'd better come, I suppose. Do the police know he's here?"

"Not yet, sir. I thought it right to inform you first."

"Where is he, the pathologist?"

"In the great hall, sir."

"Well, we can't keep him waiting. You'd better take him to Chief Inspector Grogan. I suppose there are things he may need. Hot water, for example." He looked vaguely around as if expecting a jug and basin to materialize from the air. Munter disappeared.

Ivo murmured, "You make it sound like a childbirth."

Roma swung around; her tone was a mixture of the peevish and appalled. "But surely he's not going to do the postmortem here!"

They all looked at Cordelia. She thought that Ambrose must surely know the procedure, but he too gazed at her with a look of bland, almost amused inquiry.

She said, "No. He'll just do a preliminary examination at what they call the scene of crime. He'll take the temperature of the body, try to estimate the time of death. Then they'll take her away. They don't like to move the body until the forensic pathologist has seen it and certified that life is extinct."

Roma Lisle said, "What a lot of curious information you have acquired for a girl who calls herself a secretary-companion. But of course, I forgot. You're not a secretary-companion. Ambrose tells us that you're a private eye. So perhaps you'll explain why we've all had to have our fingerprints taken. I found it particularly offensive, the way they take hold of your fingers and press them down on the pad. It wouldn't be so repulsive if you were allowed to do it yourself."

Cordelia said, "Didn't the police explain the reason? If they find any prints in Clarissa's room, they want to be able to eliminate ours."

"Or identify them. And what else are they doing, apart from grilling George? God knows they've brought enough men with them."

"Some of them are probably scientific officers from the forensic science laboratory. Or they may be what are called scene-of-crime officers. They'll collect the scientific evidence, samples of blood and body fluids. They'll take away the bedclothes and the cup and saucer. And they'll analyze the dregs of tea to find out if she was poisoned. She could have been drugged before she was killed. She was lying very peaceably on her back."

Roma said, "It didn't need a drug for Clarissa to lie peaceably on her back." Then she saw their faces. Her own went scarlet and she cried, "I'm sorry! I shouldn't have said that. It's just that I can't really believe it; I can't picture her lying there, battered to death. I haven't that kind of imagination. She was alive. Now she's dead. I didn't like her and she didn't like me. Death can't alter that for either of us." She almost stumbled to the door. "I'm going for a walk. I've got to get out of this place. If Grogan wants me, he can come and find me."

Ambrose refilled the teapot and poured himself another cup, then seated himself leisurely next to Cordelia.

"That's what surprises me about political commitment. Her cousin, the woman she was practically brought up with, is messily done to death and will shortly be carted off to be scientifically carved up by a Home Office pathologist. She's shocked, obviously. But basically she cares as little as if she'd been told that Clarissa is inconvenienced by a mild attack of fibrositis. But one mention of poor Ralston's Union of British Patriots and she's hysterical with outrage."

Ivo said, "She's frightened."

"That's obvious, but what of? Not that pathetic bunch of amateur warriors."

"They frighten me occasionally. I suppose she was right about the money and Ralston will get most of it. How much is that?"

"My dear Ivo, I don't know. Clarissa never confided the details of her personal finances; we weren't that close."

"I rather thought you were."

"And even if we had been, I doubt whether she would have told. That's one surprising fact about Clarissa. You won't believe this but it's true. She loved to gossip, but she could keep a secret when she wanted to. Clarissa liked hoarding, and that included nuggets of useful information."

Ivo said lightly, "How unexpected, and how very dangerous."

Cordelia looked at them, at Ambrose's bright malicious eyes, at Ivo's barely covered skeleton angularly disposed in his chair, at the long bony hands drooping from wrists which looked too thin and brittle to hold them, at the putty-colored face with its jutting bones turned upward to the stuccoed ceiling. She was seized with a confusion of feelings: anger, a deep unfocused pity, and a less familiar emotion which she recognized as envy. They were so secure in their sardonic, half-humorous detachment. Could anything really touch their hearts or nerves except the possibility of their own pain? And even physical pain, that universal leveler, they would meet with wry disgust or derisive contempt. Wasn't that how Ivo was facing his own death? Why should she expect them to grieve because a woman neither of them had greatly liked was lying upstairs with her face smashed in? And yet it wasn't necessary to affirm Donne's overworked aphorism to feel that something was owed to a death, that something in their relationships, in the castle itself, in the very air they breathed, had been touched and subtly altered.

Suddenly she felt very alone and very young. She was aware of Ambrose looking at her. As if he had read her thoughts he said, "Part of the horror of murder is that it does the dead out of their rights. I don't suppose anyone in this room is personally desolated by Clarissa's death. But if she'd died a natural death, at least we'd be mourning her in the sense that we'd be thinking of her with that confused mixture of regret, sentimentality, and sympathetic interest which is the normal tribute to the recently dead. As it is, all we're thinking of is ourselves. Well, aren't we? Aren't we?"

Ivo said, "I don't think Cordelia is."

The library enclosed them again in its silence. But their ears were abnormally alert to every creak, and three heads jerked upwards simultaneously at the sound of muffled footfalls across the hall and the distant thud, faint but unmistakable, of a closing door.

Ivo said quietly, "I think they're taking her away."

He moved silently behind one of the curtains and Cordelia followed. Between the wide lawns, frosted by moonlight, four dark and elongated figures, shadowless as phantoms, bent to their task. Behind them paced Sir George, stiff-legged and erect, as if his sword clanked at his side. The small procession looked like a group of mourners surreptitiously burying their dead according to some esoteric and prohibited rite. Cordelia, drained by shock and tiredness, wished she could feel some personal and appropriate response of pity. But there came into her mind instead a whisper of atavistic horror, images of plague and secret murder, de Courcy's men disposing of his victims under the cloak of night. It seemed to her that Ivo had stopped breathing. He didn't speak, but she sensed through the contact of his rigid shoulder the intensity of his gaze.

Then the curtains parted and Ambrose stood behind them. He said, "She arrived in the morning sun and leaves by moonlight. But I should be out there. Grogan should have told me they were ready to take her away. Really, that man's behavior is becoming intolerable!"

And so it was, thought Cordelia, that Clarissa left on her

final journey from Courcy Island, on that note of slightly peevish complaint.

An hour later the door opened and Sir George came in. He must have been aware of their inquiring looks, of the question which no one cared to ask. He said, "Grogan was perfectly civil, but I don't think he's formed any theories. I suppose he knows his business. That red hair must be a disadvantage—disguise, you know."

Ambrose said gravely, controlling the twitching of his mouth, "I think detection at his level is chiefly desk work. I don't suppose he does much lurking in the undergrowth."

"Must do some fieldwork, keep his hand in. He could dye it, I suppose."

He picked up *The Spectator* and settled himself at the chart table, as much at ease as if he were in his London club. The others stood and regarded him in baffled silence. Cordelia thought, We're behaving like candidates at an oral examination who'd rather like to know what questions to expect but feel that it would be taking an unfair advantage actually to ask.

The same thought must have struck Ivo. He said, "The police aren't running a competition for their favorite suspect of the year. I confess to some curiosity about their strategy and technique. Reviewing Agatha Christie at the Vaudeville is poor preparation for the real thing. So how did it go, Ralston?"

Sir George looked up from his journal and appeared to give the question serious thought. "Much as you'd expect. Where exactly was I and what was I doing this afternoon? I told them I was bird-watching on the west cliffs. Told them, too, that I'd seen Simon coming ashore through my binoculars on the way home. Seemed to think that was important. Asked about Clarissa's money. How much? Who gets it? Grogan wasted twenty minutes asking me about bird life on Courcy. Trying to put me at my ease, I suppose. A bit odd, I thought."

Ivo said, "Trying to catch you out more likely with cunning traps about the nesting habits of nonexistent species. What about this morning? Are we expected to detail every waking moment of the day?" His voice was carefully casual, but all four of them knew what it was he was asking and the importance of the reply.

Sir George took up his journal again. Without looking up he said, "Didn't say more than I needed. Told them about the visit to the church and the Devil's Kettle. Mentioned the drowning but didn't give names. No point in confusing the investigation with old history. Not their concern."

Ivo said, "You reassure me. That's rather the line I propose to take. I'll have a word with Roma when the opportunity arises, and you, Ambrose, might speak to the boy. As Ralston says, there's no point in confusing them with old, unhappy, far-off things and battles long ago."

No one replied, but Sir George suddenly looked up over his journal. "Sorry, I forgot. They want to see you now, Cordelia."

3

CORDELIA COULD UNDERSTAND why Ambrose had offered the
business room for the use of the police. It was appropriately
furnished as an office, it wasn't too large, and it kept them
well out of his way. But as she seated herself in the mahogany-
and-cane chair and faced Chief Inspector Grogan across the
desk, she wished that Ambrose had chosen any room other
than this private museum of murder. The Staffordshire figures
on the wall shelf behind Grogan's head seemed to have
grown, no longer quaintly fashioned antiques but real people,
their bland painted faces glowing and twisting into life. And
the framed Victorian broadsheets with their crudely drawn
scaffolds and death cells were intrusive in their horror, stark
celebrations of the cruelty of man to man. The room itself
was smaller than she remembered, and she felt herself closeted
with her interrogators in frightening and claustrophobic prox-
imity. She was only half aware that there was a uniformed
woman police officer sitting almost motionless in the corner

by the window, watchful as a chaperone. Did they think that she would faint or accuse Grogan of assaulting her? She wondered briefly whether it was the same anonymous officer who had helped move her clothes and belongings from the De Morgan room to her new bedroom. She had no doubt that they had been thoroughly examined before being neatly arranged on the bed.

She found herself studying Grogan for the first time. He seemed even larger than the tall, broad figure she had first watched alighting from the police launch. The strong red-gold hair was longer than one would expect on a police officer; one swath fell across his forehead and from time to time he would sweep it back with a huge hand. Despite its size, his face with its jutting cheekbones and deep-set eyes gave an impression of gauntness. Under each cheekbone a brush of hair increased the sense of rough animality, an impression oddly at variance with the excellent cut of his formal tweed suit. His skin was ruddy so that his whole appearance was of redness; even the whites of his eyes seemed bloodshot. When he moved his head, Cordelia could glimpse, under his immaculate collar, the clear dividing line between the sunburned face and his white neck. It was so marked that he looked like a man who has been decapitated and joined together again. She tried to imagine him, red-bearded, as an Elizabethan adventurer, but the image was subtly wrong. For all his strength, he wouldn't have been found among the men of action but secretly scheming in the closets of power. Might he perhaps have been discovered in that dreaded room at the Tower, working the levers of the rack? But that was unfair. She thrust the morbid images out of her mind and made herself remember what he in fact was: a twentieth-century senior police officer, bound by force regulations, restricted by Judges' Rules, doing a vital if disagreeable job, and entitled to her cooperation. Yet she wished that she weren't so frightened. She had expected to feel anxiety, but not this rush of humiliating terror. She managed to master it but was miserably aware

that Grogan, experienced as he was, had recognized it and
that it wasn't unwelcome to him.

He listened in silence while, at his request, she recounted
the sequence of events between the arrival of Sir George at
Kingly Street and her discovery of Clarissa's body. She had
handed over the collection of messages and they were spread
out on the desk before him. From time to time, as her quiet
voice rose and fell, he shifted them about as if searching for
some meaningful pattern. She was glad that she wasn't wired
up to a lie detector. Surely the needle must have leaped as she
came to those moments when, although she told no direct
untruth, she carefully omitted the facts which she had decided
not to tell: the death of Tolly's child, Clarissa's disclosure in
the Devil's Kettle, Roma's unsuccessful appeal to her cousin
for money. She didn't try to justify these suppressions by
pretending that they wouldn't be of interest to him. She was
too tired now to make up her mind about the morality of her
decision. She only knew that, even when recalling Clarissa's
battered face, there were things that she couldn't bring herself
to tell.

He made her go over her story again and again, particularly pressing her about the locking of the bedroom doors.
Was she absolutely certain that she had heard Clarissa turn
her key? How could she be so sure that she had, in fact,
locked her own door? Sometimes she wondered whether he
were deliberately trying to confuse her as a counsel for the
defense might, pretending to be obtuse, pretending that he
hadn't quite understood. She was increasingly aware of her
own tiredness, of his strong hand lying in the pool of light
from the desk lamp, the ruddy hair gleaming on the back of
his fingers, of the soft rustle as Sergeant Buckley turned the
page. She must have been speaking for well over an hour
before he finished the long interrogation and both their
voices fell silent.

Then he said suddenly, as if rousing himself from boredom,
"So you call yourself a detective, Miss Gray?"

"I don't call myself anything. I own and run a detective agency."

"That's a nice distinction. But we haven't time to go into it now. You tell me that Sir George Ralston employed you as a detective. That's why you were here when his wife died. Suppose you tell me what you've detected so far."

"I was employed to look after his wife. I let her be killed."

"Now, let's get this straight. Are you telling me that you stood by and let someone kill her?"

"No."

"Or killed her yourself?"

"No."

"Or encouraged, or helped, or paid anyone else to kill her?"

"No."

"Then stop feeling sorry for yourself. Presumably you didn't think she was in any real danger. Nor did her husband. Nor did the Metropolitan Police apparently."

Cordelia said, "I thought that they might have had a reason for skepticism."

His eyes were suddenly sharp. "You did?"

"I wondered whether Miss Lisle sent one of the notes herself, the one typed on her husband's typewriter. He was in America at the time, so he couldn't have posted it to her himself."

"And why should she do that?"

"To try to exonerate Sir George. I think she was afraid that the police might suspect him. Don't they usually think of the husband first? She wanted to make sure that he was in the clear, perhaps because she didn't want the police to waste their time on him, perhaps because she genuinely knew that he wasn't guilty. I think the Metropolitan Police might have suspected that she sent the message herself."

Grogan said, "They did more than suspect it. They tested the saliva on the flap of the envelope. It belonged to a secretor with the same blood group as Miss Lisle, and that group is rare. They asked her to type an innocuous note for them, a message which had some of the same letters and in the same order as the quotation. On that evidence they suggested, tactfully, that she might have sent the note. She denied it. But you could hardly expect them to take the death threats very seriously after that.''

So she had been right. Clarissa had sent that one message. But she might be wrong about the reason. It had, after all, been clumsily done, and had it really exonerated Sir George? But it had ensured that the police took no further interest in what they must have seen as the time-wasting mischief of an attention-seeking and probably neurotic woman. And that would have suited the real culprit very well. Had anyone suggested to Clarissa that she should send that one note herself? And had it been the only one for which she had been responsible? Could the whole sequence of quotations be an elaborate conspiracy between herself and one other person? Cordelia rejected that theory almost as soon as it came into her mind. Of one thing she was sure: Clarissa had dreaded the arrival of the messages. No actress could have simulated that fear. She had been convinced that she would die. And she had died.

Cordelia was aware that the two men were looking at her intently. She had been sitting silently, hands curved in her lap, eyes lowered, occupied with though.. She waited for them to break the silence, and when the chief inspector spoke she thought she could detect a different note in his voice which could have been respect.

"Did you deduce anything else about these notes?"

"I thought that they might have been sent by two different people, apart from Miss Lisle, I mean. I wasn't shown the first half dozen which she received. I thought it possible that they might have been different from the later communications. And most of the ones I saw, the ones I've handed over to you, can be found in the *Penguin Dictionary of Quotations*.

I think that whoever typed them had that book in front of him and typed them from the text.''

"On different machines?"

"'That wouldn't be difficult. They aren't new machines and the makes are different. There are numerous shops in London and the suburbs which sell new and reconditioned typewriters and which put out a machine or two for people to try. It would be almost impossible to trace a machine if one went from shop to shop and typed a few lines in each.''

"And who do you suggest did?"

"I don't know.''

"And what about the original anonymous correspondent, the one you might say who had the bright idea in the first place?"

"I don't know that either."

That was as far as she was willing to go. She had told them enough, perhaps too much. If they wanted motives, let them grub around for themselves. And there was one motive for the poison pen that she would never divulge. If Ivo Whittingham had kept silent about Tolly's tragedy, so would she.

And then Grogan was speaking again, leaning over the desk toward her so that the powerful body, the strong coarse voice, surged toward her, palpable as a force.

"Let's get one thing straight, shall we? Miss Lisle was battered to death. You know what happened to her. You saw the body. Now, she may not have been a good or likable woman. That has nothing to do with it. She had as much right to live her life to the last natural moment as you or I or any creature under the Queen's peace.''

"Of course. I don't see why that needs saying.'' Why did her own voice sound so small, almost peevish?

"You'd be surprised what needs saying in a murder investigation. It's the most powerful mutual protection society in the world, the trade union of the living. It's the living you'll be thinking about, wanting to protect, yourself most of all, of course. My job is to think of her.''

''You can't bring her back.'' The words, torn out of her, fell between them in all their sad banality.

''No, but I can stop someone else from going the same way. No one is more dangerous than a successful murderer. I'm boring you with platitudes because I want you to get one thing straight. You may be too bright for your own good, Miss Gray. You're not here to solve this crime. That's my job. You're not here to protect the living. Leave that to their lawyers. You're not even here to protect the dead. They're beyond needing your condescension. *On doit des égards aux vivants; on ne doit aux morts que la vérité.* You're an educated young woman. You know what that means.''

'' 'We owe respect to the living; to the dead we owe only the truth.' It's Voltaire, isn't it? But I was taught a different pronunciation.''

As soon as the words were out she was ashamed. But to her surprise his only response was a bellow of laughter. ''I bet you were, Miss Gray. I bet you were. I taught myself with a primer and a key to phonetics. But think about it. There's no better motto for a detective, and that includes female private eyes who would like to help the police but still be able to lie abed with a good conscience. It can't be done, Miss Gray. It can't be done.''

She didn't reply. After a moment Grogan said, ''What surprises me a little, Miss Gray, is how much you noticed and how carefully when you found the body. Most people, and not only young women, would have been in a state of shock.''

Cordelia thought that he was entitled to the truth, or as much as she herself understood of it. ''I know. That has surprised me too. I think what happened was that I couldn't bear to feel too much emotion. It was so horrible that it was almost unreal. My intellect took over and made it into a kind of detective puzzle because, if I hadn't concentrated on detaching myself from the horror, examining the room, noticing little things like the lipstick smear on the cup, it would have been unbearable. Perhaps that's how doctors feel at the scene of an accident. You have to keep your mind on procedures and techniques because, otherwise, you might realize that what you have lying there is a human being.''

Sergeant Buckley said quietly, "It's how a policeman trains himself to behave at the scene of an accident. Or a murder.''

Without taking his eyes from Cordelia, Grogan said, "You find that credible, then, do you, Sergeant?''

"Yes, sir.''

Fear sharpens perception as well as the senses. Glancing at Sergeant Buckley's handsome, rather heavy face, at the controlled, self-satisfied smile, Cordelia doubted whether he had ever in his life needed such an expedient against pain and wondered whether he was trying to signal his sympathy or was colluding with his superior in some prearranged interrogatory ploy.

The chief inspector said, "And what exactly did your intellect deduce when it had so conveniently taken over from your emotions?''

"The obvious things: that the curtains had been drawn although they weren't when I left, that the jewel box was missing, that the tea had been drunk. And I thought it odd that Miss Lisle had cleaned the makeup from her face but that there was a lipstick stain on the cup. That surprised me. I think she has—she had—sensitive lips and used a creamy lipstick which smears easily. So why hadn't it come off when she ate her lunch? It looked as if she must have made up her lips again before she drank her tea. But if so, why had she taken off the rest of her makeup? The balls of stained cotton wool were all over the dressing-table top. And I noticed that there wasn't as much blood as one would expect from a head wound. I thought it possible that she might have been killed some other way and the injuries to her face made afterward.

And I was puzzled about the pads over her eyes. They must have been put there after death. I mean, it wouldn't be possible for them to stay so neatly in place while her face was being destroyed."

After she finished there was a long silence. Then Grogan said, his voice expressionless, "You're sitting on the wrong side of the desk, Miss Gray."

Cordelia waited. Then she said, hoping that she wasn't doing more harm than good, "There's one thing more I ought to tell you. I know that Sir George can't have killed his wife. I'm sure that you wouldn't suspect him, anyway, but there is something you should know. When he first arrived in the bedroom and I blurted out how sorry I was, he looked at me with a kind of amazed horror. I realized that he thought for a moment that I'd killed her, that I was confessing."

"And you weren't?"

"Not to murder. Only to failure to do what I was here for."

He changed the tack of his questioning again. "Let's go back to the Friday night, the time when you were with Miss Lisle in her room and she showed you the secret drawer in her jewel box. That review of the Rattigan play. Are you sure that that is what it in fact was?"

"Quite sure."

"The paper wasn't a document or a letter?"

"It was a newspaper cutting. And I read the headline."

"And at no time did your client—and she was your client, remember—ever give you the least indication that she knew or suspected who it was who was threatening her?"

"No, never."

"And she had no enemies as far as you know?"

"None that she told me of."

"And you yourself can throw no light on why and by whom she was killed?"

"No."

It must, she thought, feel like this to be in the witness box:

the careful questions, the even more careful answers, the
longing to be released.

He said, "Thank you, Miss Gray. You've been helpful.
Not, perhaps, as helpful as I'd hoped. But helpful. And it's
early days yet. We shall be talking again."

4

AFTER CORDELIA LEFT, Grogan relaxed in his chair.

"Well, what do you think of her?"

Buckley hesitated, uncertain whether his chief wanted assessment of the last interviewee as a woman or as a suspect. He said cautiously, "She's attractive. Like a cat." Since this evoked no immediate response, he added, "Self-contained and dignified."

He was rather pleased with the description. It had, he thought, a certain cleverness while committing him to nothing. Grogan began doodling on the blank sheet in front of him, a complicated mathematical design of triangles, squares, and precisely interlacing circles spread over the page and reminding Buckley of the more obscure of his school geometry problems. He found it difficult not to fix his eyes obsessively on isosceles triangles and bisecting arcs. He said, "Do you think she did it, sir?"

Grogan began filling in his design. "If she did, it was

during those fifty-odd minutes when she claims she was taking the sun on the bottom step of the terrace, conveniently out of sight and sound. She had time and opportunity. We've only her word that she locked her bedroom door or that Miss Lisle actually locked hers. And even if both doors and the communicating one were locked, Gray is probably the only person Lisle would have let in. She knew where the marble was kept. She was up and about early this morning when Gorringe first discovered that it was missing. She has a locked cabinet in her room where she could have kept it safely hidden. And we know that the final message, like the one typed on the back of the woodcut, was typed on Gorringe's machine. Gray can type and she had access to the business room where it's kept. She's intelligent, and she can keep her head even when I'm trying to needle her into losing it. If she did have a hand in it, my guess is that it was as Ralston's accomplice. His explanation of why she was called in sounded contrived. Did you notice how she and Ralston gave almost identical accounts of his visit to Kingly Street, what he said, what she said? It was so neat it could have been rehearsed. It probably was."

But Buckley could think of an objection and he voiced it. "Sir George was a soldier. He's used to getting his facts right. And she has a good memory, particularly for important events. And that visit was important. He probably paid well, and it could have led to other jobs. The fact that they gave the same account, got the details right, speaks as much for innocence as guilt."

"According to both of them, that's the first time they met. If they are conspirators, they must have got together before then. Whatever there is between them, it shouldn't be too difficult to grub it out."

"They're an unlikely couple. I mean, it's difficult to see what they have in common."

"Politics rather than bed, I imagine. Although, when it comes to sex, nothing is too bizarre to be ruled out. Police work teaches you that if nothing else. She could have taken a fancy to being Lady Ralston. There must be easier ways of getting money than running a detective agency. And Ralston will have money, remember. His wife's, to be specific. And I don't suppose that will come before it's needed. He must be spending a packet on that organization of his—the U.B.P. or whatever they call it. And that's an odd business if you like. I suppose you can argue a case for an amateur force trained and ready to support the civil power in an emergency, but isn't that what General Walker has in hand? So what exactly do George Ralston and his geriatric conspirators think they're up to?''

As Buckley didn't know the answer and had, in fact, hardly heard of the Union of British Patriots, he wisely kept silent. Then he said, "Did you believe Gray when she said that Sir George thought that she was confessing?''

"What Miss Gray thought she saw in Sir George's face isn't evidence. And no doubt he did look amazed if he thought he heard her confessing to a murder he'd done himself.''

Buckley thought about the girl who had just left them, saw again that gentle, uplifted face, the immense and resolute eyes, the delicate hands folded like a child's in her lap. She was keeping something back, of course; but didn't they all? That didn't make her a murderess. And the idea of her and Ralston together was ludicrous and disgusting. Surely the chief hadn't yet reached the age when he needed to start believing that pathetic old lie with which the middle-aged and the elderly deceive themselves, that the young find them physically attractive. What they can do, the old goats, he told himself, is to buy youth and sex with money and power and prestige. But he didn't believe that Sir George Ralston was in that market or that Cordelia Gray could be bought. He said stolidly, "I can't see Miss Gray as a murderess.''

"It takes an effort of the imagination, I grant you. But that's probably what Mr. Blady thought of Miss Blady. Or

L'Angelier of Miss Madeleine Smith, come to that, before she so unkindly handed him his cocoa and arsenic through the basement railings."

"Wasn't there a verdict of not proven in that case, sir?"

"A fainthearted Glasgow jury who should have known better and probably did. But we're theorizing in advance of facts. We need the postmortem result, and we need to know what, if anything, was in that tea. Doc Ellis-Jones will probably get her on the slab tomorrow, Sunday or no Sunday. Once he's got his hands on the body he's quick enough at his butchering, I'll say that for him."

"And the lab, sir. How long are they likely to take?"

"God knows. It's not as if we've any idea what they're supposed to be looking for. There isn't an unlimited number of drugs which can put you out, or kill you, within a short time and with no obvious signs on the body. But there are enough to keep them busy for the next few days if this is the only murder on the stocks. We may get a clue from the p.m., of course. Meanwhile we get on with the London end. How well did any of these people know each other before they arrived on the island this weekend? What, if anything, do the Met know about Cordelia Gray and her agency? What did Simon Lessing really feel about his benefactress, and how, exactly, did his father die? Is Miss Tolgarth quite the devoted dresser-*cum*-family retainer that we're supposed to believe? What sort of money is Sir George spending on his toy soldiers? How much exactly is Roma Lisle going to get under the will and how badly does she need it? And that's just for starters."

And none of it, thought Buckley, was the kind of information people came running to give you with happy smiles. It meant talking to bank managers, lawyers, friends, acquaintances, and colleagues of the suspects, most of whom would know to a word just how far they needed to go. In theory everyone wanted murderers caught, just as in theory they all approved of hostels for the mentally ill in the community.

provided they weren't built at the bottom of their garden. It would be simpler for the police as well as reassuring to the house party at the castle if they did discover those convenient young burglars hiding terrified somewhere on the island. But he didn't believe that they existed; nor, he suspected, did anyone else. And it would be a tamely disappointing ending to the case. What glory would there be in pulling in a couple of terrified local villains who'd killed on impulse and wouldn't have the sense even to keep their mouths shut until they got a lawyer? There was an intelligence at work here. The case was exactly the kind of challenge he enjoyed and which police work so seldom provided.

"There are facts. There are suppositions. There are beliefs. Learn to keep them separate, Sergeant. All men die. Fact. Death may not be the end. Supposition. There's pie in the sky when you die. Belief. Lisle was murdered. Fact. She received anonymous communications. Fact; other people were there when they arrived. They threatened her life. Supposition; they were a bloody sight more likely to put her off her stroke as an actress. They terrified her. Supposition; that's what her husband tells us and what she told Miss Gray. But she was an actress, remember. The thing about actresses is that they act. Suppose she and her husband concocted the whole scheme, threatening messages, apparent terror and distress, breakdown in the middle of a play, calling in a private eye, the lot."

"I don't see why, sir."

"Nor do I, yet. Would any actress willingly humiliate herself onstage? God knows. Actors are an alien breed to me."

"If she knew that she was finished as an actress, could she and her husband have concocted the messages to provide a public excuse for failure?"

"Overingenious and unnecessary. Why not just pretend that her health has failed? And she didn't make the messages public. On the contrary, she seems to have taken care to prevent the news getting out. Would any actress wish her public to know that someone hated her that much? Don't they crave to be loved by all the world? No, I was thinking of something rather more subtle. Ralston somehow persuades her into pretending that her life is threatened, and then kills her, having, as it were, seduced her into conniving at her own murder. My God, that would be neat. Too neat, perhaps.''

"But why take the risk of calling in Miss Gray?''

"What risk? She could hardly discover that the letters were faked, not in one short weekend. A very short weekend as far as Lisle was concerned. Employing Gray gave the final artistic touch to the whole plan.''

"I still think he'd have been taking a risk.''

"That's because we've seen the girl. She's intelligent and she knows her job. But Ralston wasn't to know that. Who is she, after all? The proprietor of a one-woman detective agency, apparently. After Lisle first met her at the house of that friend of hers—Mrs. Fortescue, wasn't it?—she probably suggested to Ralston that they call her in. That's why she never bothered to interview the girl herself. Why trouble when the whole thing was a ploy.''

"It's ingenious, sir, but it still begs the question why Lisle should have connived at it all. I mean, what possible reason could Ralston give to persuade her to pretend that her life was threatened?''

"What, indeed, Sergeant? Like Miss Gray, I'm in danger of being too clever for my own good. But one thing I'm sure of. The murderer spent last night under this roof. And I've a choice bunch of suspects. Sir George Ralston, baronet, something of a war hero and darling of the geriatric Right. A distinguished theater critic, one even I have actually heard of. Seriously ill, too, by the look of him, which means that he'll probably die on me under the gentlest interrogation. Interrogation. Odd how one dislikes that word. Too many echoes of the Gestapo and K.G.B., I suppose. A best-selling novelist who not only owns the island but happens to be friendly with the Cottringhams, who have the ear of the lord lieutenant, the chief constable, the M.P., and anyone else who matters in the county. A respectable bookseller, ex-schoolteacher, who's probably a member of the civil rights and women's lib lobbies and who will protest to her M.P. about police harassment if I raise my voice to her. And a school kid—and sensitive with it. I suppose I should be grateful that he's not a juvenile."

"And a butler, sir."

"Thank you for reminding me, Sergeant. We mustn't forget the butler. I regard the butler as a gratuitous insult on the part of fate. So let's give the gentry in the library a respite and hear what Munter has to tell us."

5

BUCKLEY NOTED WITH IRRITATION that Munter, invited by Grogan to sit, managed in the mere act of lowering his buttocks onto the chair to suggest both that it was unseemly for him to seat himself in the business room and that Grogan had committed a social solecism in inviting him to do so. He couldn't remember ever having seen the man in Speymouth; his was certainly not an appearance one was likely to forget. Watching Munter's strong and lugubrious face on which the unease proper to his present situation was noticeably absent, he found himself prepared to disbelieve everything he heard. It seemed to him suspicious that a man should want to make himself more grotesque than nature had intended, and if this was Munter's way of thumbing his nose at the world he had better not try it on with the police.

Basically conforming and ambitious, Buckley had no resentment of those wealthier than himself; he had every intention of eventually joining them. But he despised and distrusted those who chose to earn their living by pandering to the rich and suspected that Grogan shared this prejudice. He watched them both with a wary and critical eye and wished that he were taking a more active part in the interrogation. Never had his chief's insistence that he sit silently unless invited to speak, watch carefully, and take unobtrusive shorthand notes seemed more restrictive and demeaning. Morbidly sensitive to any nuance of condescension, he felt that the glance Munter casually gave him conveyed slight surprise that he should have been allowed into the house.

Grogan, seated at the desk, leaned back in his chair so strongly that its back creaked, twirled around to face Munter, and spread his legs wide as if to assert his right to feel perfectly at home. He said, "Suppose you begin by telling us who you are, where you came from, and what precisely is your job here."

"My duties, sir, have never been precisely defined. This is not altogether an orthodox household. But I am in charge of all the domestic arrangements and supervise the two other members of staff, my wife and Oldfield, who is the gardener, handyman, and boatman. Any additional help necessary when Mr. Gorringe is entertaining or has houseguests is obtained on a temporary basis from the mainland. I look after the silver and the wine and wait at table. The cooking is generally shared. My wife is the pastry cook and Mr. Ambrose himself occasionally cooks a meal. He is fond of preparing savories."

"Very tasty, I'm sure. And how long have you been part of this unorthodox household?"

"My wife and I came into Mr. Gorringe's service in July 1979, three months after his return from a year abroad. He had inherited the castle from his uncle in 1977. Perhaps you would wish for a brief curriculum vitae. I was born in London in 1940 and educated at Pimlico primary and secondary schools. I then took a course in hotel catering and for seven years worked in hotels here and abroad. But I decided that institutional life was unsuited to my temperament and entered private service, first with an American business gentleman living in London and then, when he returned home, here in Dorset with his lordship at Bossington House. I am sure my previous gentlemen will speak for me if necessary."

"No doubt. If I were looking for a manservant you'd do very nicely. But I'll be consulting a more objective character reference source, the criminal records office. Does that worry you?"

"It offends me, sir. It doesn't worry me."

Buckley wondered when Grogan would stop this needling and get down to the main inquiry, what Munter had been doing between the ending of lunch and the finding of the body. If these preliminaries were meant to provoke the witness, they weren't succeeding. But Grogan knew his business; at least the Met had appeared to think so. He had come to Dorset burdened with something of a reputation. Now he stopped looking at Munter; his voice became conversational.

"This play. It was to be a regular event, was it? An annual drama festival perhaps?"

"I have no means of knowing. Mr. Gorringe did not confide his plans to me."

"Once was enough, I should think. It must have made a lot of extra work for you and your wife."

Munter's slow and disapproving glance around the business room was an inventory of unwelcome change: the slight rearrangement of the furniture, Buckley's jacket slung over the back of his chair, the coffee tray with the two stained cups, its surface crumbled with half-eaten biscuits. He said, "The domestic inconvenience occasioned by Lady Ralston living was nugatory compared with the inconvenience of Lady Ralston murdered."

Grogan held his pen in front of his face and peered at its tip, moving it backward and forward as if testing his eyesight.

"You found her a pleasant, likable guest, easy to get on with?"

"That was not a question to which I addressed myself."

"Address yourself to it now."

"Lady Ralston seemed a very agreeable lady."

"No trouble? No disagreements? No rows as far as you knew?"

"None, sir. A great loss to the English stage." He paused and added woodenly, "And, of course, to Sir George Ralston."

It was impossible to judge whether the statement was ironic, but Buckley wondered whether Grogan, too, had caught the clear bite of contempt. Grogan rocked back in his chair, legs stretched, and stared consideringly at his witness. Munter gazed ahead with a look of patient resignation and, after a minute of silence, permitted himself a glance at his watch.

"Right! Let's get on with it. You know what we want, a full account of where you were, what you were doing, and whom you saw between one o'clock when lunch was over and two-forty-three when Miss Gray found the body."

According to Munter's account, he had spent the whole of that time on the ground floor of the castle, chiefly moving between the dining room, his pantry, and the theater. As he had been continually busy with preparations for the play and the supper party, it wasn't always possible to say where he had been or with whom at any particular moment, although he doubted whether he had ever been alone for more than a few minutes. He said in a voice which held no trace of regret that he very much regretted not being able to be more precise, but he could not, of course, have known so detailed an account would subsequently be required. At first he had helped his wife clear away the luncheon and had then gone to check on the wine. There had been three telephone calls to answer, one from a guest who was prevented by illness from attending the performance, a second inquiring about the time the launch would leave Speymouth, a call from Lady

Cottringham's housekeeper wanting to know whether they needed any extra glasses. He had been checking on the men's dressing room when his wife had appeared backstage to ask him to look at one of the tea urns which she thought might not be working. It was unfortunate that they had to hire urns; Mr. Gorringe had a strong dislike of them and complained that they made the great hall look like a meeting of the Women's Institute, but with an audience of eighty people and the cast to provide for, the use of the urns had been necessary.

At some time, he couldn't remember precisely when, he had remembered that Mr. Gorringe had asked him to find a second music box for use in the third act of the play, Miss Lisle having expressed dissatisfaction with the one provided at the dress rehearsal. He had come here into the business room to fetch it from the walnut chiffonier. At this stage his eyes indicated what Buckley sourly thought could very well have been described as a cupboard. His Aunt Sadie had one like it, not as fancily carved on the doors or at the end of the shelves, but pretty much the same. She claimed it had been in the family for generations, kept it in the back parlour, and called it a dresser. She used it for the bits and pieces her kids brought back from holiday for her, cheap souvenirs from the Costa del Sol, Malta, and, now, from Miami. He'd have to tell her that what she'd got was a chiffonier, and she'd reply that he made it sound like a bloody ice cream.

He turned the page of his notebook. Munter's resigned voice droned on. He had taken the second music box and placed it with the first one on the props table. Shortly afterward, it could have been as late as two-fifteen, Mr. Gorringe had appeared and they had checked over the props together. By then it was time to go to the quay to meet the launch bringing the rest of the cast from Speymouth. He had gone with Mr. Gorringe to receive them and had helped with the disembarkation. Mr. Gorringe and he had escorted the gentlemen to their dressing rooms, and his wife and Miss Tolgarth had looked after the ladies. He had stayed backstage for about ten minutes and had then gone to his pantry, where Mrs. Chambers and her granddaughter were polishing glasses. He had had occasion to complain to the girl, Debbie, about a smeared glass and had supervised the arrangements to rewash them all. After that he had gone to the dining room to collect the chairs for the supper party, which was to be held in the great hall. He had been there when Mr. Gorringe put his head in to inform him of Miss Lisle's murder.

Grogan sat with his great head lowered, as if bowed with the weight of assimilating this succinct account. Then he said quietly, "You are, of course, devoted to Mr. Gorringe."

"A man is well advised to be devoted to something or to someone."

"A man is well advised to take murder seriously."

"Yes, indeed, sir. When Mr. Gorringe broke the news to me I said, 'What, in our house?'"

"Quite Shakespearean. The Macbeth touch. And no doubt Mr. Gorringe could riposte with 'Too awful anywhere'?"

"No doubt he could have, sir. Actually, what he said was that I should go to the landing stage and prevent the guests from landing. He would follow as soon as possible and explain the lamentable circumstance which necessitated the cancellation of the performance."

"The launches were then at the quay?"

"Not at that time. I judged that they were three-quarters of a mile away."

"So there was no particular hurry to warn them?"

"It was not a matter to be left to chance. Mr. Gorringe was anxious that the police investigation should not be hampered by the presence on the island of another eighty people in a state of confusion or distress."

Grogan said, "In a state of highly enjoyable excitement, more likely. Nothing like a good murder for a thrill. Or wouldn't you know?"

"I wouldn't know, sir."

"Still, it was considerate of your master—I suppose that's

what you call him—to have as his first thought the convenience of the police. Highly commendable. What was he doing, do you know, while you were wasting a certain amount of time at the quay?"

"I suppose that he was telephoning the police and acquainting his guests and the cast of the play of the fact of Lady Ralston's death. I have no doubt he will inform you if asked."

"And how exactly did he acquaint you with the fact of Lady Ralston's death?"

"He told me that she had been battered to death. He instructed me to inform the guests when they arrived that she had been killed by a blow to the head. There was no need to harrow them unnecessarily. In the event I was not required to tell them anything, as Mr. Gorringe had joined me by the time the launches arrived."

"A blow to the head. You have seen the body?"

"No, sir. Mr. Gorringe locked the door of Lady Ralston's room after the discovery. There was no occasion for any of the staff to see the body."

"But you have, no doubt, formed some opinion as to how this blow to the head was inflicted? You permitted yourself a theory, a little natural curiosity? You went so far, perhaps, as to discuss it with your wife?"

"It did occur to me to wonder whether the assault was connected with the missing marble arm. Mr. Gorringe will have told you that the display case was forced in the early hours of this morning."

"So suppose you tell us what you know about that."

"The object was brought back to the castle by Mr. Gorringe on his return from London on Thursday night and placed by him in the showcase. The showcase is kept locked, since groups of visitors are shown around the castle during the summer months on days which are announced in advance, and Mr. Gorringe's insurance company has insisted on this degree of security. Mr. Gorringe himself placed the arm in position, watched by me, and we had some conversation on its possible provenance. He then locked the showcase. The keys to the display cabinets are not, of course, kept on the key board with the house keys but in the bottom left locked drawer of the desk at which you are now sitting. The showcase was undamaged and the marble arm in place when I saw it shortly after midnight. Mr. Gorringe found it in its present state when he was on his way to the kitchen just before seven o'clock. He is an early riser and prefers to make his own morning tea and carry the tray either onto the terrace or into the library, depending on the state of the weather. We inspected the damage together."

"You saw no one, heard nothing?"

"No, sir. I was busy in the kitchen preparing the early-morning tea trays."

"And they were all there when you took up the early tea trays?"

"The gentlemen were. I understand from my wife that the ladies were also in bed. Lady Ralston's early tea was taken up later by her maid, Miss Tolgarth. At about seven-thirty Mr. Gorringe came to tell me that Sir George had arrived unexpectedly, put ashore in the small bay west of the headland by a local fishing boat. I did not myself see him until I set breakfast on the hot plate in the small breakfast room at eight o'clock."

"But anyone could have got into the house at any time after six-five when you opened up the castle?"

"The back door leading to the great hall was unlocked by me at six-fifteen. At the time I looked out over the lawn and the path leading to the beach and the coastal walk. I saw no one. But anyone could have entered and done the damage between six-fifteen and seven o'clock."

The rest of the interview was unfruitful. Munter appeared to repent of his loquacity and his answers became shorter. He had no idea that Lady Ralston was receiving poison-pen communications and had no suggestions to offer as to their origin. Shown one of the messages, he fingered the paper with fastidious distaste and said that it was the kind he and his wife commonly bought but in cream, not white. The castle writing paper had an engraved address and was of a different quality, as the chief inspector would be able to check by opening the top left-hand drawer of the desk. He had not known that Mr. Gorringe had given Lady Ralston one of his Victorian jewel caskets, nor had he been told that it was missing. He could, however, describe the casket in question since there were only two in the castle. It had been made by a silversmith of Hunt and Rosken in 1850 and was thought to have been among their pieces shown at the Great Exhibition of 1851. It had been considered for use as a prop in the third act of the play, but the larger and less valuable if more showy casket had been thought the better choice.

Grogan frowned, irritated by this display of irrelevant knowledge. He said, "There's been murder done here, bloody murder of a defenseless woman. If there's anything you know, anything you suspect, anything that later occurs to you bearing on this crime, I expect to be told it. The police are here, and here to stay. We may not always be physically present, but we'll be around; we'll be concerned with this island, concerned with what happens here, and that means concerned with you, until the murderer is brought to justice. Have I made myself clear?"

Munter got to his feet. His face was still impassive. He said, "Perfectly, sir. May I say that Courcy Island is used to murder. And the murderers commonly haven't been brought to justice. Perhaps you and your colleagues will have better luck."

After he left, there was a long silence which Buckley knew better than to interrupt. Then Grogan said, "He thinks the husband did it, or he wants us to think that the husband did it. No marks for originality. It's what we're bound to think anyway. D'you know the Wallace case?"

"No, sir." Buckley told himself that if he were to continue

working with Grogan, it would be as well to get hold of a copy of the murderers' who's who.

"Liverpool, January 1931. Wallace, William Herbert. Inoffensive little insurance agent trotting round door to door and collecting the odd bob weekly from poor sods terrified they wouldn't be able to pay for their own funerals. Taste for chess and the violin. Married a bit above himself. He and his wife, Julia, lived in genteel poverty, which is the worst poverty of the lot, in case you didn't know, and kept themselves to themselves. Then on nineteenth January, when he's out looking for the address of a prospective customer who may or may not exist, Julia gets her head savagely bashed in, in her own front sitting room. Wallace stood trial for the murder and a sturdy Liverpool jury, who probably weren't entirely unbiased, convicted. The Court of Criminal Appeal subsequently made legal history by quashing the verdict on the grounds that it was unsafe having regard to the evidence. So they let him go and he died of kidney disease two years later, a bloody sight more slowly and painfully than he would have done at the end of a rope. It's a fascinating case. Every piece of evidence can point either way, depending on how you choose to look at it. I can lie awake at night thinking about it. It ought to be compulsory study for every detective constable, a warning of how a case can go wrong if the police get it fixed in their minds that it has to be the husband."

Which was all very well, thought Buckley, but in these cases, if the criminal statistics were to be believed, it usually was the husband. Grogan might be keeping an open mind, but he had no doubt whose name featured at the head of his list. He said, "They've got a cozy little setup here, the Munters."

"Haven't they just? Nothing to do but fuss around Gorringe while he concocts his little delicacies, polish the antique silver, and wait on each other. But he lied about at least one thing. Look back to that interview with Mrs. Chambers."

Buckley thumbed back through his notebook. Mrs. Chambers and her granddaughter had been two of the first interviewed, since the woman had demanded that she be returned to the mainland in time to cook her husband's supper. She had been voluble, aggrieved, and pugnacious, viewing the tragedy as one more trick of fate designed to cause domestic inconvenience. What chiefly concerned her was the waste of food; who, she had demanded, was going to eat a supper prepared for over a hundred? Buckley had been interested, thirty minutes later, to watch her waddling down to the launch with her granddaughter, both lugging a couple of covered baskets. Some of the food, at least, would find its way down the gullets of the Chambers family. She and her granddaughter, a cheerful seventeen-year-old apt to giggle in moments of emotion, had been busy, for the most part together or with Mrs. Munter, for the whole of the critical time. Buckley privately thought that Grogan had wasted too much time on them and had resented having to record the woman's spate of irrelevancies. He found the page at last and began to read, wondering if the old man was checking up on the accuracy of his shorthand.

" 'It's disgusting, that's what it is! I always say there's nothing worse than being killed away from home and by strangers. There never was anything like this when I was a girl. It's them mods on their motorcycles, that's who it is. Great crowd of them came roaring into Speymouth last Saturday with their noisy, smelly machines. Why don't the police do something about it? That's what I want to know. Why don't you take their machines away and chuck them off the end of the pier, and their trousers too? That'd put a stop to it fast enough. Don't you waste time interviewing decent law-abiding women. Go after them motorcycling mods.' "

Buckley broke off. "That's where you pointed out that even mods could hardly motorcycle to Courcy Island, and she replied darkly that they had their little ways, they were that cunning."

Grogan said, "Not that part. A little earlier when she was rabbiting on about the domestic arrangements."

Buckley flipped back a couple of pages. " 'I'm always happy to oblige Mr. Munter. I don't mind coming to the island for the odd day and bringing Debbie if wanted. And it wasn't the girl's fault if the glasses were smeary. They've no right to send them out like that. And Mr. Munter had no call to go on at Debbie like he did. It's always the same when Lady Ralston's here. He gets his knickers in a twist when she's about, no mistake. We were here last Tuesday for the dress rehearsal and you never heard such goings-on. Asking for this, asking for the other, nothing quite to her ladyship's liking. And forty of the cast for lunch and tea, if you please. Everything had to be just so even if Mr. Gorringe wasn't here. Took himself off to London, Mr. Munter said, and I don't know as I blame him. Anyone would think she was mistress here. I said to Mr. Munter, I don't mind helping out this time, but if you're going to be stuck with this palaver next year you can count me out. That's what I said. Count me out. And he said not to worry. He reckoned that this would be the last play Lady Ralston would appear in on Courcy Island.' "

Buckley stopped reading and looked at Grogan. He told himself that he should have remembered that piece of evidence. He must have taken it down in a fugue of boredom. Black mark. His chief said quietly, "Yes, that's it. That's the passage I wanted. I'll be asking Munter for an explanation of that remark when the time's right, but not yet. It's as well to keep a few unpleasant shocks in hand. I've no doubt that Mrs. Munter will be equally discreet when she obligingly confirms her husband's story. But we'll let the lady wait. I think it's time to hear what Miss Lisle's host has to say for himself. You're a local man, Sergeant. What do you know of him?"

"Very little, sir. He opens the castle to visitors in the summer, but I imagine it's a ploy to get tax relief on the maintenance. He keeps himself to himself, discourages publicity.''

''Does he now? He'll get a bellyful of it before this case is finished. Put your head outside and ask Rogers to summon him, with, of course, the usual compliments.''

6

BUCKLEY THOUGHT that he had never seen a murder suspect as much at ease under questioning as Ambrose Gorringe. He sat back in the chair opposite Grogan, immaculate in his dinner jacket, and gazed across the desk with bright, interested eyes in which Buckley, occasionally glancing up from his notetaking, thought he could detect a gleam of amused contempt. Admittedly Gorringe was on his own ground, sitting, in fact, in his own chair. Buckley thought it rather a pity that the chief hadn't deprived him of this psychological advantage by bundling the lot of them off to Speymouth station. But Gorringe was too calm for his own good. If the husband didn't kill her, here for his money was a close runner-up.

Now being formally questioned for the first time, he repeated without discrepancies the facts he had first briefly told them when they arrived on the island. He had known Miss Lisle from childhood—both their fathers had been in the diplomatic service and had been stationed for a time at the same embassies—but they had lost touch in recent years and had seen very little of each other until he had inherited the island from his uncle in 1977. The next year they had met at a theatrical first night and she had been invited to the island. He couldn't now remember whether the suggestion had come from him or from Miss Lisle. From that visit and her enthusiasm for the Victorian theater flowed the decision to stage a play. He had known about the threatening messages since he had been with her when one of them was delivered, but she hadn't confided that they were still arriving, nor had she told him that Miss Gray was a private detective, although he had suspected that she might be when she had confronted him with the woodcut pushed under Miss Lisle's door. It had been their joint decision not to worry Miss Lisle either with that or with the news that the marble limb had been stolen. He admitted without apparent concern that he had no alibi for the crucial ninety-odd minutes between one-twenty and the discovery of the body. He had lingered over his coffee with Mr. Whittingham, gone to his room about one-thirty, leaving Whittingham on the terrace, had rested for about fifteen minutes until it was time to change, and had left his room to go to the theater shortly after two. Munter had been backstage and they had checked over the props together and discussed one or two matters relating to the after-show supper party. At about two-twenty they had gone together to meet the launch bringing the cast from Speymouth, and he had been backstage in the male dressing room until about two-forty-five.

Grogan said, "And the marble limb? That was last seen by you when?"

"Didn't I tell you, Chief Inspector? By me at about eleven-thirty last night when I went to check the tide timetable. I was interested to estimate how long the launches would take on Saturday afternoon and returning to Speymouth that night. The water can run strongly between here and the mainland. Munter saw the marble in place just after midnight.

I found that it was missing and the lock forced when I went to the kitchen at six-fifty-five this morning."

"And all the members of the house party had seen it and knew where it was kept?"

"All except Simon Lessing. He was swimming when the rest of the party were shown round the castle. As far as I know, he has never been near the business room."

Grogan asked, "What is the boy doing here, anyway? Shouldn't he be at school? I take it that Miss Lisle—Lady Ralston—was buying him a privileged education, that he isn't a day boy at the local comprehensive." The question could have sounded offensive, thought Buckley, if the carefully controlled voice had held a trace of emotion.

Gorringe replied, equally calmly, "He's at Melhurst. Miss Lisle wrote for special weekend leave. She may have thought that Webster's play would be educational. Unfortunately, the weekend has proved educational for the boy in ways she could hardly have foreseen."

"A proper little mother to him, was she?"

"Hardly that. Miss Lisle's maternal sense was, I should have thought, undeveloped. But within her capacity she genuinely cared for the boy. What you must understand about the victim in this case was that she enjoyed being kind, as indeed most of us do, provided it doesn't cost us too much."

"And how much did Mr. Lessing cost her?"

"His school fees primarily. About four thousand pounds a year I suppose. She could afford it. It all began, I imagine, because she had a conscience about breaking up his parents' marriage. If she did, it was quite unnecessary. The man had a choice presumably."

"Simon Lessing must have resented the marriage, on his mother's account if not his own. Unless, of course, he thought a rich stepmama a good exchange."

"It was six years ago. He was barely eleven when his father walked out on him. And if you're suggesting, without much subtlety I may say, that he resented it enough to bash in stepmama's face, then he waited long enough to do it and he chose a singularly inappropriate time. Does Sir George Ralston know that you suspect Simon? He probably considers himself the boy's stepfather. He'll want to take steps to see that the boy's interests are safeguarded if you're going on with that somewhat ridiculous idea.''

"I never said that we suspected him. And, in view of the boy's youth, I have agreed with Sir George that he shall be present when I speak to the boy. But Mr. Lessing is seventeen. He's no longer a juvenile in law. I find these concerted measures to protect him interesting.''

"As long as you don't find them sinister. He was extremely shocked when I broke the news to him. His own parents are dead. He was devoted to Clarissa. It's natural that we should wish to minimize his pain. After all, you're hardly here in the capacity of child-care officers.''

Grogan had scarcely glanced at his witness during this exchange. The unlined note pad which he preferred to the normal police issue was on the desk blotter in front of him, and he was sketching with his fountain pen. A careful oblong shape with two doors and two windows took shape under the huge speckled hand. Buckley saw that it was a representation of Clarissa Lisle's bedroom, something between a plan and a drawing. The proportions of the room were drawn carefully to scale, but small objects were being inserted, overlarge and carefully detailed, as a child might draw them: the jars of cosmetics, a box of cotton-wool balls, the tea tray, the alarm clock.

Suddenly and still without looking up, he asked, "What made you go to her room, sir?"

"Just after Miss Gray went to call her? Merely a chivalrous impulse. I thought that, as her host, it would be seemly if I escorted her to her dressing room. And there were things to be carried. Her makeup case for one. As we haven't much dressing-room accommodation and she was having to share with Miss Collingwood, who plays Cariola, Miss Collingwood had undertaken to be dressed and out before the star wanted the room, but Miss Lisle wasn't going to risk anyone borrowing her grease-paint. So I went to carry the box and escort the lady.''

"In the absence of her husband, who would normally perform that service?"

"Sir George had just come in to change. We met at the top of the stairs as I've already explained."

"You seem to have taken a lot of trouble for Miss Lisle." He paused and added, "One way or another."

"Walking her two hundred yards from her room to the theater hardly counts as trouble."

"But putting on the play for her, restoring the theater, entertaining her guests. It must have been an expensive business."

"I'm not a poor man, happily. And I thought that you were here to investigate a murder, not to inquire into my finances. The theater, incidentally, was restored for my satisfaction, not Miss Lisle's."

"She wasn't hoping that you might partly finance her next professional appearance? What's the theatrical jargon, be her angel?"

"I'm afraid you've been gossiping with the wrong people. That particular angelic role has never attracted me. There are more amusing ways of losing money. But if you're trying tactfully to suggest that I may have owed Miss Lisle a favor, you're perfectly right. It was she who gave me the idea for *Autopsy*, my best-seller, in case you're one of the half dozen who haven't heard of it."

"She didn't write it for you, by any chance?"

"No, she didn't write it. Miss Lisle's talents were varied and egregious but they didn't extend to the written word. The book was fabricated rather than written by an unholy triumvirate of my publisher, my agent, and myself. It was then suitably packaged, promoted, and marketed. No doubt there are sins to be laid to Clarissa's charge, but *Autopsy* isn't one of them.''

Grogan let his pen drop from his hand. He leaned back in his chair and looked at Gorringe full in the face. He said quietly, ''You knew Miss Lisle from childhood. For the last six months or so you've been intimately concerned with this play. She came here as your guest. She was killed under your roof. However she died—and we shan't know until after the postmortem—the killer almost certainly used your marble to bash in her face. Are you sure that there is nothing you know, nothing you suspect, nothing she ever said to you, that can throw any light on how she died?''

Put it any plainer, thought Buckley, and you'd have to be administering an official caution. He half expected Gorringe to reply that he would say nothing until he had seen his lawyer. But he spoke with the calm unconcern of a disinterested party who has been asked for his considered opinion and has no objection to giving it.

''My first thought—and it remains my theory—was that a trespasser had somehow gained access to the island, knowing that my staff and I would be busy with preparations for the play and that the castle would be, as it were, undefended. He climbed up the fire escape, perhaps out of mischief or devilment and with no clear idea of what he meant to do. It could have been a young man.''

''The young usually hunt in gangs.''

''Several young men, then. Or a couple if you prefer it. One of them gets in with the general idea of a prowl round while the house is quiet. That supposes a local boy, one who knew about the play. He creeps into Miss Lisle's room—she had forgotten to lock the communicating door or had thought the precaution unnecessary—and sees her apparently asleep on the bed. He is about to make his exit, with or without the jewel case, when she takes the pads off her eyes and sees him. In a panic he kills her, seizes the box, and makes his escape the same way as he came in.''

Grogan said, "Having thoughtfully provided himself in advance with the marble hand, which according to your evidence must have been taken from the display case between midnight and six-fifty-five this morning."

"No, I don't think he came provided with anything except a general intention of mischief. My theory is that he found the weapon ready to hand—forgive the atrocious pun—on the bedside table, together, of course, with the quotation from the play."

"And who are you suggesting put them there? The door to that room was locked, remember."

"I don't think there's much mystery about that, surely. Miss Lisle did."

Grogan said, "With the object of frightening herself into hysteria, or merely of providing any potential murderer who might drop in with a convenient weapon?"

"With the object of providing herself with an excuse if she failed in the play. As I'm afraid she almost certainly would. Or she may have had more devious reasons. Miss Lisle's complex personality was something of a mystery to me, as it was, I suspect, to her husband."

"And are you suggesting that this young, impulsive, unpremeditating killer then replaced the pads over his victim's eyes? That argues we have two complex personalities to elucidate."

"He could have done. You're the expert on murder, not I. But I could think of a reason if pushed. Perhaps she seemed to be staring up at him and his nerve broke. He had to cover those dead, accusing eyes. The suggestion is a little overimaginative, perhaps, but not impossible. Murderers do behave oddly. Remember the Gutteridge case, Chief Inspector."

Buckley's hand jerked on his shorthand pad. He thought, My God, is he doing it on purpose? The small audacity must surely have been deliberate. But how could Gorringe have learned of the chief's habit of referring to old cases? He glanced up, not at Grogan, but at Gorringe, and met only a look of bland innocence. And it was to him that Gorringe spoke.

"Long before your time, Sergeant. Gutteridge was the police constable shot by two car thieves in an Essex country lane in 1927. An ex-convict, Frederick Browne, and his accomplice, William Kennedy, were hanged for the crime. After killing the man, one of the thugs shot out both his eyes. It is thought that they were superstitious. They believed that the dead eyes of a murdered man, fixed on the killer's face, will bear his visage imprinted on the pupils. I doubt whether any murderer willingly looks into his victim's eyes. An interesting feature of an otherwise dull and sordid case."

Grogan had finished his drawing. The plan of the room was complete. Now, while they watched him in silence, he drew on the great bed a small sprawled matchbox figure with wisps of hair over the pillow. Last and with care, he blocked in the face. Then he put his great hand over the drawing and ripped out the page, crumpling it in his fist. The gesture was unexpectedly violent, but his voice was quiet, almost gentle.

"Thank you, sir. You've been very helpful. And now, if you've nothing else to tell us, no doubt you'll be wanting to go back to your guests."

7

When Ivo Whittingham came into the room, Buckley, embarrassed, looked quickly down and began flipping back the pages of his notebook, hoping that Whittingham hadn't caught his first look of horror and surprise. Only once before had he seen so gaunt a figure, and that was his Uncle Gerry in those last weeks before the cancer finally got him. He had felt as much affection for his uncle as he was capable of feeling, and the protracted agony of his dying had left him with one resolution: if that was what the body could do to a man, it owed something in return. From now on he would take his pleasures without guilt. He might have become a cheerful hedonist if ambition and the caution which went with it hadn't been stronger. But he hadn't forgotten either the bitterness or the pain. And Ivo Whittingham reminded him in another way. His uncle had looked at him with just such glittering eyes as if they burned with all that remained of life and intelligence. He glanced up as Whittingham seated him-

259

self, stiffly grasping the chair sides with skeletal hands. But when he spoke his voice was surprisingly strong and relaxed.

"This is unpleasantly reminiscent of a summons to one's housemaster. Good seldom came of it."

It was an irreverent beginning which Grogan was unlikely to encourage. He said curtly, "In that case I suggest that we make it as brief as possible. I take it that you knew Miss Lisle well."

"You may take it that I knew her intimately."

"Are you telling me, sir, that she was your mistress?"

"That hardly seems the right word for so spasmodic a liaison. *Mistress* suggests a certain permanence, even a measure of respectability. One is reminded of dear Mrs. Keppel and her king. It would be more accurate to say that we were lovers for a period of about six years as opportunity and her whim dictated."

"And did her husband know?"

"Husbands. Our relationship outlasted more than one marital episode. But I imagine that you're interested only in George Ralston. I never told him. I don't know whether she did. And if you're wondering whether he took his revenge, the idea is ludicrous. Why should he wait until a higher power, or fate or luck, whatever you choose to believe in, is about to rid him of me permanently? Ralston isn't a fool. And if you would like to ask whether I sent the lady on before me, the answer is no. Clarissa Lisle and I had exhausted each other's possibilities on this bank and shoal of time. But I could have killed her. I had the opportunity; I was alone in my room conveniently close all afternoon. In case you haven't already inquired, it's on the same floor as Clarissa's, a mere fifty feet away, overlooking the eastern front of the castle. I had access to the means since I had been shown the marble limb. I suppose I could have found the strength. And I think she might have opened her door to me. But I didn't kill her and I don't know who did. You'll have to take my word for it. I can't prove my innocence."

"Tell me what she was like." It was the first time Grogan had asked that question. And yet, thought Buckley, it was at the heart of every murder investigation. If it were possible to find the answer, most other questions would become superfluous.

Whittingham said, "I was going to say that you've seen her face, but, of course, you haven't. A pity. One needed to know the physical Clarissa to get any clue to what else there might have been to know. She lived intensely in and through her body. The rest is a list of words. She was egocentric, insecure, clever but not intelligent, kind of cruel as the mood took her, restless, unhappy. But she had certain skills which a gentlemanly reticence inhibits me from discussing but which weren't unimportant. She probably gave more joy than she caused misery. Since that can't be said of many of us, it's unbecoming of me to criticize her. I remember that I once sent to her the words Sir Thomas Malory has Lancelot speak to Guinevere: 'Lady, I take record of God, in thee I have had my earthly joy.' I don't take them back, whatever she may have done."

"Whatever she may have done, sir?"

"A form of words merely, Chief Inspector."

"So you mourn her?"

"No. But I shan't forget her."

There was a pause. Then Grogan asked quietly, "Why are you here, sir?"

"She asked me to come. But there was another reason. One of the Sunday papers commissioned me to do a piece on the island and the theater. What was wanted was period charm, nostalgia, and salacious legend. They should have sent a crime reporter."

"And that was enough to tempt a reviewer of your eminence?"

"It must have been, mustn't it, since here I am."

When Grogan asked him, as he had the other suspects, to describe the events of the day, Whittingham showed signs of tiredness for the first time. The body sagged in its chair like a puppet jerked from its string.

"There isn't much to tell. We had a late breakfast and then Miss Lisle suggested we see the church. There's a crypt with some ancient skulls and a secret passage to the sea. We explored both and Gorringe entertained us with old legends about the skulls and a reputed drowning of a wartime internee in the cave at the end of the passage. I was tired and didn't listen very closely. Then back to luncheon at twelve. Miss Lisle went to rest immediately afterward. I was in my room by quarter past one and stayed there, resting and reading, until it was time to dress. Miss Lisle had insisted that we change before the play. I met Roma Lisle at the head of the staircase as she came down from her room, and we were together when Gorringe appeared with Miss Gray and told us that Clarissa was dead."

"And during the morning, the visit to the church and the cave, how did Miss Lisle seem to you?"

"I think I would say, Chief Inspector, that Miss Lisle was her usual self."

Last Grogan spilled out from the folder the sheaf of messages. One of them fluttered to the floor. He bent and picked it up, then handed it to Whittingham.

"What can you tell us about these, sir?"

"Only that I knew she was getting them. She didn't tell me, but one does tend to pick up bits of theater gossip. Still, I don't think it was generally known. And here, again, I seem to be the natural suspect. Whoever sent these knew Miss Lisle and knew his Shakespeare. But I don't think I would have added the coffin and the skull. An unnecessarily crude touch, don't you think?"

"And that is all that you want to tell us, sir?"

"It's all that I can tell you, Chief Inspector."

8

IT WAS NEARLY SEVEN O'CLOCK before they got around to seeing the boy. He had changed into a formal suit and looked, thought Buckley, as if he were on the way to his stepmother's funeral instead of an interview with the police. He guessed that there was no more than eight years' difference between his age and the boy's, but it could have been twenty. Lessing looked as neatly pressed and nervous as a child. But he had himself well under control. Buckley felt that there was something vaguely familiar about his entrance, the care with which he seated himself, the serious, expectant gaze which he fixed on Grogan's face. And then he remembered. This was how he himself had looked and behaved at his final interview to join the police. He had been advised by his headmaster: "Wear your best suit, but no fountain pen or fancy handkerchief peeping coyly out of the jacket pocket. Look them straight in the eye, but not so fixedly that you embarrass them. Be slightly more deferential than you feel; they're the

ones with the job on offer. If you don't know an answer, say
so, don't waffle. And don't worry if you're nervous, they
prefer that to overconfidence, but show that you've got the
guts to cope with nervousness. Call them 'sir' or 'madam'
and thank them briefly before you leave. And for God's sake,
boy, sit up straight.''

And as the interview progressed beyond the first easy
questions, designed, Buckley could almost believe, to put the
candidate at his ease, he sensed something else, that Lessing
was beginning to feel as he had done: if you follow the
advice, the ordeal isn't so bad after all. Only his hands
betrayed him. They were broad and unpleasantly white with
thick, stubbed fingers but narrow, almost girlish nails cut very
short and so pink that they looked painted. He held his hands
in his lap, and from time to time he would stretch and pull at
the fingers as if he were routinely performing some pre-
scribed strengthening exercise.

Sir George Ralston remained standing with his back to
them, looking out the window through the partly drawn
curtains. Buckley wondered whether the intention was to
demonstrate that he wasn't influencing the boy by word or
glance. But the pose looked perverse, the more so as there
was nothing in that still darkness which he could possibly
see. Buckley had never known such silence. It had a positive
quality; not the absence of noise but a silence which sharpened
perception and gave importance and dignity to every word
and action. He wished, not for the first time, that they were at
headquarters with the sound of passing feet, of doors closing,
of distant voices calling, all the comfortable background
noises of ordinary life. Here it wasn't only the suspects who
were under judgment.

This time Grogan's doodle looked innocuous, even charming. He seemed to be redesigning his kitchen garden. Neat
rows of chubby cabbages, climbing runner beans, and fern-
topped carrots grew under his hand. He said, ''So after your
mother died you went to live with her brother and his family,

and you were there when Lady Ralston came to visit you in the summer of 1978 and decided to adopt you?''

"There was no formal adoption. My uncle was my guardian and he agreed that Clarissa would be . . . well, a kind of foster mother, I suppose. She took over the whole responsibility for me.''

"And you welcomed that arrangement?''

"Very much, sir. Life with my uncle and aunt wasn't really congenial to me.''

That was an odd word for the boy to use, thought Buckley. It made it sound as if they'd taken the *Mirror* instead of the *Times* and he hadn't been able to get his after-dinner port.

"And you were happy with Sir George and his wife?'' Grogan couldn't resist the small note of sarcasm. He added, "Life was congenial to you?''

"Very, sir.''

"Your stepmother—is that how you thought of her, as a stepmother?''

The boy blushed and glanced sideways at the silent figure of Sir George. He moistened his lips and said, "Yes, sir. I suppose so.''

"Your stepmother has been receiving some rather unpleasant communications during the last year or so. What do you know about that?''

"Nothing, sir. She didn't tell me.'' He added, "We don't . . . we didn't see a great deal of each other. I'm at school and she was often at the Brighton flat during the holidays.''

Grogan pulled one of the messages from his file and pushed it over the desk.

"That's a sample. Recognize it?''

"No, sir. It's a quotation, isn't it? Is it Shakespeare?''

"You tell me, lad. You're the one at Melhurst. But you've never seen one of these before?''

"No, never.''

"Right, then. Suppose you tell us exactly what you did between one o'clock today and two-forty-five."

Lessing looked down at his hands, seemed to become aware of his nervous methodical stretching, and grasped both sides of his chair as if to prevent himself from springing to his feet. But he gave his account lucidly and with growing confidence. He had decided to swim before the play and had gone straight to his room after lunch, where he had put on his swimming trunks under his jeans and shirt. He had taken his jersey and towel and made his way across the lawn to the shore. He had walked on the beach for about an hour because Clarissa had warned him not to swim too soon after his meal. He had then returned to the small cove just beyond the terrace and had entered the water at about two o'clock or shortly after, leaving his clothes, towel, and wristwatch on the shore. He had seen no one during either his walk or his swim, but Sir George had told him that he had watched him coming ashore through his binoculars when he himself was returning to the castle after his bird-watching. Here he again glanced around at his stepfather as if inviting corroboration and again got no response.

Grogan said, "So Sir George Ralston has told us. And what then?"

"Well, nothing really, sir. I was on my way back to the castle when Mr. Gorringe saw me and came to meet me. He told me about Clarissa." The last few words were almost a whisper.

Grogan bent his ruddy head forward and asked softly, "And what exactly did he tell you?"

"That she was dead, sir. Murdered."

"And did he explain how?"

Again the whisper. "No, sir."

"But you asked, presumably? You betrayed some natural curiosity?"

"I asked him what had happened, how she had died. He said that no one could be sure until after the postmortem."

"He's right. There's nothing you need to know except the fact that she is dead, and that it must have been homicide. And now, Mr. Lessing, what can you tell us about the arm of the dead princess?"

Buckley thought that Sir George gave an exclamation of protest; but he still didn't interrupt.

The boy looked from face to face as if the police had gone mad. No one spoke. Then he said, "You mean in the church? We visited the crypt to see the skulls this morning. But Mr. Gorringe didn't say anything about a dead princess."

"It wasn't in the church."

"You mean it's a mummified arm? I don't understand."

"It's a marble arm, a limb to be accurate. A baby's limb. Someone has taken it from Mr. Gorringe's display case, the one outside this door, and we'd rather like to know who and when."

"I don't think I've seen it, sir. I'm sorry."

Grogan had completed his kitchen garden and was separating it from the lawn by a trellis and archway. He looked up at Lessing and said, "My officers and I will be back here tomorrow. We'll probably be around for a day or two. If there's anything that occurs to you, anything that you remember which is the least unusual or likely to help, however small and unimportant it seems, I want you to get in touch. Understand?"

"Yes, sir. Thank you, sir."

Grogan nodded and the boy got to his feet, glanced for the last time at the still back of Sir George, and went out. Buckley almost expected him to turn at the door and ask whether he'd got the job.

Sir George turned at last.

"He's due back at school on Monday morning before midday. Special leave. I take it he can go."

Grogan said, "It would be helpful to us, sir, if he could stay until Tuesday morning. It's just a question of convenience. If anything does occur to him or to us, it would be helpful to be able to clear it up quickly. But obviously he can go early on Monday if you think it important."

Sir George hesitated. "Don't suppose a day will make much odds. Better for him, though, to be away from here, back at work. I'll get in touch with the school tomorrow or Monday. He'll need leave later for the funeral, but I suppose it's too early yet to think about that."

"I'm afraid so, sir."

Sir George was almost at the door when Grogan called softly, "There's one other thing, sir, which I have to ask. Your relationship with your wife. Would you say that yours was a happy marriage?"

The slim, upright figure paused for a second, hand on the doorknob. Then Sir George turned to face them. His face was twitching violently, like that of a man afflicted with a nervous spasm. Then he controlled himself.

"I find that question offensive, Chief Inspector."

Grogan's voice was still gentle, dangerously gentle. "In a murder investigation, we sometimes have to ask questions which people find offensive."

"It's meaningless unless you ask both parties. Too late for that now. Not sure that my wife had the capacity for happiness."

"And you, sir?"

He answered with great simplicity. "I loved her."

9

AFTER HE HAD GONE, Grogan said with sudden vehemence, "Let's pack up and get out of this place. It's getting claustrophobic. What time is the launch expected with Roper and Badgett?"

Buckley looked at his watch. "It should be here within fifteen minutes."

Detective Constables Roper and Badgett were to be on duty in the business room but for one night only. Their presence was almost a formality. No one at the castle had asked for police protection, nor did Grogan believe that they were in need of it. He had few enough officers without wasting manpower. The whole of the island including the secret passage to the Devil's Kettle had been searched; if the theory of the casual intruder were true, it was apparent that he wasn't now on Courcy. Tomorrow the police inquiries on the island would be complete and the investigation moved to an incident room at the Speymouth station. It was likely, thought

Buckley, to be a tedious and less than comfortable vigil for Roper and Badgett. Ambrose Gorringe had offered a bedroom and had said that the two officers should ring Munter for anything they needed. But Grogan's instructions had been clear.

"You'll bring your own flasks and sandwiches, lads, and ring for no one. You'll be beholden to Mr. Gorringe for nothing but his light and heating and the water that flushes his bog."

He pulled the bell cord. It seemed to Buckley that Munter took his time in coming.

Grogan said, "Will you tell Mr. Gorringe that we're now leaving?"

"Yes, sir. The police launch isn't yet sighted, sir."

"I'm aware of that. We shall wait for it on the quay."

When the man had gone, he said irritably, "What does he think we propose to do? Walk on water?" Ambrose Gorringe arrived within minutes to see them off the premises with formal courtesy. They might, thought Buckley, have been a couple of dinner guests, if not particularly welcome or agreeable ones. He said nothing about the event that had brought them to Courcy and made no inquiries about the progress of the investigation. Clarissa Lisle's murder might have been an embarrassing mishap in an otherwise not unsuccessful day.

It was good to be in the air again. The night was extraordinarily balmy for mid-September, and there still seemed to rise from the stones of the terrace a genial warmth like the last breath of a summer day. Briefcases in hand, they strolled together along the eastern arm of the quay. Turning to retrace their steps, they could see in the distance a stream of light from the dining-room windows and dark figures moving to and fro on the terrace, joining and then parting, pausing and then walking on as if taking part in a pavane. It looked to Buckley as if they had plates in their hands. Probably making do with the cold leftover party food, he thought, and some irrelevant quotation about baked funeral meats came into his mind. He didn't blame them for not wanting to sit together around a table, faced with one empty chair.

He and Grogan settled themselves under the canopy of the bandstand to wait for the first lights of the launch. The peace of the night was seductive. Here on the southern shore where the mainland couldn't be seen, it was easy to imagine that the island was totally isolated in a waste of sea, that they were waiting and watching for the masts of some overdue relief ship, and that the figures gliding on the terrace were the ghosts of long-dead settlers, that the castle itself was a shell, hall and library and drawing room open to the sky, the great staircase rising into nothingness, ferns and weeds pushing their way between the broken tiles. He wasn't normally imaginative, but now he deliberately indulged his tiredness by letting his mind elaborate the fantasy while he sat gently massaging his right wrist.

Grogan's voice broke harshly into the reverie. Neither the peace nor the beauty had touched him. His thoughts were still on the case. Buckley told himself that he should have known there would be no respite. He remembered the overheard comment of a detective inspector: "Red Rufus treats a murder investigation like a love affair. Gets obsessed with his suspects. Moves into their lives. Lives and breathes with the case, edgy and restless and frustrated, until it climaxes at the arrest." Buckley wondered if that was one of the reasons for his failed marriage. It must be disconcerting to live with a man who, for most of the night as well as the day, simply wasn't there.

When Grogan spoke his voice was as vigorous as if the inquiry had just begun.

"Miss Roma Lisle, cousin of the deceased, aged forty-five, shopkeeper, ex-schoolmistress, unmarried. What struck you most about the lady, Sergeant?"

Buckley dragged his mind back to the interview with Roma Lisle.

"That she was frightened, sir."

"Frightened, defensive, embarrassed, and unconvincing. Consider her story. She admits that the woodcut is hers and says that she brought it to Courcy because she thought that Ambrose Gorringe would be interested in it and would be able to advise her about its age and value. As he doesn't claim to be an authority on early seventeenth-century manuscripts, the hope was optimistic. Still, we needn't read too much into that. She found the thing, she thought it was interesting, and she brought it with her. And now for today. She tells us that she left her cousin's bedroom at about five minutes past one, went straight to the library, and stayed there until half past two when she went up to her room. It's on the floor immediately above the gallery and she didn't have to pass Miss Lisle's room to get to it. She saw and heard no one. During the hour and twenty minutes when she was in the library she was alone. Miss Gray briefly put her head round the door at about twenty past one but didn't stay. Miss Lisle remained in the library, expecting a private business call from her partner, which didn't, in fact, come through. She tells us that she also wrote a letter. Asked to produce it as a small indication of verisimilitude—not that it greatly matters—she blushes with embarrassment and says that she decided not to send it after all and tore it up. When we gently point out that there are no fragments in the library wastepaper basket she becomes even redder and confides that she took the scraps with her when she went to her room and flushed them down the W.C. All very curious. But consider something even odder. She was one of the last people to see her cousin alive; not the last, but one of the last. And she tells us that she followed Miss Lisle up to her room because she wanted to wish her good luck in the play. All very proper and cousinly. But when we point out that she'd left it rather late to get changed, she tells us that she'd decided to give the performance a miss. Would you care to propound a theory which would explain these intriguing eccentricities of behavior?"

"She was expecting a telephone call from her lover, sir,

not necessarily her partner. When it didn't come, she decided to write to him. Then she thought better of it and tore up the letter. She retrieved the fragments from the wastepaper basket because she didn't want us piecing them together and reading her private correspondence, however innocuous."

"Ingenious, Sergeant. But you see where it leaves us. At the time when, according to her, she took those scraps upstairs she couldn't have known that the police would be here to poke their inquisitive noses into anyone's private correspondence, not unless she also knew by then that her cousin was dead."

"And that last visit to Miss Lisle?"

Grogan said, "My guess is that it was less friendly than she makes out."

"But why tell us about the letter, sir? She didn't have to. Why not just say that she spent the time in the library, reading?"

"Because she's a woman who normally tells the truth. She made no pretense, for example, of liking her cousin, or being particularly grieved by her death. If she is going to lie to the police, she prefers to lie as little as possible. That way she has fewer untruths to remember and is able to persuade herself that, essentially, she isn't really lying at all. It's a sound enough principle as far as it goes. But we shouldn't read too much into that torn-up letter. She may merely have wanted to save the servants trouble, or have been afraid that they might have been curious enough to piece it together. And if Miss Roma Lisle's story is less than convincing, it's not the only one. Consider the curious reticence of the lady's maid. It sounds like the chapter heading for one of those snobbish thirties thrillers."

Buckley thought back over the interview with Rose Tolgarth. Before she had come in, Grogan had said to him, "You question the lady, Sergeant. She may prefer youth to experience. Give her a treat."

Surprised, Buckley had asked, "At the desk, sir?"

"That would seem the obvious place, unless you intend to prowl round her like a predator."

Grogan himself had greeted her and invited her to sit with more courtesy than he had shown Cordelia Gray or Roma Lisle. If she was surprised to find herself facing the younger of the two officers, she hadn't shown it. But, then, she hadn't shown anything. She had gazed at him with her remarkable eyes, with their smudgy black irises, as if she were looking into . . . what? he wondered. Not his soul, since he didn't believe that he had one, but certainly into some part of his mind which wasn't intended to be public property. All his questions had been answered politely but with the minimum of words. She had admitted that she knew about the threatening messages but refused to speculate about who might have sent them. That job, she implied, was the responsibility of the police. It was she who had made and taken up Miss Lisle's tea before she settled for her usual pre-performance rest. The routine was always the same. Miss Lisle drank Lapsang Souchong tea with no milk or sugar but with two thick slices of lemon put into the teapot before the boiling water was poured in. She had made the tea in the usual way in Mr. Munter's pantry, and Mrs. Chambers and Debbie had been with her at the time. She had taken up the tray immediately and at no time had the teapot been out of her sight. Sir George had been in the bedroom with his wife. She had placed the tea tray on the bedside cabinet and had then gone into the bathroom where there was a certain amount of tidying to be done before Miss Lisle took her bath. She had returned to the bedroom to help her mistress undress and had found Miss Gray there. After Miss Gray had returned to her own room, Sir George had left his wife and she herself had followed almost immediately afterward. She had spent the afternoon preparing the ladies' dressing room backstage and helping Mrs. Munter with the arrangements for the party. At two-forty-five she had become concerned in case Miss Gray had forgotten to call Miss Lisle and had gone herself. She had met Sir George, Mr. Gorringe, and Miss Gray outside the bedroom and had then learned of Miss Lisle's death.

They had taken her up to the bedroom and asked her to look around carefully, but without touching anything, and say whether the room was as she would expect to find it, whether there was anything which struck her as unusual. She had shaken her head. Before leaving she had stood for a moment gazing over the chaise longue, the stripped and empty bed, with a look which Buckley couldn't fathom. Sadness? Speculation? Resignation? The right word eluded him. Her eyes were open but he thought he saw her lips moving. For a moment he had the extraordinary idea that she might be praying.

Back in the business room he had asked, "You were happy working for Miss Lisle? You liked each other?" That was as tactful a way as he knew of asking whether she had hated her employer enough to bash in her skull.

She had replied quietly, "We were used to each other. My mother was her nurse. She asked me to look after her."

"And you can't think of a reason why anyone should want to kill her? All one big happy family, were they?"

The attempt at Grogan-like sarcasm had been unsuccessful. She had met it with a brand of her own.

"There's never a good reason for people to kill each other, even in happy families."

He had had little more success with Mrs. Munter. She, too, had been a polite but unrewarding witness, saying as little as possible, resisting all his blandishments to entice her into volubility or indiscretion. Ambrose Gorringe had concealed his secrets, if any, with a spate of apparently artless conjecture. Miss Tolgarth and Mrs. Munter had concealed theirs with a silence and obstinacy which just avoided being overtly uncooperative. Buckley thought that Grogan could hardly have selected two more difficult witnesses for him to practice interrogation on. Perhaps that had been the idea. The impression they apparently wanted to convey was that murder, like most of the world's violence, was a male concern from which, as women, they were only too happy to be excluded. From time to time he had found himself staring at them with what he was uncomfortably aware must have been obvious frustration. But human beings weren't like school geometry problems. If you stared at them long enough, they didn't suddenly make sense.

He said, "Miss Tolgarth admits that she didn't leave Miss Lisle until after Sir George had gone, and that accords with his evidence. Miss Gray was in her own room, so nobody saw Miss Tolgarth leave. She could have returned to the bathroom, pretended to busy herself with preparations for the bath, come back into the bedroom when Gray left, and killed her mistress then."

"The timing would be very tight, Mrs. Munter saw her downstairs in the pantry at one-twenty."

"So she says. I got the feeling, sir, that those two are standing together. I got precious little out of either of them, Rose Tolgarth in particular."

"Except one highly interesting lie. Unless, of course, the lady is less sharp-eyed than I give her credit for."

"Sir?"

"In the bedroom, Sergeant. Think. You asked her if everything looked as she would expect to find it. Her answer was a nod. But visualize that dressing table. What among all that female clutter was missing, something which we would have expected to see, given the things which, in fact, we did see?"

But the launch bringing Roper and Badgett had actually touched the quay before Buckley was able to work out the answer to the conundrum.

10

AND NOW, AT LAST, the dreadful day was over. Soon after ten
o'clock struck, one by one and with brief "Good nights,"
they had crept silently to their beds. The casual nighttime
commonplaces had become unsayable. "I'm terribly tired.
It's been a long day. Sleep well. See you all in the morning"
—all bore a weight of innuendo, tactlessness, or bad taste.
Two women police officers had moved Cordelia's things from
the De Morgan room, a touch of delicacy which would have
amused her had she been capable of being amused. The new
bedroom was on the same gallery floor but on the other side
of Simon's and overlooking the rose garden and the pool. As
she turned the key in the lock and breathed the stuffy, scented
air, Cordelia thought that it might not often be used. It was
small, dim, and cluttered and looked as if Ambrose had
furnished it strictly in period for the edification of his summer
visitors. The lightness and delicacy which he had achieved in
so much of the castle was absent. Every square inch of the

walls was covered with pictures and ornaments, and the ornate furniture, papier-mâché lined with mahogany, seemed to press in on her, dark and threatening. The room felt musty, but when she opened wide the window the sound of the sea burst in, no longer soporific and comforting but a steady menacing roar. She lay wondering whether she could summon up the energy to get out of bed and half close the window. But that was her last conscious thought before weariness took over and she felt herself drifting unresistingly down the long stream of tiredness into sleep.

BOOK FIVE

TERROR
BY
MOONLIGHT

1

AT NINE-FIFTEEN Cordelia went into the business room to ring
Miss Maudsley, wondering as she lifted the receiver whether
the police would be listening in. But monitoring private
telephone calls, even from the scene of a murder, counted as
phone tapping and for that the consent of the Home Secretary
was surely necessary. It was strange how little she knew about
a real police investigation despite Bernie's tutelage. It had
already struck her that their legal powers were a great deal
less extensive than a reading of detective fiction might suggest. On the other hand, their physical presence was far more
frightening and oppressive than she would have believed
possible. It was like having mice in the house. They might for
a time be both silent and invisible, but once they were known
to be there, it was impossible to ignore their secret and
polluting presence. Even here in the business room the force
of Inspector Grogan's rebarbative personality still lingered,
although all trace of his brief occupation had been cleared

away. It seemed to her that the police had left the room tidier than they had found it, and this in itself was sinister. As she dialed the London number it was difficult to believe that the call would go unrecorded.

It was a nuisance that Miss Maudsley in her cheap bed-sittingroom had no private telephone. The single instrument was in the darkest and most inaccessible corner of the hall at Mancroft Mansions, and Cordelia knew that she might have to wait for minutes until one of the other residents, driven mad by the insistent ring, came out to silence it. She would then be lucky if he understood English and luckier still if he were willing to trudge up four flights to call Miss Maudsley. But this morning her call was answered almost immediately. Miss Maudsley confided that she had bought her usual Sunday paper on the way home from eight o'clock mass and had been crouching on the bottom step of the stairs wondering whether to ring the castle or to wait for Cordelia's call. She was almost incoherent with anxiety and distress, and the brevity of the press report hadn't helped. Cordelia thought how chagrined Clarissa would be to learn that her fame, even after a violent death, didn't justify top billing on a day when a spectacular parliamentary scandal, the death of a pop star from a drug overdose, and a particularly brutal terrorist attack in northern Italy had presented the editor with a surplus of candidates for the front page.

Miss Maudsley, her voice breaking, said, "It says that she was . . . well . . . battered to death. I can't believe it. And it's so horrible for you. Her husband, too, of course. That poor woman. But naturally one thinks of the living. I suppose it was some kind of intruder. The paper does say that her jewelry is missing. I do hope that the police won't get any wrong ideas."

And that, thought Cordelia, was as tactful a way as any of saying that she hoped that Cordelia herself wasn't under suspicion.

Cordelia gave her instructions slowly, and Miss Maudsley made audible attempts to calm herself and listen.

"The police will be sure to check up on me and on the agency. I don't know the procedure, whether someone will call from the Dorset C.I.D. or whether they'll get the Met to do it for them. But don't worry. Just answer their questions."

"Oh, dear, yes, I suppose we must. But it's all so dreadful. Am I to show them everything? Suppose they ask to see the accounts? I did balance the petty cash on Friday afternoon, as least it didn't balance exactly, I'm afraid. Mr. Morgan, a delightful man, came to fix the name plaque. He said that he'd leave the bill until you got back, but I sent Bevis for some biscuits for him to have with his coffee and he forgot how much they cost, and we threw away the packet with the price on it."

"They're more likely to ask about Sir George Ralston's visit. I don't think the police will be interested in the petty cash. But let them see anything they ask for, except, of course, the clients' files. They're confidential. And Miss Maudsley, tell Bevis not to try to be clever."

Miss Maudsley promised in a voice which had become calmer; she was obviously making efforts to convey her total reliability to deal with whatever crises Monday might bring. Cordelia wondered which would be the more damaging, Bevis's playacting or Miss Maudsley's passionate protestations that in no possible circumstances could dear Miss Gray be capable of murder. Probably Bevis would be intimidated by the physical presence of the law from the worst excesses of his histrionic talents, unless by some ill chance he had happened recently to have viewed one of those television documentaries devoted to exposing the corruption, brutality, and racism of the police, in which case anything was possible. But at least she could be certain that whoever visited Kingly Street, it wouldn't be Adam Dalgliesh. From the rarefied and mysterious heights of hierarchy which he now inhabited, any such chore was unthinkable. She wondered whether he would read about the crime, whether he would learn that she was involved.

Nothing could have prepared Cordelia for the singularity of the rest of Sunday morning. Ambrose, as he was helping himself to his breakfast scrambled eggs, suddenly paused, spoon in hand.

"My God, I've forgotten to cancel Father Hancock! It's too late now. Oldfield will be on his way to fetch him."

He turned to explain. "He's an elderly Anglican priest who has retired to Speymouth. I usually invite him to take Sunday-morning service when I have guests. People nowadays seem to feel the need of these ministrations. Clarissa liked him to come when she was here for a weekend. He amused her."

"Clarissa!" Ivo gave a hoarse burst of laughter which shuddered his gaunt frame. "He'll probably arrive at the same time as the police. So we explain to Grogan that we aren't at his disposal for an hour or so because we'll all be at Divine Service. I can't wait to see his face. Admit it was on purpose that you didn't cancel, Ambrose."

"No, I assure you. It entirely slipped my mind."

Roma said, "He probably won't come. He'll have heard of the murder by now—it'll be all over Speymouth—and he'll assume that you don't expect him."

"Don't you believe it. If we were reduced by mass homicide to two, and Oldfield was available to fetch him, he'd come. He's nearly ninety and has his own priorities. Besides, he enjoys his sherry and luncheon. I'd better remind Munter."

He went out, smiling his secretive, complacent smile.

Cordelia said, "I wonder if I ought to change out of trousers."

Ivo seemed suddenly to have found an appetite. He spooned out a generous helping of egg. "Unnecessary, surely. I don't suppose you've brought gloves and a prayer book. Never mind; even if the props are missing we can still proceed to church in the approved Victorian fashion. I wonder whether the Munters and Oldfield will come to make a showing in the servants' pew. And what on earth will the old man find to preach about?''

Ambrose reappeared.

''Well, that's settled. Munter hadn't forgotten. Will you all be coming or have we any conscientious objectors?''

Roma said, ''I disapprove, but I don't mind putting in an appearance if the object is to irritate Grogan. We aren't expected to sing, are we?''

''Of course. There is the *Te Deum* and the responses and we have one hymn. Would anyone like to choose it?''

No one volunteered.

''Then I suggest 'God Moves in a Mysterious Way.' We meet the launch at ten-forty.''

And so the astonishing morning got under way. *Shearwater* beat the police launch to the jetty by five minutes, and Ambrose received a frail figure in cloak and biretta, who alighted with remarkable sprightliness and gazed on them benignly from moist and faded blue eyes. Before Ambrose could make the introductions the priest turned to him and said, ''I was sorry to hear of your wife's death.''

Ambrose said gravely, ''Yes, it was unexpected. But we weren't married, Father.''

''Were you not? Dear me! Forgive me, I hadn't realized. Drowned, I think they said. These waters can be very treacherous.''

''Not drowned, Father. She suffered a severe concussion.''

''I thought that my housekeeper said drowned. But perhaps I'm thinking of someone else. The war, perhaps. A long time ago, anyway. I'm afraid my memory is not what it was.''

The police launch shuddered to the quay, and they watched while Grogan, Buckley, and two other plainclothes officers alighted.

Ambrose said formally, ''May I introduce Father Hancock, who is here to take Morning Service according to the rite of the Church of England. It usually lasts an hour and a quarter.

You and your officers are, of course, very welcome to attend.''

Grogan said curtly, "Thank you, but I am not a member of your church and my men make their own arrangements in their off-duty time. I should be glad if we could again have access to all parts of the castle.''

"Of course. Munter will look after you. And I shall, of course, be available myself after luncheon.''

The church received them into its archaic, multicolored silence. Simon was persuaded to seat himself at the organ, and the rest of the party filed decorously into the high pew originally built for Herbert Gorringe. The organ was old, requiring to be pumped, and Oldfield was already there, hand at the ready. With the appearance of Father Hancock in surplice the service got under way.

Ambrose obviously took the view that his guests were dissenters, if not worse, who required a strong lead in the responses, and Ivo retained throughout an attentive gravity and showed a familiarity with the liturgy which suggested that this was his normal Sunday-morning activity. Simon managed the organ competently enough, although Oldfield let it almost run out of wind at the end of the *Te Deum* and it produced a late, noisy, and discordant amen. Roma forgot her resolve to remain silent and sang in a rich contralto only slightly out of tune. Father Hancock used the 1662 Book of Common Prayer without deletions or substitutions, and his congregation proclaimed themselves miserable offenders who had followed too much the devices and desires of their own hearts and in a slightly ragged but resolute chorus promised amendment of life. It was only at the end of the petitions, when unexpectedly he inserted a prayer for the souls of the departed, that Cordelia heard a small concerted intake of breath and the air of the church grew for a moment colder. The sermon lasted fifteen minutes and was a learned dissertation on the Pauline theology of the redemption.

As they rose to sing the hymn, Ivo whispered to Cordelia,

"That's all one asks of a sermon. No possible relevance to anything but itself."

Before luncheon, Munter served sherry, dry and chilled, on the terrace. Father Hancock managed three glasses without apparent effect and talked happily to Sir George about bird-watching and to Ivo about liturgical reform, on which Ivo showed himself surprisingly well informed. No one mentioned Clarissa, and it seemed to Cordelia that for the first time since her murder, her restless, menacing spirit was subdued. For a few precious moments the weight of guilt and misery lifted from her heart. It was possible to believe, innocently talking in the sun, that life was as well ordered, as certain, as austerely decent and reasonable, as the great Anglican compromise in which they had taken part. And when they went in to their roast ribs of beef and rhubarb tart—a conventional and rather heavy Sunday luncheon, provided, she suspected, primarily for the benefit of Father Hancock—it was a relief to have him there, to hear the thin but beautiful voice discussing such a harmless interest as the nesting habits of the song thrush, and to watch his frank enjoyment of the food and wine. Only Simon, his face flushed, drank as steadily, downing the claret as if it were water, reaching for the decanter with a shaking hand. Father Hancock seemed as spry as ever after a meal which would have reduced many a younger man to stupor, and he took his leave of them with the same serene contentment with which he had greeted them four hours earlier.

As *Shearwater* drew away, Roma turned to Cordelia and said with gruff embarrassment, "I'm going for a walk for half an hour. Would you care to come? I'd like to have a word with you."

"All right. If Grogan wants us he can send for us."

They walked together, without speaking, up the long greensward beyond the rose garden, then under the shadow of the beeches, crunching their way through the bright drifts of fallen leaves and hearing above the scuffle of their tramping feet the strengthening pulse of the sea. After five minutes they emerged from the trees and found themselves on the edge of the cliff. To their right was a concrete bunker, part of the 1939 defenses of the island, its low entrance almost blocked with leaves. They moved around it and settled their backs against its rough-textured wall, looking down through a green-and-gold pattern of beech leaves to the narrow strip of beach and the glitter of the sea-washed shingle.

Cordelia didn't speak. The walk had been at Roma's request. It was for her to say what was on her mind. But she felt curiously peaceful and at ease with her companion, as if none of their differences could weigh against the fact of their common femininity. She watched as Roma picked up a beech twig and began methodically shredding it of leaves.

Without looking at Cordelia, she said, "You're supposed to be an expert in these things. When do you suppose we can get away? I've got a shop to look after; my partner can't manage indefinitely on his own. The police can't keep us here, surely. The investigation could take months."

Cordelia said, "They can't legally hold us at all unless they arrest us. Some of us will have to attend the inquest. But I should think you could leave tomorrow if you wanted to."

"And what about George? He'll need some help. Is he going to sort out her things, jewelry, clothes, makeup, or does he expect me to?"

"Hadn't you better ask him?"

"We can't even get into her bedroom. The police still have it sealed. And she's brought drawers of stuff with her. She always did, even for a weekend. And then there'll be all the clothes in the Bayswater flat and at Brighton, suits, dresses, her furs. He can hardly dump it all on Oxfam."

Cordelia said, "They'd be surprised, certainly. But I expect they'd find a good use for it all. They could sell the clothes in their gift shops." She would have found this female chat about Clarissa's wardrobe bizarre if she hadn't realized that Roma's concern about her cousin's clothes masked a deeper concern—Clarissa's money. Again there was silence.

Then Roma said gruffly, "Did you know that I'd asked Clarissa for a loan just before she was killed and that she'd turned me down?"

"Yes. I was there when she told Sir George."

"And you haven't told the police?"

"No."

"That was decent of you, considering that I haven't been particularly pleasant to you."

"What has that to do with it? If they want that kind of information, they can get it from the person concerned: you."

"Well, they haven't got it so far. I lied. I'm not proud of it and I'm not even sure why. Panic, I suppose, and a feeling that it would suit them to pin the murder on me rather than on George or Ambrose. One's a baronet and war hero and the other's rich."

"I don't think they want to pin it on anyone except the guilty person. I don't take to either of them, Grogan or Buckley. But I think they're honest."

Roma said, "It's odd. I've never much liked or trusted the police, but I always took it for granted that, faced with a crime as serious as murder, I'd cooperate with them up to the hilt. I want Clarissa's murderer caught, of course I do. So why do I feel so defensive? Why do I act as if Grogan and Buckley are in league against me? And it's humiliating to find oneself lying, lying and terrified, and ashamed."

"I know. I feel the same."

"It looks as if George hasn't told them about our quarrel either. Nor has Tolly, apparently. Clarissa sent her out while we were talking, but she must have guessed. What do you think she has in mind, blackmail?"

Cordelia said, "I'm sure not. But I think she knows. She was in the bathroom while I was there, and she probably overheard. Clarissa was pretty vehement."

"She was vehement with me, vehement and offensive. If I were capable of killing her, I'd have done it then."

They were silent for a moment; then she said, "What I can't get used to is the way we all carefully avoid discussing who it was who killed her. We don't even confide what we've told Grogan. Since the murder, we've behaved to each other like strangers, telling nothing, asking nothing. Don't you find it strange?"

"Not really. We're stuck here together. Life will be intolerable if we start hurling accusations or recriminations at each other or divide into cliques."

"I suppose so. But I don't think I can go on, not knowing, not even talking about it, pretending to make polite conversation, when we're all thinking the same thing, avoiding each other's eyes, wondering, locking our doors at night. Did you lock yours?"

"Yes. I wasn't sure why. I don't think for one moment that there's a homicidal maniac on the island. Clarissa was always the intended victim. She wasn't killed by mistake. But I did lock my door."

"Against whom? Who do you think did it?"

Cordelia said, "One of us who slept in the castle on Friday night."

"I know that. But which one?"

"I don't know. Do you?"

Roma's twig was a thin, denuded wand. She threw it away, found another, and began again the work of methodical destruction.

"I should like it to be Ambrose if anyone, but I can't believe it. Wasn't it George Orwell who wrote that murder, the unique crime, should arise only from strong emotions? Ambrose never felt a strong emotion in his life. And he hasn't the courage or the ruthlessness. He isn't capable of that much hatred. He likes to play with the toys of violence: a tag end of executioner's rope, a bloodstained nightdress, a pair of Victorian handcuffs. With Ambrose, even the horror comes secondhand, disinfected by time and charm and quaintness. And it can't be Simon. He never even saw the marble limb, and, anyway, he'd have confessed by now. He's a weakling like his father. He wouldn't have the psychological strength to stand up to Grogan for five minutes if the going got rough. And Ivo? Well, Ivo's dying. He's nearly served his life sentence. He may feel that he's out of the reach of the law. But where's his motive? I suppose George is the main suspect, but I don't believe that either. He's a professional soldier, a professional killer if you like. But he wouldn't do it in that way, not to a woman. It could be the Munters, singly or together, or even Tolly, but I can't think why. That leaves you and me. And it wasn't me. And, if it's any comfort to you, I don't think it was you either."

Cordelia said, "Tell me about Clarissa. You spent a lot of your holidays with her as a child, didn't you?"

"Oh, God, those awful Augusts! They had a house on the river at Maidenhead and spent most of the summer there. Her mother thought that Clarissa ought to have young company, and my parents were glad to have me fed and boarded free. Oddly enough, we got on quite well together then, united I suppose by our fear of her father. When he came down from London she lived in terror."

"I thought that she adored him, that he was an overindulgent devoted papa."

"Is that what she told you? How typical of Clarissa! She couldn't even be honest about her own childhood. No, he was a brute. I don't mean he physically ill-treated us. In some ways that would have been more endurable than sarcasm, a cold adult anger, contempt. I didn't understand him then, of course. Now I think I do. He didn't really like women. He married to get himself a son—he had the egotism that can't imagine a world in which he hasn't at least a vicarious immortality—and he found himself with a daughter, an invalid wife who'd no intention of breeding again, and a job in which divorce wasn't an option. And Clarissa wasn't even pretty when she was a child. His coolness and her fear killed any spontaneity, any affection, even any intelligence which she might have shown. No wonder she spent the rest of her life obsessively looking for love. But, then, don't we all?''

Cordelia said, "After I was told something about her, something she'd done, I thought that she was a monster. But perhaps no one is, not entirely, not when you know the truth about them.''

"She was a monster all right. But when I think of Uncle Roderick, I can understand why. Hadn't we better be getting back? Grogan will suspect us of conspiracy. We can probably scramble down to the beach from here and walk back by the sea.''

They trudged back along the edge of the surf. Roma, her hands sunk in her jacket pockets, walked ahead, splashing through the small receding waves, seeming oblivious of the wet trouser bottoms flapping against her ankles, of her sodden shoes. The way back was longer and slower than the walk through the copse, but at last they turned the headland of a small bay and the castle was suddenly before them. They stopped and watched. A young man in bathing trunks and carrying a rough wooden box was climbing down the fire escape from the window of Cordelia's first bedroom. He climbed carefully, hooking his arms around the rungs, being careful not to touch them with his hands. Then he glanced around, walked to the edge of the rocks, and with a sudden violent gesture flung the box out to sea. Then he stood poised for a moment, arms raised, and dived. About thirty yards from the end of the terrace rocked a boat, a different boat from the police launch. A diver, sleek and glittering in his black suit, rested on the gunwale. As soon as the box hit the water he twisted his body and dropped backward out of sight.

Roma said, "So that's what the police are thinking.''

"Yes. That's what they're thinking.''

"They're after the jewel casket. And suppose they do manage to dredge it up.''

Cordelia said, "It will be bad news for someone on this island. I think that they'll find that it still holds Clarissa's jewels."

But what else might it hold? Would the notice of Clarissa's performance in *The Deep Blue Sea* still be in the secret drawer? The police had taken very little interest in that single square of newsprint, but suddenly it seemed to Cordelia that it must have had some significance. Wasn't there just a possibility that it had a bearing on Clarissa's death? The thought at first seemed absurd, but it persisted. She knew that she wouldn't be satisfied until she had seen a duplicate. The obvious first step was to call at the newspaper office in Speymouth and examine the morgue. She knew the year, Jubilee Year, 1977. It shouldn't be too difficult. And at least it would give her something positive to do.

She was aware that Roma was standing absolutely still, her eyes fixed on the lone swimmer. Her face was expressionless. Then she shook herself and said. "We'd better go in and face another round of what, with Chief Inspector Grogan, passes for the third degree. If he were openly impertinent, or even brutal, I'd find it less offensive than his veiled masculine insolence."

But when they passed through the hall and were drawn by the sound of voices into the library, they were told by Ambrose that Grogan and Buckley had left the island. They were said to be meeting Dr. Ellis-Jones at the Speymouth mortuary. There would be no more questioning until Monday morning. The rest of the day was their own to get through as best they could.

2

BUCKLEY THOUGHT that Sunday afternoon was a hell of a time for an autopsy. He didn't exactly enjoy them whenever he had to attend, but Sunday, even when he was on duty, had about it a lethargic postprandial calm which called for a comfortable chair in the sergeants' mess and a desultory reading over of reports rather than an hour spent on his feet while Doc Ellis-Jones sliced, sawed, cut, weighed, and demonstrated with his gloved and bloody hands. It wasn't that Buckley felt squeamish. He didn't in the least care what indignities would be practiced on his own body once he was dead, and he couldn't see why anyone should be more perturbed by the ritual dismemberment of a corpse than he had been as a lad watching his Uncle Charlie in that exciting shed behind his butcher's shop. Come to think of it, Doc Ellis-Jones and Uncle Charlie shared the same expertise and went about their business in much the same way. This had surprised him when, as a newly appointed constable fresh out of regional training school, he had attended his first postmortem. He had expected that it would be more scientific, less brutal, and far less messy than it had, in fact, proved to be. It had occurred to him then that the main differences between Doc Ellis-Jones and Uncle Charlie were that Uncle Charlie worried less about infection, used a smaller variety of somewhat cruder instruments, and treated his meat with more respect. But that wasn't surprising when you considered what he charged for it.

He was glad to get out at last into the fresh air. It wasn't that the p.m. room stank. It would have been less objectionable to him if it had. Buckley strongly disliked the smell of disinfectant which overlaid rather than masked the smell of putrefaction. The smell was elusive but persistent and tended to linger in his nose.

The mortuary was a modern building on upper ground to the west of the little town, and as they made their way to their Rover they could see the lights coming on like glow worms along the curving streets and the dark form of Courcy Island lying supine like a half-submerged and sleeping animal, far out to sea. It was odd, thought Buckley, how the island seemed to draw closer or recede, depending on the light and the time of day. In the mellow autumnal sunshine it had lain in a blue haze, looking so near that he could imagine it possible to swim to that multicolored and tranquil shore. Now it had drawn far into the Channel, remote and sinister, an island of mystery and horror. The castle was on its southern shore and no lights beckoned. He wondered what the small company of suspects was doing at this moment, how they would face the long night ahead. It was his guess that all but one of them would sleep behind locked doors.

Grogan came up to him. Nodding toward the island, he said, "So now we know what one of them knew already, how she died. Stripped of Doc Ellis-Jones's technical chat about the mechanics of force and the local absorption of kinetic energy in injuries to the head, not to mention the interesting and characteristic pattern in which the skull disintegrates under the weight of impact, what have we? Much as we expected. She died from a depressed fracture of the front of the skull made with our old friend, a blunt instrument. She was probably lying on her back at the time, much as Miss Gray found her. The bleeding was steady but almost entirely internal, and the effect of the blow was intensified by the fact that the bones of her skull are thinner than normal. Unconsciousness supervened almost immediately and she died within five to fifteen minutes. The subsequent damage was done after death; how long after, he can't unfortunately say. So we have a murderer who sits and waits while his victim dies and then . . . what? Decides to make sure? Decides that he didn't much like the lady and may as well make that fact plain? Decides to cover up how she died by giving her more of the same thing? You aren't going to tell me that he waited for ten minutes or so before deciding to panic?''

Buckley said, ''He could have spent the time searching for something and been enraged when he didn't find it. So he took out his frustration on the corpse.''

''But searching for what? We haven't found it either, unless it's still there in the room and we've missed its significance. And there's no sign of a search. If the room was searched, it was done with care and by someone who knew what he was about. And if he was looking for something, my guess is that he found it.''

''There's still the lab report to come, sir. And they'll have the viscera within the hour.''

''I doubt whether they'll find anything. Doc Ellis-Jones saw no sign of poison. She may have been drugged—we mustn't theorize too far ahead of the facts—but my guess is that she was awake when she died and that she saw the face of her killer.''

It was extraordinary, thought Buckley, how cold the day became once the sun had gone. It was like moving from summer to winter in a couple of hours. He shivered and held open the car door for his chief. They moved slowly out of the parking lot and turned toward the town. At first Grogan spoke only in laconic spurts.

"You've heard from the coroner's officer?"

"Yes, sir. The inquest's fixed for two o'clock on Tuesday."

"And the London end? Burroughs is getting on with those inquiries?"

"He's going up first thing in the morning. And I've told the divers we'll be needing them for the rest of the week."

"What about that bloody press conference?"

"Tomorrow afternoon, sir. Four-thirty."

Again there was silence. Changing gear to negotiate the steep and twisting hill which ran down to Speymouth, Grogan suddenly said, "The name Commander Adam Dalgliesh mean anything to you, Sergeant?"

There was no need to ask, "Commander of what force?" Only the Met had commanders. Buckley said, "I've heard of him, sir."

"Who hasn't? The commissioner's blue-eyed boy, darling of the establishment. When the Met, or the Home Office come to that, want to show that the police know how to hold their forks and what bottle to order with the *canard à l'orange* and how to talk to a Minister on terms level with his Permanent Secretary, they wheel out Dalgliesh. If he didn't exist, the force would have to invent him."

The gibes might be unoriginal, but there was nothing secondhand about the dislike. Buckley said, "It's a bit old-fashioned, isn't it, sir, all that stuff?"

"Don't be naive, Sergeant. It's only unfashionable to talk like that anymore, but that doesn't mean that they've changed their thinking or their actions. He could have had his own force by now—probably be chairing the Association of Chief Police Officers—if he hadn't wanted to stick to detection. That and personal conceit. The rest of you can struggle in the muck for the prizes. I'm the cat who walks alone and all places are alike to me. Kipling."

"Yes, sir." Buckley paused and then asked, "What about the commander?"

"He knows the girl, Cordelia Gray. They tangled together in a previous case. Cambridge, apparently. No details offered and none asked for. But he's given her and that agency a clean bill. Like him or not, he's a good copper, one of the best. If he says that Gray isn't a murderess, I'm prepared to take that as evidence of a sort. But he didn't say that she's incapable of lying, and I wouldn't have believed him if he had."

He drove on in a moody silence. But his mind must have been mulling over yesterday's interviews. After a space of ten minutes in which neither of them spoke, he said, "There's one thing which struck me as intriguing. You probably noticed it yourself. They all described the visit on Saturday morning to the church and the crypt. They all mentioned that story about the drowned internee. But it was done a little too casually; the mere mention of an unimportant trifle; just a short excursion we happened to fancy before lunch. As soon as I invited them to dwell on the incident they reacted like a bunch of virgins who'd had an interesting experience in the Marabar Caves. I suppose the allusion is wasted on you. Sergeant?"

"Yes, sir."

"Don't worry. I'm not degenerating into one of those literary cops. I'll leave that to Dalgliesh. We did *A Passage to India* as a set book when I was at school. I used to think it overrated. But no knowledge is wasted in police work, as they used to tell me at training school, not even E. M. Forster apparently. Something happened in the Devil's Kettle which none of them is prepared to talk about and I'd like to know what."

"Miss Gray found one of the messages."

"So she says. But I wasn't thinking of that. It's probably a long shot, but we'd better find out more about that 1940 drowning. I suppose Southern Command would be the starting point.''

Buckley's thoughts went back to that white, scientifically butchered body, to a nakedness which had been totally unerotic. And more than that. For a moment, watching those gloved and probing fingers, he had felt that no woman's body would ever excite him again. He said, ''There was no rape and no recent intercourse.''

''That hardly surprised us. Her husband hadn't the inclination and Ivo Whittingham hadn't the strength. And her murderer had other things on his mind. We'll call it a day, Sergeant. The chief constable wants a word with me first thing tomorrow. No doubt that means that Sir Charles Cottringham has been having a word or two with him. That man's a nuisance. I wish he'd stick to amateur theatricals and leave real-life drama to the experts. And then we'll get back to Courcy Island and see if a night's sleep has refreshed their memories.''

3

AT LAST the interminable hours dragged to dinner time Cordelia came in from a last and solitary walk with barely time to shower and change. By the time she went down, Ambrose, Sir George, and Ivo were already in the dining room. They were all seated before Simon appeared. He was wearing a dark suit. He looked at the others, flushed, and said, "I'm sorry. I didn't realize that we were going to change. I won't be long." He turned to the door.

Ambrose said with a touch of impatience, "What does it matter? You can dine in your swimming trunks if it makes you feel more comfortable No one here cares what you wear"

Cordelia thought that it wasn't the happiest way of putting it. The unspoken words hung on the air. Clarissa would have cared; but Clarissa wasn't there. Simon's eyes slewed to the empty chair at the top of the table. Then he sidled to a chair beside Cordelia

Ivo said, "Where's Roma?"

"She asked for soup and chicken sandwiches in her room. She says she has a headache."

It seemed to Cordelia that everyone was simultaneously doubting the reality of the headache while mentally congratulating Roma on having hit on so simple an expedient for avoiding this, their first formal dinner together since Clarissa's death. The table had been rearranged, perhaps in an attempt to minimize the trauma of that empty chair. The two end places hadn't been laid, and Cordelia and Simon sat facing Ambrose, Ivo, and Sir George, almost, it seemed, eyeball to eyeball, while an expanse of mahogany stretched gleaming on either side. Cordelia thought that the arrangement made them look like a couple of vive-voce candidates facing a not particularly intimidating panel of examiners, an impression which was strengthened by Simon's suit in which, paradoxically, he looked less cool and more formally overdressed than did the other three in their frills and dinner jackets.

Neither Munter nor his wife was present. Bowls of vichyssoise were already set at each place, and the second course was under covers on the sideboard hot plates. There was a faint smell of fish, an unlikely choice for a Sunday. It was obviously to be a convalescent's dinner, blandly inoffensive, unexciting to the palate or the digestion. It was, thought Cordelia, a nice point of culinary etiquette, the choice of menu for a house party of murder suspects dining together the day after the crime.

Ivo's thoughts must have been running with hers, for he said, "I wonder what Mrs. Beeton would reject as the most inappropriate meal for this kind of occasion. My choice would be borscht followed by steak tartare. I can't decide on the pudding. Nothing too crude, but it needs to be richly indigestible."

Cordelia said in a low voice, "Don't you care at all?"

He paused before replying as if her question merited careful thought. "I don't like to think that she suffered or was in terror even for a moment. But, if you mean do I care that she's no longer alive, then no, I don't really care.''

Ambrose had finished pouring the Graves. He said, ''We'll have to serve ourselves. I told Mrs. Munter to take the evening off and get some rest, and Munter hasn't shown himself since luncheon. If the police want to interview him again tomorrow they'll be unlucky. It happens about every four months, and invariably if I've had a house party. I'm not sure whether it's a reaction to the excitement, or just his way of discouraging me from too much entertaining. As he's usually considerate enough to wait until my guests have left, I can't really complain. He has compensating qualities.''

Sir George said, ''Drunk, is he? I thought he might take to the bottle.''

''I fear so. It usually lasts three days. I did wonder whether the violent death of one of my guests would break the pattern, but apparently not. I suppose it's his release from some intolerable internal boredom. The island isn't really congenial to him. He has an almost pathological dislike of water. He can't even swim.''

Ambrose, Ivo, and Cordelia had moved to the sideboard. Ambrose lifted a silver lid to reveal thin fillets of sole in a cream sauce.

Ivo asked, ''Why, then, does he stay?''

''I've never asked him for fear that the same question might occur to him. Money, I suppose. And he likes solitude even if he would prefer it not to be guaranteed by two miles of sea. He has only me to please. An easy job on the whole.''

''And easier now that Clarissa's dead. I take it you won't be going ahead with the drama festival?''

''Not even, my dear Ivo, as a memorial to her.''

They then seemed to realize that the exchange, even though Sir George was seated too far away to overhear, was in poor taste. Both of them glanced at Cordelia. She felt a little angry with Ambrose.

Helping herself to *haricots verts*, she said on impulse, ''I was wondering whether he might have found a way to augment his wage, perhaps a little smuggling on the side. The Devil's Kettle would be a useful unloading point. I noticed that he keeps the trapdoor bolt well oiled, and he'd hardly need to do that if you don't show the place to summer visitors. And on Friday night I saw a light flashing at sea. I thought that it might be acknowledging a signal.''

Ambrose laughed as he carried back his plate, but when he spoke the thin note of spite was unmistakable. "Clever Cordelia! You're wasted as an amateur. Grogan would be glad to enroll you in the ranks of official snoopers. Munter may have his private arrangements, but he doesn't confide in me and I certainly have no intention of inquiring. Courcy is traditionally a smuggler's haven and most sailors in these parts do a little amateur smuggling. It wouldn't amount to much—a few casks of brandy, an occasional bottle of scent. Nothing as spectacularly naughty as drugs, if that's what you have in mind. Most people like a little tax-free income, and a touch of risk adds to the fun. But I don't advise you to confide your suspicions to Grogan. Let him get on with the investigation he has in hand.''

Ivo said, "What about the lights Cordelia saw?"

"Warning off his pals, I expect. He'd hardly want the stuff landed with the island swarming with police.''

Ivo said evenly, "Except that Cordelia saw the signal on Friday. How could he know that the police would be here next day?''

Ambrose shrugged, unworried. "Then it couldn't have been the police he feared. Perhaps he knew or guessed that we were being favored with the company of a private eye. Don't ask me how he knew. Clarissa didn't confide in me and I shouldn't have told Munter even if she had. But it's my experience that little goes on under any roof that a good servant doesn't learn first.''

They rejoined Sir George. He had already helped himself to sole and was eating with a stolid determination but with no evident enjoyment. Cordelia pondered on Munter. She thought it unlikely that he had guessed her secret or that he would have altered his plans if he had. It was more possible that with the castle full of guests he had felt the time unpropitious for the reception of his loot: too many people about, too much extra work, the possibility that he would find it difficult to slip away unnoticed. Perhaps he hadn't been able to get a message to his confederates or the message had gone astray. Or had there been an unexpected arrival on the island, someone he feared particularly, or someone who might have known of the Devil's Kettle, might even have visited it? There was only one person who fitted that bill: Sir George.

The meal seemed endless. Cordelia sensed that they all wished it over but that no one wanted to appear to hurry or to be the first to leave. Perhaps that was why they appeared to be eating with deliberate slowness. She wondered whether it was the absence of staff that made the occasion so portentous; they might be the remnants of some deserted and soon to be beleaguered garrison stoically eating their last meal with traditional ceremony, ears tuned for the first distant shouts of the barbarians. They ate and drank but were silent. The six candles in their branched entwined stems seemed to burn less brightly than on their first evening so that their features, half shadowed, were sharpened into caricatures of their daytime selves. Pale etiolated hands reached out to the fruit bowl, to furred and flushed peaches, the curved shininess of bananas, apples burnished so that they looked as artificial as Ambrose's candlelit skin.

The french windows had been shut against the chill of the autumn night and a thin wood fire crackled in the immense grate. But surely those fitfully leaping flames couldn't account for the oppressive heat of the room. It seemed to Cordelia that it was getting hotter by the minute, that the heat of the day had been trapped and thickened, making it difficult to breathe, intensifying the smell of the food so that she felt faintly nauseated. And in her imagination the room itself changed; the Orpens splurged and spread into amorphous colors, so that the walls appeared to be hung with crude tapestries, and the elegantly stuccoed roof raised smoked hammer beams to a black infinity, open to an everlastingly starless sky. She shivered despite the heat and reached for her wineglass as if the physical feel of cool glass could strengthen her hold on reality. Perhaps only now were the full horror of Clarissa's death and the strain of the police interrogation taking their physical toll.

One candle wavered as if blown by an invisible breath, flickered, and went out. Simon gave a gasp, then a long, terrified moan. Hands, half lifted to mouths, became motionless. They turned in a single movement and stared at the window. Silhouetted againt the moonlight reared an immense form, its black arms flailing, hurling itself against the window. Its anger came to them faintly, something between a wail and a bellow. As they gazed in fascinated horror it suddenly ceased its frantic beating and was for a moment still, quietly looking in at their faces. The gaping mouth, raw as a wound, seemed to suck at the window. Two gigantic palms, fingers splayed, imprinted themselves on the glass. The pressed, distorted features dissolved against the window into a mess of slowly draining flesh. Then the creature gathered its strength and heaved. The doors gave, and Munter, wild-eyed, almost fell into the room. The night air rushed cool and sweet over their faces, and the distant sighing of the waves became a surging tide of sound as if the swaying figure had been borne in on them by the force of a violent storm, bringing the sea with him.

No one spoke. Ambrose got to his feet and moved forward. Munter brushed him aside and shambled up to Sir George until their faces almost touched. Sir George stayed in his seat. Not a muscle moved. Then Munter spoke, throwing back his head and almost howling the words, "Murderer! Murderer! Murderer!"

Cordelia wondered when Sir George would move, whether

he would wait until Munter's fingers were actually at his throat. But Ambrose had moved behind and had seized the shuddering arms. At first the contact seemed to calm Munter. Then he gave a violent wrench.

Ambrose said breathlessly, "Could one of you help?"

Ivo had begun peeling a peach. He seemed totally unconcerned. He said, "I'd be no use in this particular emergency, I'm afraid."

Simon got up and grasped the man's other arm. At his touch Munter's belligerency left him. His knees buckled and Ambrose and Simon moved closer, supporting his sagging weight between them. He tried to focus his eyes on the boy, then slurred out a few words, guttural, unintelligible, sounding hardly English. But his final words were clear enough: "Poor sod. God, but she was a bitch, that one."

No one else spoke. Together Ambrose and Simon urged him to the door. He gave no further trouble but went as obediently as a disciplined child.

After they left, the two men and Cordelia sat in silence for a minute. Then Sir George got up and closed the french windows. The noise of the sea became muted, and the wildly flickering candles steadied and burned with a clear flame. He returned to the table, selected an apple, and said, "Extraordinary fellow! I was at Sandhurst with a chap who drank like that. Sober for months at a time, then paralytic for a week. Torpedoed in the Med in the winter of 'forty-two. Foul weather. Picked up from a raft three days later. Only one of the party to survive. He said that it was because he was pickled in whiskey. D'you suppose Gorringe lets Munter have the key to his cellar?"

"I shouldn't think so." Ivo sounded amused.

Sir George said, "Extraordinary arrangement, a butler who can't be trusted with the keys. Still, I suppose he has other uses. Devoted to Gorringe obviously."

Ivo asked, "What happened to him, your friend I mean?"

"Fell in his own swimming pool and drowned. The shallow end. Drunk at the time, of course."

It seemed a long time before Ambrose and Simon reappeared. Cordelia was struck with the boy's pallor. Surely coping with a drunken man couldn't have been so horrifying an experience.

Ambrose said, "We've put him to bed. Let's hope he stays there. I must apologize for the performance. I've never known Munter to behave before in such a spectacular way. Will someone please pass the fruit bowl?"

After dinner they gathered in the drawing room. Mrs. Munter had not appeared and they poured their own coffee from the glass percolator on the sideboard. Ambrose opened the french windows and one by one, as if drawn by the sea, the guests walked out onto the terrace. The moon was full, silvering a wide swath to the horizon, and a few high stars pinpricked the blue-black of the night sky. The tide was running strongly. They could hear it slapping against the stones of the quay and the distant whisper of the spent waves hissing on the shingle beach. The only other sound was the muted footfalls of their walking feet. Here in this peace, thought Cordelia, it would be easy to believe that nothing mattered, not death, nor life, nor human violence, nor any pain. The mental picture of that splotch of battered flesh and congealed blood which had been Clarissa's face, scored as she thought forever on her mind, became unreal, something she had imagined in a different dimension of time. The disorientation was so strong that she had to fight against it, to tell herself why she was here and what it was she had to do. She came out of her trance to hear Ambrose's voice. He was speaking to Simon.

"You may as well play if you want to. I don't suppose a half hour of music would offend anyone's susceptibilities. There must be something appropriate, somewhere between a music-hall medley and the Dead March from *Saul*."

Without replying, Simon went over to the piano. Cordelia followed him into the drawing room and watched while he sat, head bowed, silently contemplating the keys. Then, suddenly hunching his shoulders, he brought down his hands and began playing with quiet intensity, and she recognized the slow movement of Beethoven's "Moonlight Sonata."

Ambrose called from the terrace, "Trite but appropriate."

He played well. The notes sang into the silent air. Cordelia thought it interesting that he should play so much better with Clarissa dead than he had when she was alive.

When he had finished the movement she asked, "What's going to happen, about your music I mean?"

"Sir George has told me not to worry, that I can stay on at Melhurst for a final year and then go to the Royal College of the Academy if I can get in."

"When did he tell you this?"

"When he came to my room after Clarissa was found."

That was a remarkably quick decision, thought Cordelia, given the circumstances. She would have expected Sir George to have other things on his mind just then than Simon's career.

The boy must have guessed her thoughts. He looked up and said quickly, "I asked him what would happen to me now and he said that I wasn't to worry, that nothing would change, that I could go back to school and then on to the Royal College. I was frightened and shocked and I think he was trying to reassure me."

But not so shocked that he hadn't thought first of himself. She told herself that the criticism was unworthy and tried to put it out of her mind. It had, after all, been a natural childish reaction to tragedy. What will happen to me? How will this affect my life? Wasn't that what everyone wanted to know? He had at least been honest in asking it aloud.

She said, "I'm glad, if that's what you want."

"I want it. I don't think she did. I'm not sure I ought to do something she wouldn't have approved of."

"You can't live your life on that basis. You have to make your own decisions. She couldn't make them for you even when she was alive. It's silly to expect her to make them now that she's dead.''

"But it's her money.''

"I suppose it will be Sir George's money now. If it doesn't worry him I don't see why it need worry you.''

Watching the avid eyes desperately gazing into hers, Cordelia felt that she was failing him, that he was looking to her for sympathy, for some reassurance that he could take what he wanted from life and take it without guilt. But wasn't that what everyone craved? Part of her wanted to respond to his need; but part of her was tempted to say, "You've taken so much. Why jib at taking this?''

She said, "I suppose if you want to salve your conscience about the money more than you want to be a professional pianist, you'd better give up now.''

His voice was suddenly humble. "I'm not all that good, you know. She knew that. She wasn't a musician, but she knew. Clarissa could smell failure.''

"Oh, well, that's a different issue, whether you're good enough or not. I think you play very well, but I can't really judge. I don't suppose that Clarissa could either. But the people at the colleges of music can. If they think you're worth accepting, they must think you have at least a chance of making a career in music. After all, they know what the competition's like.''

He looked quickly around the room and then said, his voice low, "Do you mind if I talk to you? There are three things I must ask you.''

"We are talking.''

"But not here. Somewhere private.''

"This is private. The others don't seem likely to come in. Is it going to take long?''

"I want you to tell me what happened to her, how she looked when you found her. I didn't see her, and I keep lying

awake and imagining. If I knew, it wouldn't be so awful.
Nothing is as awful as the things I imagine.''

"Didn't the police tell you? Or Sir George?"

"No one told me. I did ask Ambrose but he wouldn't say."

And the police would, of course, have had their own
reasons for keeping silent about the details of the murder. But
they had interviewed him by now. She didn't see that it
mattered anymore whether he knew or not. And she could
understand the horror of those nightly imaginings. But there
was no way in which she could make the brutal truth sound
gentle. She said, "Her face was battered in."

He was silent. He didn't ask how or with what.

She said, "She was lying quite peacefully on the bed,
almost as if she were asleep. I'm sure she didn't suffer. If it
were done by someone she knew, someone she trusted, she
probably didn't even have time to feel afraid."

"Could you recognize her face at all?"

"No."

"The police asked me if I'd taken anything from a display
cabinet, a marble arm. Does that mean they think it was the
weapon?"

"Yes." It was too late now to wish that she'd kept quiet.
She said, "It was found by the bed. It was . . . it looked as if
it had been used."

He whispered, "Thank you," but so quietly that she had
difficulty in hearing him.

After a moment she said, "You said there were three
things."

He looked up eagerly as if glad that his mood had been
broken. "Yes, it's Tolly. On Friday when I went swimming
while the rest of you toured the castle, she waited for me on
the shore. She wanted to persuade me to leave Clarissa and
live with her. She said that I could go straightaway and that
she had a room in her flat I could have until I'd found myself
a job. She said that Clarissa might die."

"Did she say how or why?"

"No. Only that Clarissa thought she was going to die and that people who thought that often did die." He looked straight at her. "And next day, Clarissa did die. I don't know whether I ought to tell the police what happened, about waiting for me, what she said."

"If Tolly was actually planning to murder Clarissa, she'd hardly warn you in advance. She was probably trying to tell you that you couldn't rely on Clarissa, that she might change her mind about you, that she might not always be there."

"I think she did know. I think she guessed. Ought I to tell the chief inspector? I mean, it is evidence, isn't it? Suppose he found out that I'd been keeping something back?"

"Have you told anyone?"

"No. Only you."

"You must do what you think is right."

"But I don't know what's right! What would you do if you were in my place?"

"I wouldn't tell. But then I have a reason. If you feel that it's right to tell, then tell. If it's any comfort to you, I don't think the police will arrest Tolly on that evidence alone, and they haven't any other, at least as far as I know."

"But she'd know that I must have told them! What would she think of me? I don't think I could face her after that."

"You might not have to. I don't suppose she'll stay on now that Clarissa's dead."

"So you would tell if you were me?"

Cordelia's patience snapped. It had been a long day, ending in the trauma of Munter's dramatic appearance, and she was weary in spirit as well as body. And it was difficult to sympathize with Simon's obsessive self-concern.

"I've told you. I wouldn't tell. But I'm not you. It's your responsibility and you can't force it on anyone else. Surely there's something you're capable of deciding for yourself."

She regretted the unkindness almost as soon as the words were out of her mouth. She turned her eyes from his scarlet face and stricken, doglike eyes and said, "I'm sorry. I shouldn't have said that. I suppose we're all on edge. Wasn't there a third thing you wanted to ask?"

He whispered, his mouth trembling, "No. There's nothing else. Thank you." He got up and closed the piano. He added quietly and with some attempt at dignity, "If anyone asks about me, I've gone to bed."

Unexpectedly, Cordelia found that she, too, was close to tears. Torn between irritation and pity and despising her own weakness, she decided to follow Simon's example. The day had gone on long enough. She went out on the terrace to say good night. The three black-clad figures were standing apart, silhouetted against the iridescence of the sea, motionless as bronze statues. At her approach they simultaneously turned, and she could feel the concentrated gaze of three pairs of eyes. No one moved or spoke. The moment of moonlit silence seemed to her portentous, almost ominous, and as she said her good nights the thought that for the past twenty-four hours she had tried to suppress surfaced in all its stark and frightening logic. "We are here together, ten of us on this small and lonely island. And one of us is a murderer."

4

CORDELIA FELL ASLEEP almost as soon as she had closed her book and put out the bedside light. But her awakening was as sudden. She lay for a moment confused and then put out her hand and found the switch. Her wristwatch, curled on the bedside table, showed her that it was just after three-thirty, far too early, surely, for her to have waked naturally. She thought that her sleep had been pierced by some sound, perhaps the shriek of a night bird. The moonlight screamed through the half-drawn curtains, cutting a swath of light over the ceiling and walls. The silence was absolute except for the pulse of the plangent sea, louder now than in the stir of the daylight hours. Her mind, still drugged with sleep, took hold of the tag end of a dream. She had been back in Kingly Street, and Miss Maudsley had been showing her with pride a newly rescued kitten. As is the way of dreams, she found it unsurprising that the kitten should be sleeping in a carved cradle with a red canopy and side curtains, a miniature of

313

Clarissa's bed, or that, when she peered into the cot and pulled aside the shawl, she should see, not a kitten, but a baby, and should know that this was Miss Maudsley's illegitimate child and that she must be very tactful and not betray that she knew. She smiled at the memory, put out the light, and tried to relax into sleep.

But this time it was elusive. Once awake, she was restless. Her mind busied itself again with the mystery and horror of Clarissa's death. Image succeeded image, unsought but insistent, disconnected in time but horribly clear: Clarissa's satin-clad body gleaming palely under the crimson canopy; Clarissa gazing down into the swirl of water at the Devil's Kettle; Clarissa's slim figure passing to and fro on the terrace, pale as a ghost; Clarissa standing on the pier and stretching her arms bat-winged in welcome; Clarissa removing her makeup, turning on Cordelia one naked and diminished eye in a freakish, strange, discordant gaze which seemed now to hold a look of sad reproach.

Her mind held that last picture as if unwilling to let it fade. Something about it was significant, something that she ought to have known or remembered. And then the realization came. She saw again the dressing table, the balls of cotton wool smeared with makeup, the smaller pads shifting across the mahogany, blackened with mascara. Clarissa had used a special lotion to cleanse her eyes. But those pads hadn't been on the dressing table when her body was discovered. Perhaps she hadn't troubled to remove her eye makeup. Was that something which the forensic pathologist would be able to detect even beneath that shattered and swollen flesh? But why should she take off her powder and foundation and leave her eyes under a weight of shadow and mascara, particularly as she proposed to rest them under the moistened pads. But wasn't there another possibility, that she had kept on all her makeup because she was expecting a visitor and that it had been the visitor who had wiped her face clean before smashing it to pulp? And that implied a man. A man was surely the most likely secret visitor. But Clarissa was too obsessed with her appearance to meet even a woman with a naked face. Still, wouldn't a woman be more likely to realize that she must use the special pads to remove the eye makeup? Tolly would have known it certainly. But Roma? Roma's eyes were devoid of mascara, and in the urgency and terror of the moment she would be unlikely to make a close inventory of the bottles on the dressing table. A man was still the most likely to make such a mistake, except perhaps Ivo, with his knowledge of theatrical makeup. The strangest part of it all was surely Tolly's silence. The police must have questioned her about the makeup, must have asked her if everything on the dressing table looked normal. And that meant that Tolly had held her tongue. Why and for whom?

It was impossible now to will herself to sleep. But she must have dozed at last, if only fitfully, for it was nearly four when she next awoke. She was too hot. The bedclothes lay heavily on her like the weight of failure, and she knew that there would be no more sleep that night. The sea was louder than ever, the air itself seeming to throb. She had a vision of the tide rising inexorably over the terrace, sweeping into the dining room, floating the heavy table and the carved chairs, rising to cover the Orpens and the stuccoed ceiling, creeping up the stairs until the whole island was covered except for the slender tower, rising like a lighthouse above the waves. She lay rigidly, longing for the first flush of day. It would be Monday, a working day in Speymouth. She would be able to get away from the island, if only for a few hours, to visit the local newspaper office, to try to trace the cutting about Clarissa's Jubilee performance. She had to have something positive to do, however unlikely to prove successful and significant. It would be good to feel free, free of Ambrose's ironic, half-secret smile, Simon's misery, Ivo's gaunt fortitude; free most of all from the eyes of the police. She had no doubt that they would be back. Yet, short of arresting her, there was nothing they could do to prevent her spending a day on shore.

Now it seemed that the morning would never come. She gave up the attempt at sleeping and got out of bed. She pulled on her jeans and guernsey, went to the window, and drew back the curtains. Below her lay the rose garden, the last overblown heads drooping on their spiky branches, bleached pale by the moon. The water on the pond looked as solid as beaten silver, and she could see clearly the smudge of lily leaves, the gleam of their blossoms. But there was something else on the surface, something black and hairy, an immense spider crawling, half submerged, spreading and waving its innumerable hairy legs under the shimmering water. She gazed in fascinated disbelief. And then she knew what it was and her blood ran cold.

She wasn't aware of her flight down to the gate which led from the passage to the garden. She must have banged on bedroom doors as she ran, indiscriminately, aware only that she might need help, not waiting for a response. But others must have been sleeping lightly. By the time she reached the door into the garden and was straining upwards to shoot back the top bolt, she was aware of muffled footsteps padding down the passageway, a confused murmur of voices. And then she was standing at the edge of the pool with Simon, Sir George, and Roma beside her and viewing clearly for the first time what it was she knew that she had seen: Munter's wig.

It was Simon who threw off his dressing gown and waded into the pool. The water came up to his thrashing arms. He gulped, then dived. The rest of them watched and waited. The water had scarcely steadied after the flurry of his disappearance when his head shot up, sleek as a seal's. He called, "He's here. He's caught on some wire netting where the lilies are rooted. Don't come in. I think I can free him."

He disappeared again. Almost at once they saw two black shapes surfacing. Munter's bald head, face upwards, looked as swollen as if it had been in the water for weeks. Simon pushed the body toward the side of the pool, and Cordelia and Roma bent and tugged at the sodden sleeves. Cordelia knew that it would be easier to take his hands, but the bloated fingers, yellow as udders, repelled her. She bent over his face and shifted her grasp to his shoulders. The eyes were open and glazed, the skin as smooth as latex. It was like pulling a dummy from the water, some discarded manikin with a sawdust-stuffed body, waterlogged and inert in its ridiculous formal coat. The clown's mask with its sagging jaw seemed to be gazing into hers with a look of piteous inquiry. She could imagine that she smelled his breath, stinking with drink. She was suddenly ashamed of the repugnance which had rejected the sad remnant of his humanity, and in a spasm of pity she grasped his left hand. It felt like a taut bladder, fleshless and cold. And it was in that moment of touch that she knew he was dead.

They tugged him onto the grass. Simon pulled himself out of the water. He folded his dressing gown under Munter's head, forced back his neck, and felt in the gaping mouth for dentures. There were none. Then he fastened his mouth over the thick lips and began the kiss of life. They watched silently. No one spoke, even when Ambrose and Ivo came up quickly and stood among them. There was no sound but the squelch of sodden clothes as Simon bent to his task and the regular gasp of his intaken breath. Cordelia glanced at Sir George, wondering a little at his silence. He was gazing down at the bloated, inverted face, at the half-shut and unseeing eyes, with a look of great intensity, almost of incredulous recognition. And in that moment, Cordelia's heart jolted. Her eyes met his and she thought they flashed a warning. Neither spoke, but she wondered whether he had shared her revelation. There came into her mind an old incongruous picture: the music room at the convent, Sister Hildegarde stretching wide her mouth and eyes in an anticipatory mime, raising the white baton. "And now, my children, the Schumann. Happy, happy! Mouths wide. *Ein munteres Lied* "

She dragged her mind back to the present. There was no time to think about her discovery or to explore its implications. She forced herself to look again at the sodden lump of flesh on which Simon was so desperately working. He was close to exhaustion when Ambrose bent and felt for the pulse at Munter's wrist. He said, "It's no good. He's dead. And he's icy cold. He's probably been in the water for hours."

Simon didn't reply. He went on mechanically pumping breath into the inert body as if performing some indecent and esoteric rite.

Roma said, "Ought we to give up? I thought you were supposed to go on for hours."

"Not when the pulse has gone and the body's cold."

But Simon took no notice. The rhythm of his harsh, indrawn breath and the antics of his crouched body seemed to have become more frantic. It was then that they heard Mrs. Munter's voice, low but harsh: "Leave him be. He's dead. Can't you see that he's dead?"

Simon heard her. He stood up and began to shiver violently. Cordelia took his dressing gown from under Munter's head and wrapped it around his shoulders.

Ambrose turned to Mrs. Munter. "I'm so very sorry. When did it happen, do you know?"

"How can I tell?" She paused, then added, "Sir. I don't sleep with him when he's drunk."

"But you must have heard him go out. He can't have walked steadily or quietly."

"He left the room just before three-thirty."

Ambrose said, "I wish you had let me know."

Cordelia thought, he sounds as peevish as if she were proposing to take a week's holiday without consulting him.

"I thought you paid us to protect you from trouble and inconvenience. He'd made enough for one night."

There seemed to be nothing to say. Then Sir George came forward and beckoned to Simon. "Better get him indoors."

There was a new note in Mrs. Munter's voice. She said quickly, "Don't bring him into the servants' flat, sir."

Ambrose said soothingly, "Of course not, if that's how you feel."

"That's how I feel." She turned and walked away.

The rest of the party looked after her. Then Cordelia ran and caught her up.

"Please let me come with you. I don't think you should be alone."

She was surprised that the eyes lifted to hers could hold so much dislike.

"I want to be alone. There's nothing the likes of you can do. Don't worry, I'm not going to kill myself." She nodded toward Ambrose. "You can tell him that."

Cordelia returned to the group. She said, "She doesn't want anyone with her. She says to tell you that she'll be all right."

No one answered. They were still standing in a circle, looking down on the body. Dressing-gowned as they were, their feet muffled by slippers, they loomed over the corpse like a group of oddly clad mourners: Sir George in shabby checked wool, Ivo's dark green silk through which his shoulders stuck like wire hangers, Ambrose's somber blue faced with satin, Roma's padded and flowered nylon, Simon's brown bathrobe. Watching the circle of bent heads, Cordelia half expected them to raise in concert and wail a threnody in the thin air.

Then Sir George roused himself and turned to Simon. 'Shall we get on with it?"

Ivo had wandered a little way along the edge of the pool and was contemplating the remnants of the water lilies as if they were some rare marine vegetation in which he had a scientific interest. He looked up and said, "But ought you to move him? Isn't it usual not to disturb the body until the police arrive?"

Roma cried, "But that's only in a case of murder! This is

an accident. He was drunk, he staggered, and he fell in
Ambrose told us that Munter couldn't swim."

"Did I? I can't remember. But it's perfectly true. He
couldn't swim."

Ivo said, "You told us so at dinner. But Roma wasn't
there."

Roma cried, "Someone told me, Mrs. Munter perhaps
What does it matter? He was drunk, he fell in, and he
drowned. It's perfectly obvious what happened."

Ivo resumed his contemplation of the water lilies. "I don't
think anything is ever perfectly obvious to the police. But I
daresay you're right. There's enough mystery without making
more. Are there any marks of violence on the body?"

Cordelia said, "Not that I can see."

Roma said obstinately, "We can't leave him here. I think
we should take him indoors." She looked at Cordelia as if
inviting her support.

Cordelia said, "I don't think it matters if we move him. It
isn't as if we had found him like this."

They all looked at Ambrose as if waiting for instructions
He said, "Before we move him, please come with me, all of
you. There's something we have to decide."

5

THEY FOLLOWED HIM toward the castle. Only Simon glanced behind him at the ungainly lump of cold flesh, still spread-eagled, which had been Munter. His glance conveyed an embarrassed regret, almost a look of apology, that they should have to desert him, leave him so uncomfortably circumstanced.

Ambrose led them into the business room and switched on the desk lamp. The atmosphere was at once conspiratorial; they were like a gang of dressing-gowned schoolchildren planning a midnight prank.

He said, "We have a decision to make. Do we tell Grogan what happened at dinner? I think we ought to agree about that before I telephone the police.

Ivo said, "If you mean do we tell the police that Munter accused Ralston of murder, why not say so plainly?"

Simon's hair, plastered over his brow and dripping water into his eyes, looked unnaturally black. He was shivering under the dressing gown. He looked from face to face, astounded. "But he didn't accuse Sir George of . . . well, of any particular murder. And he was drunk! He didn't know what he was saying. You all saw him. He was drunk!" His voice was getting dangerously close to hysteria.

Ambrose spoke with a trace of impatience. "No one here thinks it of any importance. But the police may. And anything that Munter did or said during the last hours of his life will obviously interest them. There's a lot to be said for saying nothing, for not complicating the investigation. But we have to give roughly the same account. If some tell and the others don't, those who opt for reticence will obviously be placed in an invidious position."

Simon said, "Do you mean that we pretend that he didn't come in through the dining-room windows, that we didn't see him?"

"Of course not. He was drunk and we all saw him in that state. We tell the police the truth. The only question is, how much of the truth?"

Cordelia said quietly, "It isn't only Munter's shouted accusation at Sir George. After you and Simon took Munter out, Sir George told us about an army friend of his who had drunk in just that compulsive way . . ."

Ivo finished the sentence for her, "And had been drowned in just that way. The police will find that an interesting coincidence. So unless Sir George told you both the same story on a different occasion—which I take it he didn't— Cordelia and I are already in what you might call an invidious position."

Ambrose took in this information in silence. It seemed to give him some satisfaction. Then he pronounced, "In that case the choice would seem to be: do we all give a truthful account of the evening's proceedings, or do we omit Munter's shout of 'Murderer' and the story about Ralston's unfortunate friend?"

Cordelia said, "I think we should tell the truth. Lying to the police isn't as easy as it sounds."

Roma said, "You speak from experience, perhaps."

Cordelia ignored the note of malice and went on, "They'll question us closely. What did Munter say when he burst in? What did the rest of us talk about when Ambrose and Simon were helping him to bed? It isn't only a question of omitting embarrassing facts. We have to agree on the same lies. That's apart from any moral considerations."

Ambrose said easily, "I don't think we need complicate the decision with moral considerations. Doing evil that good may come is a perfectly valid option whatever the theologians tell you. Besides, I imagine that we all did a little judicious editing in our interviews with Grogan. I did. He seemed to feel that my staging the play for Clarissa required explaining, so I told him that she gave me the idea for *Autopsy*. An ingenious but quite unnecessary lie. So our first decision is easy. We tell the truth, or we agree on a story. I suggest we take a secret ballot."

Ivo said quietly, "Here, or do we all repair to the crypt?"

Ambrose ignored him. He turned first to where Simon stood, his chattering mouth half open, his washed face pale under the feverish eyes, and thought better of it. He said to Cordelia with formal courtesy, "Would you be good enough to bring me two cups from the kitchen? I think you know the way."

The short journey, the incongruous errand, seemed to her of immense significance. She walked down the empty passages and into the kitchen and took down two breakfast cups from the dresser with grave deliberateness as if an unseen audience were watching the grace of every movement. When she got back to the business room it seemed to her that no one had moved.

Ambrose thanked her gravely and placed the cups side by side on the desk. Then he went out to the display cabinet and returned, carrying the round board with its colored marbles, Princess Victoria's solitaire board. He said, "We each take a marble. Then we close our eyes—no peeping, I implore you—and drop it into one of the cups. We'll make it easy to remember. The left cup for the more sinister option, the right for righteousness. You'll see that I've even aligned the handles appropriately so there's no excuse for confusion. When we've heard the five marbles drop we open our eyes. It's convenient that Roma wasn't at dinner. There's no possibility of a tie."

Sir George spoke for the first time. He said, "You're wasting time, Gorringe. You'd better ring for the police now. Obviously we tell Grogan the truth."

Ambrose took his marble, selecting it with some care and examining its veining as if he were a connoisseur of such trifles. "If that's what you want, that's what you vote for."

Ivo said, "Do you then intend to take a second ballot to decide whether we tell the police about the first ballot?"

But he took a marble. Sir George, Simon, and Cordelia followed. She closed her eyes. There was a second's silence, and then she heard the first marble tinkle into a cup. The second followed almost immediately, then a third. She stretched out her hands. They were briefly brushed by ice-cold fingers. She felt for the cups and placed a hand on each so that there could be no mistake. Then she dropped the marble into the right-hand cup. A second later she heard the last marble fall. The sound was unexpectedly loud; it must have been dropped from a height. She opened her eyes. Her companions were all blinking as if the period of darkness had lasted for hours, not seconds. Together they looked into the cups. The right-hand one held three marbles.

Ambrose said, "Well, that simplifies matters. We tell the truth, apart, of course, from mentioning this little divertissement. We came together into the business room and you all sat here together, appropriately subdued, while I rang the police. We've only spent a few minutes, so there will be no embarrassing hiatus of time to account for."

He replaced the marbles, after carefully scrutinizing each one, handed the two cups to Cordelia, and took up the telephone receiver. As she was returning the cups to the

kitchen, two thoughts chiefly occupied her. Why had Sir
George waited until the ballot was inevitable before announc-
ing that he favored the truth, and which of the two of them
had dropped a marble into the left-hand cup? She did briefly
wonder whether anyone could have transferred someone else's
marble in addition to dropping his own, but decided that this
would have required some sleight of hand even if done with
open eyes. Her own ears were exceptionally sharp, and they
had detected only the four clear tinkles as the other marbles
fell.

Ambrose was apparently practicing a policy of togetherness.
He waited until she returned before ringing the Speymouth
police station. He said, "It's Ambrose Gorringe speaking
from Courcy Island. Will you tell Chief Inspector Grogan that
my butler, Munter, is dead? He was found in the pool here,
apparently drowned."

Cordelia thought that the statement was notable for being
brief, accurate, and carefully noncommittal. Ambrose for
once was keeping an open mind on the cause of Munter's
death. The rest of the conversation was monosyllabic. Ambrose
eventually replaced the receiver. He said, "That was the duty
sergeant. He'll let Grogan know. He says not to move the
body. The less interference the better until the police arrive."

There was silence in which it seemed to Cordelia that they
all simultaneously recognized that they were cold. It wasn't
yet half past six, and while it might appear unfeeling to
express a wish to return to bed and hopeless to expect to sleep
once there, it was unreasonably early to get dressed and face
the day.

Ambrose said, "Would anyone care for tea or coffee? I
don't know what's likely to happen about breakfast. You may
get none unless I cook it, but I assure you I'm perfectly
competent. Is anyone hungry?"

No one admitted to being hungry. Roma shivered and
hunched herself deeper into her padded nylon dressing gown.

She said, "Tea would be welcome, the stronger the better. And then I, for one, am going back to bed."

There was a general murmur of acquiescence.

Then Simon spoke. "There's something I forgot. There's some kind of box down there. I felt it when I released the body. Ought I to bring it up?"

"The jewel casket!" Roma turned, reanimated, the desire for bed apparently forgotten. "So he had it after all!"

Simon said eagerly, "I don't think it's the casket. It felt larger, smoother. He must have dropped it as he fell."

Ambrose hesitated. "I suppose we ought to wait until the police arrive. On the other hand, I have a curiosity to see what it is, if Simon has no objection to a second immersion."

So far from objecting, the boy, shivering as he was with cold, seemed impatient to get back to the pool. Cordelia wondered if he had temporarily forgotten that sprawled body. She had never seen him so animated, almost frantic. Perhaps it was the result of being, for once, the center of the action.

Ivo said, "I think I can contain my curiosity. I'm going back to bed. If anyone is making tea later, I'd be grateful if you'd bring up a cup."

He left on his own. Roma was apparently cured of both her headache and her tiredness. They returned to the pool. The fading moon was tissue thin and the sky was streaked with the first light of day. The air rose in a thin mist from the water and struck them with a damp autumnal chill. Bereft of the moonlight's bleak enchantment and the sense of unreality which moonlight bestows, the body looked at once more human and more grotesque. The flesh of the left cheek, resting against the stones, was pressed upwards to distort the eye so that it seemed to be leering at them, ironic and knowing. From the drooling mouth a trickle of bloodstained saliva had hung and dried on the stubble of the chin. The sodden clothes looked as if they had already shrunk, and a thin stream of water still ran from the trouser legs and dripped slowly into the pool. In the uncertain light of the first dawn it seemed to Cordelia that his life blood was seeping away, unregarded and unstanched. She said, "Can't we at least cover him up?"

"Of course." Ambrose was at once solicitous. "Could you fetch something from the house, Cordelia? A tablecloth, a sheet, a towel, or even a coat would do. I'm sure you'll find something suitable."

Roma turned on him, her voice harsh. "Why send Cordelia? Why should she be expected to run all the errands round here? She's not paid to take your orders. Cordelia isn't your servant. Munter was."

Ambrose looked at her as if she were an unintelligent child who had for once succeeded in making a sensible remark. He said calmly, "You're perfectly right. I'll go myself."

But Roma, in angry spate, was beyond appeasement. "Munter was your servant and you can't even bring yourself to say you're sorry he's dead. You don't care, do you? You didn't care about Clarissa and you don't care about him. Nothing touches you as long as you're comfortable and saved from boredom. You haven't said a word of regret since we found his body. And who are you, for God's sake? Your grandfather made his money out of liver pills and gripe water. You haven't even the excuse of caste for not behaving like a human being."

For a second Ambrose's body froze, and two moons of red appeared on the smooth cheeks, then as quickly faded, leaving him very pale. But his voice hardly altered. "The only human being I know how to behave like is myself. I shall grieve for Munter in my own time and place. This hardly seems an appropriate moment for a valediction. But if its absence offends you I can always emulate Prince Hal. 'What! old acquaintance! could not all this flesh/Keep in a little life? Poor Jack, farewell,/I could have better spared a better man.' And if it's any comfort to you, I would rather see all of you, with one possible exception, dead at the bottom of my pool than lose Carl Munter. But you're right about

Cordelia. One is too ready to take advantage of competence and kindness.''

After he left there was an embarrassed silence. Roma, her face blotched, her chin creased with stubborn anger, stood a little apart. She had the truculent, slightly defensive air of a child who knows that she has said something indefensible but who is not altogether ungratified by the result.

Suddenly she swung round and said gruffly, ''Well, at least I managed to provoke a human reaction from our host. So now we know where we stand. I take it that Cordelia is the privileged one among us whom Ambrose would be reluctant to see dead at the bottom of his pool. Even he isn't entirely immune to a pretty face, apparently.''

Sir George stared down at the water lilies. ''He's upset. Natural, after all. Hardly the time to quarrel among ourselves.''

Cordelia felt that she ought to make some comment but, unable to think of anything appropriate, remained silent. She was puzzled by Roma's outburst, which she hardly felt was the result of concern or affection for herself. It could, she supposed, have been a gesture of feminine solidarity or a blast against male arrogance. But she suspected that it was more likely a spontaneous release of pent-up terror and shock. Whatever the cause, the result had been interesting. And Ambrose had been remarkably apt with his quotation from *Henry IV*. Was that because he was a natural lover of Shakespeare, or because he had recently been spending some time looking though the Shakespearean section of the *Penguin Dictionary of Quotations*?

They heard Ambrose's returning footsteps on the stones. He was carrying a folded red-checked tablecloth. While they watched he shook it out, then let it fall gently over the body. Cordelia thought that, as a temporary shroud, it was hardly the most appropriate covering he could have found. He knelt and tucked it solicitously around the body as if making it comfortable. Still no one spoke.

Then Sir George turned to Simon and barked out his order. "Right boy. Let's get on with it."

Simon had already judged the depth of the pool, and this time he dived. His body cleft the water in a neat curve, parting the water lilies. There was a flurry and a brief commotion. And then his sleek head broke the surface and he raised both his arms high. Between them he held a dark wooden box about twelve inches by nine. A few seconds later he pushed his burden into Ambrose's waiting hands and was drawing himself up over the side of the pool. He gasped, "It was caught under the netting. What is it?"

For reply Ambrose opened the lid. The music box, watertight, had emerged a little scratched but otherwise undamaged. The cylinder slowly turned, and a tinkle of sweet disjointed notes plucked out a familiar tune, one which Cordelia had last heard during the final rehearsal, "The Blue Bells of Scotland."

They listened silently until the tune was at an end. Then there was a pause and the next tinkle began, soon to be identified as "My Bonnie Lies Over the Ocean."

Ambrose closed the box. He said, "The last time I saw this it was with the other music box on the props table. He must have been taking it back to the tower room. This would be the direct route from the theater to the tower."

"But why? What was the hurry?" Roma frowned at the box as if its appearance had disappointed her expectations.

Ambrose said, "There was no hurry. But he was drunk and I suppose he was acting irrationally. Munter shared my slight obsession with order, and he strongly disliked any of the things in the castle being used as theatrical props. I suppose his muddled brain thought that this was as good a time as any to start putting things to right."

Cordelia thought that Sir George had been remarkably silent. Now he spoke for the first time. "What else has he moved? What about the other box?"

"That was kept in the cupboard in the business room. As

far as I can remember, one box was there, the second with the clutter in the tower room.''

Sir George turned to Simon. ''Better get dressed, boy. You're shivering. There's nothing else to do here.''

It was a dismissal, almost brutal in its peremptoriness. Simon seemed to realize for the first time that he was cold. His teeth began to chatter. He hesitated, nodded, then shambled off.

Roma said, ''That boy has more talents than I gave him credit for. And how, incidentally, did he know what Clarissa's jewel box was like? I thought you only gave it to her when she arrived on Friday morning.''

Cordelia said, ''I suppose he knows in the same way as you and I know: because we've been to her room and been shown it.''

Roma turned to go. ''Oh, I realized, of course, that he must have been in her room. I was just wondering when exactly.'' She added, ''And how did he know that Munter was carrying the box when he fell? It could have been lying there on the bottom for months.''

''It was a safe assumption, surely, given the position of the body and the fact that it and the box were both caught by the netting.'' Ambrose's voice held a lightness and a determined incuriosity which Cordelia sensed was a little too controlled, a little too careful. He added, ''Why not leave the questions to Grogan? One amateur detective in the house is surely enough. And accusations of murder come more appropriately from the police, don't you feel?''

Roma turned away, hunching her shoulders more deeply into the collar of her dressing gown. ''Well, I'll get back to bed. Perhaps I could have some tea in my room, too, when you get around to making it. And when I've had my stint with Grogan I'll relieve you of my presence here. Either the Courcy curse is still operative, or in your paradise death is becoming infectious.''

Ambrose watched while she slumped away and disappeared

into the shadows of the arches. He said, "That woman could be dangerous."

Sir George was still staring after her departing back. "Only unhappy."

"With a woman that amounts to the same thing. And with those beefy swimmer's shoulders, she shouldn't wear a padded dressing gown. And she shouldn't choose that shade of blue, or any blue for that matter. I suppose that we may as well see whether the second music box is back where it's normally kept."

In the business room he knelt and opened the doors of a walnut chiffonier. Cordelia could see that it contained a number of box files, two carefully wrapped parcels, which could have been ornaments as yet unpacked, and a box of dark wood similar in size to the first. He placed it on the table and raised the lid. The box plucked out the tune "Greensleeves."

Sir George said, "So he did return it. Odd. Probably couldn't rest until he'd started putting things to rights."

Cordelia said, "Except that he's changed them around. This one belonged in the tower room."

Ambrose's voice was unexpectedly sharp. "How can you possibly know?"

"Because I saw it there on Friday afternoon while Clarissa was rehearsing. I went to explore the tower and found the room. I couldn't be mistaken."

"They look very alike."

"But they play different tunes. I opened the box in the tower, this box. It played 'Greensleeves.' The one used at the rehearsal played the Scottish medley. You know. You were there."

Sir George said, "So yesterday afternoon he fetched this one from the tower and not from the business room." He turned to Ambrose. "Did you know that, Gorringe?"

"Naturally not. I knew that we had two boxes and that one was kept here, the other in the tower room. I didn't know which was which. They aren't a particular passion of mine.

When Munter told me what he also told the police, that he
hadn't left the ground-floor apartments and that he'd fetched a
music box from the business room, I saw no reason to doubt
him."

Cordelia said, "When Clarissa or the producer first asked
for a music box, Munter acted as one would expect. He
fetched the nearer and less valuable box. Why trouble to go
all the way to the business room? He wouldn't have gone to
the tower room if Clarissa hadn't rejected the first box."

Ambrose said, "The only entrance to the tower is from the
gallery. Munter lied to the police: at about two o'clock
yesterday he was within a few feet of Clarissa's door. That
means he could have seen someone entering or leaving. The
police may feel that he could have gone in to her himself,
locked door or no locked door. And that's why he was so
obsessive about returning the boxes, each to the room he said
he'd taken it from. He needn't have troubled, of course. I
don't see how anyone could have known the truth. It was pure
chance that you, Cordelia, wandered into the tower and found
the second box. Whether the police believe you is, of course,
another matter."

Cordelia said, "It wasn't altogether chance. If Clarissa
hadn't ordered me out of the theater I should have watched
the rehearsal to the end. And I don't see why the police
shouldn't believe me. They may find it easier to believe that I
was curious to explore the tower room than that you, who are
so fond of your Victoriana, didn't know precisely where you
kept each of your music boxes." As soon as she had spoken,
she wondered whether this frankness had been wise; spoken
to her host, it had hardly been courteous.

But Ambrose accepted the comment without offense. He
said easily, "You're probably right. I doubt whether they'll
believe either of us. After all, they have only our word for it
that Munter lied. And it's very convenient for us, isn't it: a
dead suspect who can't now deny what any of us chooses to

say about him? 'The butler did it.' Even in fiction, so I'm led to believe, that solution is regarded as unsatisfactory.''

Sir George lifted his head. ''I think the police launches are arriving.''

He must, thought Cordelia, have remarkable ears for an aging man. Hers had caught nothing. And then she sensed rather than heard the throb of engines. They looked at one another. For the first time Cordelia saw in their eyes what she knew they must be recognizing in hers, the flicker of fear.

Ambrose said, ''I'll meet them at the quay. You two had better get back to the body.''

Sir George and Cordelia were alone. If it were to be said, it had to be said now, before the police questioning began. But it was hard to get out the words, and when she did they sounded harsh, accusatory.

''You recognized that drowned face, didn't you? You think he could have been Blythe's son?''

He said, unsurprised, ''It did strike me, yes. Never occurred to me before.''

''You'd never seen Munter like that before, his face upturned, dead and drowned. That's how you last saw his father.''

''What made you think of it?''

''Your face when you looked down at him. The war memorial he decorates every Armistice Day. The words he shouted out at you: 'Murderer, murderer!' It was his father he meant, not Clarissa. And I think he muttered in German to Simon. And his Christian name. Didn't Ambrose say he was Carl? And his height. His father died slowly because he was so tall. But, most of all, his name. *Munter* is German for *Blythe*. It's one of the few German words I know.''

She had seen that look of strained endurance on his face before, but all he said was ''Could be. Could be.''

She asked, ''Are you going to tell Grogan?''

''No. None of his business. Not relevant.''

''Not even if they arrest you for murder?''

"They won't. I didn't kill my wife." Suddenly he said, quickly as if the words were forced out of him, "I don't believe I deliberately let them kill him. May have done. Difficut to understand one's motives. Used to think it was all so simple."

Cordelia said quickly, "You don't have to explain to me. It's none of my business. And you were a very young officer at the time. You can't have been in command here."

"No, but I was on duty that evening. Should have discovered that something was afoot, should have stopped it. But I hated Blythe so much that I couldn't trust myself to go near him. That's one thing you never forget or forgive, cruelty when you're a child and defenseless. I shut my mind and my eyes to anything that concerned him. May have shut them deliberately. You could call it a dereliction of duty."

"But no one did. There was no court-martial, was there? No one blamed you."

"I blame myself." There was a moment's silence; then he said, "Never knew he was married. No mention of a wife at the inquest. There was talk of a girl in Speymouth but she never showed herself. No talk of a child."

"Munter probably wasn't born. And he could have been illegitimate. I don't suppose we shall ever know. But his mother must have been bitter about what happened. He probably grew up believing that the army had murdered his father. I wonder why he took a job on the island: curiosity, filial duty, the hope of revenge. But he couldn't have expected that you would turn up here."

"He might have hoped for it. He took the job in the summer of 1978. I married Clarissa that year and she has known Ambrose Gorringe nearly all her life. Munter probably kept track of me. I'm not exactly a nonentity."

Cordelia said, "The police have made mistakes before now. If they do arrest you I shall feel free to tell them. I shall have to tell them."

He said quietly, "No, Cordelia. It's my concern, my past, my life."

Cordelia cried, "But you must see how it will look to the police! If they believe me about the music box, they'll know that Munter was in the gallery a few feet from your wife's room at about the time she died. If he didn't kill her himself, he could have seen the person who did. Taken with that shout to you of 'Murderer,' it's damning unless you tell them who Munter was."

He didn't respond but stood as rigid as a sentry, his eyes gazing into nothingness.

She said, "If they arrest the wrong person, it's double injustice. It means that the guilty one goes free. Is that what you want?"

"Would it be the wrong person? If she hadn't married me she'd be alive today."

"You can't know that!"

"I can feel it. Who was it said we owe God a death?"

"I can't remember. Someone in Shakespeare's *Henry the Fourth*. But what has that to do with it?"

"Nothing, I expect. It came into my mind."

She was getting nowhere. Beneath that apparently guileless and inarticulate front of personality he harbored his private undercover agent, a mind more complex and perhaps more ruthless than she had imagined. And he wasn't a fool, this deceptively simple soldier. He knew precisely the extent of his danger. And that could mean that he had his own suspicions, that there was someone he wanted to protect. And she didn't think that it would be either Ambrose or Ivo.

She said helplessly, "I don't know what you want of me. Am I to carry on with the case?"

"No point, is there? Nothing can frighten her ever again. Better leave it to the professionals." He added awkwardly, "I'll pay, of course, for your time so far. I'm not ungrateful."

Ungrateful for what? she wondered.

He turned and looked down at Munter's body. He said,

"Extraordinary business, putting that wreath on the war memorial every year. Do you suppose Gorringe will keep up the tradition?"

"I shouldn't think so."

"He should. I'll have a word with him. Oldfield could see to it."

They turned to make their way across the rose garden, then stopped. Coming across the lawn toward them in the pale apricot light, their footfalls absorbed by the soft grass, were Grogan and his coterie of officers. Cordelia was caught unawares. Facing their silent, inexorable advance, their bleak, unsmiling faces, Cordelia resisted the temptation to glance at Sir George. But she wondered whether he shared her sudden and irrational vision of how the two of them must look to the police: as guilty and discomfited as a couple of poachers surprised by the gamekeepers with their dead spoils at their feet.

BOOK SIX

A CASE CONCLUDED

1

MUNTER'S BODY WAS TAKEN AWAY with a speed and efficiency which Cordelia thought almost unseemly. By ten o'clock the metal container with its two long side handles had been slid from the jetty onto the deck of the police launch with as little ceremony as if it had held a dog. But what, after all, had she expected? Munter had been a man. Now he was a weight of latent putrefaction, a case to be given a file and a number, a problem to be solved. She told herself that it was unreasonable to expect that the men—police officers? mortuary attendants? undertaker's staff?—would bear him away with the solemnity appropriate to a funeral. They were doing a familiar job without emotion and without fuss.

With this second death the suspects had been able to watch the police at work. They did it discreetly from the window of Cordelia's bedroom, watching while Grogan and Buckley walked slowly around the body like a couple of marine scientists intrigued by some bedraggled specimen washed up by the tide. They watched while the photographer did his job, hardly seeming to notice or speak to the police, occupying himself with his own expertise. And this time Dr. Ellis-Jones didn't appear. Cordelia wondered whether this was because the cause of death was apparent or he was busy elsewhere with another body. Instead, a police surgeon arrived to certify that life was extinct and to make the preliminary examination. He was a large and jovial man, dressed in sea boots and a knitted jersey, patched on both elbows, who greeted the police like old drinking companions. His cheerful voice rose clearly on the quiet morning air. It was only when he knelt to rummage in his case for his thermometer that the watchers at the window silently withdrew and took refuge in the drawing room, ashamed of what had suddenly seemed an indecent curiosity. And it was from the drawing-room windows, less than ten minutes later, that they saw Munter's body borne through the archway and across the quay to the launch. One of the bearers said something to his mate and they both laughed. He was probably complaining about the weight.

And with this second death even the police questioning didn't take long. There was, after all, not a great deal that anyone could tell, and Cordelia guessed how suspiciously unanimous that little must sound. When it was her turn she went into the business room weighed down by the conviction that nothing she said would be believed. Grogan stared at her across the desk, his pale, unfriendly eyes red-rimmed as if he had gone without sleep. The two music boxes were on the desk in front of him, carefully positioned side by side.

When she had finished her account of Munter's appearance at the dining-room windows, of the finding of his body and the recovery of the music box, there was a long silence. Then he said, "Why exactly did you go up to the tower room on Friday afternoon?"

"Just curiosity. Miss Lisle didn't want me at the rehearsal

and Mr. Whittingham and I had finished our walk. He was tired and had gone to rest. I was at a loose end.''

"So you amused yourself by exploring the tower?"

"Yes."

"And then you played with the toys?'' He made it sound as if she were a tiresome child who hadn't been able to keep her hands off someone else's kiddy car. She realized with a mixture of anger and hopelessness the impossibility of explaining, of making him understand that impulse to set the whole childish menagerie working, to drown wretchedness with a cacophony of sound. And even if she had confided the cause of her distress—Ivo's telling her of the death of Tolly's child—would her story have sounded any more plausible? How did one explain to a policeman, perhaps to a judge, a jury, those small, seemingly irrational compulsions, the pathetic expedients against pain, which hardly made sense to oneself? And if it were difficult for her, so egregiously privileged, how did those others cope—the ignorant, the uneducated, the inarticulate—faced with the esoteric and uncompromising machinery of the law?

She said, "Yes, I played with the toys."

"And you are absolutely certain that the music box you found in the tower room played the tune 'Greensleeves'?'' He smacked his great palm down on the lid of the left-hand box, then lifted the lid. The cylinder turned and the delicate teeth of the long comb once more picked out the nostalgic, plaintive tune.

She said, "I'm absolutely sure."

"Externally, they're very alike. The same size, the same shape, the same wood, almost the same pattern on the lids."

"I know. But they play different tunes."

She could understand the frustration and the irritation which he was keeping so tightly under control. Had she liked him better, she might have sympathized. If she were telling the truth, Munter had lied. He had left the ground floor of the castle some time during that critical hour and forty minutes.

The only entrance to the tower was from the gallery floor. He had been within feet of Clarissa's door. And Munter was dead. Even if Grogan believed him innocent, even if some other suspect was brought to trial, her evidence about the music box would be a gift for the defense.

He said, "You didn't mention your visit to the tower when you were questioned yesterday."

"You didn't ask me. You were chiefly interested in what I did and saw on Saturday. I didn't think it important."

"There's nothing else that you didn't think important?"

"I've answered all your questions as honestly as I can."

He said, "Perhaps. But that isn't quite the same thing, is it, Miss Gray?"

And the small voice of her own conscience, in collusion with him, indicted her. Have you? Have you?

Suddenly he leaned across the desk and put his face close to hers. She thought she could smell his breath, sour and tainted with beer, and had to force herself not to draw back.

"What exactly happened on Saturday morning in the Devil's Kettle?"

"I've told you. Mr. Gorringe told us the story of the young internee who was left to drown. And I found that quotation from the play."

"And that's all that happened?"

"It seems to me enough."

He sat back and she waited. He didn't speak.

At last she said, "I should like to go to Speymouth this afternoon. I want to get off the island."

"Who doesn't, Miss Gray?"

"That's all right, is it? I don't have to ask permission? I mean, you can't stop me from going where I like unless you arrest me."

He said, "That, no doubt, is what you'd advise your clients if you had any. And you'd be perfectly right. We can't stop you. But you must be in Speymouth tomorrow at two o'clock for the inquest. It won't take long, just a formality.

We'll be asking for an adjournment. But you were the one who found the body. You were the last person to see Miss Lisle alive. The coroner will want you there.''

She wondered whether it was intended to sound like a threat. She said, "I'll be there."

He looked up and said, so gently that she almost believed him to be sincere, "Enjoy yourself in Speymouth, Miss Gray. Have a good day."

2

IT WAS AFTER TWELVE-THIRTY when she was released. Having strolled out to join the others who were drinking their pre-luncheon sherry on the terrace, she learned that Oldfield had already gone to the mainland to fetch the post and supplies. Ambrose was expecting a parcel of books from the London Library. Cordelia asked if *Shearwater* could be ordered for her for two o'clock and he agreed without curiosity, merely inquiring when she would like the launch to be at Speymouth quay for the return journey. Cordelia ordered it for six o'clock.

She wasn't hungry for luncheon, nor, apparently, was anyone else. Mrs. Munter had provided a cold buffet in the dining room, too much food, most of it intended for the party, set out indiscriminately in an appetite-stifling mass. The wonder was, thought Cordelia, that she had bothered at all. No one had spoken of her since the finding of her husband's body. She too had been interviewed by the police but had spent most of the morning secluded in her flat or moving silently and unnoticed from pantry to dining room. Cordelia doubted whether Ambrose was greatly concerned about her, and there was no one else to care. She decided to see if she was all right, to ask, before setting out, whether there was anything she could do for her in Speymouth. She doubted that her intrusion would be welcomed. What was there, after all, that she or anyone could do? But at least she could ask.

She didn't trouble to sit down but cut herself slices of cold beef and put them between bread. Then, making her excuses to Ambrose, she helped herself to an apple and a banana and took her picnic onto the beach. Already her mind was moving away from this claustrophobic island toward the mainland. She felt like a refugee, waiting to be rescued from some plague-ridden and violent colony, watching with desperate eyes for the boat which would bear her away from the smell of rotting corpses, the shouting and tumult, the bodies strewn on the shore, toward the safety and normality of home. The mainland which she had seen recede with such high hopes only three days earlier now shone in the imagination with all the effulgence of a promised land. It seemed to her that two o'clock would never come.

Shortly before one-thirty she made her way along the tiled passage past the business room to the baize door which she knew must lead to the servants' flat. There was no bell or knocker, but while she was wondering how to attract attention, Mrs. Munter came quietly up behind her, carrying on her hip a basket of washing. Without speaking, she held open the door and Cordelia passed before her down a shorter passageway and into a small sitting room to her right. Like all other Victorian architects, Godwin had ensured that from none of their rooms could the servants overlook their betters, whether the family were disporting themselves indoors or out. The single window gave a view only of a wide yard with, beyond it, the stable block with its charming clock tower and weather vane. Across the yard was slung a washing line from which drooped a pair of Munter's huge pajamas. They seemed to Cordelia pathetic and embarrassing, and she averted her eyes as if detected in a morbid curiosity.

The room itself was starkly furnished, not uncomfortable, but, despite the artful simplicity of the Art Nouveau furniture, almost devoid of character. There was a television set in the corner but no books or pictures and no photographs or ornaments on the dresser. It was as if the inhabitants had no past to remember, no present to celebrate. And no third person, apparently, ever sat here. There were only two easy chairs, one on each side of the elegantly carved iron grate, and only two upright chairs set opposite each other at the dining table.

Mrs. Munter didn't invite her to sit down. Cordelia said, "I didn't mean to bother you. I just wanted to see that you are all right. And I'm going into Speymouth shortly. Is there anything I can get or do for you?"

Mrs. Munter swung her basket of washing down on the table and began folding the clothes. "There's nothing. I'll be with you on the boat likely enough. I'm leaving, miss. I'm getting off the island."

"I know how you must feel. But if you're frightened I could share a room with you tonight."

"I'm not frightened. What is there to be frightened of? I'm leaving, that's all. I never liked being here and now that he's gone I don't have to stay."

"Of course not, if that's how you feel. But I'm sure Mr. Gorringe wouldn't want you to do anything in a hurry. He'll want to talk to you. There are bound to be, well . . . arrangements."

"There's nothing to talk about. He's been a good enough master but it was Munter he wanted. I came with Munter. Now we're separate."

Separate, thought Cordelia, finally and forever. There had been no mistaking the note of satisfaction, almost of triumph. And she had come to the flat out of an embarrassed compassion, inexperienced as she might be, to try to give comfort. None, it appeared, was wanted or necessary. But surely there would be wages outstanding, offers of help to be made, funeral arrangements to be discussed. Ambrose would surely want to reassure her that she could stay on at the castle as long as it suited her. And, of course, there would be the police, Grogan and his ubiquitous experts in death, trained in suspicion and mistrust. If Munter had been deliberately pushed to his death, she could have done it. With one undetected murderer already on the island, what better time to get rid of an unwanted husband? Cordelia didn't doubt that Grogan, faced with this ungrieving widow, would place her high on his list of suspects. And the police were bound to see this hurried departure as highly suspicious.

She was wondering whether she ought to say a word of warning when Mrs. Munter spoke. "I've spoken to the police. They've no call to keep me. They know where they can find me. Mr. Gorringe can see to the funeral arrangements. It's no concern of mine."

"But you were his wife!"

"I never was his wife. He wasn't the marrying kind, nor am I. I'll be leaving in the launch as soon as Oldfield is ready."

"Are you all right for money? I'm sure that Mr. Gorringe..."

"I don't need his help. Munter had money. He had ways of making a bit on the side and I know where he kept it. I'll take what's due to me. And I'll be all right. Good cooks don't starve."

Cordelia felt totally inadequate. She said, "No indeed. But have you somewhere to go, for tonight I mean?"

"She'll be staying with me."

Tolly came quietly into the room. She was wearing a dark blue fitted coat with padded shoulders and a small hat pierced with one long feather. The outfit was reminiscent of the thirties and gave her a slightly raffish smartness. She was carrying a bulging suitcase bound with a strap. She moved

unsmiling to Mrs. Munter's side—it was impossible for
Cordelia to think of her by any other name—and the two
women faced her together.

Cordelia felt that she was seeing Mrs. Munter clearly for
the first time. Until now she had hardly noticed her. The
strongest impression she had made was of an unobtrusive
competence. She had been an adjunct to Munter, little more.
Even her appearance was unmemorable: the coarse hair,
neither fair nor dark, with its stiff, corrugated waves; the
stolid body; the stumpy, workworn hands. But now the thin
mouth which had given so little away was taut with an
obstinate triumph. The eyes which had been so deferentially
downcast stared boldly into hers with a look of challenging,
almost insolent confidence. They seemed to say, "You don't
even know my name. And now you never will." Beside her
stood Tolly, unchanged in her self-contained serenity.

So they were going away together. Where, she wondered,
would they live? Presumably, since she'd offered Simon a
room, Tolly had a house or flat somewhere in London where
she had made a home for her child. Cordelia had a sudden
and disconcertingly clear picture of them, not living there
surrounded by memories, but installed in a neat suburban
house within convenient distance of the tube and the shopping
center, net curtains looped across the bay window, hindering
inquisitive eyes, a small front garden railed against unwelcome
intruders, against the past. They had thrown off their servitude. But surely that servitude must have been voluntary.
Both were adult women. Surely it wasn't the fear of unemployment that had kept them from their freedom. They could
have left their jobs whenever it suited them. So why hadn't
they? What was the mysterious alchemy that kept people tied
together against all reason, against inclination, against their
own interests? Well, death had parted them now, one from
Clarissa, the other from Munter; parted them very conveniently,
the police might think.

Cordelia thought, I'm seeing both of them clearly for the

first time and still I know nothing about them. Some words of Henry James fell into her mind. "Never believe that you know the last word about any human heart." But did she know even the first word, she who called herself a detective? Wasn't it one of the commonest of human vanities, this preoccupation with the motives, the compulsions, the fascinating inconsistencies of another personality? Perhaps, she thought, we all enjoy acting the detective, even with those we love; with them most of all. But she had accepted it as her job; she did it for money. She had never denied its fascination, but now, for the first time, it occurred to her that it might also be presumptuous. And never before had she felt so inadequate for the task, pitting her youth, her inexperience, her meager store of received wisdom against the immense mysteriousness of the human heart.

She turned to Mrs. Munter. "I should like to have a word with Miss Tolgarth alone. May I, please?"

The woman didn't reply but looked at her friend and was given a small nod. Without speaking, she left them.

Tolly waited, patient, unsmiling, her hands folded before her. There was something which Cordelia would have liked to ask first, but she didn't need to. And she was less arrogant now than when she had first taken the case. She told herself that there were questions she had no right to ask, facts she had no right to be told. No human curiosity, no longing to have every piece of the jigsaw neatly fitted into place as if her own busy hands could impose order on the muddle of human lives, could justify asking what she knew in her heart was true, whether Ivo had been the father of Tolly's child. Ivo, who had spoken of Viccy with knowledge and love, who had known that Tolly had refused to accept any help from the father; Ivo, who had taken the trouble to get in touch with the hospital and learn the truth about that telephone call. How strange to think of them together, Ivo and Tolly. What was it, she wondered, that they had wanted of each other? Had Ivo been trying to hurt Clarissa or assuage a deeper hurt of his

own? Was Tolly one of those women, desperate for a child,
who prefer not to be burdened with a husband? The birth of
Viccy, if not the pregnancy, must surely have been deliberate.
But none of it was her business. Of all the things that human
beings did together, the sexual act was the one with the most
various of reasons. Desire might be the commonest, but that
didn't mean that it was the simplest. Cordelia couldn't even
bring herself to mention Viccy directly. But there was something she had to ask.

She said, "You were with Clarissa when the first of the
messages came, during the run of *Macbeth*. Would you tell
me what they looked like?"

Tolly's eyes burned into hers with a somber, considering
stare, but not, she thought, with resentment or dislike.

Cordelia went on, "You see, I think it was you who sent
them, and I think she might have guessed and known why.
But she couldn't do without you. It was easier to pretend.
And she didn't want to show the messages to anyone else.
She knew what she had done to you. She knew that there
were things even her friends might not forgive. And then
what she hoped would happen did happen. Perhaps there had
been some change in your life which had made you feel that
what you were doing was wrong. So the messages stopped.
They stopped until one of the small number of people who
had known about them took over. But then they were different
messages. They looked different. Their purpose was different.
And their end was different and terrible."

Still there was no reply.

Cordelia said gently, "I know I've no right to ask. Don't
answer me directly if you'd rather not. Just tell me what those
first messages were like and I think I shall know."

Then Tolly spoke. "They were written by hand in capital
letters on lined paper. Paper torn from a child's exercise
book."

"And the messages themselves. Were they quotations?"

"It was always the same message. A text from the Bible."

Cordelia knew that she was lucky to have gained so much. And even this confidence wouldn't have been given if Tolly hadn't recognized some sympathy, some empathy, between them. But there was one more question which she thought she might risk.

"Miss Tolgarth, have you any idea who it was who took over?"

But the eyes looking into hers were implacable. Tolly had told all she intended to tell.

"No. I concern myself with my own sins. Let others look to theirs."

Cordelia said, "I shall never pass on to anyone what you've just said to me."

"If I thought that you would, I wouldn't have told you." She paused, and then asked in the same even tone, "What will happen to the boy?"

"To Simon? He told me that Sir George will keep him on at Melhurst for his final year and that he'll then try for a place at one of the colleges of music."

Tolly said, "He'll be all right now she's gone. She wasn't good for the young. And now, if you'll excuse me, miss, I'd like to help my friend finish her packing."

3

THERE WAS NOTHING MORE to be said or done. Cordelia left the two friends together and went to her bedroom to get ready for the afternoon's excursion. As her object was to search for the newspaper review, her full scene-of-crime kit was hardly necessary, but she slipped a hand magnifying glass, a pocket torch, and a notebook into her shoulder bag and pulled her guernsey over her shirt. It might be cold on the boat on the return trip. Last she wound the leather belt twice around her waist and buckled it tightly. As always, it felt like a talisman, a girding on of resolution. As she crossed the terrace from the western front of the castle, she saw that Mrs. Munter and Tolly were already making their way toward the launch, both of them carrying a case in either hand. Oldfield must only recently have landed. He was still dragging his crates of wine and groceries onto the jetty, helped rather surprisingly by Simon. Cordelia thought that the boy was probably glad of something to do.

Suddenly Roma appeared from the dining-room windows and hurried down the terrace in front of her. She went up to Oldfield and spoke to him. The canvas post bag was on top of his trolley, and he unbuckled it and took out the bundle of letters. Drawing close to them, Cordelia could sense Roma's impatience. It looked as if she might snatch the bundle from Oldfield's gnarled fingers. But then he found what she was wanting and handed her a letter. She almost ran from him, then slowed to a walk, and, without noticing Cordelia's approach, tore the envelope open and read the letter. For a moment she stood absolutely still. Then she gave a sob, so high that it was almost a wail, and began stumbling along the terrace, pushed past Cordelia, and disappeared down the far steps to the beach.

Cordelia paused for a moment, uncertain whether to follow. Then she called to Oldfield to wait for her, that she wouldn't be long, and ran after Roma. Whatever the news, it had devastated her. There might be something she herself could do to help. Even if not, it was impossible just to board the launch and set off as if the scene had never happened. She tried to silence the small resentful voice which protested that it couldn't have occurred at a more inconvenient time. Was she never to be allowed to get off the island? Why should she always have to be the one to act as universal social worker? But it was impossible to ignore such distress.

Roma was stumbling and reeling along the shore, her hands flung out before her, groping in the air. Cordelia thought that she could hear a high continued scream of pain. But perhaps it was the cry of the gulls. She had almost caught up with the fleeing figure when Roma tripped, fell at full length on the shingle, and lay there, her whole body shaking with sobs. Cordelia came up to her. To see the proud and reserved Roma in such an abandonment of grief was as physically shocking as a blow to the stomach. Cordelia felt the same rush of impotent fear, the same helplessness. All she could do was to kneel in the sand and put her arms around Roma's shoulders,

hoping that this human contact might at least help to calm
her. She found herself softly cooing as she might to a child or
an animal. After a few minutes the dreadful shaking ceased.
Roma lay so still that, for a second, Cordelia feared that she
had ceased to breathe. Then she heaved herself clumsily
upright and threw off Cordelia's arm. Having walked unsteadily
into the surf, she bent and began splashing her face. Then she
stood upright for a moment, looking out to sea, before
turning to face Cordelia.

Her face was grotesque, bloated like a long-drowned visage, the eyes like gummed slits, the nose a bulbous mess.
When she spoke her voice was harsh and guttural, the sounds
forcing themselves through swollen vocal cords.

"I'm sorry. That was a disgusting exhibition. I'm glad it
was you, if that's any comfort."

"I wish I could help."

"You can't. No one can. As you've probably guessed, it's
the usual commonplace sordid little tragedy. I've been chucked.
He wrote on Friday night. We only saw each other on
Thursday. He must have known then what he was going to
do."

She pulled the letter from her pocket and held it out.

"Go on, read it! Read it! I wonder how many drafts it took
to produce this elegant, self-justifying piece of hypocrisy."

Cordelia didn't take the letter. She said, "If he hadn't the
decency and courage to tell you to your face, he isn't worth
crying over; he isn't worth loving."

"What has worth to do with love? My God, why couldn't
he have waited?"

Waited for what? thought Cordelia. For Clarissa's money?
For Clarissa's death?

She said, "But if he had, could you ever have been sure?"

"Of his motive, you mean? Why should I care? I haven't
that kind of pride. But it's too late now. He wrote a day too
soon. Oh, God, why couldn't he have waited? I told him that
I'd get the money. I told him!"

A wave, larger than its fellows, broke at Cordelia's feet and rolled a woman's silver evening sandal among the brighter seawashed stones. She found herself looking at it with an artificial intensity, making herself wonder what sort of woman had worn it, how it had come to be in the sea, from what wild party on what yacht it had been lost overboard. Or was its owner out there somewhere, a slim, half-clad body turning in the waves? Any thought, even that thought, helped to shut out the harsh unnatural voice which might any moment say those fatal words which couldn't be taken back and which neither of them would be able to forget.

"When I was a child I went to a coeducational school. All the children paired off. When the friendship cooled, they used to send each other what they called a chuck note. I never had one. But then I never had a boyfriend. I used to think it would be worth getting the chuck note if only I'd had the friendship first, just for one term. I wish I could feel that now. He was the only man who has ever wanted me. I think I always knew why. You can only deceive yourself so far. His wife doesn't much enjoy sex and I was a free fuck. All right, don't look like that! I don't expect you to understand. You can get love whenever you want it."

Cordelia cried, "That isn't true; not of me, not of anyone!"

"Isn't it? It was true of Clarissa. She only had to look at a man. One look, that's all it ever took. All my life I've watched her using those eyes. But she won't any more. Never again. Never, never, never."

Her anguish was like an infection, strong and feverish and smelling of sweat. Cordelia could feel its contamination in her own blood. She stood on the shingle, afraid to approach Roma since she knew that physical comfort would be unwelcome, reluctant to leave her, miserably aware that Oldfield would be getting impatient.

Then Roma said gruffly, "You'd better go if you want to catch the launch."

"What about you?"

"Don't worry. You can escape with an easy conscience; I shan't do anything stupid. That's the euphemism, isn't it? Isn't that what they always say? Don't do anything stupid. I've been taught my lesson. No more stupidity, Roma! I can tell you what will happen to me, in case you're interested. I'll take Clarissa's money and buy myself a London flat. I'll sell the shop and find myself a part-time job. From time to time I'll take a foreign holiday with a woman friend. We shan't much enjoy each other's company, but it will be better than traveling alone. We'll devise little treats for ourselves, the theater, an art show, dinner at one of those restaurants where they don't treat solitary women as pariahs. And in the autumn I'll enroll for evening classes and pretend an interest in throwing pots or the Georgian architecture of London or comparative religion. And every year I shall get a little more fussy about my comforts, a little more censorious of the young, a little more fretful with my friend, a little more right-wing, a little more bitter, a little more lonely, a little more dead."

Cordelia would have liked to say, "But you'll have enough to eat. You'll have your own roof over your head. You won't die of cold. You'll have your strength and your intelligence. Isn't that more than three-quarters of the world enjoys? You're not a Victorian shell gatherer, waiting for a man to give purpose and status to your life. There doesn't even have to be love." But she knew that the words would be as futile and insulting as telling a blind man that there was always the sunset.

She turned and walked away, leaving Roma still staring out to sea. She felt like a deserter. It seemed discourteous to hurry, and she waited until she reached the terrace before breaking into a run.

4

NO ONE SPOKE during the passage to the mainland. Cordelia sat in the prow of the launch, fixing her eyes on the gradually approaching shore. Mrs. Munter and Tolly settled themselves together in the stern, their bags at their feet. When *Shearwater* finally berthed, Cordelia waited until they had left before herself getting up. She watched while the two women, side by side but still unspeaking, made their slow way up the hill toward the station.

The town was less crowded and less busy than on the Friday morning, but it still held its slightly archaic air of cheerful sunlit domesticity. What she found extraordinary was to be so unnoticed. She had half expected that people would turn to stare at her, that she would hear the whispered word *Courcy* at her back, that she would bear an all-too-visible mark of Cain. How marvelous it was to be free of Grogan and his minions, at least for a few blessed hours, no longer one of that apprehensive, self-regarding coterie of suspects, but an

ordinary girl walking an ordinary street, anonymous among
the early-afternoon shoppers, the last holiday visitors, the
office workers hurrying back to their desks after a belated
lunch. She wasted a few minutes in a chemist's shop behind a
charming Regency façade buying a lipstick which she didn't
need, taking more than usual care over her selection. It was a
small gesture of hope and confidence, a salute to normality.
The only mention she saw or heard of Clarissa's death was a
couple of placards advertising national dailies with the words
ACTRESS MURDERED ON COURCY ISLAND written, not printed,
under the paper's name. She bought one at a kiosk and found
a brief account on the third page. The police had given the
minimum of information, and Ambrose's refusal to speak to
the press had obviously frustrated them in making much of a
story. Cordelia wondered whether, in the end, it would prove
to have been wise.

She learned from the newsagent that there was now only
one local paper, the *Speymouth Chronicle*, which came out
twice a week on Tuesday and Friday. The office was at the
northern end of the esplanade. Cordelia found it without
difficulty. It was a white converted house with two large
windows, one painted with the words *Speymouth Chronicle*
and the other filled with a display of newspaper photographs.
The front garden had been paved to provide a parking space
for half a dozen cars and a delivery van. Inside she found a
blond girl of about her own age presiding at a reception desk
and simultaneously coping with a small switchboard. At a
side table an elderly man was sorting pictures.

Her luck held. She had feared that old copies of the paper
might be kept elsewhere or might not be readily available to
the public. But when she explained to the girl that she was
researching into provincial theater and wanted to look up the
reviews of Clarissa Lisle's performance in *The Deep Blue
Sea*, no questions were asked and no difficulties made. The
girl called out to her companion to keep an eye on the desk,
ignored a light on the switchboard, and took Cordelia through

a swinging door and down a steep flight of ill-lit stairs to the basement. There she unlocked a small front room from which the exciting musty smell of old newsprint rose to the nostrils like a miasma. Cordelia saw that the back numbers were bound in folders filed in chronological order on steel shelves. In the middle of the room was a long trestle table. The girl switched on the light and two fluorescent tubes glowed into harsh brightness.

She said, "They're all here, going back to 1860. You can't take anything away and you mustn't write on the papers. Don't slip off without telling me. I have to come and lock up after you've finished. Okay? See you later then."

Cordelia approached her task methodically. Speymouth was a small town and was unlikely to have a permanent theater company. It was almost certain, therefore, that Clarissa had played with a repertory company during the summer season, most likely between May and September. She would begin her search with those five months. She found no mention of the Rattigan play in May, but she did note that the summer repertory company, based in the old theater, opened with each new offering on a Monday and played for two weeks. The first reviews appeared on a page devoted to the arts in each Tuesday's edition, a commendably quick response for a small provincial paper. Presumably the reviewer telephoned his copy from the theater. The first mention of *The Deep Blue Sea* appeared in an advertisement in early June, which stated that Miss Clarissa Lisle would be guest star for the two weeks beginning July 18. Cordelia calculated that the notice would appear on the arts page, invariably page nine, on July 19. She lugged the heavy bound volume containing the editions from July to September onto the table and found the paper for that date. It was larger than the normal edition, consisting of eighteen pages instead of the usual sixteen. The reason was made apparent on the first page. The Queen and the Duke of Edinburgh had visited the town on the previous Saturday as part of their Jubilee Year provincial tour, and the Tuesday edition had been the first one following the visit. It had been a big day for Speymouth, the first royal visit since 1843, and the *Chronicle* had made the most of it. The account of the first page stated that further pictures were shown on page ten. The words struck a chord of memory. Cordelia was now almost sure that the reverse side of the notice she had seen had been not newsprint but a picture.

But now that success was so close she felt a sudden loss of confidence. All she would discover would be the review by a provincial reporter of a revival which hardly anyone in Speymouth would now remember. Clarissa had said that it was important to her, important enough to keep in the secret drawer of her jewel box. But that, with Clarissa, could have meant anything. Perhaps she had liked the notice, met the reviewer, enjoyed on the occasion a brief but satisfactory love affair. It could have been as sentimentally unimportant as that. And what possible relevance could it have to her death?

And then she saw that the sheet she wanted wasn't there. She checked twice. No careful turning of the newspaper disclosed pages nine and ten. She bent back the thick wedge of newsprint where it was gripped by the binder. Down the margin of page eleven she thought she could detect a thin impression as if the paper had been faintly scored with a knife or razor blade. She got out her magnifying glass and moved it slowly over the bound edges. Now she could see it clearly, the telltale mark, in some places actually cutting the paper, showing where the sheet had been excised. She could detect, too, minute shreds of paper where the edge of page nine was still clasped in the binder. Someone had been here before her.

The girl at the desk was busy with a customer inquiring, but without any visible signs of grief, how she went about inserting a death notice and how much extra a nice bit of verse would cost. She handed over a child's exercise book and pointed out the rounded, laboriously formed letters. Cordelia, always curious about the idiosyncrasies of her fellow human beings and for a moment forgetting her own concerns, edged closer and slewed her eyes to read:

The pearly walls were shining,
St. Peter whispered low,
The golden gate was opened,
And in walked Joe.

This piece of extremely dubious theology was received by the girl with a lack of interest which suggested that she had read its like before. She spent the next three minutes attempting to explain what the probable cost would be, including the extras if the notice was boxed and surmounted with a wreathed cross, a consultation which was punctuated by long considering silences as they both contemplated samples of the designs on offer. But after ten minutes all was satisfactorily decided and she was then able to turn her attention to Cordelia, who said, "I've found the right edition but the sheet I think I want isn't there. Someone's cut it out."

"They can't have. It isn't allowed. That's the archives."

"Well, they have. Is there another copy?"

"I'll have to tell Mr. Hasking. They can't go cutting the morgue about. Mr. Hasking will be in a rare state about that."

"I'm sure. But I do need to see that page urgently. It's page nine of the edition of July nineteenth, 1977. Haven't you any other back numbers I could look through?"

"Not here. The chairman might have a set up in London. Cutting up the morgue! Mr. Hasking sets great store by those old copies. That's history, that is, he says."

Cordelia asked, "Can you remember who last asked to see them?"

"There was a blond lady from London last month. Writing a book about seaside piers, she said. They blew this one up in 1939 so the Germans couldn't land, then the council hadn't any money to build it again. That's why it's so stumpy. She said they used to have a music hall on the end when she was a girl and artistes used to come down from London in the season. She knew a lot about piers."

Cordelia thought that a better-equipped or more efficient private detective would have come with photographs of the victim and suspects for possible identification. It would have been useful to know whether the blond woman who was so knowledgeable about piers looked like Clarissa or Roma. Tolly, unless she had disguised herself, surely an unnecessarily dramatic ploy, was obviously out. She wondered whether Bernie would have thought of photographing the house party unseen, prepared for just such an eventuality. She hadn't herself felt such a tricky procedure to be possible or useful. But she did, after all, have the Polaroid in her kit on the island. Perhaps it would be worth a try. She could come back tomorrow.

She said, "And is the pier lady the only one who has recently asked to see the archives?"

"While I've been here. But, then, I've only been on the desk a couple of months. Sally could have told you about anyone before that, but she's left to get married. And I'm not always on the desk. I mean someone could've come when I was in the office and Albert was on the desk."

"Is he here?"

The girl looked at her as if astounded at such ignorance. "Albert? Of course he isn't. Albert's never here Mondays." She looked at Cordelia with sudden suspicion. "Why d'you want to know who else has been here? I thought you were just after seeing that review."

"I am. But I was curious who could have cut out that page. As you said, these are important records. And I wouldn't like anyone to think it was I. You're quite sure there isn't a copy anywhere else in the town?"

Without looking around, the elderly man who was still arranging new photographs in the display frame with a deliberation and an eye for artistic effect which suggested that the job could well take the rest of the day made his suggestion.

"July nineteenth, 'seventy-seven, did you say? That's three days after the Queen's visit. You could try Lucy Costello. She's kept press cuttings on the royal family for the last fifty years. Isn't likely she'd have missed the royal visit."

"But Lucy Costello's dead, Mr. Lambert! We had an article about her and her press cuttings the day after they buried her. Three months ago, that was."

Mr. Lambert turned around and spread out his arms in a parody of patient resignation. "I know Lucy Costello's dead! We all know she's dead! I never said she wasn't dead. But she's got a sister, hasn't she? Miss Emmeline's still alive as far as I know. She'll have the cuttings books. Isn't likely she'd throw them out. They may have buried Miss Lucy but they haven't buried her press cuttings with her, not that I know of. I said to try her. I didn't say speak to her."

Cordelia asked how she could find Miss Emmeline. Mr. Lambert turned away again to his photographs and spoke gruffly, as if regretting his former loquacity. "Windsor Cottage, Benison Row. Up the High Street, second left. Can't miss it."

"Is it far? I mean, ought I to take a bus?"

"You'd be lucky. Catch yer death, you would, waiting for that number twelve. Ten minutes' walk at most. No trouble for a young 'un."

He selected a picture of a portly gentleman wearing a mayoral chain, whose sideways glance of salacious bonhomie suggested that the official banquet had more than fulfilled expectations, and positioned it carefully beside a photograph of a well-endowed and decidedly underclad bathing beauty, so that his eyes appeared to be gazing down her cleavage. Cordelia thought that here was a man who enjoyed his work. She thanked him and the girl for their help and set out to find Miss Emmeline Costello.

5

MR. LAMBERT HAD BEEN RIGHT about the distance. It was almost exactly ten minutes' brisk walk to Benison Row. Cordelia found herself in a narrow street of Victorian houses curving about the town. Although there was a pleasing unity in the age, architecture, and height of the cottages, they were charmingly individual. Some had bow windows; others had been fitted with wooden window boxes from which a profusion of variegated ivy, geraniums, and aubrietia trailed their bright pattern against the painted stucco; and the two at the end of the row had bay trees in painted tubs set each side of the gleaming front door. Each had a narrow front garden set behind wrought-iron railings which, perhaps because of their delicate ornamentation, had escaped being sacrificed for scrap iron in the last war. Cordelia realized that she had never before seen a row of houses with their railings complete, and they gave to the street, which was outwardly so English in its small-scale prettiness, a touch of charming but alien eccentricity. The little gardens rioted with color, the warm, deep reds of autumn seeming to burst against the railings. Although it was late in the season, the air was a potpourri of lavender and gillyflowers. There were no cars parked at the curb, no throat-catching tang of petrol fumes. After the bustle and hot smells of the High Street, walking into Benison Row was like stepping back into the cozy simplicity of another and legendary age.

Windsor Cottage was the fourth house down on the left-hand side. Its garden was plainer than the rest, a neat square of immaculate lawn bordered with roses. The brass door knocker in the shape of a fish gleamed brightly in every scale. Cordelia rang the bell and waited. There was no sound of hurrying footsteps. Again she rang, this time a longer peal. But there was silence. She realized with a pang of disappointment that the owner was out. It had, perhaps, been stupidly sanguine to expect that Miss Costello would be waiting at home simply because she, Cordelia, wanted to see her. But the disappointment dragged at her spirit and filled her with a restless impatience. She was convinced now that the missing news cutting was vital, and only in this neat little house was there a chance of finding it. The prospect of having to return to the island with this clue unexplored, her curiosity unsatisfied, appalled her. She began pacing up and down outside the railings, wondering how long it might be worth waiting, whether Miss Costello would return, perhaps from shopping, or had shut up the house and gone away for a holiday. And then she noticed that the two upper windows were open at the top, and her spirits rose. A middle-aged woman came out of the next-door house, looked up the road as if expecting someone, and was about to close the door when Cordelia ran forward.

"Excuse me, but I was hoping to see Miss Costello. Do you know if she's likely to be back this afternoon?"

The woman replied pleasantly, "She'll be at the washateria, I expect. She always does her washing on Monday afternoons.

She shouldn't be long, unless she decides to have tea in the town.''

Cordelia thanked her. The door closed. The little street sank back into silence. She leaned against the railings and tried to wait in patience.

It wasn't long. Less than ten minutes later she saw an extraordinary figure turn the corner into Benison Row and knew at once that this must be Miss Emmeline Costello. She was an elderly woman, trundling after her a canvas-covered shopping trolley from the top of which bulged a plastic-covered bundle. She walked slowly but upright, her thin figure obliterated by a khaki army greatcoat so long that its hem almost scraped the pavement. Her small face was as softly puckered as an old apple and further diminished by a red-and-white-striped scarf bound around her head and tied under her chin. Over it had been pulled a knitted purple cap topped with a bobble. If such a superfluity of clothing was necessary on a warm September day, Cordelia could only wonder how she dressed in winter.

As Miss Costello came up to the gate, Cordelia moved to open it for her and introduced herself. She said, ''Mr. Lambert of the *Speymouth Chronicle* suggested that you might be able to help me. I'm looking for a cutting from an old edition of the paper—July nineteenth, 1977. Would it be an awful nuisance if I looked through your sister's collection? I wouldn't trouble you, but it really is important. I've tried the newspaper morgue but the page I want isn't there.''

Miss Costello might present to the world an appearance of almost intimidating eccentricity, but the eyes which looked into Cordelia's were sharp, bright as beads, and accustomed to making judgments, and when she spoke it was in a clear, educated, and authoritative voice, which immediately and unmistakably defined her precise place in the complicated hierarchy of the British class system.

''When you're eighty-five, my child, don't live on top of a hill. You'd better come in and have some tea.''

In just such a voice had Reverend Mother greeted Cordelia when she had first arrived, tired and frightened, at the Convent of the Holy Child.

She followed Miss Costello into the house. It was apparent that nothing would be done in a hurry, and as a supplicant she could hardly insist that it be. She was shown into the drawing room while her hostess went off to remove several layers of her outer clothing and to make tea. The room was charming. The antique furniture, probably brought from a larger family home, had been selected to suit the room's proportions. The walls were almost covered with small family portraits, water-colors, and miniatures, but the effect was of an ordered domesticity, not of clutter. A mahogany wall cupboard inlaid with a pattern of rosewood held a few choice pieces of porcelain, and on the mantel shelf a carriage clock ticked away the moments. When Miss Costello reappeared, wheeling a trolley before her, Cordelia saw that the tea service was in green decorated Worcester and that the teapot was silver. It was an occasion, she thought, on which Miss Maudsley would have felt perfectly at home.

The tea was Earl Gray. As she sipped it from the elegant shallow cups, Cordelia had a sudden and irresistible impulse to confide. She couldn't, of course, tell Miss Costello who she was or what she was really seeking. But the peace of the room seemed to enclose her with a warm security, a comforting respite from the horror of Clarissa's death, from her own fears, even from loneliness. She wanted to tell Miss Costello that she came from the island, to hear a sympathetic human voice saying how awful it must have been, a comforting elderly voice assuring her in the remembered tones of Reverend Mother that all would be well.

She said, "There's been a murder on Courcy Island. The actress Clarissa Lisle has been killed. But I expect you know. And now Mr. Gorringe's manservant has been drowned."

"I have heard about Miss Lisle. The island has a violent history. I don't suppose these will be the last deaths. But I haven't read the newspaper account, and, as you see, we don't have a television set. As my sister used to say, there's so much ugliness now, so much hatred, but at least we don't have to bring it into our sitting room. And at eighty-five, my dear, one is entitled to reject what one finds unpleasing.''

No, there was no comfort to be had here in this seductive but spurious peace. Cordelia was ashamed of the momentary weakness that had sought it. Like Ambrose, Miss Costello had carefully constructed her private citadel, less beautiful, less remote, less extravagantly self-indulgent, but just as self-contained, just as inviolate.

Neither excitement nor impatience had impaired Cordelia's appetite. She would have been grateful for more than the two thin slices of bread and butter provided, particularly as the meagerness of the meal bore no relation to its length. It was surprising that Miss Costello could take so long drinking two cups of tea and nibbling her share of the food. But at last they had finished.

Miss Costello said, ''My late sister's press cuttings are in her room upstairs. She was a dedicated monarchist''—here Cordelia thought she detected a nuance of indulgent contempt— ''and there is scarcely a royal occasion during the last fifty years which escaped her attention. But her main interest was, of course, in the House of Saxe-Coburg-Gotha. I shall leave you to search on your own if I may. I am unlikely to be able to help you. But please don't hesitate to call if you feel that I could.''

It was interesting but not altogether surprising, thought Cordelia, that Miss Costello hadn't troubled to inquire what she was seeking. Perhaps she regarded such a question as vulgar curiosity or, more likely, feared that it might only provoke one more intrusion of the disagreeable into her ordered life.

She showed Cordelia into the front bedroom. Here Miss Lucy's obsession was immediately apparent. The walls were almost covered with photographs of royalty, some of them half effaced with scribbled signatures. On a long shelf over the bed was closely ranged a collection of coronation mugs, and a glass-fronted display cabinet was filled with other memorabilia, crested and decorated teapots, cups and saucers, and engraved glass. The whole of the wall facing the window was fitted with shelves holding a collection of scrapbooks. Here was the famous collection.

Each of the books was marked on the spine with the dates covered, and Cordelia was able, without difficulty, to find July 1977. The local press photographers had done justice to Speymouth's big day. There was hardly an aspect of the royal visit which had gone unrecorded. There were pictures of the royal arrival, the mayor in his chain, the curtseying mayoress, the children with their miniature Union Jacks, the Queen smiling from the royal car, hand raised in the distinctive royal wave, the Duke at her side. But there was no cutting which precisely fitted Cordelia's memory of the shape and size of the missing piece. She sank back on her heels, the book open before her, and felt for a moment almost sick with disappointment. The microdots of grinning, anticipatory, self-satisfied faces mocked her failure. The chance of success had been slight, but she was chagrined to realize how much hope she had invested in it. And then she saw that hope was not yet lost. On the bottom shelf was stacked a row of stout manila envelopes, each with the year written on it in Miss Lucy's upright hand. Opening the top one, she saw that it also contained press cuttings, perhaps duplicates sent to Miss Lucy by friends eager to help with her collection or cuttings she had rejected as unworthy of inclusion but hadn't liked to throw away. The envelope for 1977 was plumper than its fellows as befitted Jubilee Year. She tipped out the medley of cuttings, most already fading with age, and spread them around her.

Almost immediately she found it: the remembered oblong shape, the heading "Clarissa Lisle Triumphs in Rattigan Revival," the third column cut down the middle. She turned

it over. She didn't know what she had expected, but her first
reaction was one of disappointment. The whole of the reverse
was taken up with a perfectly ordinary press photograph. It
had been shot across the esplanade and showed the opposite
pavement thronged with smiling faces, a row of children
squatting on the curb, their flags at the ready, their more
adventurous elders perched on window ledges or clinging to
lamp posts. At the back of the crowd two stout women with
Union Jacks around their hats stood on the steps of a house,
holding up a sagging banner with the words *Welcome to
Speymouth*. Royalty hadn't yet arrived, but the picture conveyed
the sense of happy expectation. Cordelia's first irrelevant
thought was to wonder why Miss Costello had rejected it.
But, then, there had been so many pictures to choose from,
many in which the Queen was actually shown. But what
possible interest could this not particularly distinguished photograph, this record of local patriotism, have for Clarissa
Lisle? She looked at it more closely. And then her heart
leaped. To the right of the photograph was the slightly blurred
figure of a man. He was just stepping out into the road,
obviously intent on some private business, oblivious of all the
excitement around him, his preoccupied face staring past the
camera. And there could be no doubt about it. The man was
Ambrose Gorringe.

Ambrose in Speymouth in July 1977. But that had been the
year of his tax exile. Surely he had had to stay overseas for
the whole of the financial year; she could remember reading
somewhere that even to set foot in the United Kingdom
would vitiate the nonresident status. But suppose he had
sneaked back—and this picture proved that he must have
done—wouldn't that make him liable for all the tax he had
avoided, all the money he must have spent on restoring the
castle, acquiring his pictures and porcelain, beautifying his
private island? She would have to find an expert, discover
what the legal position was. There would be firms of solicitors in Speymouth. She could consult a lawyer, put a general

question on tax law; there would be no need to be specific. But she had to know, and there wasn't much time. She glanced at her watch. Already it was ten minutes to five. The launch would be waiting for her at six o'clock. It was essential to get some kind of confirmation before she returned to the island.

As she gathered up the unwanted cuttings and replaced them in the envelope and went downstairs to find Miss Costello, her mind was busy with this new knowledge. If Clarissa had realized the significance of that press photograph, why hadn't anyone else? But, then, why should they? Ambrose hadn't lived on the island in 1977. He had probably visited it only rarely; it was unlikely that his face would be known locally. Those who knew him best lived in London and were unlikely ever to see the *Speymouth Chronicle*. And he had written his best-seller under a pseudonym. Even if someone living locally did recognize the picture, he was unlikely to realize that this was A. K. Ambrose, the author of *Autopsy*, who was supposed to be spending a year in tax exile. It was hardly the kind of thing one advertised. No, it had been his appallingly back luck that Clarissa had been playing in Speymouth that week and had wanted to read her notice. And Clarissa had extorted her price for silence. Oh, it would have been subtly managed; there would have been nothing crude or blatant about this blackmail. Clarissa would have laid down her terms with charm, even a tinge of amused regret. But the price would have been demanded, and it had been paid. So much was clear to her now: why Ambrose had tolerated the disruption of his life by the players, why Clarissa made use of the castle as if she were its chatelaine. Cordelia told herself that none of this proved that Ambrose was a murderer, only that he had a motive. And she held the proof of it in her hand.

Afterward it was to strike her as strange that never for one moment did she consider taking the cutting at once to the police. First she must get confirmation; then she must confront Ambrose. It was as if this murder investigation had nothing to do with the police. It was a matter between herself and Sir George who had employed her, or perhaps between herself and the woman she had failed to protect. And Chief Inspector Grogan's arrogant masculine voice rang in her ears: "You may be too bright for your own good, Miss Gray. You're not here to solve this crime. That's my job."

She found Miss Costello in her small back kitchen, folding her linen ready for ironing. She was happy for Cordelia to take away the cutting and said so without bothering to look at it or to take her attention from her pillowcases. Cordelia asked whether she could recommend a firm of local solicitors. This request did evoke a swift upward glance from the shrewd eyes, but still she asked no questions. Escorting her guest to the door, she merely said, "My own advisers are in London, but I have heard that Blake, Franton, and Fairbrother are considered reliable. You will find them on the esplanade about fifty yards east from the Victoria memorial. You would be wise to hurry. Little useful activity, professional or otherwise, goes on in Speymouth after five o'clock."

6

MISS COSTELLO WAS RIGHT. By the time Cordelia arrived panting, at the polished Georgian door of Messrs. Blake, Franton, and Fairbrother it was shut firmly against any further clients for that day. The lower rooms were in darkness, and although there was a light in the second story, a nameplate on the side of the door showed that this part of the house was a separate flat. Even if it hadn't been, she could hardly disturb a strange solicitor in his private house for advice on what was, after all, on the face of it, hardly an urgent matter. Perhaps there was a firm which remained open until six; but how to find it? There was always the yellow pages, if the post office provided this directory in the provinces. She was ashamed to discover that, Londoner as she was, this was a fact she didn't know. And even if she could find a directory which gave the names of local solicitors, there would be the difficulty of locating the offices without a town map. She seemed to have come on this excursion singularly ill equipped.

As she stood irresolute, a young man came up bearing a carton of vegetables and pressed the bell of the flat. He said, "Closed, are they?"

"Yes, as you see. I wanted a solicitor in a hurry. It's rather urgent."

"Yeah, that's the thing about solicitors. If you have to have 'em it's usually urgent. You could try Beswick. He's got an office in Gentleman's Walk. About thirty yards down the street and turn left. He's about halfway up on the right."

Cordelia thanked him and ran. Gentleman's Walk was easily found, a narrow cobbled street of elegant early eighteenth-century houses. A brass nameplate, polished to the point of being almost indecipherable, identified James Beswick, Solicitor. Cordelia was relieved to see that a light still shone behind the translucent glass and that the door opened to her touch.

Seated at the desk was a fat, rather untidy woman with immense scarlet-rimmed spectacles, wearing a tightly belted suit in a brightly patterned cretonne of overblown roses and intertwined vine leaves which gave her the look of a newly upholstered sofa. She said, "Sorry, we're shut. Call or ring tomorrow, ten o'clock onward."

"But the door was open."

"Literally, but not figuratively. I should have locked it five minutes ago."

"But since I'm here . . . it's very urgent. It won't take more than a few minutes, I promise."

A voice from an upper room called out, "Who is it, Miss Magnus?"

"A client. A girl. She says it's very urgent."

"Is she comely?"

Miss Magnus jerked her spectacles to the end of her nose and looked at Cordelia over the rims. Then she shouted up the stair, "What's that got to do with it? She's clean, she's sober, and she says it's urgent. And she's here."

"Send her up."

The footsteps receded. Cordelia, suddenly assailed by doubts, asked, "He is a lawyer, isn't he? A good one?"

"Oh, yes, he's that all right. Nobody's ever said that he isn't a good lawyer."

The emphasis on the last word was ominous. Miss Magnus nodded at the staircase. "You heard him. First floor to the left. He's feeding his tropical fish."

The man who turned to her from the window was tall and gangling with a lean, creased, humorous face and half spectacles worn low on his long nose. He was sprinkling seed from a packet into an immense fish tank, not shaking it from the packet but pinching small quantities between his fingers and dropping the seed in a careful pattern on the surface of the water. There was a tumble of red and bright blue as the fish swirled together and snapped at the food. He pointed as one of the fish streaked to the surface in a blaze of polished bronze. "Look at him. Isn't he a beauty? That's the dawn tetra, an expensive little fellow from British Guiana. But perhaps you prefer the glowlight tetra. There he is, lurking under the shells."

Cordelia said, "He's very beautiful, but I don't much enjoy tropical fish in tanks."

"Is it the fish or the tanks or the conjunction you object to? They're perfectly happy, I assure you, at least one assumes so. Their small world has been artistically and scientifically devised for their comfort, and they get their food regularly. They sow not, neither do they reap. Ah, there's a beauty! Look at that flash of gold and green."

Cordelia said, "I wanted some information urgently. It isn't about my affairs, it's just a general inquiry. You do give that kind of advice?"

"Well, it isn't usual. I'm not sure that it's wise. Solicitors are rather like doctors. You can't really generalize or deal in hypothesis; each case is unique. You have to know all the circumstances if you're really going to help. That's an interesting analogy, come to think of it; and I'll go further. If your

doctor tells you to go abroad at once you can always settle for
sunny Torquay instead. If your solicitor suggests you go
abroad, you'd be wise to make for Heathrow immediately. I
hope you're not in that precarious situation.''

"No, but it's about going abroad that I've come to consult
you. I want to know about tax avoidance.''

"Do you mean tax avoidance, which is legal, or tax
evasion, which isn't?''

"The first. Suppose I came into a very large sum of
money, all of it in one tax year. Could I avoid paying tax if I
went abroad for twelve months?''

"That depends what you mean by 'came into a large sum
of money.' Are you talking about an inheritance, a gift, a
football-pool win, a sale of property, or shares, or what?
You're not contemplating a bank raid, are you?''

"I mean earned income. Money I received by writing a
successful play or a novel, or painting a picture or acting in a
film.''

"Well, if you were sensible you would arrange your con-
tracts so that the money wasn't all received during the one
financial year. That would be a matter for your accountant
rather than for me.''

"But suppose I didn't expect it to be so successful.''

"Then you could avoid paying tax on it by becoming
non-resident for the whole of the subsequent financial year.
Money earned in that way is taxed retrospectively as you
probably know.''

"Could I come home for a holiday or a weekend?''

"No. Not even for a day.''

"Suppose I needed to. I might be homesick.''

"I should strongly advise you not to. Tax exiles can't
afford the luxury of homesickness.''

"But if I did come back?''

He sighed. "If you really want an authoritative answer I
would have to do some delving to see if there is any case law.
And as I say, it's more a question for a tax accountant than

for me. My present view, for what it's worth, is that you would become liable for tax on the income received during the whole of the preceding year."

"And if I concealed the fact of my return from the Inland Revenue?"

"Then you could be prosecuted for attempted fraud. Probably they wouldn't bother with that if the amount wasn't large, but they would see that they got the tax due. I mean, they're in the business of getting their hands on tax properly due."

"How much would that be?"

"Well, the present top rate on earned income is sixty percent."

"And in 1977?"

"Ah, in those unregenerate days it was rather more. Eighty percent or more on an income of over twenty-four thousand of taxable income. Something like that."

"So they might ruin me?"

"Bankrupt you, you mean? Indeed they might, if you were so ill advised as to spend all your previous year's income in advance in the confident expectation that it wouldn't be taxable. Death and taxation catch up with us all."

"Thank you. You've been very kind. Can I pay now? If it's more than two pounds I'm afraid I'll have to give you a check. I have a check card."

"Well, it hasn't taken very long, has it? And I think Miss Magnus has balanced the petty cash and locked away the box. Suppose you have this consultation on me."

"I don't think that would be right. I ought to pay for your time."

"Then put a pound in the doggy box and we'll call it quits. When you've written your best-seller you can come back and I'll give you some proper advice and charge you very high for it."

The doggy box was on his desk, the brightly painted model of a lugubrious spaniel holding between its paws a collecting tin bearing the name of a well-known animal charity. Cordelia folded in a couple of pound notes with the mental promise that she would charge only one to Sir George's account.

And then she remembered. There probably wouldn't be any account. Perhaps she would return to the office poorer than when she had left. Sir George had reassured her that she would be paid, but how could she charge him for so tragic a failure? It would be too like blood money. And how on earth would her bill be worded? It was strange how many small complications the huge complication of murder threw up. She thought, Even in the midst of death we are in life, and the petty concerns of life don't go away.

SHE REACHED THE HARBOR with two minutes to spare. She was surprised and a little disconcerted to find that the launch wasn't waiting but told herself that Oldfield must have been kept by some job on the island; she was, after all, a little ahead of time. She sat on the bollard to wait, glad of the chance to rest, although her mind, stimulated by the excitements of the day, soon drove her to action. She got up and began restlessly pacing the harbor wall. Below her a sluggish tide sucked at the verdurous stones and a swag of seaweed spread its gnarled and drowned hands under the darkening surface. Daylight was fading and the warmth died with the light. One by one the houses climbing the hill lit their glowing oblongs behind drawn curtains and the winding streets became festive with sparkling necklaces of light. The late shoppers and holiday makers had gone home, and she heard only the occasional echo of a solitary footfall on the harbor wall. The little town, as if regretting its hours of unseasonable frivolity, was settling into a chill autumnal calm. The smells of summer were forgotten, and a rank watery smell rose from the harbor.

She looked at her watch. She saw that it was six-fifteen, and the time was immediately confirmed by the striking of a distant church clock. She walked to the harbor mouth and gazed toward the island. There was no sign of the launch, and the sea was empty except for two or three late-returning boats gliding with slackened sails toward their moorings.

Still she paced and waited. Seven-fifteen. The evening sky, layered in mauve and purple, had flamed into darkness, and the moon, pale as a tissue, shed a trembling path of light over the sea. In the distance, Courcy Island crouched like an animal against the paler hue of the sky. Night had distanced it. It was hard now to believe that only two miles of water separated that black and ominous shore from the lights, the gathered domesticity of the town. Looking out at it, she shivered. Ambrose's story came back into her mind with the primitive atavistic force of a childhood nightmare. She could understand why so many local fishermen down the ages had thought the island accursed. Almost she could picture that desperate sailor, fighting the onset of the plague and the fury of the sea, wild-eyed and exultant on his way to his dreadful vengeance.

It was after seven-thirty now. Whether by accident or by design, Oldfield wasn't going to come. But at least she could leave the quay to ring the island and inquire without the fear of missing him. She remembered seeing two telephone boxes near the Victoria statue. Both were free, and when she had shut herself into the first she was glad to find that it hadn't been vandalized. It was irritating that she hadn't made a note of the castle number, and for a moment she feared that Ambrose's obsession with privacy might have caused him to be ex-directory. But the number was listed, although under Courcy Island, not his name. She dialed and could hear the ringing tone. Then the receiver was lifted, but no one replied to her voice. She thought that she could detect the sound of breathing but told herself that this must be imagination. She said again, "It's Cordelia Gray here. I'm ringing from Speymouth. I was expecting the launch at six o'clock." Still there was no reply. She spoke again, more loudly, but there was nothing but silence and the impression, eerie but unmistakable, that there was someone there, someone who had lifted the receiver but who had no intention of speaking. She replaced the hand piece and dialed again. This time she got the engaged signal. The receiver had been taken off the rest.

She made her way back to the harbor, though now with little hope that the launch would be in sight. Then she saw that there were lights and signs of activity on one of the moored vessels. Standing on the edge of the quay, she looked down at a shabby but sturdy wooden boat with a crudely constructed cabin amidships, brown sails, and an outboard motor. The port and starboard lamps were lit, and there was a dragnet heaped in the stern. It looked as if the sailor was preparing for a night's fishing. And he must, she thought, have a small galley. The salty, mouthwatering tang of fried bacon rose from the cabin above the fainter pervasive smell of tar and fish. As she gazed down, a stocky and bearded young man squeezed through the cabin door and looked up, first at the sky and then at her. He was wearing a patched jersey and sea boots and was biting into a thick sandwich. With his cheerful, ruddy face and shock of black hair he looked like an amiable buccaneer.

On impulse she called down to him, "If you're setting out, could you land me on Courcy Island? I'm staying there and the launch hasn't come for me. It's terribly important that I get back tonight."

He moved along the boat, still munching the wedge of greasy bread, and looked up at her with eyes which were shrewd but not unfriendly. He said, "They say there's someone murdered there. A woman, isn't it?"

"Yes, the actress Clarissa Lisle. I was staying there when it happened. I'm still supposed to be staying there. They should have sent the launch for me at six. I must get back tonight."

"A murdered woman. That's nothing new for Courcy Island. I'll be fishing off the southeast point. I'll take you if you're sure you want to go." Neither his voice nor his face betrayed any particular curiosity.

She said quickly, "I'm quite sure. I'll pay for the petrol, of course. That's only fair."

"No need. The wind's free. There'll be enough of it out in the bay. You can crew if you like."

"I'm not sure that I know how. But I'll put on the right rope when you tell me."

He transferred the sandwich to his left hand, wiped the right on his jersey and held it out to help her aboard.

She said, "How long do you think it will take us?"

"The tide's running against us. Best part of forty minutes. Maybe more."

He disappeared into the cabin and she waited, seated in the bow, willing herself to patience. A minute later he reappeared and handed her a sandwich, two rashers of bacon, greasy and strong-smelling, wedged between thick slices of crusty bread. Until she bit into it, almost dislocating her jaw in the process, Cordelia hadn't realized just how hungry she was. She thanked him. He said with a trace of boyish satisfaction at the evident success of his catering arrangements, "There'll be cocoa once we get under way."

He clambered along the outside of the cabin toward the stern. A minute later the engine shuddered and the small boat began to creep from the quay.

7

IT WAS ALMOST IMPOSSIBLE to believe that she had first seen Courcy Castle only three days earlier. In that short span of time she seemed to have lived through long, action-packed years, to have become a different person. Surely it had been some excitable expectant child who had gasped in wonder at her first sight of those sunlit walls, those patterned battlements, that high, luminous tower. But now, as the little boat turned the headland, she almost gasped again. The castle was ablaze with light. Every window shone, and from the tower, scored with pencil-slim lines of light, the high window threw a strong beam like a warning beacon over the sea. The castle seemed buoyant with light, lifted above the rocks to float in motionless serenity under an indigo sky, obliterating the nearer stars with brightness. Only the moon held her place, wan as a circle of rice paper, moving behind a thin veil of cloud.

She stood on the quay until the boat had drawn away. For a

moment she was tempted to call out to the boy to stay, at least within call. But she told herself that she was being ridiculous and fanciful. She wouldn't be alone with Ambrose. Even if Ivo was too sick to be much support, Roma, Simon, and Sir George would be there. And even if they weren't, why should she be afraid: She would be facing someone with a motive. But motive alone didn't make a murderer. And she agreed in her heart with Roma. Ambrose hadn't the nerve, the ruthlessness, the capacity for hatred, which drove a man to the ultimate crime.

Light lay across the terrace like a sheet of silver. She trod it as if on air, as if she, too, were buoyant, moving silently toward the open french windows of the drawing room. And then Ambrose appeared and stood watching her approach, a dark figure silhouetted against the light. He was wearing a dinner jacket and holding a glass of red wine in his left hand. The picture had the clarity and distinction of a painting. She found herself admiring the artist's technique: the careful positioning of the body, the artful blob of red in the glass cunningly and deftly painted in to emphasize the dark vertical lines of the figure, the splash of white at the shirt front, the dominant eyes which gave a focus and meaning to the whole composition. This was his kingdom, his castle. He was in command. He had illuminated it as if to celebrate and exult in his mastery. But when she came up to him his voice was light and casual. He might have been welcoming her home after an afternoon's shopping on the mainland. But wasn't that precisely what he thought he was doing?

"Good evening, Cordelia. Have you eaten? I didn't wait dinner, such as it is. I cooked myself some soup and an herb omelet. Would you care for one?"

Cordelia moved into the drawing room. Here only the wall lights and one table lamp were lit, making a cozy circle of light by the fire. The corners of the room were dark, and long shadows moved like fingers over the carpet and the walls.

The fire must have been lit for some time. A single large log was burning steadily.

She slipped off her shoulder bag and asked, "Where is everyone?"

"Ivo's in bed, not at all well, I'm afraid. He'll be going home tomorrow if he's fit for the journey. Roma has left. She was anxious to get back to London. Sir George had one of his mysterious calls to a meeting at Southampton and she took the launch with him. They won't be returning, although they'll both be in Speymouth tomorrow for the inquest. Simon said that he wasn't hungry. He's gone to bed."

So they were alone after all, alone except for the sick Ivo and a boy. She asked, hoping that her voice didn't betray her dismay, "Why wasn't the launch at Speymouth? Oldfield was supposed to meet me at six."

"He or I must have misunderstood. He'll be back with *Shearwater*, but not until the morning. He's visiting his daughter in Bournemouth for the night."

"I did ring, but whoever answered put down the receiver."

"I'm afraid that's been my stock response to the telephone today. Too many calls, too many reporters."

They stood together in front of the fire. She took the newspaper photograph from her bag and held it out to him. "I went to Speymouth to find this."

He didn't touch it or even glance at it. "I did wonder. I congratulate you. I didn't think you'd succeed."

"Because you'd already cut it out of the newspaper morgue?"

He said calmly, "Yes, I destroyed it about a year ago. It seemed a sensible precaution."

"I found another."

"So I see." Suddenly he said gently, "You look tired, Cordelia. Hadn't you better sit down? May I get you some claret or brandy?"

"I'd like a glass of claret, please."

She had to keep her mind clear, but the thought of the wine was irresistible. Her mouth was so dry that she could hardly frame her words. He fetched a glass for her from the dining room, poured her wine, and refilled his own glass, then sat with the decanter close at hand. They settled themselves on each side of the fireplace. It seemed to Cordelia that no chair had ever been more welcoming or as comfortable, no wine had ever tasted so good. He began to speak as calmly and unemotionally as if they were sitting together after dinner, discussing the ordinary events of an unremarkable day.

"I came back to visit my uncle. I was his heir and he wanted to see me. I don't think he understood that I couldn't return and still have a tax-free year. That wasn't the way his mind worked. It would never have occurred to him that a man could spend a year of his life doing what he didn't want to do, living where he didn't want to live, because of money. I wish you'd known him. You would have liked each other. It wasn't difficult getting here unnoticed. I flew from Paris to Dublin and took an Aer Lingus flight to Heathrow. Then I traveled by rail to Speymouth and rang the castle for my uncle's servant, William Mogg, to meet me after dark with the launch. They'd lived together here for nearly forty years. I asked Mogg not to tell anyone that he'd seen me, but it wasn't necessary. He never spoke of his master's business. Three months after my uncle died he turned his face to the wall and followed him. So you see, there wasn't really any risk. He asked me to come. I came."

"And if you hadn't, perhaps he would have altered his will."

"Unkind, Cordelia. You probably won't believe me, but I wasn't influenced by that disagreeable possibility. I didn't even believe that it was a possibility. I liked him. I seldom saw him—he didn't encourage visits even from his heir—but when I did pay my annual homage there was something between us which both of us recognized. Not love. I think he loved only William Mogg, and I'm not sure that *I* know what the word means. But whatever it was, I valued it. And I valued him. He had toughness, obstinacy, courage. He was his own man. He lay in that immense bedroom like some ancient chieftain gazing out over the sea and fearing nothing; nothing, nothing. And then he asked me to get for him something he fancied, a last taste of blue Stilton. He can't have tasted it for thirty years. He and William Mogg practically lived off the island, making their own butter and cheese. God knows what put that need into his mind. He could have asked Mogg to get it for him. But he didn't; he asked me.''

"So that's why you went to Speymouth?"

"That's why. If I hadn't done that simple act of filial kindness, Clarissa wouldn't have seen that press photograph, wouldn't have forced me into staging *The Dutchess of Malfi*, would still be alive. Odd, isn't it? It makes nonsense of any theory of the beneficent governance of human life. But then I learned that lesson when I was eight and my mother died because she was one minute late for the plane home and the one she caught crashed. It was a matter, you see, of whether the Paris traffic lights were red or green. We live by chance and we die by chance. With Clarissa, if you look back far enough, it was a matter of eight ounces of blue Stilton. Evil coming out of good, if those two words mean something to you.''

Ivo had asked her much the same question. But this time she wasn't expected to answer.

He went on, ''A man should have the courage to live by his beliefs. If you accept, as I do absolutely, that this life is all that we have, that we die as animals, that everything about us is finally lost irrevocably, that we go into the night without hope, then that belief must influence how you live your life.''

"Millions of people live with that knowledge and still live good and kindly and useful lives.''

"Because goodness and usefulness and kindness are expedient. I have my share of them. It is necessary for comfort to be at least a little liked. And perhaps some of the virtuous unbelievers still retain a vestigial hope or fear that there could be an afterlife, a measure of reward or punishment, a rebirth. There isn't, Cordelia. There isn't. There's nothing but darkness, and we go into it without hope."

Remembering how he had sent Clarissa into her darkness, she gazed, appalled, at the gently smiling face with its look of spurious sorrow, as if the full knowledge of what he had done had only now come home to her.

"You smashed in her face! Not once; time and time again! You could make yourself do that!"

"It wasn't agreeable. And if it's any consolation to you, I had to close my eyes. And it seemed to go on for so long. The sensation was horribly specific, softness cushioning the brittleness of bones. And so many bones. I could feel them splintering like smashing a tin of toffee in childhood. Our old cook used to let me make it. Smashing it when it had cooled was the best part. And when I opened my eyes and made myself gaze, Clarissa wasn't there. Of course, she hadn't been there before, but once her face was gone I couldn't even remember what she had looked like. More than anyone else I know, Clarissa was her face. That demolished, I knew afresh what I'd always known: the ridiculous presumption of supposing that she had a soul."

Cordelia told herself, I won't be sick. I won't. I won't. And I must stay calm. I mustn't panic.

His voice came to her faintly but very clearly. "When I was sixteen and first came to this island as a schoolboy, I knew for the first time what I wanted of life. Not power, not success, not sex, with men or women. That has always been to me an expense of spirit in a waste of shame. It wasn't even money, except as it contributed to my passion. I wanted a place. This place. I wanted a house. This house. I wanted this view, this sea, this island. My uncle wanted to die on it. I wanted to live on it. It's the only real passion I've ever known. And I wasn't going to let a nyphomaniac second-rate actress take it from me."

"And so you killed her?"

He refilled her glass and his own, then looked at her. She had the feeling that he was measuring something: her probable response, his need to confide, perhaps even how much time remained to them. He smiled, and the smile was one of genuine amusement which almost broke into a laugh. "My dear Cordelia! Do you really believe that you're sitting here sipping Château Margaux with a murderer? I congratulate you on your sangfroid. No, I didn't kill her. I thought you understood that. I haven't that brand of courage or ruthlessness. No, she was dead when I battered in her face. Someone had been there before me. She couldn't feel it, you see. Nothing matters, nothing exists, as long as you can't feel it. It wasn't living flesh that I beat to a pulp. It wasn't Clarissa."

But of course. What had made her so blind? She had reasoned all this out before. Clarissa must have been dead when he raised the marble limb and brought it down, the limb of a dead princess who, by chance, had borne the same name as that other child, who more than a century later had died, uncomforted by her mother, in a London hospital bed.

He said, "There was no upwards spurt of blood. How could there be? She was already dead. It isn't so very difficult to strike when the kill has been made. No blood, no pain, no guilt. All I did was to cover up for the murderer. Admittedly my motive was mainly self-interest. I needed to find and destroy that vital scrap of newsprint. I knew that it would be somewhere in the room. That was one of her little tricks, to keep it near her, to take it out of her handbag occasionally and pretend to read the review. But you should credit me with some disinterested concern for the killer. It pleased me to concoct for him a way of escape if he had the guts to take it. After all, I did owe him something."

"She could have taken photocopies of the photograph."

"Perhaps, although it wasn't likely. And what would it matter if she had? They'd be found with her effects at home, trivia to be thrown away with the detritus of her essentially trivial life, the half-used jars of face cream, the dead love letters, the hoarded theater programs. And even if George Ralston had found it and realized its significance—an unlikely eventuality—he wouldn't have done anything. George wouldn't have seen it as his business to do the work of the Inland Revenue. I came back here for one day and one night to be with a dying old man. Would you, or anyone you know, use that knowledge to inform on me?"

"No."

"And will you now?"

"I must. It's different now. I have to tell; not the tax people, the police. I have to."

"Oh, no, you don't, Cordelia! No, you don't! Don't try to fool yourself that you no longer have the responsibility of choice."

She didn't answer.

He leaned forward and refilled her glass. "It wasn't the possibility of other copies that worried me. What I couldn't risk was the police finding that one copy in her room. And I knew that if it were there to find, they'd find it. They'd be looking for a motive. Everything in that room would be collected, docketed, scrutinized, examined. There was a chance, of course, that they'd take the cutting at its face value, a critic's notice kept for purely sentimental reasons. But why that particular notice, a not-very-important play in a provincial theater? It's never safe to rely on the stupidity of the police."

She said with great sadness, "So it was Simon. Poor Simon! Where is he now?"

"In his room. Perfectly safe, I assure you. Don't you want to know what happened?"

"But he couldn't have planned it. Not Simon. He couldn't have meant it."

"Planned it, no. Meant it? Who's to say what he meant? She's just as dead, isn't she, whatever he meant? What he told me was that she invited him to her room. He was to say that he was going for a swim, put on his swimming trunks under his jeans and shirt, wait until thirty minutes after she'd gone to rest, then knock three times at the door. She'd let him in. She said there was something she wanted to talk to him about. There was, of course. Herself. Whatever else did Clarissa ever want to talk about? He, poor deluded fool, thought she was going to tell him that he could go to the Royal College, that she'd pay for his musical education."

"But why send for Simon? Why him?"

"Ah, that I doubt whether we shall ever know. But I can make a guess. Clarissa liked to make love before a performance. Perhaps it gave her confidence; perhaps it was a necessary release of tension; perhaps she knew of only one way to stop herself thinking."

"But Simon! That boy! She couldn't have wanted him!"

"Perhaps not. Perhaps, this time, she only wanted to talk, wanted companionship. And, with all respect to you, my dear Cordelia, she had never looked to a woman for that. But she may have thought that she was doing him a service in more ways than one. Clarissa is totally incapable of believing that a man existed—a normal man anyway—who wouldn't take her if he could get her. To do her justice, my sex hasn't done much to disabuse her of the idea. And what better time for Simon to begin his privileged education than on a warm afternoon after, I pride myself, an excellent luncheon and when she needed a new sensation, a divertissement, to take her mind off the performance ahead? And who else was there? George, poor chivalrous booby, would lie to the death to protect her reputation, but my guess is that he hasn't touched her since he discovered that he was a cuckold. I'm no use to her. And Whittingham? Well, Ivo has had his turn. And can you imagine her wanting him even if he had the strength? It would be like handling the dry skin of death, infecting your tongue with the taste of death, smelling corruption in your nostrils. Given dear Clarissa's peculiar needs, who was there but Simon?''

"But it's horrible!"

"Only because you're young, pretty, and intolerant. It would have done no harm with a different boy and at a different time. He might even have thanked her. But Simon Lessing was looking for a different kind of education. Besides, he's a romantic. What she saw in his face wasn't desire; it was disgust. Of course, I could be wrong. She may not have thought it out very clearly. Clarissa seldom did. But she asked him to come to her. And as with me and my uncle, he came.''

She said, "What happened? How did you find out?"

"I lied to Grogan about the time I left my room. I changed at once and quickly so that just after twenty minutes to two I was passing Clarissa's door. At that moment Simon looked out. The encounter was completely fortuitous. We stared at each other. His face was ghastly, ashen white, the eyes glazed. I thought he was going to collapse. I pushed him back into the bedroom and locked the door. He was wearing only his swimming trunks, and I saw his shirt and jeans in a heap on the floor. And Clarissa was lying sprawled on the bed. She was dead.''

"How could you be sure? Why didn't you get help?"

"My dear Cordelia, I may have led a sheltered life, but I know death when I see it. I did check. I felt for a pulse. None. I drew the corner of my handkerchief across her eyeball, a disagreeable procedure. No response. He had brought the jewel box crashing down on her head and smashed the skull. The box was actually lying there on her forehead. Oddly enough, there was very little bleeding, a small smudge on his forearm where the blood had spurted upwards, a thin trickle running from her left nostril. It had almost dried when I saw her, and yet she had been dead for only ten minutes. It looked like a crooked gash, a disfig-

urement above the gaping mouth. That's one last humiliation which none of us can do anything about, looking
ridiculous in death. How she would have hated it! But,
then, you know. You saw her.''

Cordelia said, ''You forget. I saw her later. I saw her when
you'd finished with her. She didn't look ridiculous then.''

''Poor Cordelia! I'm sorry. I would have spared you that if
I could. But I thought it would look suspicious if I went up
early to call her myself. That's something I've learned from
popular fiction. Never be the one to find the body.''

''But why? Did he say why?''

''Not very coherently. And I was more concerned to get
him away than to discuss the psychological complications of
the encounter. But neither of them had got what they wanted.
She must have seen the shame and the disgust in his eyes.
And he saw the loss of all his hopes in hers. She taunted him
with his sexual failure. She told him that he was as useless to
her as his father had been. I think it was at the moment when
she lay there, half naked on the bed, smiling up at him,
mocking him and his dead father together, destroying all his
hopes, that his control snapped. He seized the jewel casket,
the only weapon to hand, and brought it down.''

''And after that?''

''Can't you guess? I told him precisely what he must do. I
schooled him in his story to the police. He was to say that
he'd gone to swim after lunch as he had told us all that he
would. He'd walked along the beach until about an hour after
the end of the meal and had then entered the water. He had
started off back to the castle at about a quarter to three to
dress for the play. I made sure that he had it by heart. I took
him into Clarissa's bathroom and washed off the small spot of
blood. Then I dried the basin with toilet paper and flushed it
down the W.C. I found the newspaper cutting. It didn't take
long. Her handbag or the jewel box were the two obvious
places. Then I took him next door and instructed him how to
get down the fire escape from your bathroom window, being

careful not to touch any of the rungs with his hands. He was like a dutiful child, obedient, extraordinarily calm. I watched while he managed the fire escape, carrying the box under his arm, then as he went to the edge of the cliff and hurled it out to sea as I'd instructed him. And if the police do succeed in dredging it up, they'll find that the valuable jewels are missing. I took them out and flung them into another part of the sea. Forgive me if I don't demonstrate my confidence in you by saying precisely where. But it would never have done if all that the police found missing in the casket was one reputed sheet of newsprint. Then he dived and I watched him strike out strongly toward the west cove."

"But someone else was watching, too: Munter from the tower room window, the only window which overlooks the fire escape."

"I know. He managed to make that plain to us in his drunken ramblings when Simon and I were helping him to his room. It wouldn't have mattered. Munter was absolutely safe. I told Simon not to let it worry him. Munter would have taken any secret of mine to the grave."

Cordelia said, "He took it to the grave conveniently early. And could you really trust a drunkard?"

"I could trust Munter, drunk or sober. And I didn't kill him. Nor, as far as I know, did Simon. That death, at least, was accidental."

"What did you do next?"

"I had to work quickly. But the haste and the risk were remarkably stimulating. My plotting of this real-life mystery was almost as ingenious as it was in *Autopsy*. I cleaned the makeup from Clarissa's face so that the police wouldn't suspect that she'd invited a visitor to her room. Then I set out to destroy the evidence of how precisely she was killed and to substitute a weapon which Simon couldn't have brought with him because he didn't know it existed, a weapon which would deceive the police into thinking that the murder was connected with the threatening quotations. I didn't tell Simon what I proposed and didn't touch the body until he'd left. His ignorance was his greatest safeguard. He didn't have to act or pretend. He knew nothing about the marble. He never saw Clarissa's shattered face."

"And you had the limb with you, I suppose, in the inside pocket of your cloak?"

"I had both of them ready, the marble and the note. I was intending to put them in the casket which Clarissa would open in the second scene of act three. It would have had to be done under cover of the cloak and at the last minute, requiring some sleight of hand. But I think I might have managed it. And I assure you the result would have been spectacular. I doubt whether she would have got through the scene."

"And is that why you took the job of assistant stage manager and occupied yourself with the props?"

"That's why. It was natural enough. People assumed that I wanted to keep an eye on my belongings."

"And after you'd destroyed Clarissa's face, I suppose you took Simon's clothes to the cove, also hiding them under your cloak."

"How well you understand duplicity, Cordelia. I should have liked to leave them farther down the shore, but there wasn't time. The small cove beyond the terrace was as far as I could manage. And then I entered the theater by the arcade and checked the props with Munter. I should mention that I didn't have to worry unduly about fingerprints when I was in Clarissa's room. This is my house. The furniture and the objects, including the marble, belong to me. It was perfectly reasonable that they should bear my prints. But I did wonder about my palm print on the communicating door. That could have shown that I was the last person to touch it. That's why I took good care to open it after we found the body."

"And the threatening quotations, you sent those, too? You took over when Tolly stopped?"

"So you know about Tolly. I think I've underestimated you, Cordelia. Yes, it wasn't difficult. Poor Tolly took to religion as an opiate for grief, and I continued the good work but in a rather more artistic form. It was only then that Clarissa called the police. It wasn't a development I welcomed, so I suggested a little ploy to her that effectively scotched their interest. Clarissa really was an extraordinarily stupid woman. She had instinct but absolutely no intelligence. My success depended on two things about Clarissa: her stupidity and her terror of death. So when Tolly's little notes with their remarkably apt biblical reference to millstones around necks ceased, I initiated my own brand of unpleasantness with the occasional help of Munter. The object was, of course, to destroy her as an actress and give me back my privacy, my peaceable island. It was only as an actress that Clarissa had any power over me. She would never return to Courcy if its theater was the scene of her final humiliation. Once her confidence and her career were effectively and totally destroyed, I should be free. To do her justice, she wasn't a common blackmailer. She didn't need to be. She first saw that newspaper cutting in 1977. Clarissa liked to pamper her ego with discreditable secrets about her friends, and this was one she hugged to herself for three years before she needed to make use of it. It was my bad luck that the restoration of the theater and the crisis in her career should coincide. Suddenly there was something she wanted of me. And she had the means to get it. I assure you that the blackmail was carried out with the greatest delicacy and discretion."

Suddenly he leaned toward her and said, "Look, Cordelia, it isn't going to be possible to shield him for much longer. He's beginning to drink. You must have seen it. And he's making mistakes. That gaffe which Roma noticed, for example. How could he have known what the jewel box was like if he hadn't seen or handled it? And there will be others. I like the boy and he's not without talent. I've done all I can to save him. Clarissa destroyed his father, and I didn't see why she should add the son to her list of victims. But I was wrong about him. He hasn't the guts to see this through. And Grogan is no fool."

"Where is he now?"

"I told you. In his room as far as I know."

She looked into his face, at the smooth, womanish skin burnished by the light of the fire, the eyes like black coals, the perpetually half-smiling mouth. She felt the persuasive force flowing toward her, rooting her into the comfort of her chair. And then, as if the claret had mysteriously cleared her mind, she knew exactly what he was doing. The careful explanations, the wine, the almost companionable chat, the seductive comfort folded like a shawl around her tiredness; what were they but a ploy to waste time, to keep her at his side? Even the place had conspired with him against her: the cheerful domesticity of the fire, the sense of unreality induced by the long restless shadows, the windows wide to the disorienting blackness of the night and the ceaseless sleep-inducing susurration of the sea.

She snatched up her shoulder bag and ran from the room, through the echoing hall, up the wide staircase. She flung open the door of Simon's bedroom and switched on the light. The bed was made, the room empty. She fled like a wild creature from room to empty room. Only in one did she see a human face. In the soft glow of his bedside lamp, Ivo was lying on his back, staring at the ceiling. As she came up to him he must have sensed her desperation. But he smiled sadly and gave a small rueful shake of the head. There was no help here.

There was still the tower to search, that and the theater. But perhaps he wasn't any longer in the castle. The whole island was open to him, cliffs and uplands, meadows and woodlands, the black unsearchable island holding like a shell in its dark intricacies the everlasting murmur of the sea. There was still the business room and the kitchen quarters, unlikely as it was that he had taken refuge there. She sped down the tiled passage and flung herself at the business-room door. And then she stood, arrested. The second display cabinet, the one which held the small mementos of Victorian crime and horror, had been violated. The glass had been smashed. Staring down, she saw that something was missing: the handcuffs. And then she knew where she would find Simon.

8

SHE FLUNG HER SHOULDER BAG on the desk of the business room, taking with her only her pocket torch. There was only one other thing she wished to have, the leather belt. But it was no longer around her waist. Somewhere and somehow during the day's activities she had lost it. She had a memory of hurriedly putting it on in the women's cloakroom of a chain store where she had stopped on her way to Benison Row. In her anxiety to find Miss Costello she must have buckled it insecurely. As she ran across the lawn and into the darkness of the wood, she wished that she still felt the reassuring strength of that private talisman clasped around her waist.

The church loomed before her, numinous and secret in the moonlight. No lights shone from the open door, but the faint gleam from the east window was enough to light her to the crypt even without the aid of her pocket torch. And that door, too, was open with the key in the lock. Ambrose must have told him where it could be found. The strong, dusty smell of the crypt came up to meet her. She didn't pause to find the switch but followed the shifting pool of light from her pocket torch past the rows of domed skulls, the grinning mouths, until it shone on the heavy iron-bound door which led to the secret passage. This too was open.

She dared not run; the passage was too twisting, the ground too uneven. She remembered that the passage lights were on a time switch and pressed each button as she passed, knowing that in a few minutes the lights would go out behind her, that she was moving from brightness into the dark. The way seemed interminable. Surely that small party, only two days earlier, hadn't traveled as far as this. She had a moment of panic, fearing that she might have found and taken a hidden turning and be lost in a maze of tunnels. But then she saw the second flight of steps, and there gleamed before her the low-roofed cavern above the Devil's Kettle. The single bulb suspended in its protective grille was shining steadily. The trapdoor was up, the lid resting against the wall of the cave. Cordelia knelt and gazed down into Simon's face. It strained up at her, the eyes wide and staring, the whites showing, like the eyes of a terrified dog. His left arm was stretched above his head, the wrist handcuffed to the top rail. His hand drooped from the bar of the handcuff, not the strong hand she remembered coming down on the piano keys, but as tender and pale as the hand of a child. And the steadily rising water, flapping like black oil against the cave walls and glazed with light from the cavern above, was already up to his shoulders.

She climbed down beside him. The cold cut her thighs like a knife. She said. "Where's the key?"

"I dropped it."

"Dropped it or threw it? Simon, I have to know where."

"I just dropped it."

Of course. He would have no need to hurl it far. Handcuffed and helpless as he was, he couldn't retrieve it now, however close it lay and however tempted or desperate he might be.

She prayed that the bottom of the cave would be rock, not sand. She had to find the key. There was no other way. Her mind had already done its rapid calculation. Five minutes to get back to the castle, another five to return. And where would she find a tool box, a file sufficiently strong to cut through the metal? Even if there were someone in the castle able and willing to help her, there still wasn't time. If she left him now she would be leaving him to drown.

He whispered, "Ambrose told me I'd be in prison for the rest of my life. That or Broadmoor."

"He lied."

"I couldn't stand it, Cordelia! I couldn't stand it!"

"You won't have to. Manslaughter isn't murder. You didn't mean to kill her. And you aren't mad." But how clearly the words of Ambrose fell into her mind. "Who's to say what he meant? She's just as dead, isn't she, whatever he meant?"

Any additional light was welcome. She switched on her torch, resting it on the top rung. Then she gulped in a lungful of air and lowered herself carefully under the gently heaving surface. It was important not to disturb the sea bed more than she could help. The water was icy cold and so black that she could see nothing. But she felt with her hands, scraping them along the bottom, feeling the gritty sand, the spurs of sharp unyielding rock. A swath of seaweed wound itself around her arm like a soft detaining hand. But her slowly creeping fingers found nothing that could have been the key.

She came up for air and gasped, "Show me where exactly you dropped it."

He whispered through his bloodless, chattering lips, "About here. I held my right hand out like this. Then I let it fall."

She cursed her folly. She should have taken more trouble to discover the exact place before disturbing the sand. Now she might have lost it forever. She had to move gently and slowly. She had to stay calm and take her time. But there wasn't any time. Already the water was up to their necks.

She lowered herself again, trying methodically to cover the

area he had indicated, letting her fingers creep like crabs over the surface of the sand. Twice she had to come up for air and see briefly the horror and the despair in those staring eyes. But·on the third attempt her hand found the stub of metal and she brought up the key.

Her fingers were so cold that they felt lifeless. She could hardly grasp the key and was terrified that she might drop it, that she might not be able to fit it into the lock.

Watching her shaking hands, he said, "I'm not worth it. I killed Munter, too. I couldn't sleep and I was there, in the rose garden. I was there when he fell in. I could have saved him. But I ran away so that I wouldn't have to look. I pretended that I hadn't seen, that I hadn't been near."

"Don't think about that now. We've got to get you out of here, get you warm again."

The key was in the lock at last. She was fearful that it might not work, that it might not even be the right key. But it turned easily enough. The bar of the handcuff loosened. He was free.

And then it happened. The trapdoor crashed down in an explosion of sound as physical as a blow cleaving their skulls. The noise seemed to thunder through the island, shaking the iron ladder under their rigid hands, lifting the water at their throats, and bursting it against the walls of the cave in a tidal wave of concentrated fury. It seemed that the cave itself must split open to let in the roaring sea. The burning flashlight, dislodged from the top rung of the ladder, curved in a shining arc before Cordelia's horrified eyes, gleamed for a second under the swirling water, and then died. The darkness was absolute. And then, even before the echo of that crash had rumbled into silence, Cordelia's ears caught a different sound, the hideous rasp of metal against metal, once and then repeated, a noise so dreadful in its implication that she threw back her sea-drenched head, and almost howled her protest into the blackness.

"Oh, no! Please God, no!"

Someone—and she knew who it must be—had kicked down the trapdoor. Someone's hand had shot home the two bolts. The killing ground had been sealed. Above them was unyielding wood, surrounding them the rock face, at their throats the sea.

She raised herself and pressed with all her strength against the wood. She bent her head and strained against it with her shoulders. But it didn't move. She knew that it wouldn't. She was aware of Simon dragging himself up beside her, of his palms beating ineffectually against it. She couldn't see him. The darkness was as thick and heavy as a blanket, an almost palpable weight against her chest. He was aware only of his terrified moans, long drawn out and tremulous as the waiting sea, of the rank smell of his fear, of the harsh indrawing of his breath, of a thudding heart which could have been his or hers. She reached out for him with her hands. They moved in what was meant to be comfort over his wet face, knowing only by their warmth which of the drops were seawater and which were tears. She felt his trembling hands on her face, her eyes, her mouth. He said, "Is this death?"

"Perhaps. But there's still a chance. We can swim for it."

"I'd rather stay here and have you close to me. I don't want to die alone."

"It's better to die trying. And I won't try without you."

He whispered, "I'll try. When?"

"Soon. While there's still air enough. You go first. I'll be behind you."

It was better for him that way. The first one through would have an easier passage, unhampered by the leader's thrusting feet. And if he gave up, there was the hope that she might have the strength to push him through. For a second she wondered how she would cope if the passage narrowed and his inert body blocked her escape. But she put the thought away from her. He was now less strong than she, weakened by cold and terror. He must go first. The water was now so high that only a fragile ribbon of light marked the exit. Its beam lay pale as milk on the dark surface. With the next wave that, too, would go and they would be trapped in utter darkness with nothing to point the way out. She tugged off her waterlogged jersey. They let go of the ladder, joined hands, and paddled to the middle of the cave where the roof was highest, then turned on their backs and gulped in their long last lungfuls of air. The rock face almost scraped Cordelia's forehead. Water, cool and sweet, fell on her tongue like the last taste of life. She whispered, "Now," and he let go of her hand without hesitation and slid under the surface. She took her final gulp of air, twisted, and dived.

She knew that she was swimming for her life, and that was almost all she knew. It had been a moment for action, not for thought, and she was unprepared for the darkness, the icy terror, the strength of the inflowing tide. She could hear nothing but a pounding in her ears, feel nothing but the pain above her heart and the black tide against which she fought like a desperate and cornered beast. The sea was death, and she struggled against it with all she could muster of life and youth and hope. Time had no reality. It could have been minutes, even hours, that passage through hell, yet it must have been counted in seconds. She wasn't aware of the thrashing body in front of her. She had forgotten Simon, forgotten Ambrose, forgotten even the fear of dying in the struggle not to die. And then, when the pain was too great, her lungs bursting, she saw the water above her lighten, become translucent, gentler, warm as blood, and she thrust herself upward to the air, the open sea, and the stars.

So this was what it was like to be born, the pressure, the thrusting, the wet darkness, the terror, and the warm gush of blood. And then there was light. She wondered that the moon could shed so warm a light, gentle and balmy as a summer day. And the sea, too, was warm. She turned on her back and floated, arms widespread, letting it bear her where it would. The stars were companionable. She was glad they were there. She laughed aloud at them in her joy. And it wasn't in the least surprising to see Sister Perpetua there bending over her in her white coif. She said, "Here I am, Sister. Here I am."

How strange that Sister should be shaking her head, gently but firmly, that the coiffed whiteness should fade and that there should be only the moon, the stars, and the wide sea. And then she knew who and where she was. The struggle still wasn't over. She had to find the strength to fight this lassitude, this overwhelming happiness and peace. Death, which had failed to seize her by force, was creeping on her by stealth.

And then she saw the sailing boat gliding toward her on the moonlit stream. At first she thought that it was a sea phantom born of her exhaustion and no more tangible than the white-coiffed face of Sister Perpetua. But it grew in form and solidity, and as she turned toward it she recognized its shape and the tousled head of its owner. It was the boat which had brought her back to the island. She could hear it now, the swish of the waves under the keel, the faint creaking of wood, and the hiss of the air in its sail. And now the stocky figure was standing back against the sky to fold the canvas in his arms and she heard the splutter of the engine. He was maneuvering to draw alongside. He had to drag her aboard. The boat lurched, then steadied. She was aware of a sharp pain dragging at her arms. And then she was lying on the deck and he was kneeling beside her. He seemed unsurprised to see her. He asked no questions, only pulled off his jersey and folded it around her.

When she could speak she gasped, "Lucky for me you were still here."

He nodded toward the mast and she saw, buckled around it like a talisman, the narrow strip of leather.

"I was coming to bring you that."

"You were bringing me back my belt!"

She didn't know why it was so funny, why she had to fight the impulse to break into wild hysterical laughter.

He said easily, "Oh, well, I had a fancy to land on the

island by moonlight, and Ambrose Gorringe is none too keen on trespassers. I had it in mind to leave the belt on the quay. I reckoned you'd find it soon enough in the morning."

The moment of incipient hysteria had passed. She struggled upright and gazed back at the island, at the dark mass of the castle, as impregnable as rock, all its lights extinguished. And then the moon arrived from behind a cloud and suddenly it glowed with magic, each separate brick visible yet insubstantial, the tower a silver fantasy. She gazed enchanted at its beauty. And then her numbed brain remembered. Would he be watching for her, there on his citadel, binoculars raised, eyes scanning the sea for her bobbing head? She could picture how it might have been: her exhausted body dragging itself ashore through the squelch of the shingle and the drag of the receding waves, her bleared eyes looking up only to meet his implacable eyes, his strength confronting her weakness. She wondered if he could have brought himself to kill in cold blood. She thought that it would have been difficult for him. Perhaps it would have been impossible. How much easier to kick shut the trapdoor, to shoot back the bolts and leave the sea to do your work for you. She remembered Roma's words: "Even his horror is second-hand." But how could he have let her live, knowing what she did?

She said, "You saved my life."

"Saved you a bit of a swim, that's all. You'd have made it. You're close enough to the shore."

He didn't ask why, almost naked, she should be swimming at such an hour. Nothing seemed to surprise or disconcert him. And it was only then that she remembered Simon. She said urgently, "There are two of us. There was a boy with me. We've got to find him. He'll be here somewhere. He's a very strong swimmer."

But the sea stretched in a calm, moonlit emptiness. She made him wait and search for an hour, tacking slowly up and **down the shoreline with the sails** furled, the engine gently purring. She lay slumped against the gunwale and stared desperately, watching for any movement on the sea's calm face. But at last she accepted what she had known from the beginning. Simon had been a strong swimmer. But weakened by cold and terror and perhaps by some despair which went beyond them, he hadn't been strong enough. She was too tired now to feel grief. She was hardly aware even of disappointment. And then she saw that they were making slowly for the quay.

She said quickly, "Not to the island, to Speymouth."

"You'll be wanting a doctor, then?"

"Not a doctor, the police."

Still he asked no questions, but put the boat about. After a few minutes with warmth and energy flowing back into her limbs, she tried to get up and give him a hand. But she seemed to have no strength in her arms.

He said, "Better go into the cabin and get some rest."

"I'd rather stay here on deck if that's all right."

"You'll not be in my way."

He fetched a pillow and a heavy coat from the cabin and tucked her up beside the mast. Looking up at the pattern of unregarding stars, hearing the flap of the canvas as the boom swung over, and soothed by the swish of the waves under the slicing hull, Cordelia wished that the journey could go on forever, that this respite of peace and beauty between the horror passed and the trauma to come might never end.

And so in a companionable silence they sailed together toward the harbor, feeling the peace of the night flowing between them. Cordelia must have slept. She was dimly aware of the boat gently bumping the quay, of being carried ashore, of his hands under her breasts, of the strong sea smell of his jersey, of a heart beating strongly against her own.

9

THE NEXT TWELVE HOURS remained in Cordelia's memory only as a confused impression of time passing but disoriented, of a limbo in which individual pictures and people stood out with startling and unnatural clarity as if a clicking camera had spasmodically recorded them, fixing them instantaneously and forever in all their capricious banality.

A huge teddy bear on the desk at the police station, humped against the wall at the end of the counter, squint-eyed, with a tag around its neck. A cup of strong, sweet tea slopping into the saucer. Two sodden biscuits disintegrating into mush. Why should they produce so clear an image? Chief Inspector Grogan in a blue jersey with frayed cuffs wiping egg off his mouth, then looking down at his handkerchief as if sharing her wonder that he should be eating so late. Herself huddled in the back of a police car and feeling the rough tickle of a blanket on her face and arms. The foyer of a small hotel, smelling of lavender furniture polish, with a lurid print of the death of Nelson above the desk. A cheerful-faced woman, whom the police seemed to know, half supporting her up the stairs. A small back bedroom with a brass bedstead and a picture of Mickey Mouse on the lamp shade. Waking in the morning to find her jeans and shirt neatly folded on the bedside chair and turning them over in her hands as if they belonged to someone else; thinking that the police must have gone back to the island the night before and how odd they hadn't taken her with them. One old man silently sharing the breakfast room with her and two women police officers, paper napkin tucked into his collar, a vivid red birthmark covering half his face. The police launch butting its way across the bay against a freshening wind with herself, like a prisoner under escort, wedged between Sergeant Buckley and a policewoman in uniform. A sea gull hovering above them with its strong curved beak, then dropping to settle on the prow like a figurehead. And then a picture which jerked all the unrealities into focus, brought back all the horror of the previous day, and clamped it around her heart like a vise: the solitary figure of Ambrose waiting for them on the quay. And among all these disjointed images there was the memory of questions, endless repetitive questions, of a ring of watching faces, of mouths opening and shutting like automatons. Afterward she could recall every word of the dialogue although the place had slipped forever from her mind, whether it had been the police station, the hotel, the launch, the island. Perhaps it had been all of those places and the questions had been asked by more than one voice. She seemed to be describing events that had happened to someone else, but to someone she knew very well. It was all clear in the mind of that other girl, although it had happened so long ago, years ago, so it seemed when Simon had been alive.

"Are you sure that when you first arrived at the trapdoor it was up?"

"Yes."

"And the door itself resting back against the wall of the passage?"

"It must have been if the trapdoor was open."

"If? But you said it was open. You're sure you didn't open it yourself?"

"Quite sure."

"How long were you with Simon Lessing in the cave before you heard it crash down?"

"I can't remember. Long enough to ask about the key to the handcuffs, to dive and find it, to set him free. Less than eight minutes perhaps."

"Are you sure that the trapdoor was bolted? Did you both try to lift it?"

"Me at first; then he joined me. But I knew it wasn't any good. I heard the scrape of the bolts."

"Is that why you didn't try very hard, because you knew that it wasn't any good?"

"I did try hard. I pressed my shoulders against it. I suppose it was a natural reaction, to try. But I knew it wasn't any use. I heard the bolts being shot home."

"You heard that small sound against the rush of the incoming tide?"

"There wasn't very much noise in the cave. The tide spouted in quietly like water into a kettle. That's what was so frightening."

"You were frightened and you were cold. Are you sure you would have had the strength to push open the door if it had fallen accidentally?"

"It didn't fall accidentally. How could it? And I heard the bolts."

"One or two?"

"Two. The scrape of metal against metal. Twice."

"You realize what that means? You understand the importance of what you're saying?"

"Of course."

They made her go back with them to the Devil's Kettle. It

was neither kind nor merciful; but, then, they weren't in the business of being kind or merciful. There were bright lights trained on the trapdoor, a man kneeling and dusting it for prints with the careful delicate strokes of a painter. Then they raised it, not resting it against the rock face but balancing it upright on its hinges. They stood back and, after no more than a couple of seconds, it crashed down. She shivered like a puppy, remembering another such crash. They asked her to raise it. It was heavier than she had expected. Underneath was the iron ladder leading down to death, the ray of bright daylight shining from a crescent exit, the slap of dark, strong-smelling water against the rock. They even made her go down, then shut the trapdoor gently over her. As they had instructed, she pushed her shoulders against it and was able without much strength to force it open. One of the officers climbed down into the cave and they closed the trapdoor and gently shot back the bolts. She knew that they were testing how much she could have heard. Then they asked her to balance the trapdoor on its hinges and she tried but couldn't. They asked her to try again, and when she failed they said nothing. She wondered if they thought that she wasn't trying. And all the time she saw, in her mind's eye, Simon's drowned body with its gaping mouth and glazed eyes, turning and twisting, sucked to and fro like a dead fish in the ebbing tide.

And then she was sitting in a corner of the terrace, alone except for the unspeaking, unsmiling woman police officer, waiting beside the police launch which would take her away from the island forever. Her typewriter and hand baggage were at her feet. There was still a wind but the sun had come out. She could feel its comforting warmth on her back and was grateful. She had thought that, since yesterday, she would never be warm again.

A shadow fell across the stones. Ambrose had come up silently to stand beside her. The waiting policewoman was out of earshot, but he spoke as if she were not there, as if they were totally alone. He said, "I missed you last night. I was worried about you. The police tell me that they found a hotel for you. I hope that it was comfortable.''

''Comfortable enough. I can't remember much about it.''

''You've told them everything, of course. Well, that's obvious from the mixture of coolness, speculation, and slight embarrassment with which they've regarded me since they made their untimely if not unexpected visit late last night.''

''Yes, I've told them''

''I can almost smell their exhilaration. It's understandable. If you aren't lying or mistaken or mad, they're onto a very good thing. Promotion gleams like the Holy Grail. They haven't arrested me, as you see. The situation is unusual, requiring tact and care. They'll take their time. At the moment I imagine that they're still testing the trapdoor, trying to decide whether it could have crashed down accidentally, whether you really could have heard the bolts shot home. After all, when they returned here last night, in a state I might say of some excitement, they found the trapdoor closed but not bolted. And I don't think they'll get any identifiable prints from the bolts, do you?''

Suddenly she felt an immense and overpowering anger, almost cosmic in its intensity as if one fragile female body could hold all the concentrated outrage of the world's pitiable victims robbed of their unvalued lives. She cried, ''You killed him, and you tried to kill me. Me! Not even in self-defense. Not even out of hatred. My life counted for less than your comfort, your possessions, your private world. My life!''

He said with perfect calmness, ''If that's what you believe, a certain resentment is reasonable. But you see, Cordelia, what I'm saying to the police and to you is that it didn't happen. It isn't true. No one tried to kill you. No one shot back those bolts. When you reached the trapdoor you found it closed. You raised it just wide enough to slide through and climb down to Simon, but you didn't prop it up completely. You closed that door after you; either that or you partly raised it and it accidentally fell. You were terrified, you were cold and you were exhausted. You hadn't the strength to shift it.''

"And what about the motive, the photograph in the *Chronicle*?"

"What photograph? It was unwise of you to leave it in your shoulder bag on the business room table. A natural oversight in your anxiety about Simon, but highly convenient for me. Don't tell me you haven't yet discovered that it's missing."

"The police are checking with the woman who gave it to me. They'll know that I did have a press cutting. Then they'll begin searching for a duplicate."

"Which they'll be lucky to find. And even if they do and the copy, after four years, is as clear as the one you so carelessly lost, I shall still have my defense. Obviously I have a double somewhere. Is that so unusual? Finding any real proof that I was in the United Kingdom in 1977 will get more difficult with every month that passes. In a year or so I should have felt safe even from Clarissa. And even if they can prove I was here that doesn't make me a murderer or a murderer's accomplice. Simon Lessing's death was suicide and it was he, not I, who killed Clarissa. He confessed the truth to me before he disappeared. He fractured her skull, beat her face to a pulp in his hatred and disgust, then made his escape through the bathroom window. And last night, unable any longer to face the truth of what he'd done or its consequences, he tried to kill himself. Despite your heroic attempt to save him, he succeeded. It was fortunate that he didn't take you with him. I had no hand in any of it. That, Cordelia, is my story, and nothing you choose to fabricate can disprove it.''

"Why should I want to fabricate? Why should I lie?"

"That's what the police asked me. I had to reply that the imagination of young women is notoriously fertile and that you had, after all, been through an appalling experience. I added that you are the proprietress of a detective agency which—forgive me, I'm judging from externals—isn't exactly prospering. You'd have to spend a fortune to get the kind of publicity that this case will bring you if it ever comes to trial."

"Hardly the kind of publicity anyone would want. Failure."

"Oh, I wouldn't be too depressed about that. You showed admirable courage and intelligence. 'Above the call of duty' is how poor George Ralston would put it. I think that George will feel that he's had value for money." He added, "If you persist in going on with this, it will be my word against yours. Simon's dead. Nothing can touch him further. It isn't going to be comfortable for either of us."

Did he think that she hadn't thought of that, of the long months of waiting, the interrogations, the trauma of the trial, the speculative eyes, the verdict which could brand her as a liar, or worse, a publicity-crazed hysteric? She said, "I know. But, then, I'm not much use to comfort."

So he was going to make a fight for it. Even as he watched her rescue last night he must have been planning, scheming, perfecting his lies. He would use every ounce of his skill, his reputation, his knowledge, his intelligence. He would hold onto his private kingdom until his last breath. She glanced up at him, at the half smile, the calm, almost exultant confidence. Already he was rejoicing in the release from boredom, buoyant with the euphoria of success. He would buy the best advice, the most prestigious lawyers. But essentially it would be his fight and he wouldn't yield an inch now or later.

If he succeeded, how would he live with the memory of what he had done? Easily enough. As easily as Clarissa had lived with the memory of Viccy's death, Sir George with his guilt over Carl Blythe. You didn't need to believe in the sacrament of penance to find expedients for coping with guilt. She had hers; he would contrive his. And was it so very remarkable, what had happened to him? Somewhere, every minute of every day, a man or woman is suddenly faced with an overwhelming temptation. It had gone ill with Ambrose Gorringe. But what had he been able to draw upon at the core of his being which could give him the strength to resist? Perhaps if you opted out long enough from human concerns, from human life with all its messiness, you opted out also from human pity.

She said, "Please leave me. I want you to go away."

But he didn't move. After a moment she heard him say, quietly and gently, "I'm sorry, Cordelia. I'm sorry." And then, as if aware for the first time of that silent uniformed watcher, he added, "Your first visit to Courcy Island hasn't been as happy for you as I hoped. I wish it could have been otherwise. Please forgive me."

She knew that this was the only admission that he would ever make. It had no validity in law. It would never be given in evidence. But she believed, almost despite herself, that it had been sincere.

She watched him as he walked briskly toward his castle. At the doorway Chief Inspector Grogan appeared and moved out to meet him. Without speaking they went inside together.

Still she sat and waited. A uniformed officer, painfully young and with the face of a Donatello angel, came across to her. He blushed and said, "There's a telephone call for you, Miss Gray. In the library."

Miss Maudsley was trying hard not to sound fussed, but her voice was close to panic. "Oh, Miss Gray, I do hope it's all right to call you. The young man who answered said that it was. He was so helpful. But I wondered when you'll be coming home. There's a new case just in. It's terribly urgent, a lost Siamese kitten, a seal point. It belongs to a child who is just out of hospital after her leukemia treatment and she's had it only a week. It was a coming-home present. She's dreadfully distressed. Bevis is at another audition. If I go there's no one to look after the office. And Mrs. Sutcliffe has just rung. Her Pekinese, Nanki-Poo, is lost again. She wants someone to go round at once."

Cordelia said, "Put a notice on the door to say that we'll be open at nine o'clock tomorrow. Then lock up and start

looking for the kitten. Ring Mrs. Sutcliffe and tell her I'll call
round this evening about Nanki-Poo. I'm just on my way to
the inquest, but Chief Inspector Grogan will ask for an
adjournment. It shouldn't take long. And then I'll catch the
mid-afternoon train."

Putting down the receiver, she thought, And why not? The
police would know where to find her. She wasn't yet free of
Courcy Island. Perhaps she never would be. But she had a job
waiting for her. It was a job that needed doing, one that she
was good at. She knew that it couldn't satisfy her forever, but
she didn't despise its simplicities; almost she welcomed them.
Animals didn't torment themselves with the fear of death, or
torment you with the horror of their dying. They didn't
burden you with their psychological problems. They didn't
whine about their condition. They didn't surround themselves
with possessions or live in the past. They didn't scream with
pain because of the loss of love. They didn't expect you to lie
for them. They didn't try to murder you.

She walked through the drawing room and out to the
terrace. Grogan and Buckley were waiting for her, standing
motionless, Grogan at the prow of the police launch, Buckley
at the stern. In their still intensity they looked like unweaponed
knights standing guardian over some fabled vessel, waiting to
bear their king to Avalon. She paused and regarded them,
feeling the concentrated gaze of their unwavering eyes, aware
that the moment held a significance which all three recognized but which none of them would ever put into words.
They were struggling with their own dilemma. How far could
they rely on her sanity, her honesty, her memory, her nerve?
How far dare they trust their reputations to her fortitude when
the going got rough? How would she acquit herself if the case
ever came to trial and she found herself standing in that
loneliest of places, the witness box of the Crown Court? But
she felt distanced from their preoccupations as if nothing that
they could do or think or plan had any relevance to her. It
would all pass as they and she would pass. Time would take

their story and fold it with the half-forgotten legends of the island, Carl Blythe's lonely death, Lillie Langtry sweeping down the great staircase, the crumbling skulls of Courcy.

Suddenly she felt inviolate. The police would have to make their own decisions. She had already made hers, without hesitation and without a struggle. She would tell the truth, and she would survive. Nothing could touch her. She hitched her bag more firmly on her shoulder and moved resolutely toward the launch. For one sunlit moment it was as if Courcy Island and all that had happened during that fateful weekend was as unconcerned with her life, her future, her steadily beating heart, as was the blue uncaring sea.